OVERWHELMING ACCLAIM FOR VICKI HINZE'S NOVELS

ACTS OF HONOR

"Gripping and adrenaline-charged, Hinze's plot will appeal to fans who like their suspense razor-sharp."—*Publishers Weekly*

"Absolutely riveting."—*Philadelphia Inquirer*

"An excellent story of awakening love."—*Miami Herald*

"Powerful, tender, passionate. Read ACTS OF HONOR."
—Stella Cameron, *New York Times* bestselling author of *Key West*

"Vicki Hinze speaks in a voice unique to the genre. ACTS OF HONOR reads like a mystery with touches of Tom Clancy. If you seek a story with characters of depth, a different twist, tingling suspense, and bittersweet love, buy ACTS OF HONOR."—*Reader to Reader*

"An electrifying, supercharged thriller."
—Meryl Sawyer, bestselling author of *Half Moon Bay*

"You'll be on the edge of your seat until the very end. If you like a healthy dose of intrigue with your romance, you'll enjoy this new military thriller by Ms. Hinze."
—*Interludes*

Turn the page for more praise . . .

"[A] tautly crafted thriller . . . A roller-coaster ride of sizzling suspense, deadly betrayal, and courage . . . A great read."
   —Merline Lovelace, Colonel, USAF (Ret)
      author of *Call of Duty*

"When it comes to the military romance sub-genre . . . Vicki Hinze is one of the top guns . . . DUPLICITY has cross-genre appeal . . . If justice prevails, Ms. Hinze will quickly reach the top of multiple bestselling lists."
   —Harriet Klausner, *Painted Rock Reviews*

"A fast-paced novel with plenty of twists and turns, and a lot of great insight into the world of the military . . . You will not be disappointed with this action-packed thriller."
   —*Interludes*

SHADES OF GRAY

"The complications here go beyond the usual hurdles and make the romance more touching for being hard-won. And if the main action seems far-fetched, just read *The New York Times*."—*Publishers Weekly*

"SHADES is very fast-paced, filled with the kind of intrigue and plot twists that make for a great action movie . . . a great read if you're a fan of Clancy-type novels and movies. I enjoy books that combine intrigue with romance and found SHADES to be a perfect combination of the two."
—*The Middlesex News* (MA)

"A great story line that easily could sell as a romance or an action thriller. Hinze is clearly one of the leaders of military romances that emphasizes action, suspense, and romance. A winner for fans of romantic suspense."
   —*Affaire de Coeur*

St. Martin's Paperbacks titles
by Vicki Hinze

Shades of Gray
Duplicity
Acts of Honor
All Due Respect

ALL DUE RESPECT

VICKI HINZE

St. Martin's Paperbacks

ALL DUE RESPECT

Copyright © 2000 by Vicki Hinze.

Cover photograph © David Hanover / Stone; Photo illustration by Herman Estevez.

ISBN: 0-312-97513-9

Printed in the United States of America

St. Martin's Paperbacks edition / October 2000

St. Martin's Paperbacks are published by St. Martin's Press, 175 Fifth Avenue, New York, NY 10010.

10 9 8 7 6 5 4 3 2 1

This book is dedicated to all who serve;
to Seekers,
who have discovered the most worthy journey is
the one within and, enlightened,
willingly bear the costs and the pain of reaching out to
ease the way and light the path for others.

Acknowledgments

My gratitude to my family, who tolerated me while I explored the issue of abuse. I'm grateful for your steadfast support, and your constant reminders during the writing of this book, that the challenge of abuse has not been a part of my world for many, many years.

My gratitude to the team at St. Martin's Paperbacks for the opportunity to share my perceptions and perspectives through nine projects. Thank you for the entire experience. The heart knows.

My gratitude to those who shall remain nameless by choice for sharing their often painful memories, thoughts, and views on both the issues of abuse and missiles. Because you dared, others have an opportunity to see that constructive solutions are possible.

My gratitude to the VIPs in my life, Lorna, Laverne, Cindy, Joyce, Darlene, Micki, Bev, Gin, and Marge, and Mary for never letting "good enough" be good enough, and for your steadfast caring and sharing of your many talents and expertise.

My gratitude to the Halos for all the reasons you know, and those you've yet to imagine.

My gratitude to the members of Aids4Writers@ egroups.com, my writing group. Your questions about writing keep me honest and on my toes, always provoking thought. I'm richer for the experience.

May all the life lessons learned at your knees now shine through me as a beacon of truth for others.

Author's Note

MY purpose in writing these novels is to offer readers an opportunity to peek into the military world and to experience some of the challenges our service members and civil servants endure for all of us. Yet I consider it vital to do no harm, to include nothing to further jeopardize or to create a need for further sacrifices from them or their families. Much is already demanded of both.

For these reasons, I've implemented creative license, as I did in *Shades of Gray, Duplicity,* and *Acts of Honor,* and altered known technologies and some standard means of operation. Grayton Air Force Base exists only within these pages, and the Rogue missile is a fabricated compilation of other missile systems and a guess on where the technology will be in a few years. I hope you'll agree with me that protecting those who serve us warrants these deviations, and you'll be as grateful to them as I am for their service and commitment to fighting our wars—those declared, and undeclared.

Blessings,
Vicki Hinze

ALL DUE RESPECT

Chapter One

~

MY God, he'd found her.

Unable to believe her eyes, Dr. Julia Warner-Hyde
turned her back to him, squeezed her eyes shut. *Calm down.
Think. Think!*

She darted a frantic gaze up then down the shore, out
on the churning Gulf of Mexico. Sand. Water. Deserted
picnic area. Not even a trash receptacle close enough to
hide behind.

He's found you, Julia. Accept it. You have to face him.

Face him? She couldn't face him. She didn't want to
face him—or anyone who reminded her of the past.

*No matter how hard you try, some things you can't out-
run. Your history is one of them. You've got to accept that,
too.*

She did. But *now*?

The water crept up on the beach, soaking her shoes.
Maybe it wasn't him. Maybe it was an optical illusion.
Maybe the bleak glare off the water or the blinding reflection of the sugar-white sand had tricked her. The stiff sea
breeze was burning her eyes and blurring her vision. She
could have seen a resemblance where there wasn't one.

Squinting back over her shoulder, she double-checked.
Six two, mid-thirties, black hair. Same familiar body and
resolute stride. He sidestepped the beachside park's picnic
area, the brisk wind plastering his windbreaker against his

white shirt and jeans-clad hip, and moved straight toward her.

It was definitely him.

The fine hair on her neck stood on end and the chill cut through to her bones. Damn it, she'd been so careful. How had he found her? How had *anyone* found her?

Had to be Intel or the OSI, Julia.

Since she'd left the lab and come here to teach first grade, the Office of Special Investigations had been keeping tabs on her and briefing every Department of Defense honcho with a vested interest on her activities. She would resent that, but she couldn't do it with conviction and a clear conscience. If an agent hadn't breached protocol three years ago and warned she was in danger, she'd be dead now. Still, their keeping tabs on all former employees didn't explain why her former Black World coworker, Dr. Seth Holt, was in Grace, Alabama, and not in his lab in New Orleans, designing ballistic missiles. What did this visit mean? Would she have to leave Grace now, too?

Seth stopped in front of her. "Hello, Julia."

She crossed her arms over her chest and stared up at him, doing her damnedest to control her fear. "What are you doing here?"

His eyebrows inched up on his forehead. "I expected a 'Hello, Seth. It's good to see you,' but I guess you still haven't mastered the rudiments of tact."

Tact? He wanted tact from a woman who was terrified her whole life was about to be ripped to shreds—again? Or did he think she was the world's biggest sucker? This wasn't a friendly visit; the grim slash of his mouth and jut of his jaw proved it, not to mention his finding her. This visit had purpose. Risks with grave consequences. And that had to be horrible news for her.

"We need honesty, not tact." He'd always said honesty made their relationship special. Shifting uncomfortably, she edged back from the creeping water. "Now, why are you here, Seth?"

He fisted a hand in his jacket pocket and professional distance filled his eyes. "I need your help."

Definitely sucker bait. Seth Holt never allowed himself to need anyone, or anything from anyone. He was the most self-sustained, self-sufficient man ever born. "You prefer working alone," she reminded him.

"Not when I'd fail and innocent people would pay the price."

So he wasn't here to ruin her new life. That should be good news, but it wasn't. It meant his back was against the proverbial wall in a professional crisis. And his crisis carried the capability of destroying many lives. Seth worked in the Black World: that shadowy and undiscussed segment of the military where everything—personnel, missions, and weaponry—was classified Top Secret or higher. He designed and developed new technologies and weapon systems that were incorporated into existing weaponry packages and used in covert military operations. Operations that typically remained classified for years after they occurred, if not forever. When Seth Holt said innocent people, he didn't mean a sprinkling of civilians. He meant all the citizens of the United States.

"What price?" She asked the question but, former rocket scientist to current rocket scientist, she understood, and Seth knew it.

"Millions could pay with their lives."

Her skin crawled, and she wished that just once she could recall Seth's damage-assessment estimates being exaggerated. But they had always been logical and uncannily accurate. He never elevated risks or potential—not even when refusing to do so had cost him the funding of a project. Even dead certain his request for funds to develop his own missile-defense sensor design would be denied, Seth had called it exactly as he'd seen it and, knowing it, made his "millions could pay with their lives" all the more chilling.

He sat down on the first of three tables. His feet on the bench and his arms braced against his knees, he stared

across the beach to the rough water, blowing right out the
window the stereotype of a rocket scientist and engineer as
a squirrely old man with inch-thick glasses and a bowed
back. He looked more like a bodybuilder; he had to be still
spending an hour a day at the gym. Though he wore his
hair longer now, it was still that rich, deep black, contrast-
ing starkly with his green eyes and sharp features. He
looked . . . wonderful.

She hated it.

Her pulse quickened, and she hated that, too—and it
surprised her. Seth was gorgeous, true, but he always had
been, and looking at him before never had affected her.

Considering your situation back then, this surprises you?

It didn't. But maybe her reaction to him was a sign.
Maybe she was finally healing.

*You've got to be kidding, Julia. No human being can
heal that much.*

Certain her conscience was right, she sat on the picnic
table beside Seth, propped her feet on the bench, and
looked out at the water, giving herself a moment to absorb
the gravity of this visit.

The gulf was rough, choppy, and whitecaps rolled into
froth at the sandy shore. The wind carried a salty tang and
the lack of sun and the slate-gray sky only reinforced her
gloomy mood. His showing up here rattled her through to
the soles of her feet, but it had cost him a lot to come to
her, and it didn't take a rocket scientist to know it. For
some reason, that helped her calm down. "How can I help
you?"

A frown creased the skin between his heavy brows and
his square jaw tightened. "I've been advised against this
but, before I get specific, I have to ask you something."

Advised. Definitely work-related. Strangely disappointed, she worked to not tense up, taking this one breath
at a time. "Okay."

"I want to be clear. I am not prying into your personal
life. I just . . . Oh, hell, Julia. The truth is, I need to know

who you are now." He leveled her with a steady look. "This situation . . . It's sensitive."

A sensitive crisis and he needed to know if he could still trust her. After the way she'd walked out on him without notice, his questioning her shouldn't have hurt. And yet it did. But she couldn't blame him. She had earned his doubt. "All right."

"Why did you leave without saying good-bye?" He looked her straight in the eye. "Was it something I said or did?"

She had hurt him. Amazing, because she hadn't realized she *could* hurt him. Professionally, yes, but not personally. And why, on realizing she could hurt him personally, had he had to ask her the one question she couldn't answer honestly?

Regret bit her hard, and she worked to give him *a* truth, if not *the* truth. "I loved working with you." Hoping what she could tell him would be enough, she fingered the mini-flashlight on her key ring, avoided his eyes. "Leaving was my only option. I didn't like it, but I had no choice, Seth." And she had lived with the guilt and regret to prove it.

He stared at her, seeking the truth. "Why?"

She squeezed her eyes shut. "I can't tell you that."

"It had nothing to do with me or work?"

"No." Oh, God. A half-truth and now he knew her reasons had been personal.

Seth looked torn between pressing her and clamming up. A few beats passed and, oddly, he opted to press. "Did your husband's job transfer here?"

She should tell him about Karl, yet she couldn't make herself do it. In waltzing back into her life as abruptly as she'd waltzed out of his, Seth had caught her unawares, and for a split second, she had been mentally transported back into her kitchen in New Orleans, back to Karl, the man she had married who supposedly had loved her. Now the old memories rushed in and crushed down on her. A shudder rippled through her. She stiffened against it, furious that just thinking of him still terrified her. She respected and admired Seth but, God, how she hated her memories. That life was over, finished, and she resented like hell any part of it intruding into the new life she'd struggled and sacrificed to build.

If there was any good news in this, it was that word of Karl's being in prison evidently hadn't filtered back to Seth or to others in the field—and she would rather it not filter back now. The truth was gruesome, the grapevine merciless. Seth might understand about Karl but, then again, he might not. And even if his opinion shouldn't matter to her, it did. She didn't want to risk losing his respect.

She had lost everything once. Every single thing. It had hurt like hell and nearly had killed her, but somehow she had dredged up the courage to start over. She didn't want to regress—couldn't afford to regress—and go through any of it again. She *wouldn't* regress or go through any of it again. "I earned five times what Karl earned as a cop. If you were me, would you quit because Karl transferred?"

"No, but then I'm not you."

Terrific. She'd let tension unleash her temper and now Seth knew her reason for leaving his lab was personal *and* work-related. Brilliant move. "Karl's job wasn't a factor."

"I take it Karl is fine, then?"

"Yes, he's fine." True as far as she had gone. During her last check with his arresting officer, Detective LeBrec, that's exactly what he had told her. *Karl is fine.* So, okay, LeBrec had added *unfortunately.* But nothing compelled her to relate that to Seth. "I chose to come here and to teach."

Clearly struggling to understand, Seth asked, "Did you know anyone here, before coming to Grace?"

Coming to Grace. If she told Seth she had come here for a fresh start on an omen seeking grace, he would forget needing her help and insist she be mentally evaluated. Seth worked with proven entities, with facts, not with omens, or with those who followed them. "No."

"Why first grade, Julia? Why not college? I thought you gave up teaching after graduate school."

Because kids have to learn to lie, just as they have to learn to hate. Because little kids weren't yet corrupt, and if she could teach them that everything—*everyone*—deserves respect before they became corrupt, then she stood a chance of preventing others from going through the hell she'd been through. "I did give it up. But now I'm back." She shrugged. "It's what I wanted."

"I don't get it. You loved your work in the lab. I know you did."

She had, and she'd had enough of this. She really had tried to ease Seth's mind and to assure him he had played no part in her decision to leave the lab. God forbid he ever learn the truth. But she couldn't stand his digging into her past anymore. She just couldn't. "I said, it's what I wanted." She cooled her gaze, signalling him to back off. "Now, what do you want?"

His expression stiffened. Still resting his elbows on his bent knees, he leaned forward. "I've developed a system that will return a hostile, in-flight smart bomb to its launch site."

He had to be kidding. But he didn't look like he was kidding, and she'd never known Seth to kid around about his work. He was talking about an extremely innovative missile-defense system here. Until now, attempts to develop a missile-defense system had centered on interceptor "kill" missiles, where an incoming, hostile missile was rammed into and detonated by a outbound, friendly missile. So far, even that program hadn't produced a stellar performance. Its personal best was a couple of hits and a truckload of near misses, and a near miss was a failure. Depending on the type of warhead the hostile missile carried, a near miss allowed catastrophic damage to occur. But Seth was talking about taking the entire ballistic-missile-defense program in a whole new direction. One refining and manipulating technology so an attack resulted in a self-inflicted wound. Excitement bubbled in Julia, overtaking the tension. "Is it successful?"

"The prototype is."

"Seth, that's wonderful." She smiled. "Will it negate the need for traditional 'kill' missile interceptors?"

"If we're lucky."

Pursing her lips, she tilted her head. "Are you going to be lucky?"

"Maybe." He glanced at a pelican perching on a dockside pier post. "They're calling it Project Home Base." He followed the pelican's move down to the next post. "The contract to develop it is about to be awarded."

"So why do you look so glum? You should be flying high."

"I hold several patents on the system."

"Okay." Not unusual. Seth had often held patents on their previous projects. So had she.

"Because I stand to profit personally—financially, I mean—I can't head the project."

That had happened before, too. "So they'll assign someone else to head it and you'll be assigned to the project as a consultant." She shrugged. "What's the problem?"

"No one else is qualified to head it."

He meant that no one he trusted was qualified to head it. Julia stilled her jangling keys. Seth was saying more than she was hearing. Not atypical between them, but she was out of practice at reading between his lines. "You're worried about this for another reason."

Nodding, he confirmed her fears. "Two, actually."

When he didn't say any more, she resisted an urge to nudge him, then realized the problem. "To disclose them to me, you're going to have to breach security."

Expelling a sigh, he looked back at her. "Is your clearance still valid?"

"You know it's not, Seth." For all the good it had done her, when she had moved, she'd been extremely careful not to leave a trail. Seth had to have contacted the OSI or Intel to find her. No one except those who already knew what had happened would advise him not to pry into her personal life to determine who she was and what she stood for now. Seth had to know it all. Every sordid detail.

Heat crept up her neck to her face, and she flushed hot. He probably had been testing her, asking about Karl, to see if she would admit what had happened. And maybe she should have, but she just wasn't that brave. That brave, or that strong.

"I'm going to trust you, Julia." Seth laced his fingertips. "I'm not sure why, but I'm going to trust you."

The hurt ran deep. Didn't he understand that she wouldn't have left as she had unless it had been completely necessary? Didn't he know her better than this?

Obviously not. "You're going to trust me because you know you can—and because you don't have a choice." Anything with the potential to kill millions rated as a crisis in her book, and no doubt in the OSI and Intel's, too. They had authorized Seth to breach security and talk to her. Otherwise, he would never do it. Ever.

Now just how should she feel about that? Relieved, or worried?

Damn worried, she decided. If they'd authorized disclosure to her, then the news had to be godawful.

"I do still trust you," Seth said. "But I'm not comfortable with the risks of being wrong."

She frowned at him. "What makes you think I'm comfortable with your dropping back into my life, dumping this problem in my lap? I left, remember? I don't get involved in these professional crises anymore."

He slid off the edge of the table and shifted in the sand, half burying his loafers, then stopped directly in front of her. His jacket brushed against her knees. "I'm worried for two reasons. One, my professional reputation and financial security are on the line." His expression turned dark, clouded. "And two, I've already noted what could be program irregularities."

"Someone on the project is corrupt?"

"It's possible. During Slicer Industries' development of the prototype, I picked up on two minor incidents that could be significant. I'm just not sure."

"But you're sure enough to be concerned."

"Of course."

Of course. With Seth, any irregularity pertinent to his project or to a potential project, no matter how slight, warranted concern.

"What these two incidents were isn't important," he said. "What is important is that if this project is funded—which it will be—then I need someone I trust heading it." He lifted his gaze from her shoulder to her eyes. "I need you, Julia."

Oh, damn. She didn't want to be in this position. Why had he put her in it, forcing her to choose? "I can't," she said before realizing the words had left her mouth. "I wish I could, but that isn't my life anymore." God, she felt disloyal, like an ungrateful traitor. Why did refusing him make her feel so rotten and hurt so badly?

Because, aside from your uncle Lou, Seth Holt is the only man in your life who always backed you up and never demanded anything in return. He's always been special.

Julia shut out her nagging conscience. The last thing she wanted was a man carrying "special" status in her life. "Look, Seth. If you suspect corruption, then why not contact the lab commander, the general, or the OSI?" By regulations, the Office of Special Investigations and the general and lab commander *should* be notified, and they both knew it.

"Colonel Ed Pullman is the lab commander."

"The gutless wonder from the TDY trip to Edwards?" A Colonel Pullman had headed their team on a temporary duty trip to the desert Air Force base to test the Rogue missile. He'd been spineless.

"That's the one," Seth confirmed. "And I can't go to the OSI yet. I don't have hard evidence." The wind blew his hair down over his broad forehead. "If I report this without hard evidence, people's careers and lives will be destroyed. Innocent or guilty. I can't do that to them, Julia."

Many could and would. But not Seth. He wouldn't risk wrongly accusing anyone. And any accusation he levied would be investigated under the standard premise of guilty until proven innocent. Considering the stakes were national security, the Department of Defense—or the government, for that matter—had no other choice. "Does this technology fall under the Black Operations umbrella?" Black World technology often had dual uses, military and civilian applications. In the lab, Black Ops signified military applications only.

He shifted on his feet, clearly uncomfortable. "It's . . . extremely sensitive."

Definitely Black Ops. Of course, Black Ops. So the project would be considered violated, too. Congress could pull the funding, demand extensive modifications, or scrap the entire project. Without a missile-defense program, the United States would remain extremely vulnerable. Very disturbing thought, considering the findings about the Chinese having access to secret nuclear warfare technology. "I see."

"Not yet. You're missing a key element," he said. "I need your help to protect us."

Us. Americans. *All* Americans. Resisting an urge to drag specifics out of him, she patiently persisted. "From what?"

"You remember the Rogue missile?"

"Of course." The most advanced missile in the U.S. arsenal. Five thousand pounds of explosives. A hundred sixty-six bomblets that scatter when disbursed. A warhead capable of carrying conventional, chemical, biological, or nuclear ordnance. A new metal alloy construction and a stealth system that made the Rogue undetectable by standard countermeasures, such as early-warning satellite launch-detection systems that alert ground-based radar when a hostile missile is inbound. Seth held two system patents on the Rogue. Julia held one. "What's wrong with it?" A system malfunction? Some overlooked flaw in the design?

"Nothing is wrong with it. The Rogue works just fine."

"So what's the problem?"

Seth's expression turned grave. "We no longer have sole possession of it."

The heat seeped from Julia's body. Chills rippled up her

back, down her arms, and her left biceps began to spasm. She rubbed it, shoulder to elbow. "H-how?"

"I don't know. That's for Intel to determine. What I do know is, if a hostile faction launches a Rogue against us, with Home Base I can minimize the damage."

"But Home Base is still a simple seeker missile. The Rogue isn't some mousy missile, carrying a five-hundred-pound bomb, for God's sake. How can you negate the impact of a hostile Rogue with a simple seeker missile?"

"First, the Rogue is even more powerful than you know. After you left the lab, I modified its booster-ignition and explosives systems. That expanded its kill and damage zones substantially. Secondly, Home Base isn't a simple seeker."

"Well, what is it?"

A pleased-with-himself smile hovered on Seth's lips. When a woman jogging along the shore ran out of earshot, he continued. "With Home Base, I can determine if the Rogue is live ordnance or a decoy. I can track it, forecast its trajectory, and most importantly, if it's a smart bomb I can reverse its trajectory while it's in flight, return it to its home base, and detonate it."

Damn. Julia brushed her windblown hair back from her eyes. He really had taken a totally innovative approach in his design of this missile-defense system. "You can actually track, forecast, and return it to its own launch site? Even a Rogue?"

"Theoretically, yes."

"Magnetic energy?" Altering it could abort a launch.

"No. Existing arms treaties prohibit the use of an adequate power source."

Julia played out defense strategy scenarios. He couldn't alter the trajectory, only reverse the existing programming. "So anyone launching against the U.S. would, in effect, be attacking themselves?"

"Yes. And depending on its warhead type and payload—which I can't determine—when they attack themselves, they're going to damage or destroy everything within a hundred-kilometer radius of their chosen launch site."

A hundred kilometers? Three years ago, the zone was the size of two football fields, end to end. Now it was a hundred kilometers. "How? Isn't the zone dependent on the missile's payload and capability?"

"Home Base is also armed," he said. "Kill zone is roughly thirty kilometers. Damage zone, a hundred kilometers."

Visions of the aftereffects of a hydrogen bomb detonating flashed through her mind. She didn't dare ask with what Home Base was armed. Not with a hundred-kilometer damage zone. But factoring in compliance with existing international arms treaties, it had to be armed with some new explosives technology.

Seth's eyes gleamed. "Do you see how valuable this technology would be to hostile factions?"

"Oh, yes." Devastation. Destruction. The creation of a wasteland. A moron could see the danger—and the challenge. Corrupted, the Home Base technology would fail, and the hostile Rogue would hit its U.S. target. Worse, with the Home Base technology, a hostile faction could reprogram any smart-bomb missile the U.S. launched to return to its U.S. home base and detonate.

"We both know traditional interceptors only have an eighty-percent success rate. That leaves a big window of vulnerability, Julia. We need an actual missile-defense system. Right now, several countries are capable of targeting us and we have no functional, effective response. Home Base will give us both. Naturally, it's equally important that *only* we have this defense system." Seth's worry crept into his voice. "One well-placed, hostile Rogue could cripple this country."

"And kill millions." Julia shuddered. Seth hadn't exaggerated the damage-assessment estimates.

What if a hostile faction targeted a metropolitan area? Take out even segments within a hundred-kilometer radius of a metro area, and that would wipe out a lot of Americans and a lot of resources. And if the hostile Rogue carried a chemical, biological, or nuclear warhead, then the damage-assessment estimates soared.

Millions. Literally.

When her heart dropped down from her throat and back into her chest where it belonged, she responded. "I understand why you need someone you can trust." But could she do it? Could she risk helping him?

Karl's in jail. It's safe. Considering the risks to others, how can you not do it?

Her conscience made a strong case with valid points. If she refused and something happened, she would never forgive herself. Millions *could* die.

"Well?" Seth interrupted her internal debate. "Will you help me?"

She swallowed her fears about stepping back into her old life. It would be hard. There would be so many reminders, so many demons, waiting to confront her on every street corner. She couldn't avoid them. But the stealth system, which prohibited the Rogue from being detected and tracked by standard countermeasure devices, carried her patent, and refusing Seth and turning away, denying her responsibility, would only create more demons.

She couldn't live with more demons.

Staring out at the water, she accepted the inevitable. She would just have to find a way to deal with this. Just as she'd had to learn to deal with the other challenges.

One demon at a time. One challenge at a time. One breath at a time.

"Julia?"

She looked into Seth's eyes and couldn't refuse him. "Yes. When the contract is awarded, I'll take a leave of absence from school and head the project."

"Good." He sighed his relief. "Good."

Julia's mind chugged ahead. "But how are you going to get me back into the system?" Knowing he hadn't forgotten, she still felt compelled to remind him. "I walked out without notice. They're not just going to let me come back."

"Normally, they wouldn't. But there's a new program and, under specific conditions, we're allowed to bypass competitive bids on certain slots and hire direct."

"Specific conditions?"

"Extreme threats to national security," he said. "The Rogue is loose, Julia."

That qualified in her book. "What about my security clearances?"

"They'll be in place within a couple of days."

A couple of days? It normally took weeks.

He'd already started processing them.

Seemed he had an answer for everything, and she wasn't at all sure she liked it. It made her feel manipulated, and she hated that. She stared at him until he looked at her. "You knew I'd say yes."

"I prayed you would say yes," he corrected her. "And I prepared for it."

"Of course." It wasn't manipulation. It wasn't. Seth always prepared. He was rock-solid, and always had been. It was a damn shame more men hadn't emulated him. Karl, in particular. "When will the contract be awarded?"

"I'm not sure exactly," he said. "Is it critical?"

"It is to me," she said. "I have a special student, Jeff. His mother died a few months ago and I suspect his father is emotionally abusing him." Jeff had become the son Julia never had, and never would have. She couldn't just leave him. He needed her—almost as much as she needed him. "I have to talk to him, file a report with the school counselor, and then work with her and the authorities to stop the abuse. I'm all he's got, Seth. I can't leave him, knowing that's going on. I won't."

"Of course not," he said. "You've got a week, maybe two. I'll get you set up and find you an apartment near Grayton."

"Grayton?" Her confusion carried in her tone.

"Grayton Air Force Base," he said. "It's about thirty miles north of Hurlburt Field, on the Florida gulf coast."

"You mean, I don't have to go back to New Orleans?"

"No." He blinked hard, then grunted. "I guess I forgot to mention I'd transferred."

"Yes, you did." No New Orleans. No demonic memories to confront. No new demons. She smiled her relief when she really wanted to weep it. "What brought that on? The transfer, I mean." He was king of the lab; well treated, and seldom questioned.

The smile left his face and his eyes clouded. "I could say I transferred to pursue other professional endeavors."

Her official reason for leaving. The barb hit its mark.

"But the fact is," he went on, "Grayton's the new location of the Battle Management Center. Its lab is under the direct command of the Ballistic Missile Defense Organization."

"I see." Still stinging from his "professional endeavor" remark, Julia scooted off the table, down to the sand, and dusted her backside with her hand. "I'd better get back to school."

He looked down at her. "Thanks for bailing me out on this."

How could she refuse? That she didn't want to refuse him concerned her. "You present a compelling case."

"Yeah, unfortunately, I do." Seth sighed. "I've missed working with you, Julia."

They'd worked together like hand to glove, finishing each other's thoughts and sentences, instinctively agreeing on what to test next in their designs, on which battles to fight with the honchos and which ones to postpone. They had shared a unique relationship, based on trust and steeped in mutual respect. Neither intruded, but both were there if needed and called on. She'd hated losing that, resented losing him, and, for once, she let down her guard and admitted it openly. "I've missed you, too, Seth."

Sand lifted by the wind stung her foot. Julia swiped at it. "Is Home Base the sensor design you were working on privately before I left the lab?"

"No. Different systems, different tasking. But mine can piggyback on Home Base. At least, I hope one day it will."

"So it hasn't been funded."

"Not yet."

That had to be disappointing for him. To invest that much into something, to know it would work, and to have it put on permanent hold for a lack of money had to gnaw at him. It gnawed at her for him. "I'm sorry."

"Me, too." He let out a sigh. "I'm still perfecting it on my own. Who knows? Maybe its time will come." He shrugged, then stilled, staring at her key chain. "You'll need to get rid of that before you come to the lab." He nodded at the miniature black flashlight dangling from her key chain. "They've become terrorists' new weapon of choice."

Julia methodically challenged its potential uses. Only one passed her barrage of tests. "Scanners mistake explosives for batteries?"

"For the moment." Seth nodded.

Meaning, scanner modifications in progress had a solution on the near horizon. Thank God. Having to fear every flashlight in the country incited nightmares, and she already had all of those she could handle.

Sometimes, knowing these little tidbits could drive a person to paranoia. Unfortunately, if you knew them, odds were it wasn't paranoia but a clear and present danger routinely encountered by service members in the field.

"Julia." Seth sounded hesitant. "Your coming to Grayton will be okay with Karl, won't it?"

The question caught her off guard. Was it a deliberate second chance to confess about Karl? Even if it was, she couldn't do it. Doing her best to cover, act nonchalant, she smiled. "No problem at all." It wouldn't be, since Karl wouldn't know it.

"Good. I'll be in touch." Seth turned and walked toward the parking lot.

Julia watched him go, unsure if his asking twice about Karl meant Seth knew what happened or he was fishing to find out. If she asked, he would tell her. Seth never lied. But she didn't want that Pandora's box opened. And maybe that wasn't what had her uneasy. Maybe it was the angle of his head or the stillness in him, getting to her. Maybe it was because he had delivered the news about the Rogue she had helped design now being in hostile hands or the possible corruption on Home Base, a project not yet even developed. Or it could be that tidbit about terrorists using flashlights to house explosives.

Or it could be just the man himself.

Damn it, it could be. He was special. He always had been special, and that made him dangerous.

In the last three years, she had come a long way on the road back to becoming more of her old self. A very long way. But she hadn't come far enough, or remained innocent or unchanged by her experiences enough, to risk trusting another man.

Not even Seth.

Men with good intentions could get you killed just as fast as those with bad intentions. And it was all but impossible to tell the difference between them. Hadn't she married Karl Hyde believing he was a good man? A really good man? Hadn't he seemed kind and gentle and loving— all the things she wanted in a husband? And hadn't her experience with him proven that any man could deceive any woman he chose to deceive?

It had. Karl had seemed all those good things and more, and he had ended up being a heartless bastard with a black soul. He'd ended up in jail. And, thanks to him, she had barely escaped with her life, and she was still being threatened.

Those truths made the bottom line with any man the same. Give him your trust and odds are good you'll end up dead.

That was a lesson learned she would never forget. And it applied even to Seth Holt.

Chapter Two

A week later, Seth sat in his office as perplexed about what had triggered the massive changes in Julia's life as he had been before he had gone to Grace.

All his life, he had done his damnedest to avoid asking for favors, but he had searched for her on his own since she'd left, and he had failed to find her. When he had noted irregularities on the project, he'd had no choice but to go to the OSI, meet with Agent 12, and ask for his help to locate her.

Though neither publicly acknowledged it, Seth and Agent 12 had a history. Before Seth had left active duty in the Air Force and had gone civilian to work in the lab, he and Agent 12, who had been Lieutenant Colonel Matthew Grant back then, had worked in Special Forces together. Because the Rogue was loose and in hostile hands, and because Seth had invoked the crunch-time code they had used on convert operations in critical circumstances, Matthew had agreed that Julia could be trusted and they needed her to help Seth save their asses, and he had told Seth where to find her: Grace, Alabama.

Julia, teaching first grade in a tiny gulf coast town that didn't warrant a pinprick on most maps and could never offer her the opportunities she'd had in his lab.

Seth cranked back in his chair and lifted his feet to the corner of his desk. She had often surprised him, but this move confounded him. Julia was bright; a genius gifted with common sense and vision. Reserved, in a way, and beautiful, though she had never been a wrench-your-neck-looking-at-her kind of woman. She was too serious, smiled too seldom for that. But she had this way of making a man feel important, strong and weak at the same time. By the time he figured out she was strong and vulnerable, she'd snagged him. And she'd snagged plenty. Half his engineers, contractors, and all of the guys in the lab had been crazy about her. Oddly enough, the other women hadn't seemed envious. They had been protective of her. Seth never had figured that out.

Now, she had the same somber brown eyes. The same sleek, stubborn chin, and chestnut-brown hair the sun streaked gold—every bit as beautiful as the day she had last walked out of his lab—but for someone miserable enough to leave the research-and-development work she loved to "pursue other professional endeavors," she hadn't seemed a damn bit happier. Less rigid, but no happier. And if she wasn't happier, then why had she left?

And why had she nearly gone into cardiac arrest when she had seen him on the beach? She'd looked . . . haunted.

Too much just didn't make sense. Matthew had access to Julia's Intel reports and would have enlightened Seth, but his commander nixed that by reclassifying her file Eyes Only. Seth couldn't slot the logic for that smooth move, and Matthew couldn't explain, but Julia had been distant and secretive at Grace. Actually, she had been damn scared. She had never been afraid of Seth, and he didn't like her being afraid of him now. What triggered her fear?

One thing was clear. Speculating wouldn't give him any answers . . . but talking to her might. It was worth a shot. He lifted the phone and dialed her number.

She answered on the third ring. "Hello."

"Julia, it's me, Seth." He thumbed the pages of a magazine. "Notification came in today. The contract has been awarded."

"That's terrific."

She sounded down. Julia didn't get down, except maybe when alone. "The realtor's ready to hang me, but I finally found the right apartment for you. It's ready and waiting."

"When do I need to be there?"

Worried. Definitely worried. He tossed the copy of *Scientific American* onto his desk and frowned at the cover. "What's wrong, Julia?"

"Nothing. I'm fine."

Right words, wrong tone. The woman was anything but fine. "Is it Jeff?" She had said that student was special to her. Whether or not she knew it, she loved the boy; Seth had heard it in her voice. And even knowing Jeff had been abused and needed loving, Seth envied Jeff Julia's love, and condemned himself for the envy.

"I'm worried about him," she said. "He's not supposed to stay alone after school."

A latchkey kid? In first grade? "Isn't that against the law?"

"Yes. He has to be twelve," she said. "I wrote his father a note about it, but Jeff came to school again today with his BAMA key ring. William Camden ignored the note."

So Jeff was a fan of the Alabama ball team, too. Seth mentally stored that detail. "I'm sorry to hear that."

"An observer joined us on the playground and Jeff said some crazy-sounding things. Until this incident, I thought it was part of the grief. His mother died a few months ago."

"What did he say?"

He asked the observer if he was mad at me. The man said no. Jeff looked at me and said, 'If he gets mad, just yell. I've got my listening ears on.' "

"Nothing crazy about it," Seth said. "Grief-stricken kids don't think mad men hit. Abused kids do."

"You're right. I talked to Jeff for a long time." Strain muted her voice. "He is being emotionally abused."

Curious about Jeff's special-to-Julia status, Seth had done some checking on the boy and had sensed abuse— he'd seen shades of himself in Jeff—but the confirmation, still made him sick. "What have you done about it?"

"Reported it to the school counselor, who reported it to the authorities. Now Camden's out for my blood and my job. I'd give him both, if he'd just stop hurting Jeff."

She would. Jeff was lucky to have an ally. Seth hadn't, and making his way on his own had been hell.

"Now Camden's really ticked off and he knows I'm leaving. What if he takes out his anger at me on Jeff?"

"He won't." Seth stared across his office at the glass-panel wall. The inner lab was dark; the glass reflective. Cold determination lined his face. "Call Jeff for me, Julia. I'm going to see him."

"You can't do that."

"Of course I can," Seth said. "I am."

"But you don't have any authority—"

"I don't need any," Seth interrupted. "Jeff needs a friend. I'm going to be one."

"Camden will have a fit. He'll blame Jeff for your interfering, and things will get worse."

"I'll handle Camden. You just prepare the way for me with Jeff, so I'm not a stranger. He'll be nervous around me."

"You're a big man, and Jeff is tiny. He thinks all men get mad, and mad men hit."

"Then don't you think the sooner he learns different, the better?"

She hesitated, then said, "Okay, I'll call. But be careful. I don't want Camden coming after you, too."

Julia's concern felt good. Too good. "I will." Seth beat down the hope that Camden *would* come after him. He'd welcome any excuse to give the man an attitude adjustment.

"You're special for caring, Seth." Her voice dropped low, husky. "You've always been special."

Seth started to respond, then thought better of it. For five years, he had loved this woman and never had said a word because she was happily married. From his parents, Seth knew happy marriages were a rare and special thing. The world already had too much ugliness in it for a man to deliberately ugly up a rare and special thing. Still, he would remember her "you're special" for a long time to come.

ONLY on the gulf coast could a kid play shirtless in his front yard in November.

Seth leaned against the Lexus and glanced away from Jeff down the oak-lined street. Nice neighborhood. Pretty two-story, white clapboard house with a wide front porch and a hurricane fence enclosing the yard. At least Jeff wasn't going home alone after school to a rough neighborhood. Not that his safety was assured here, but his odds seemed better.

Jeff tossed the football up in the air and then caught it. He hadn't yet noticed Seth, and that worried him. The boy could be taken by surprise. But Seth liked seeing him play as if he didn't have a worry in the world and he wished down to his bones that was true.

Julia had been damn upset, scared Camden would lash out at Jeff over her report. Seth had calmed her down but, during every minute of their conversation, he had gotten more and more angry at Camden. For hurting a defenseless kid, and for upsetting Julia.

Jeff dropped the ball. When he picked it up, he saw Seth and grinned from ear to ear. "You're Dr. Seth," he said, running up to the fence. "Dr. Julia told me you were coming to see me."

"Dr. Julia?"

Jeff nodded. "So we don't get her and Mr. Warner mixed up. He's a teacher, too."

". . . Ah, I see." Julia had paved the way, all right, including a photo or Jeff wouldn't have recognized him on sight. Where had she gotten one? Regardless, Jeff didn't seem at all wary of Seth and for that he felt grateful. "I wanted to talk with you. Dr. Julia was a little worried about you bringing your house key to school."

"I have to have it when I get home to get in."

"Didn't she send your dad a note about that?"

"I gave it to him." Jeff looked up at Seth, round-eyed. "I promise."

"Well, what did he say?"

Biting his lip and avoiding Seth's eyes, Jeff swayed side to side. "I dunno."

"Yes you do."

A resigned sigh hiked his slim shoulders and Jeff shuffled his foot in the sandy dirt, kicking up a little cloud of dust. "Do I have to tell you?"

"Yes, you have to tell me."

Blinking hard, Jeff tucked his head to his chest and mumbled, "Goddamn your mother for dying, and goddamn you."

"*What?*"

"I'm sorry for cussing, Dr. Seth, but that's what he said." The boy's cheeks blistered and his eyes filled with tears. "I hate it when he cusses."

What Jeff hated was his father cussing him. Seth didn't give a tinker's damn for it, either. He'd never in his life hugged a kid, but he wanted to hug Jeff. How many times had Camden pulled this stunt, damning them? "Losing your mom's still hard, isn't it?"

"I miss her."

Three little words, but ones so powerful they threatened to knock Seth to his knees. "I know. My mom died when I was six, too. I still miss her." And he still felt guilty about her death. At least Jeff had been spared that.

"Dr. Julia's sure Mom misses me, too." Doubt riddled the boy's voice. He pushed away from the fence and stared down at the dirt. "But I think she might be too hurt to miss me."

Confused, Seth pressed him. "What do you mean, buddy?"

"My mom's burning in hell." Jeff studied the sand-crusted toe of his sneaker. "Dad says she'll burn there forever." He choked down a sob rooted in hopelessness. "Every time I close my eyes I see her on fire."

The depth of the kid's suffering stabbed through Seth's

heart, and every instinct in his body urged him to beat the hell out of Camden for doing this to the boy. But that was a selfish response. Seth had to focus on what was best for Jeff.

He squatted so they could see eye to eye. "I have a question for you, Jeff. It's not a test or anything, just a question," Seth said. "Do you believe in God?"

The boy rolled his gaze. "Everybody believes in God. They gotta cuz He's everybody's father and Mom said."

Universal, Mom being the ultimate authority on everything. "What else did she tell you about Him?"

"That He loves us and always will, no matter what."

So far, so good. "I think she's right."

"She was real smart." Pride tinged Jeff's voice.

Seth smiled to lend weight to what he was about to say, hoping the boy would find comfort in it and maybe, just maybe, a little peace. "What she told you is how we know she's not burning in hell, Jeff."

Hope filled his face, but doubt quickly chased it. "Then how come Dad said she was?"

Because he's like my father was. He's a cruel and selfish bastard who has no idea how much he's hurting you. Because even if he did know how much he was hurting you, he wouldn't give a tinker's damn. Because making you feel worse makes him feel better. Stronger. Like more of a man.

Seth thought it all, and said none of it. Instead, he searched for a reasonable explanation that wasn't hard on Jeff's dad. If Seth came across hard, the boy would feel compelled to defend his father. Sad, but that's the way it always worked. The parent abused, the kid protected.

"When somebody you love dies, you miss them. Your dad hurts way down deep, but he can't go around crying all the time, so he acts angry with your mom for leaving you both."

Jeff's jaw dropped open and his eyes stretched wide. "You mean, Mom *wanted* to die?"

"No, she loved you too much to ever want to leave you." Sensing Jeff's doubt and confusion, Seth lifted a leaf from the ground and then dusted away the grains of sand clinging to it. They showered against his shoes. "It's like this leaf." He pinched it between his forefinger and thumb. "It was green and on a tree limb up there." He pointed to a wintering oak. "But when it was time, the leaf turned brown and fell off."

Understanding dawned in Jeff's eyes. "Grass turns brown, too."

"In a way, everything does." Seth smiled. "People are born and, when it's time, they die."

"But the leaves and grass don't burn in hell. Just people do." A frown creased the skin between Jeff's brows. "So if God loves us, then how come He's burning Mom?"

"He isn't, son," Seth said softly. The little skeptic shrugged, and Seth countered, offering logic. "Think about it. If God is everybody's father, then He's your mom's father, too." Seth slung an arm over his bent knee. "Now if you were a father who loved your children—no matter what—would you make them burn in hell forever?"

Jeff didn't hesitate. "No."

"Neither would God, Jeff," Seth said. "Your mom isn't burning in hell, son. She's watching over you from heaven."

Confusion muddied his relief. "But Dad says—"

"I know. But you've thought this through for yourself now. You know the truth in here." Seth gently touched Jeff's chest through the fence, felt his heart pound against his fingertips. "People say and do all kinds of things when they're in pain. They keep hoping *something* will make them feel better."

Jeff's lip trembled. "It makes me hurt."

Rage threatened Seth, but he swallowed it back down. More rage, Jeff did not need. "Your dad hurts you?"

"When he says stuff." Jeff dragged in a deep breath that lifted his chest. "He doesn't love me. I don't know why." Jeff glanced at Seth. "Is something wrong with me?"

"No, it's just grief. It's not your fault."

"Maybe it is." He bowed his shoulders and stared at

Seth's shoes, as if confessing the most shameful, unmentionable sin. "Dad says only Mom wanted me and then she died. Now, he's stuck with me."

Camden was a real piece of work. A bastard, through and through. "I don't know a lot about kids, Jeff. But I know a good one when I see one, and you're a good one. Don't you ever let anyone tell you different."

"It's hard to remember."

It was. Particularly when you heard you were lousy a lot more often. Seth's voice went thick. "Are you scared he'll hurt you, buddy?"

Jeff stared off into the pin oaks. The wind slicked his hair back from his face. "Maybe. He—he used to hurt my mom." Turning, Jeff stared hard, willing Seth to believe him. "But he was always real sorry. Mom told me he was."

Seth sincerely doubted it, but he kept his opinion to himself. Jeff needed the lie. "Okay, but no more nightmares of your mom burning, because she's not. She never was. I said so, and I never lie."

"Dr. Julia told me." A weak smile touched Jeff's lips, and he swatted at a mosquito buzzing his neck.

Seth's smile froze on his face. It wasn't just dust and dirt, Jeff was bruised. Even under the armpit. He'd been grabbed and jerked. Hard.

The front door creaked open, and a man stepped out onto the porch. Had to be Camden. Mid-twenties, brown hair, CPA slump in his shoulders. He topped out at about five eight and moved with a giveaway swagger that pegged him as a severe sufferer of the little, big-man syndrome. *So you're short. Act tough, bluster and bully, and people will consider you important.*

Seth pretended not to see him but made sure his voice was loud enough to carry. "I told Dr. Julia I'd check on you everyday while she's away."

"You did?" Jeff's smile got broader. "Every day?"

Camden's grimace deepened. "Yeah," Seth said. "You know how women are. Worrywarts."

"Yeah." Jeff's nod nearly cracked his neck. "Worry-warts."

Seth bit back a smile. Jeff loved it. Knowing Julia was worrying about him made him feel safe, as if he mattered. And, of course, he did. "So is that okay with you?"

"It's not okay with me." Camden came off the porch and walked three steps down the sidewalk, toward the fence.

Seth looked down at the man, debating. He couldn't hit him; he'd kill him. And though he had left the Special Forces, his hands and feet were still considered lethal weapons. Camden might deserve killing, but if Seth did it, then he'd be in prison. He couldn't help the boy from prison. He had to give diplomacy a try. It'd set a better example for Jeff, and keep Julia off his back.

Seth turned a cool gaze on Camden. "Why would you object?" he asked, letting the implication that Camden had something to hide hang between them.

He went red. "Who the hell are you?"

"Dr. Seth Holt." Seth didn't offer to shake the man's hand, not that Camden had ventured within reach. He'd stopped a good twelve feet away.

"I don't want you around my son."

"Last I checked, this was a public sidewalk." Seth folded his arms across his chest. "Are you saying I'm committing a crime by standing on a public sidewalk?"

"I'm saying I want you to stay away from my kid."

Seth glanced down and saw that Jeff had paled. Not wanting to upset the boy, he softened his expression and his voice. "Jeff, you've got some dirt on your face. I don't want to have to tell Dr. Julia your face was dirty. How about you go wash it up, so I can tell her you were spit-shine clean?"

He dropped his voice so only Seth could hear. "Are you and Dad gonna . . . talk?"

Seth nodded.

"Don't hurt him, okay?"

Damn it. "I won't."

The little skeptic gave him the once-over. "You look awfully mad."

"I know, but mad men don't always hit."

"Promise?"

Gritting his teeth, Seth staved off a sigh. "Yeah, I promise."

Jeff ran up the walk, giving his father a wide berth, paused on the porch to look back and double-check Seth, then went on into the house.

When the door slammed shut, Seth turned his attention back to Jeff's father. "Camden, let me be perfectly clear. Jeff is my friend, and I am going to check on him every day. That isn't negotiable."

"The hell you say. You can't stick your nose in my personal business."

"I'm using every ounce of restraint I possess to keep from kicking your ass for beating on a kid," Seth warned him. "Now, I can check on Jeff without you causing any grief, or you can cause grief, I'll kick your ass, and then check on him anyway." Seth shrugged. "Your choice. I'm up for either."

Camden's Adam's apple bobbed in his throat. "Don't come on my property. You come on my property, I'll have you arrested for trespassing."

Seth stiffened his stance. "You'll let me see Jeff whenever and wherever or I'll have the cops riding your back, nonstop."

"Don't threaten me, Holt."

"No threat." Seth would report the bruises to the social worker *and* to the cops and he'd call them daily for a report. In his experience, cops had a low tolerance level for men who beat up on kids. "It's a solemn promise. I saw the bruise."

Camden paused on the first step up to the porch and looked back at Seth. "What?"

"I saw the bruise." Seth let his anger seep into his voice. "Don't hurt the boy anymore."

"He fell playing football."

"Sure he did." Seth grimaced. "It's a little tricky to bruise your inner and outer arm, your armpit, and your ribs by falling down, Camden."

"He did fall," Camden insisted.

"Okay, fine. Let's keep this simple. I don't give a damn how he gets bruised, if I see another one on him, I'm holding you responsible."

"What gives you the right—"

"You grab the boy hard enough to leave a bruise that covers half his body and you want to talk to me about rights?" *Losing it. Control slipping. Promised Jeff.* Seth took in a deep breath and dropped his voice to just above a whisper. "I'm holding you responsible."

"Okay. All right. You can see him."

Typical. Back a little, big-man against the wall and he folds, provided you're big enough to stomp him.

The front door swung open and Jeff ran outside, up to the fence, and then cranked back his neck. "This okay?"

Seth leashed his rage, forced himself to relax, and then looked down at Jeff's upturned face.

He'd washed it, all right. But only it. A thin rim of mud circled his jawline. The face was clean, but his throat and neck were dust covered and mud splotched from water droplets. Seth nearly laughed. "Looks good to me."

Camden slipped into the house.

"Dr. Seth?"

"Yes, Jeff?"

He licked at his lips, then stared up at Seth. "Thank you for checking on me."

Hell, when a kid looked up at you as awed as if you were Michael Jordan, what was a measly couple hours of driving time and a few phone calls? "No problem, buddy. That's what friends are for."

"Yeah, buddy." Jeff smiled.

The warmth in it captured a corner of Seth's heart, and he smiled back. "Yeah."

Jeff tapped the tip of his shoe against the metal fence, and his smile faded. "Dr. Seth?"

"What is it, Jeff?"

"Buddies don't lie to buddies, right?"

"Buddies don't lie period."

"I didn't have my listening ears on, but I heard Dad when he yelled at you." Jeff rubbed at his bruise. "I didn't fall playing football."

Admitting that took guts. And of all the people in the world he could have chosen to trust, Jeff had picked him. The kid had courage—and he'd snagged another corner of Seth's heart.

Honored and humbled, Seth squatted down. He curled his fingers through the wire fencing and around Jeff's tiny ones, and then looked the boy straight in the eye. "I know, son."

Jeff's eyes stretched wide. "He told you?"

"No." Hard to admit even to Jeff, even after all these years. But necessary. "My dad used to get mad and hit, too."

"Did you have to live with him?"

"No. I lived with strangers." Twenty-three foster homes in twelve years.

"You didn't have nobody to love you, neither?"

"Just myself," Seth said, then winked at Jeff. "But now I've got a buddy."

"Yeah, two buddies. Me and Dr. Julia."

Seth smiled, wishing that were true.

JULIA stared through the windshield at the four-story beige brick building. Deep down, she felt the stir, the old surge of excitement and enthusiasm she had always felt on entering a lab. But this return was temporary, and this lab was unlike any she had worked in before—it had windows.

Someone rapped on her car window.

Startled, she darted her gaze, saw Seth, and chided herself for being so jumpy. Her living on an adrenaline rush, being ready at all times for fight or flight, once had been normal, but she couldn't afford the costs of stressing her nerves anymore.

She grabbed her keys out of the ignition, her purse from the passenger's seat, and then got out of the blue Camry she had bought before moving to Grace—and had reregistered three times since in three different states, creating a paper trail away from her true location.

A lot of good that did.

" 'Morning." Seth closed her door behind her. "Did you have any trouble finding the place?"

"None at all." Julia shifted around him and moved to the sidewalk. "The maps you faxed over were great."

Seth stepped to her side. "Is the apartment okay?"

It was beautiful. Lots of pastels and cushy furniture. Definitely feminine, welcoming, and it had great locks. On the knobs and keyed dead bolts that slid a full inch into the metal door's frame. "It's perfect." The best thing about it was that Seth had leased it and put all the utilities—including the phone—in his name. She really would get a break from Karl and his threats.

At least until some uninformed, well-intentioned soul made the connection between her and Seth and passed it along.

She gave Seth a broad smile. "Thanks for stocking the pantry and fridge." What a nice surprise to arrive thirsty and tired and find something to drink and no need for immediate shopping. Julia hated immediate shopping. She had just finished doing some the night she had been attacked and nearly had died. Too many bad memories there. "How did you know my favorite brands?"

"We worked together for over two years, Julia. You brought your lunch every day. It didn't take a genius."

She supposed not, though for the life of her she couldn't recall even which kind of soda Seth preferred. God, but she had been unconscious in those days.

No. Not unconscious. Preoccupied with staying healthy and sane, and then with staying alive.

"You look stressed." Seth steered her toward the lab's entrance. "Is everything okay?"

She forced herself to smile. "I'm just a little nervous

about being back in this environment. A lot changes in three years."

"You'll be up to speed in a couple of days." He passed her a name badge. "Clip this to your collar on the left."

That, she hadn't forgotten. She took it and attached the clasp to her jacket lapel. Thin laminated plastic, but it felt strange. "Why is it so heavy?"

"There's a chip inside. It allows security to track you anywhere in the building."

They knew who was where at all times. Considering the nature of the work, that was clever and, in a sense, comforting, but it also felt damned invasive. "Why are there windows in the lab?"

"There aren't. Just in the outer-rim offices. They're bulletproof," he assured her. "Not a security threat."

Seth seemed displeased about the lack of windows away from the outer-rim offices, which made no sense. After all his years of working in secure labs, he should be used to it. Though many did suffer physical and emotional challenges due to the lack of natural sunlight and fresh air. It was a hazard of the job that a couple weeks' rest and relaxation typically cured. Those not cured transferred out to jobs that required less secure environments.

They stopped at the back of a line of four people waiting to get through security's entrance checkpoint.

When they stepped up to the desk, a brash young lieutenant greeted them. " 'Morning."

"Lieutenant Dean," Seth said. "This is Dr. Hy—"

"Warner," Julia interrupted. "Dr. Julia Warner." She smiled and offered him her hand. "It's nice to meet you, Lieutenant."

"Thank you, ma'am."

Seth looked at her strangely, but said nothing about her dropping Karl's name. "I'll show her the ropes."

The lieutenant nodded, Seth swiped his ID card in the system's slot, and when the light turned green, he crossed the threshold of a metal archway.

Julia followed suit, clipped the badge back to the lapel

of her navy suit jacket, and then followed Seth, her heels clicking softly on the gray tile.

The inner building was a maze of long and winding corridors that all looked alike: bare white walls, gray tile floors, and closed doors. "It would take six months to stop getting lost in here." Julia stepped around two colonels who had paused to talk in the hallway. A map of the place would help tremendously, but Security would veto one being drafted, much less one being distributed for use.

"It's not bad, really." Seth chuckled. "Just visualize the layout. The center of the building is the inner lab. The vault surrounds it. There's only one corridor leading to it, no windows, and one door. Security is far more extensive and sophisticated here than the lab in New Orleans."

"How extensive and sophisticated?" Already, her every move was being monitored by a chip in her ID badge. And she would have to be blind not to see the cameras at every intersecting corridor and door.

"Very." Seth led on. "The offices out here are for the general lab. Lots of dual technologies being developed. Secure, but not—"

"I understand." Dual-technology programs had civilian and military applications. The projects in the outer lab weren't Black Box projects developed solely for military use. Black Box projects were developed in the inner lab, and unless you headed the program or you were the sole-source contractor's project representative, you knew only the portion of the project you worked on. You might have a general understanding of the overall mission, but more than likely, you knew only your own specific personal mission. In the general lab, you were more apt to know not only both the civilian and military applications of your entire project, but those of the others being developed around you.

Seth stopped at a junction in the corridor. A studious security guard stood sentry at a small podium-type desk. " 'Morning, Dr. Holt."

"Good morning, Sergeant Grimm." Seth smiled. "This

is Dr. Warner. She'll be working with me in the vault for a while."

The sergeant skimmed Seth with a handheld scanner, then moved to scan Julia. "Welcome to the zone, ma'am."

Julia smiled at the reminder. People often referred to the vault as the Twilight Zone because, in it, strange and bizarre ideas were considered the norm. "Thank you."

He finished scanning and then nodded toward the card-system machine attached to the wall near his shoulder.

Seth inserted his ID card, then walked through.

Julia followed.

They moved on, down yet another seemingly endless, winding corridor. "We've walked at least a mile." And she had the screaming arches to prove it. "How much farther?"

"We've walked just under half a mile, actually." They stopped again. "I'll explain more once we're inside."

She nodded, staring at the two glass cylinders behind Seth. Bordered by solid walls, the cylinders ran from ceiling to floor. You either went through them, or turned around.

"They're not glass," Seth said. "They're sound-and-bulletproof, and strong enough to sustain the force of a reasonable explosion." He shrugged. "Perfectly safe."

Julia gave him a sidelong look. "Define *reasonable*."

Seth laughed and motioned for her to follow his lead.

She stepped to the side of the cylinder and inserted her card into the appropriate slot. With a little high-pitched whir, it sucked the card inside. The cylinder's door opened. When she'd moved inside, the door sealed shut. Locked in, she noted the absence of air flow: a necessary precaution against biological or chemical invasion, if not exactly comfortable. A moment passed, and another, and then the door in front of her glided open. She stepped out and dragged in a deep breath of crisp air.

"Don't forget your card." Seth motioned toward the machine.

He looked a little green around the gills. Wondering

why, she stepped aside, and then pulled her card from the tray. "You okay?"

"Yeah." He grabbed his card. "I just hate this damn thing."

Evidently, being locked inside the cylinder unnerved him. Funny, how differently people react to things. To her, it was a rare place. One where she felt safe.

Seth smiled sheepishly. "Almost there."

"Good. People have children in less time than it takes to get into this place."

"It's not that bad, Julia."

"No, it's that good." It was time-consuming and irritating, but the precautions were definitely warranted.

They walked down yet another deserted gray corridor to the next checkpoint. This one was unmanned, though cameras littered the wall, covering every possible angle.

Passing through, they took the first right, and then stopped at a set of double doors. Two machines hung side by side on the wall next to them. Seth stepped up to the first machine and centered his forehead against a plate glass, as if he were peeking inside. Given a green light, he moved to the second machine and placed his palm flat against a pad that resembled a small computer screen.

Julia mimicked him. Iris and palm print scanners. "Biometrics?"

"Enhanced biometrics," he corrected. "Including facial-structure scans."

Something in his tone alerted her. "And what else?"

"That's classified." The double doors opened. "We're here."

Julia looked at the doors, then above them. "After all that, just one camera at the entrance to the vault?"

Seth laughed. "We've been in the vault since we went through the transporter—the glass cylinder."

"Oh." Julia wanted to cringe but refused to do it. She should have realized that. *Transporter* was an apt slang name for the cylinder. Working in the vault's inner lab was like working in another world. "Just how thick are the walls in this place?"

"Well over eighteen feet."

Not an exact response, which meant he had no intention of stating specifics, but the footage cited was thick enough to sustain a direct hit from any missile known to man, except for the Rogue, without concerns of penetration compromising the vault's integrity.

The double doors closed behind them. Julia looked around. Offices on the outer perimeter, the inner lab in the center of the complex. A handful of men and women sat at their workstations. Same gray tile floors and white walls as everywhere else, but the lab didn't feel abandoned. Pulsating energy, it felt alive.

"Come on," Seth said. "I'll give you the nickel tour. Maybe we'll run into Dempsey."

"Who's Dempsey?" Julia looked at the lab tables with pure envy. Everything imaginable, right at the fingertips. And for the thousandth time, she felt that hollow ache of loss at having to leave her work behind. The lab had been the one place she had felt comfortable. The one place she hadn't felt compelled to lock doors and constantly look back over her shoulder.

The only place she had been safe.

"Dempsey Morse," Seth said, pausing at the water fountain to get a quick drink. "He represents Slicer Industries on the team."

Home Base's contractor. "Ah, I see."

"We have a briefing set up for ten. You'll definitely meet him then. I think you'll like him. Dempsey's sharp. A UCLA graduate with about twenty years' experience. A little gruff, but a good man to have on our side."

"Sounds charming."

"Right."

Ignoring him, Julia looked around. Three offices, a conference room, an employee's lounge, several sets of rest rooms, a showering facility, and a detox sterilization chamber formed the outer perimeter, and the hub—the inner lab—at the complex's center. An admin section stood in the southeast corner, across from the three offices. In it, she saw an unmanned desk—administrative assistance was banned in the inner lab—a keyed copier that tracked who made copies, when, how many, and of what, and a one-way fax. Anything could come into the Black Box, but nothing went out.

"The computers in here are on a closed system," Seth said. "No networking to the outside, no Internet access. We have two offices outside the vault with access and e-mail. You can use those, but on nothing regarding the project, of course."

"Electronic mail wasn't a big deal before I left."

"It is now."

As she had thought. In three years, a lot had changed.

Seth ducked in through an open door. "Your office. Mine's next door."

"Terrific." She stepped inside and sat down at her desk. It felt good. Strange, but good. Almost like home.

"Why don't you settle in? Files on the desk there relate to the project and team members. Specific project files, you'll have to sign out one by one. Greta handles that for us. You'll meet her at the briefing."

"Fine."

A frown knit Seth's brow. He seemed hesitant. Finally, he worked his way up to asking what he wanted to know. "Julia, why have you dropped—" He stopped suddenly. "Never mind."

He looked at her, seeking encouragement to finish his question. Knowing what it was—why she'd dropped Karl's surname—she didn't give it.

"Well." He motioned to the far wall. "Conference room is on the other side of the lab. See you there at ten."

Julia nodded, and then watched him through the glass wall, giving her a view of the lab. He walked straight to his office. Seth had done everything in the world to make her comfortable—at the apartment and here. He even had quelled his curiosity about her name change. Grateful for that small mercy, she shoved her hair back from her face and looked around.

The office was decent. About twenty feet long and twelve wide. Tiled, like everything else, but the far white wall had been decorated with a mural of an English garden. Pretty scene. And her desk even faced the door.

Seth had remembered. He'd often remarked on her "fetish" for seeing what was coming. He had no idea how on-target he had been, of course, and it wasn't so much *what* but *who*. His not knowing had been one of the reasons they had worked together with such comfort and ease.

Don't be a coward, Julia. There were a lot of reasons you were at ease with Seth. Admit it.

There were. She loved his honesty. Knowing that if Seth said something, she could bank on it. Anyone could. He always played straight. And he had courage. When necessary, he would go toe to toe with anyone short of God, and yet he genuinely respected other people's ideas, views, and opinions. He seldom teased, but often laughed.

You always loved Seth's laughter.

She had. For some strange reason, in it she heard hope. After she had left, when times had gotten really, really tough and the urge to quit trying overwhelmed her, she would hear Seth's laughter in her mind and find the strength she needed to keep struggling. Without his laughter, she might have given up.

Special.

Yes, but only in a general sense. Nothing personal or remotely intimate. She'd have to be crazy to ever let herself get personal or intimate again.

Julia, Julia, Julia. Wake up, woman. You already have.

No way. No damn way. Not now, not ever again. She'd nearly died, for God's sake.

Whatever you say.

Oh, shut up.

Her conscience had to be wrong about this. Had to be.

Slightly nauseous, she stretched to the stack of files, pulled out one labeled Profiles, and dug in, eager to get her mind off Seth and familiarize herself with the team and the project.

"Okay," she said, lifting a page with an unsteady hand. "First, let's get a fix on you, Dempsey Morse . . ."

Chapter Three

JULIA entered the conference room promptly at ten.

Seven people were already seated, waiting for her. Seth had taken the chair at the foot of the table, leaving the opposite end free for her. As project head, she would occupy that seat in the future, but not wanting to exert authority before it had officially been given to her, or before introductions, she walked on and sat down in the empty chair at Seth's right.

From the gleam in his eyes, Seth understood. He should. This was a management technique she had learned from him.

"Everyone, this is Dr. Julia Warner," Seth said. "You have her profile before you." He nodded to the single sheet of paper on the conference table at each seat.

"Julia, this is the team." Seth started on his left. "Dempsey Morse."

"Welcome to the zone, Doctor."

Morse was shorter than Seth, about fifty, and round bellied. He had nice eyes. Gray-blue with a kind twinkle in them. He looked pleasant natured, and Julia hoped he was; though she had her doubts. Dempsey Morse had been married and divorced four times. But that could be the job. It was demanding, and hell on a family. Morse was profiled to be sharp, devoted, and disciplined. That sounded good in her book. "Thank you, Mr. Morse," she said. "It's good to be here."

"Dempsey."

She nodded, then looked to the man at his side.

"Cracker." The youngest member of the team, a chilling twenty-three, swiped a hand over his shaved head. "I do computers."

An understatement, if ever she'd heard one. Cracker was a computer-guru genius. He didn't drink or smoke. He wasn't married, had no permanent relationships going, and he considered computing a recreational activity as well as his life's work. He could hack into, or block out, any known security system, and had earned his nickname by proving it to the CIA. In a little friendly rivalry competition, the Defense Intelligence Agency bet the CIA that he could crack their security system. He'd won—which came as no surprise to the DIA because he had already cracked their system. "Hi, Cracker," Julia said, then glanced on around the table.

"Greta." A pretty redhead introduced herself. Her hair was short and spiky, a little on the funky side, yet her clothing was extremely conservative. "Booster systems specialist and secure-file liaison."

"Hello, Greta." Thirty-five, beautiful, brainy, and no wedding ring. Why hadn't Seth latched onto her?

The thought came, and an unexpected streak of jealousy came with it. Tight-chested and surprised, Julia banished both. The idea of Seth and Greta—or him and any woman, for that matter—should not make Julia jealous. Ridiculous reaction.

Ridiculous. It was *not* personal. She looked on.

"Mr. Sandlis." The oldest member of the team, hovering sixty, paused rapping his pen against the tabletop to push his glasses up on his nose. "Trajectory specialist."

Julia nodded and her gaze locked on a forty-year-old man with dark, leathery skin and even darker eyes.

"Marcus." He slumped in his chair. "Explosives."

A shiver prickled up Julia's spine, and she quickly

looked away, to the gorgeous African-American woman dressed in red, who could pass for thirty though she was over forty.

"Linda," she said in a rich, husky voice. "Interceptor/Tracker specialist and Saudi widow." She sighed. "Again."

"Ouch." Julia flinched. Seth had told her about Linda being married to Mac, an active-duty Air Force pilot, who had just been deployed for his fourth remote tour in Saudi Arabia. "Sorry to hear it."

"Sorry to have to say it." Linda sighed deeper. "Again."

Julia sent her an empathetic look. The long separations during remote tours, when the spouse and family were left behind, were part of the norm for military families, but that didn't make them, or the readjustments on returning home from them, easier for the service members or their families. In Linda's case, she was being left behind for the fourth time in just over three years with two rebellious teenage sons who seemed bent on driving her nuts by pushing every boundary possible to see what they could get away with while their dad was away. "If you need a shoulder, mine's here."

Genuine appreciation shone in Linda's eyes. "Thanks."

"Anytime," Julia said, then addressed the entire team. "I'm looking forward to working with all of you. Right now, the U.S. lacks a missile-defense system and is vulnerable to attack. When we're done, we'll have the most advanced system in operation worldwide. We can feel good about the security that system offers and what it means in real terms to Main Street America." She offered them a smile.

Marcus and Dempsey Morse didn't smile back.

It was an interesting group with impressive credentials. With the exception of Dempsey Morse and Mr. Sandlis, who offered no first name, none of the team offered their surname, and all around they had avoided disclosing their official titles. Seth definitely had compiled another winning team. She glanced over at him and tugged at her right earlobe.

Understanding lit in his eyes, and he tugged back.

It was a signal common between them in the old days, and he had remembered. She almost laughed out loud, and she probably would have, but something about him wasn't . . . right.

She scanned him and her gaze stuck at his collar. His ID badge. The overhead light glared on it, so she couldn't see it clearly, but she could tell the man pictured did not have black hair. She checked, and everyone else had their badges. So whose did Seth have?

More importantly, who had his?

Seth took over, spoke a few words about the day's goals, and then ended the meeting.

It had been brief. A formality, really. A chance for her to meet the team and officially take over the project.

They filed out of the conference room and returned to their offices and workstations. Julia lingered, intending to ask Seth about the badge, but he pulled Linda aside and asked her something about her kids. From his tone, it sounded serious and, not wanting to interrupt, Julia decided to wait until they had finished their conversation to talk to him about his badge. Waiting should be safe enough. They were in the inner lab, for God's sake.

She walked on to her own office, thoughtful, and sat down at her desk. Seth had seemed genuinely interested in Linda and her children, and he certainly had been genuinely concerned about Jeff. What if when Julia's troubles had started she had gone to Seth with them? What if she hadn't felt so ashamed and embarrassed and certain her problems had been her fault? She had refused to even acknowledge there were problems until it was too late. But what if she hadn't?

Seth would have helped her. Just as he had helped her with Jeff. Just as he helped Linda. Julia wouldn't have had to deal with—

Stop it. Just stop it. Done is done.

She squeezed her eyes shut. Done *was* done. Dragging Seth into hell with her would have been a stupid thing to do. It couldn't have worked out much worse than it had for her, but involving Seth would only have made him intimate friends with misery, too. She'd done the right thing, keeping him out of it.

Letting go of the past, she reached for a file.

The rest of the morning breezed by with Julia rereading the profiles, looking for personal strengths and potential weaknesses in the team members that could create challenges. More often than not, problems originated with the staff, not the work, and if she could spot weaknesses and negate them, she would take a lot of pressure off herself and spare the whole team headaches.

At noon, she scarfed down a sandwich at her desk and shifted her focus to policy changes that had occurred during her absence. Those, she had to get a grip on quickly. Nothing could sabotage a program faster than breaching policy, stepping on toes, and ticking off powerful people.

Finally, about four, she began reviewing the actual project files. By tomorrow night, she estimated, she'd be up to speed.

She could have made the transition sooner, but none of the project files she needed to review could be removed from the vault, and no crisis on the horizon warranted her pulling an all-nighter. Her day officially ended at sixteen thirty—four-thirty P.M. Naturally, she would work until her usual six.

Just after five, Seth appeared in her doorway. "Julia."

The concern in his voice jerked her attention from the file in her hands to him. Long ago, she had become accustomed to Seth's shielding his emotions, to his expression appearing dark, remote, and distant. But now it looked ten times darker than Marcus's and the worry she had seen in Seth's eyes at the beach had doubled. That chilled her to the bone. "What is it?"

He closed her office door, then turned and jammed a fist into his pocket. "We've got a serious problem."

With Seth, serious meant *serious*. Her skin crawled. And what he had told her at the picnic area came to mind.

Millions could pay with their lives.

Julia prodded him. "What's wrong?"

"Someone's made copies of Home Base's sensor codes."

"Who?" They had a keyed copier, for God's sake.

"According to the log"—Seth's grim expression turned sickly and cold fury glinted in his eyes—"me."

Julia mentally flashed back to the conference room, to the briefing. To Seth's name badge. "Oh, hell." She stared up at him. "We're being set up."

Chapter Four

W E need to lock down the vault."

Julia considered it, then rubbed her hands together atop her desk. "I think that would be a mistake, Seth."

"A mistake?" He paced between her visitor's chair and office door. "Don't you understand? They've got the damn sensor codes."

"I understand." Grave news. Home Base's sensor codes controlled its sensory perceptions, much like a human's eyes and ears. It collected visual, audio, and magnetic energy data, verified it, and then transmitted the verified data back to them—one day, to the duty monitor at the Battle Management Center—giving them a clear picture, except for the type of warhead of the incoming hostile missile's capability.

Definitely grave news. Dangerous news. "Sit down, okay?" She motioned to the green visitor's chair, and then waited.

"Sit down?" He leaned against her desk. "We need to move on this."

"Seth," she said more firmly. "Sit down."

He stared at her as if she'd lost her mind, and then plopped down on the leather chair. Air gushed out of it. "We're wasting time."

"No we're not." She leaned toward him. "If we lock down the lab, odds double that we'll never find out who copied the codes." Convinced she was right, she pressed on. "We need to keep this quiet."

"Quiet?" Seth dragged a hand through his hair. It gleamed black in the fluorescent light. "Julia, would you think? Whoever took those codes—"

"Can't do a damn thing with them until the project is developed and activated."

"What if they get to whoever's got the Rogue? Hostiles could develop the technology before we do. We'd have no damn defense."

The thought chilled her to the marrow of her bones. "Not with only the codes. They'd need more. System designs, specs, schematics." She spun through scenarios. "Look, I agree that we've got a serious problem, but we can't react out of fear—not if we want to identify the thief."

Seth visibly calmed down and some of the color returned to his face. "We're compelled to notify Security and the OSI. How do you propose we do that and keep this quiet?"

"We don't break protocol, we just slow it down a little." Julia lifted a pen from the blotter. She always thought better with a pen in her hand. "You noted irregularities before the project was funded. Who assisted you in developing the prototype and is now on the team?"

"Dempsey Morse, Cracker, and Marcus. Everyone else is new."

"Then it seems plausible that one of them copied the codes."

"That's a hell of an assumption."

"Yes, it is." She slumped back. "But irregularities manifested then and now. We're too new into the project for someone unfamiliar with it to have gathered much info outside their own areas. Crossover seems far more probable." She waited for that disclosure to sink in, and then went on. "Also, during the briefing this morning, I noticed your ID badge wasn't yours."

"What?" Startled, Seth looked down to the badge. "It's mine."

"Now it is. Then, it wasn't," Julia insisted. "The photo caught my eye."

"Whose was it?"

"I couldn't tell. The lights caused a glare," she said. Now, of course, she wished she had immediately pursued finding out. But she had blown that opportunity.

Withholding a sigh, she looked over at Seth. "I intended to ask you about it, but you were talking with Linda and it sounded serious. I didn't want to interrupt. Then, the truth is, I got involved and forgot about it." Not an admirable or easy thing to admit, but honest.

"So someone switched the badge, and then switched it back? While I was in the inner lab?" Seth snorted. "Julia, that sounds absurd."

"Nevertheless, it's what I think happened. I know the photo wasn't yours." She reached over to her cup of tea, and took a sip. Fear dried out the throat in a hurry. "Did you deliberately remove your badge at any time before the briefing?"

"No, I didn't."

"Okay, then who had the opportunity to switch badges with you?"

"It could have been any of them. I met with all three separately before the briefing. And with Linda."

Linda, who was frustrated and stressed out at again being a Saudi widow.

Seth frowned. "It's hard to believe someone could have switched the badge and then switched it back without me noticing."

"Not really." Julia set her teacup down and missed its warmth against her fingers. Inside, she felt ice-cold. "They taught us how it's done in counterterrorism training, remember?"

Seth blinked, grimaced, and then blinked again, looking totally disgusted with himself. As if he'd made a foolish mistake and regretted it. "Yeah, I remember."

Knowing Seth would beat himself up over this for a long time to come without added assistance, Julia turned the topic, focusing on finding a solution rather than dwelling on a mistake that couldn't be changed. "So who did you meet with twice—once to switch the badges, and then after the briefing, to switch them back?"

His grim expression turned grimmer. "All of them, including Linda."

Figured. Nothing could be easy in these situations. The thief would see to that. "Locking down the lab won't tell us anything, Seth. But it will tell the thief plenty."

"We sure as hell can't ignore it."

"No, we can't. We've had a security breach and we need to do the right thing." He wasn't going to like this. How could he? He looked guilty as hell of committing the crime.

And he could be guilty.

Oh, but she hated thinking it, much less testing the possibility for credibility, but in the past three years, he could have changed. Seth could have orchestrated this. "We can delay a little, but then we need to contact the OSI."

He blew out a long breath, rubbed his palms over his thighs. "You're right." His tone deepened, became more somber. "It's going to look bad for me, Julia."

"Yes, it will." She stared him straight in the eye, hating herself for doubting his innocence. Yet doubt was there—and it *should* be there. Hadn't he trained her to consider all possibilities, every eventuality, regardless of who was involved? "But no matter how it looks, we have to fulfill our duties, Seth. We can't compromise them or our integrity." They would have nothing left, including no self-respect.

He sat silent.

And she worried. What if he asked her to keep the breach confidential until he could prove his innocence? Would she? Could she? She shouldn't. Certainly she shouldn't, and yet . . . She swallowed hard. Oh, but she hoped he didn't ask.

"My words to you. I remember." He gripped the chair arms. "I meant them then, and they're just as true now. We can't compromise." He swallowed hard. "We have no choice."

Through her relief, she felt his resignation, grasped what doing the right thing was costing him personally. And she wondered. If in his position, would she have his courage? She hoped she would, but she couldn't be sure. Maybe no one could be sure until they were in that position.

He hauled himself out of the chair. His knees cracked, and a muscle in his cheek twitched. "For the record, I didn't do it."

The flicker of doubt flamed. Never before had Seth felt it necessary to defend himself on ethical issues to her, or to remind her that he had established the ethic. Why now?

Her heart told her that he sensed her skepticism and wanted to put it to rest, and she wanted to give him the benefit of the doubt, to trust him. But her head refused to let her do it. She tried to take that leap of faith—*really tried*—but the lessons she had learned against trusting on faith alone had been ingrained until they were as much a part of her as her DNA. She couldn't do it, especially when she alone wouldn't suffer the consequences of making the wrong choice. It wasn't right to jeopardize unsuspecting others who had entrusted her with the responsibility of making those decisions wisely. That responsibility wasn't a coat she could just take off and stuff in the closet because suddenly wearing it had become uncomfortable. It wasn't right.

It wasn't safe.

Hoping for reassurance and not getting it clearly disappointed Seth, but he quickly shielded it behind remote indifference. "No sense in delaying." He lifted the phone receiver, punched down the secure-line button, and then dialed the Office of Special Investigations.

"Agent 12, please." Seth looked at the files on her desk, at the bare foot she rubbed with the toe of her pump-shod one. He looked at the mural—anywhere and everywhere, except into her eyes.

Julia hated hurting him. He had always been good to her, always had been open and honest. His laughter had helped her heal.

Seth is an ethical man, for God's sake.

But is he an innocent one?

That, she didn't know. Worse, she couldn't prove it. And until she could . . .

"Do you have some time on your schedule?" Seth's fingers clamped around the phone's receiver. His knuckles went white. "Dr. Warner-Hyde—Dr. Warner," he corrected himself, "and I need a few minutes." He let out a sigh. "Yes, I'm afraid it is." He cranked his neck back, let his gaze drift across the dimpled ceiling. "We've had a security breach."

He paused to listen, and then added, "Yeah, we'll be right over."

JULIA and Seth took the steps two at a time and entered the unnumbered brick building housing Grayton Air Force Base's Office of Special Investigations.

Seth opened the door and Julia stepped through. Heat blasted her in the face. Evidently, the OSI office was having trouble with the base's master climate control adjusting to the swift temperature changes outside, too. At the lab, people had been complaining. Yesterday they needed heat and had air-conditioning. Today, they needed air-conditioning and had heat. She walked across the reception area to the first of two desks.

An older woman, wearing silver-rimmed glasses on the tip of her nose, looked up at them. "May I help you?"

Seth answered. "Agent 12, please."

She skimmed a subtle look at their name badges. "Just a moment." Lifting the phone receiver, she punched in a series of numbers, paused, and then said, "Drs. Holt and Warner have arrived."

Julia glanced over to the armed soldier standing guard behind a glass booth. The overhead light glinted on the metal butt of his holstered gun.

"Yes, sir. I'll send them right in." The receptionist—Mrs. Anderson, according to her name plate—cradled the phone then tipped her gray head toward the first of two hallways. "He'll meet you in the conference room," she said. "Left corridor, second door on the right."

Julia nodded, and then started down the long corridor beside Seth.

Photos of former OSI commanders dressed in dark blue Class-A uniforms lined the wall. All men, all broad shouldered, all brigadier generals. Considering the responsibilities that went with commanding investigations of everything from petty crimes to computer-information theft, project corruption, security breaches, and murders occurring on Air Force installations, Julia supposed the commanders needed broad shoulders—and the clout that comes with rank. Not all crimes were committed by service members of lesser rank than the criminologists investigating them, and some suspects were civil servants, dependents of active-duty or retired service members, and some were civilians. The crime that had brought them here could have been committed by any or all of the above.

At the second door, they stopped, and Seth rapped.

"Come in." A man's voice carried through the wood.

Recognizing it as that of the agent who had breached protocol and saved her life, Julia tensed.

"Julia?" Seth motioned for her to go inside.

She entered and, needing a moment to collect herself, she avoided looking at Agent 12 by focusing on the only other thing in the room: a conference table surrounded by twelve chairs with worn leatherette cushions.

"Agent 12." Seth offered his hand. "Thanks for taking time to see us."

Agent 12. Typically, it wasn't necessary or wise to know more about an OSI agent than his number. Interacting with one generally signaled serious trouble; something service members and civil servants alike attempted to avoid. Julia hadn't even known his number, only that he was an OSI agent. Prepared now, she glanced up at him.

Definitely the same man. Older than her and Seth's thirty-seven, about forty-six, with blond hair, blue eyes, and a boy next-door face that hadn't seemed to age since their first meeting. He was dressed in civilian clothes, a brown suit, which was a common OSI agent practice. Rank anonymity leveled the field and eliminated intimidation barriers between lower- and higher-ranked suspects or witnesses and agents.

"It's good to see you, Dr. Holt." Agent 12 shook and released Seth's hand, and then turned to her. "You must be Dr. Warner."

"Yes." Julia clasped and shook. Not a hint of recognition in his eyes. None. He looked at her as if she were a complete stranger. Convenient amnesia must be a job skill an agent developed with practice. He was good at it. "How are you?"

He motioned for them to sit and returned to his chair. "Any better and it'd kill me."

A lie, and they all knew it. Things were rough all over. In the last six years, the military had suffered a forty percent drawdown in forces and a budget strung so tight that a minor, unanticipated conflict outside U.S. borders sent the administration scurrying to Congress to beg for money and stretched resources and personnel so thin that CONUS— the continental U.S.—was left vulnerable. Things were definitely rough all over.

"So," Agent 12 said, "tell me about this security breach."

Julia let Seth talk, and he did so at length.

The longer she sat there listening, the more intensely her head ached. Partly from pretending she had never seen Agent 12 before, and—she glanced at her watch—partly because she, Agent 12, and Seth had been cloistered in the secure briefing room for over an hour already. Every known detail about the sensor-code theft had been related. Every potential challenge that could arise had been thoroughly discussed. For the past ten minutes, Seth and Agent 12 had been rehashing events and the potential impact of the stolen sensor codes.

Julia recognized the pattern's methodology. Agent 12 absorbed all the data, sifted through, doubled back for verifications and clarifications—no doubt factoring in intelli-

gence report contents he had access to that they did not—
and then formed a plan of action. If jackhammers weren't
having a field day inside her head, she might have appreciated the intricacies of the mental process. Instead, she
couldn't focus beyond doubting Seth and hoping Agent 12
drew some conclusions soon. If she wanted to get through
the headache—the guilt for doubting Seth would take
longer—before it got to the migraine, throw-your-guts-up
stage, then she needed food, medication, a hot bath, and a
cold glass of juice. And she needed them fast.

Agent 12 looked up from a legal pad of scribbled notes
only he and God could possible decipher. "So, in your professional opinions, the sensor-codes theft poses a real and
serious danger, but not an immediate threat. Am I clear on
that?"

Seth responded. "Yes."

"Can we reprogram the codes?"

"We can, but we'll lose maximum effectiveness," Seth
responded succinctly. "The systems are interdependent.
Change one, and you've got to change them all to maintain
the highest precision probability ratings."

"It'd be a nightmare to do," Julia added. "But if necessary, we have the ability to make it happen."

"True." Seth nodded. "But maybe not before the hostiles
do and they inflict serious damage on us."

Agent 12 fixed his gaze on his pad. "All right. Here's
what we're going to do." He leaned back in his chair,
gripped its arms, and then laid out his plan of action. "Officially, the OSI is investigating. But no word of the matter
is to leave this room. Tell no one that the codes have been
copied."

"Not even Colonel Pullman?" Julia asked. The lab commander should know about this.

"Isn't he still TDY to Switzerland?"

"Yes, he is," Seth said. "Two more weeks."

Agent 12 nodded. "Then, at the moment, he has no need
to know."

Julia saw the logic in that. Pullman was thousands of

miles away, unable to do anything, so why drag him into the net and risk further comprising security? "What about lab Security or the Home Base team members?" she asked. She knew the answer, but she wanted it official.

"No, not a word about the theft," Agent 12 confirmed. "And no one is to know an investigation is in progress. That's vital."

"Is this the best possible course of action?" Julia squinted against the harsh glare of the fluorescent lights. "Being unaware, another team member could divulge crippling information to the thief."

"I hope so." Agent 12 gave her a solemn nod. "When the theft seems to go unnoticed, the thief is going to doubt that he or she stole the right sensor codes. If the right codes had been stolen, then the lab would be locked down and a formal investigation launched. Security, OSI agents, Intel, a team from the Inspector General's office—everyone would be swarming the place, crawling up everyone's backside and down their throats, right?"

"Yes," Julia answered. They would be in everyone's face with microscopes, digging into professional and personal relationships, sifting through every tidbit of data, much of which would prove insignificant but had to be investigated and verified to be dismissed.

"So the absence of an investigation, and of anyone seeming to notice a theft in a high-security area has occurred, makes doubt gnaw at the thief. He needs confirmation." The agent gave her a steely look. "When he seeks it, he tips his hand. We'll know it."

"It's our best shot," Seth agreed.

"That's the way I see it." Agent 12 stood up. "Keep me posted on anything unusual. Even if it seems trivial. Sometimes what seems insignificant makes the case."

Julia gathered her purse. "Nothing about a theft in a Black World vault's inner lab is insignificant, Agent 12."

"True." He nodded an apology. "I'll have someone review the Security films. Maybe we got lucky and the cameras picked up your badge being switched, Dr. Holt. If not—"

"I know." Seth dipped his chin. "I'm guilty until proven innocent."

"I'm afraid so." Agent 12 turned his gaze to Julia. "Theoretically, I should pull Dr. Holt's clearances until this matter is resolved."

Julia glimpsed Seth out of the corner of her eye. He fully expected she would ask Agent 12 to do exactly that. And she should. But she hesitated, wavering, and then did the only thing she could tolerate doing, though she cursed herself as a damn fool for it. "I'll accept responsibility. As I said, I noted the badge had been switched before the theft. As far as I'm concerned, Dr. Holt has already been proven innocent of the security breach."

She'd said and meant it. Now she had to hope she could live with it—without regret, and without creating more demons.

WHY had she done it?

Seth closed the Lexus's passenger door, glanced at Julia through the window, and then walked around the hood and got in on the driver's side. He still couldn't figure it out.

Julia hadn't accepted personal responsibility for him out of a sense of loyalty. When it came to security breaches, she had no loyalty. She might not be convinced he was guilty, but she doubted he was innocent. No way had he misinterpreted that.

She sat silently, staring straight ahead, her purse in her lap. Something strange was going on with her, right down to her name. Jeff and the kids called her Dr. Julia. Understandable. Dr. Warner-Hyde was a mouthful for six-year-old kids, and confusing, with a "Mr. Warner" also teaching at the same school. But why had she introduced herself as "Warner" and dropped "Hyde" from her surname at Grayton?

Seth cranked the engine, pulled out of the OSI parking lot, and then headed back across base toward the office. At the intersection of Powell Drive and General Mayes Boulevard, he braked at the four-way stop. A blue truck crossed the intersection. His headlights shone against its door.

The silence in the Lexus was deafening; even the blinker flashing sounded like thunder. This wasn't the companionable silence he and Julia had enjoyed. This silence was stone-cold, tense, and anything but comfortable.

Seth punched down on the gas pedal, hooked a left, and fell into line behind the truck. He couldn't blame her for doubting him. After all, he had trained her to doubt—particularly on security-breach incidents. Julia always had seemed wary of others' motives, but he couldn't fault her for that, either. Long before he had joined the Special Forces, wariness had proven its value as an essential survival skill.

So, she doubted him. He couldn't condemn her for it, and he hadn't. Not verbally, anyway. But she sensed it; hence, the silence. He wasn't being fair.

Bent on making things right, he passed the credit union and stopped at the traffic light by the service station. He glanced at the dashboard clock, and then over at Julia. Still stiff and wooden. "It's nearly seven. Do you want to grab some dinner?"

"I don't think so. It's been a long day and my head is killing me."

He shouldn't have asked but, damn it, he wanted the tension between them to end. And he wanted answers. He *needed* answers. She worried about trusting him, but he worried about trusting her, too. His financial and professional reputations were on the line—even more so now than when he had gone to her for help. "Maybe you'd feel better if you ate."

"I'll pass, Seth."

Dead end. He couldn't force her to tell him anything, and odds were she wouldn't, but he had to ask. It didn't take much of a stretch to imagine Julia being radically different from the person she had been three years ago.

Is she different?

Torn between wanting to know and fearing what he would discover, Seth accepted that he had no choice but to find out. Because he had met with one other person both before and after the briefing. One other person who had both access and the opportunity to pull the double switch with the badges. One other person he would be a damn fool not to consider a viable suspect, because she had wanted to keep the sensor theft quiet.

Julia.

Chapter Five

THE migraine won.

Julia crawled into bed moaning, sank back against the pillow, and draped a cold washcloth over her forehead and eyes. Her stomach rolled, her every pulse beat throbbed with the force of a hammer strike against her temples, at the backs of her eyes. If she moved to pull up the covers or turn off the nightstand's lamp, she would throw up. And that would trigger an all-night vigil of vomiting and pain. Taking the oral medication Dr. Flynn had prescribed would be an exercise in futility. She had waited too long. Now a muscle in her left arm knotted, raising a lump the size of a lemon, and it throbbed, too.

You know better than to get stressed. You know better.

"Oh, shut up." The headache would run its course, as so many had in the past three years, and the muscle spasms in her arm and shoulder would eventually stop, too. Until then, she was damned to suffer them both. Just one more challenge in a long list of them. Some legacy.

One breath at a time.

At least Seth hadn't pushed her for answers tonight. But he had again assured her that he hadn't copied the sensor codes and he had confessed that, when in his office, he often kept his badge on his desk. He took it off because, when he worked at the computer, it dug into his arm. And he had wrangled a commitment from her for dinner at Antonio's restaurant tomorrow night after work.

His questions would come then.

They were inevitable. She might as well let him ask the damn things, and have it done and over. But, God, she didn't want him to look at her with pity. Or with morose curiosity. Or without the respect she had always seen in his eyes.

Yet how could she avoid it? What could she tell him?

Anything—except the truth. She would have to lie.

To Seth? To Seth, whose laughter gave you strength when you had none and you needed it to survive? You're going to lie to Seth?

Her stomach heaved.

The vigil had started.

SETH stood on the porch, outside the front door. "I know it's late, Camden, but I want to see him."

"Damn it, Holt, he's asleep." Camden scratched his head, shrugged a robe-clad shoulder. "So was I."

Seth resisted an urge to sigh. "Look, I thought we had an understanding about this."

"Understanding? I call it blackmail."

"And I call your bruising Jeff a felony," Seth countered. "You can let me peek in on him, or I call the cops and complain and they'll check on him—every two hours. Your choice."

Cinching the belt on his blue robe, Camden frowned, opened the door, and then led Seth upstairs to Jeff's room.

It was spotless. Toys shelved against the wall, nothing tossed on the carpeted floor. Even his lunch box had been placed on his desk chair. Weird for a six-year-old boy. And Jeff lay on a twin bed, scrunched up under a quilted crimson bedspread with BAMA stamped in white lettering all over it.

Camden stayed in the hallway.

Jeff opened his eyes. "Dr. Seth."

"Hey, buddy." Seth smiled into Jeff's droopy eyes. "Sorry I woke you."

"I wasn't sleeping," he whispered, glancing at the door to make sure they were alone.

"Pretending, huh?"

Jeff nodded against the pillow. "Dad said you forgot me, but I knew you didn't." He reached out from under the covers and patted Seth's chest. "I knew the truth in here."

Jeff had remembered what Seth had told him. His heart swelled and the boy snagged the whole thing. "I'd never forget you," Seth said, knowing it was true. Before Jeff could ask, Seth added, "That's a promise."

"Cuz we're buddies." Jeff flung himself into Seth's arms, then hugged him hard.

So this was what hugging a kid was like. The soapy-kid smell, the tiny arms stretching to reach and fasten around your neck. The sense of total trust. Damn, but it rattled a man. Deep. Seth patted Jeff's back, his own throat thick. "Yeah. We're buddies."

"I love you, Dr. Seth."

Tears burned the back of Seth's nose, stung his eyes. Since he was six, he had waited to hear those words come his way—without sex being a factor and it being hormones talking—and they never had. Not until now. Not until Jeff.

Seth blinked hard, and hugged gently. Jeff made him feel protective, but the boy also pulled at something softer in Seth that he wasn't sure how to tag. Still, he understood what it meant at gut level. He'd go to the wall and scale it or tear it down for this kid. Anywhere, anytime. Go up against anyone. And yet giving Jeff the words wouldn't be easy. Doing something alien never comes easy. But the boy needed the words—and, Seth realized, he needed to give them.

Still, just thinking about saying it had his chest in a vise, his throat stuffed with sandpaper, and his gut full of concrete. But determined, he squeezed his eyes shut, and took the plunge. "I love you, too, Jeff."

DURING the night the phone rang.

Fingering her way across the nightstand, Julia peeked

out from under the cold washcloth and lifted the receiver. "Hello." She sounded half-dead. She felt worse.

"Nowhere to run, nowhere to hide. Not from me, sugar." The man's grated whisper disintegrated into an eerie warning. "You should know better than to even try."

Oh, God. Terror ripped through her veins. Julia flung the receiver onto the sheets and stared at it as if it were a hissing rattler. Hearing his sardonic laughter through the receiver, she grabbed the phone and slammed it on its hook, jerked the plug out of the wall, and then slung it down on the carpeted floor. It bounced and settled with a dull thunk.

Tears blurred her eyes, stole her breath, and a disappointment so deep it felt as if it were cutting her in two slashed through her body. There would be no break from the threats.

Karl had found her.

Chapter Six

JULIA stared into the bathroom mirror and groaned. A corpse had more color than she did this morning.

She slathered on extra makeup to hide the dark circles under her eyes and her deathly pallor, dressed, and then dragged herself into work by nine.

Her gray suit looked drab, but she needed the comfort of quiet to recover. Finally, just before dawn, she had stopped heaving, but her insides were still shaky.

As soon as she left the Camry to approach the building, something Seth had said in the car the night before niggled at her. If when in his office he often kept his badge on his desk, then anyone could have made the first switch. But the sensor codes had been copied at 1040 and Seth had left the building for lunch at 1100. So the second switch, where the thief had returned Seth's badge, had to have occurred during that twenty-minute time span.

If she were committing treason by stealing Top Secret information, what's the first thing she would do?

Get the codes out of the building.

Yeah. Before the second switch. Before anyone noticed the copies had been made. Before any irregularity had been noted and Security shut down the lab.

So, who on the first-switch suspect list also left the building between 1040 and 1100?

Good question.

After clearing the lab's first Security checkpoint, she stopped at the second one. Sergeant Grimm was on duty. He lifted the handheld scanner to run his check, and she asked, "Sergeant, where is the Security office?"

He backed away. "First corridor to the right after you come out of the transporter."

"Thanks." Julia went through the cylinder, and then to the Security office.

A female sergeant who appeared about six months pregnant sat at the reception desk. "May I help you, Dr. Warner?"

Word was out. Everyone in the building knew her name and credentials, and they'd likely already started a betting pool on where she had been for the past three years. *Merciless gossip grapevine.* "Yes, please. Who is responsible for inner-lab security?"

"That would be Colonel Mason, ma'am. But I can probably help you with whatever you need."

"Great." Julia thought fast. "I'm looking for clarification on a specific security procedure. There appears to be conflicting instructions in the regs."

The smile faded. "I'd better get the colonel."

Julia smiled. "Thank you." Conflicts in the regulations usually signaled sticky wickets, often with legal repercussions. No one voluntarily became involved. At least that hadn't changed.

"This way, Dr. Warner." The sergeant led Julia to the colonel's office.

The colonel stood and offered his hand. "Bob Mason."

Julia clasped it firmly and shook. Mason was a huge man, barrel-chested and broad-nosed. His crew cut was short and his complexion ruddy.

"Have a seat, Doctor." He waved to a chair.

Grateful, Julia sat down. After the exercise of walking through the building to his office, she found her insides weren't just shaky from last night's vigil, they rattled. "Thank you."

"We have a problem on a reg?"

"No, we don't." Julia smiled. "I'm sorry, but I didn't want to discuss this with anyone else."

His eyes sparkled interest. "So what do you want to discuss, Doc?"

"I need a list of everyone who was in the inner lab yesterday morning between nine and eleven. Is it possible to get that information?"

"Sure." Smelling a situation in the making, his interest deepened. "Do we have a problem?"

"Not at present, no."

"Can I feel confident that if we develop a problem, I'll be notified immediately?"

"You can bank on it." As soon as Agent 12 gave her an approving nod, she would gladly dump the works in Colonel Mason's lap.

The overhead light glinted on his watch. "May I ask why you want this list?"

"Certainly." She smiled again.

He paused, waited, and when it became evident she wasn't going to elaborate, he laughed. Deep and hard. "I can ask all I want, but you're not going to answer."

Her cagey response amused him. She'd take amusement, so long as she got her list. "I'll answer if I must," she said. "But at this time, I would prefer not to have to do it."

"It is for professional purposes."

Personal purposes would violate the Privacy Act. A huge, huge taboo. "Yes, sir."

He nodded. "That works for me." He turned to his computer, booted up, and keyed in a request. In short order, a list began printing. "I take it you'd prefer this not to come to Colonel Pullman's attention."

The lab commander. "With all due respect, sir, I'd prefer to keep it a private matter, between us."

Mason pursed his lips. "Is he still at that high-level WMD symposium in Switzerland?"

She didn't have to scan her memory through the military's many acronyms to translate *WMD*. Weapons of mass destruction were all too familiar to her. "Yes, he is."

"Sounds intensive."

"I'm sure it is, sir." Her heart rate ratcheted. Maybe, just maybe, Mason would go along with her request.

The list finished printing. He retrieved the pages from the printer's tray and then passed them to her. "I'm a little reluctant to divert a man's focus when it's on something as important as WMDs, so this'll be staying between us. At least for now."

Julia took the list but didn't look at it, or show her relief that he had agreed to keep the gutless wonder, Pullman, out of the loop. She stood up and shook Mason's hand and, because he had just placed an inordinate amount of trust in her, she smiled. "Thank you, Colonel."

"You're welcome, Doc. It was worth the laugh." He smiled back. "People have you pegged as serious, but they're wrong."

"Are they?" Seemed right as rain in her book. She was damn serious.

"You've got a wicked sense of humor."

"Thanks," she said, then thought better of it. "I think."

He laughed again, and she left his office.

Near the transporter, she stepped to the side of the corridor and checked the list, scanning for first-switch access. As expected, all four people Seth had named had opportunity. Now, she held evidence proving it.

Scanning the list again, she checked for sign-outs during the twenty-minute time span the thief had to get the codes out of the building and pull the second switch, giving Seth back his badge.

Linda had signed out for the day at 1020—before the theft. Cracker hadn't left the inner lab until after four. When a lockdown could occur at any moment, it seemed highly unlikely that he would sit on the codes inside the lab for five hours. If caught with the codes, Cracker would be arrested for treason. The man was a genius not an idiot.

Cracker and Linda were innocent.

But both Dempsey Morse and Marcus had signed out during the twenty minutes in question, had had the opportunity to pull both ends of the badge switch, and had had the opportunity to get the codes out of the building before a possible lockdown.

Both had had opportunity and means, yes. But what about motive?

ANTONIO'S restaurant was enjoying a quiet night. A fire roared in the dining room's grate, but no motive revealed itself in the flames, or in Julia's records search that day.

She ordered herself to let go of some tension before her head or arm flared up again, and stared into the fire.

"You okay?" Seth asked.

"Frustrated." She looked across the table at him, knowing she didn't need to explain. She had filled Seth in first thing that morning. They both had been in motive search-mode ever since.

"You've looked peaked all day." He glanced at her plate. "Let go, and enjoy your dinner."

She nodded, grateful for the short reprieve. And it would be short. Seth's personal questions for her were inevitable; she knew it. Yet, she still had no idea how to answer them.

Over the years, he had looked at her in many ways. With amusement, pride, disappointment, doubt, and once, she'd thought, with longing, though that had to have been a trick of the light. Name an emotion, and at some time or another Seth likely had focused it on her—with two exceptions: hatred and pity. If she had to choose one of them, she'd choose hatred. Pity appalled her.

She had moved mountains, suffered month after month of agony alone, to make sure she never saw it. All of that suffering couldn't have been for nothing. She had to have endured it for something. Pity. She hated even the sound of the word. Even the look of it, when written down on a page. She had refused to feel it for herself, for Karl, for the loss of her beloved work; refused by sheer will and determination. She had kept her secrets. Hid them, at times, even from herself. And she had to go on hiding them. Especially from Seth. His opinion shouldn't matter that much, but it did. He respected her. He always had, and she would not lose that. She had so little left to lose.

"You're still not eating." Seth's jacket cuff brushed against the edge of the white linen tablecloth. "Don't you like the food?"

A passing waiter's eyebrows shot up. If not stressed to the max, Julia would have smiled. Antonio's was Grayton's finest for Italian dining, a four-star restaurant, which was saying something, considering its location. And the linguine and white clam sauce tasted as delicious as it smelled; the best she had ever eaten. "It's outstanding." She sipped at her iced tea.

The restaurant was nearly empty, the staff discreet. White columns ran ceiling to floor, their bases covered in thick ivy. Positioned between the tables, they gave diners the illusion of privacy but not of seclusion. Julia liked the feel—and being seated facing the entrance.

Seth definitely hadn't forgotten.

She set her glass back to the pristine tablecloth. "Go ahead, Seth."

He paused, his fork in midair. "What?"

Julia resisted a smile, though only heaven knew why she felt the urge, knowing what was coming. "You've had that I-have-a-thousand-questions look on your face all day." She dabbed at her chin with her napkin. "Go ahead and ask them."

"Okay." He took a drink of water from his glass. When he set it down, a chip of ice slid down the outside of it, spotting the cloth. "Why did you do it?"

She dredged up a wry grin. "Could you be a little more specific?"

"Why did you leave without telling me you were going?"

"It wasn't personal, Seth. Don't think for a second it was. I told you, I had no choice."

"We were coworkers, but I thought we were also friends." He snagged a sesame roll from the bread basket and ripped it in two. "Damn it, Julia. What we had was more than friendship. We were . . . I don't know. Connected. We were connected. You could have called, dropped me a postcard—something to let me know you were alive."

While she had drawn strength from his laughter, he had worried that she'd been dead. Unnerved by how close he had come to being right, she reached for her water glass. "I'm sorry. I didn't realize it would bother you so much." True, she hadn't, yet honesty forced her to add, "But even if I had known, I wouldn't have been able to contact you." Feeling an overwhelming need to touch him, she placed her hand over his, atop the table. "I am sorry, Seth."

His fingertips trembled. "Why couldn't you contact me?"

Because I was unconscious in the hospital. Because for six months and twenty-seven days I had to go to physical therapy to regain the use of my left arm. Because I learned firsthand the true meaning of man's inhumanity to man, and I didn't want to see or talk to anyone—least of all, a man.

Her hand shook. Hard. She pulled it back and hid them both under the table, out of sight. Fighting a tremor in her voice, she managed to get out the truth. "It was impossible for me to contact anyone."

He stilled, his eyes alert and searching. "Why?"

She squeezed her fists until her nails bit into her palms. Vintage male. Why did he have to push? Why couldn't he just accept what she had given him?

Resentment gushed up from that secret place where she kept strong emotions buried. She knew the costs of letting them loose. Dissatisfaction, depression, despair. Migraines and muscle spasms. *Pain.* A price too high to pay. "Isn't knowing I couldn't contact you enough?"

Considering it, Seth took two bites of his lasagna and then changed the topic, asking a question of his own. "How does Karl feel about your coming here?"

Definitely suspicious about Karl. "Fine." Another lie. God help her, she was buried herself in half-truths and lies. "Why do you ask?"

A waiter refilled their glasses. In the silence, the fire hissed and crackled and spat out sparks, as if it too knew she'd been dishonest and protested.

"Because you've changed your name."

How much did Seth know? How much did he suspect? Julia's throat went dry. Maybe the OSI or Intel hadn't told him the whole sordid story. Or maybe they had and Seth wanted her to admit it. That, she refused to do. She had been humiliated enough in this ordeal. "Yes, I changed my name." She lifted her gaze to his, hoping he wouldn't dare to push her on this.

Seth pushed. "Why?"

"It's less cumbersome."

He took a slow sip of wine, watching her over the rim of his glass. She was as outwardly reactive as an ace poker player. The woman had learned well. But she was hiding something; that was evident. And it was something significant or she wouldn't feel so threatened by his questions. He recognized threatened when he saw it, and she was hanging on to the cliff's edge by her fingernails, fearing the truth coming out, and fearing him.

He hated that. Hated anyone fearing him, but especially Julia.

This was a new experience between them. One he hoped to get rid of and never see again. "So why not Dr. Julia Hyde? Why Warner?"

She rolled her gaze. "It was a personal choice, Seth. Not a decision affecting the Second Coming." She stiffened in her seat. "Look, working in the zone with a name like Dr. Hyde isn't going to encourage anyone to take me seriously. I'm heading an innovative and very-important-to-your-career project that's vital to the country, and it's careening toward crisis mode. I need serious authority and credibility."

Fat chance. He knew her. And she never had given a tinker's damn what anyone else thought. Respect for her work. Certainty that a project would help preserve peace and prevent war. That's what mattered to Julia. Yet maybe she had thought she would gain more respect as Dr. Warner than Dr. Hyde. Not impossible—especially with her working in the zone. But he wasn't sucker enough to believe that was the whole truth. "Remnants of Jekyll and Hyde?"

She blinked hard, then let out a stumbling, "Yes."

A lie. But he'd let her have it. Whatever was going on with her and her husband would surface soon enough. Yet there was something he couldn't let slide until she chose to enlighten him. A matter on which he couldn't accept half-truths or scapegoat answers.

He sighed, dropped his napkin to his plate, and then pulled an envelope out of his jacket's inner pocket. "You haven't wanted to explain much. I'm not trying to be an intrusive pig, just letting you know I'm not obtuse. While I respect your privacy, I'm going to have to insist you explain this." He passed the envelope.

Julia stared at the gray envelope as if it had been contaminated with anthrax and touching it would be lethal. "What is it?"

"It's a bill for your cell phone." Seth hated her sounding afraid, but he had to force this issue. "It was forwarded to the office from your home in Grace."

Julia squeezed her eyes shut. "I didn't have the apartment address yet." She took the envelope. "I'll file a change of address with the company first thing in the morning."

"That isn't the problem." Seth watched her closely. She sounded calm, but looked on the verge of hysterics.

"What is the problem?"

She knew exactly. She was stalling him, grasping for time to concoct a plausible answer. Knowing it put a sharp bite in his tone. "The problem is, this bill is in my name."

Chapter Seven

JULIA couldn't hold Seth's gaze.

She tried, but she just couldn't do it. Now, she understood why the bill had been delivered to him at the office and why he had opened it.

God, when filing her forwarding address with the post office, why hadn't she thought of that? *Why?*

"Well, Julia?" Seth riveted her with an uncompromising gaze.

She stared at a column beyond his left shoulder. "I need the phone for emergencies."

"I don't care why you have the phone. I want to know why it's in my name."

Tears she refused to cry blurred her vision. Damn it, why had he had to find out? In this whole, lousy, drawn-out mess, couldn't she get even one break? Just one lousy break?

She finally managed to look at him. "Because I didn't want anyone to be able to trace the number to me."

Seth's eyes narrowed and his square jaw clenched. That response he clearly hadn't expected, but *uncompromising* still seemed etched in his face. He would demand answers.

"Who are you hiding from?" A frown creased his brow. "How long have you been using my name? And how else are you using it?"

Because the last two questions were less complex than

the first, Julia answered them. "Only for the cell phone. And I've been using it for about three years."

"Since you left?"

"Actually, no. Several months later." After she had gotten out of the hospital.

"Talk to me, Julia." Seth lifted his glass. The fire's flames reflected in it. "I want to understand."

She risked making eye contact. "I needed the protection. I've never been late paying the bills. Never. And no one—except for Jeff—has the number. No one else ever has had it."

She sounded desperate, near panic, and she felt worse. Even in the cool restaurant, her whole body felt clammy and the spicy smells of the food had grown overpowering. She was barely holding down the bites she'd managed to swallow.

Seth stared at her, long and hard. "You should have asked first, Julia."

His dark expression hadn't lightened, but something gentle flickered in his eyes. An understanding of sorts, or maybe acceptance. Not forgiveness yet, but not the black-thunder kind of hell-raising she had been expecting and dreading since she had put the phone in his name. "I couldn't ask." She let him see the truth in her eyes, pleaded for understanding. "You would have insisted on knowing why, and I . . ." Her voice trailed off. Some things just couldn't be explained.

"You what?" he asked. "You didn't want to tell me? Couldn't tell me?" He shoved his plate aside, clearly upset. "What you're saying is, we've depended on each other in the lab for years but, outside it, you can't trust me with the truth."

Surprise streaked through her. "No. No, Seth. You've got it all wrong. You were already at risk. I couldn't put you in more danger." The words spilled out before she thought to stop them.

Seth went statue still. "Are you saying you left New Orleans to protect me?"

"Yes." Oh, God. She hadn't meant to say it. How could she have blurted that out? How had she gotten into this tangle? Julia stiffened, determined to regain control of this situation. "No."

"Well, excuse me, sugar, but that's damn confusing."

Icy rage blasted through her. "Do *not* call me 'sugar.' Ever. I hate it."

Surprised by the vehemence in her voice as much as Seth, she squeezed her eyes shut, wishing a hole would magically appear beneath her chair and suck her down.

"I apologize." Regret flitted across Seth's face but anger still clipped his tone. "I didn't mean to offend you."

"I know." She nodded, embarrassed that she had come uncorked at such an innocent remark. "I shouldn't have snapped. It's just, well, that particular term"—even now she couldn't make herself call it an endearment—"is a hot button for me." She forced herself to look into his eyes. "I'm sorry, Seth."

"It's okay." He set his glass aside. "But which is the truth? Yes, you left to protect me or, no, you didn't?"

"Both are true."

He silently stared.

She slumped in defeat. "I left to protect you, but mostly I left to protect me."

"From whom?"

She pinched her lips together, gave him a negative nod. That question she couldn't answer. Not without opening a Pandora's box that had to stay sealed for both their sakes.

"Okay, then." Seth rested his hands on the table. "When exactly did you realize you needed a cell phone for protection?"

She had to keep it together. She could do it. From the beginning, she figured one day she would get caught. True, as time passed and she hadn't, the fear had subsided, but she had always known that the possibility still existed. "The day I left New Orleans." Haunted by memories, she blinked hard and looked into Seth's eyes. Her hell had started long before then, but on that day, hell and horror had merged forces and descended on her.

Just thinking of it had her leaping from being on edge to raw-nerved. Too raw to sit there another moment. "Can we go outside?" She crossed her chest with her arms, rubbed her left one hard to fight off muscle spasms and chills. "I—I need fresh air."

It wasn't Antonio's. It was the subject matter that had her gasping. Stressed, chilled, and gasping. Sweet heaven, she was going to have to tell Seth the truth.

Well, at least part of it. She wasn't brave or strong enough to relive it all again. Could anyone be brave or strong enough to look into a past like hers without shutters? Willingly gaze into eyes filled only with pity?

She couldn't imagine it. Yet, from the set of Seth's jaw, and judging by his persistence, it appeared he intended to force her to do exactly that.

God, give her strength.

SETH paid the bill, then went outside to meet Julia.

She wasn't in the nook just outside the door, or in Antonio's garden. Bordered by tall-standing oaks and blossoming Christmas azaleas, the softly lit alcove's white wicker rockers stood empty. Seth continued the search, but failed to find her. As a last resort, he checked the parking lot. She stood at the passenger's door of his black Lexus.

Evidently, Dr. Warner had decided she didn't want to talk after all. Seth hated putting her on the spot. Physically, Julia was a small woman. The top of her head hit him about mid-chest. But he tended to forget her diminutive size because the woman had presence. She walked into a room and it came to life. She spoke, people listened. She wasn't frail or retiring or shy—or pushy. She just was, and those around her sensed that what she was mattered.

She got attention with her presence. She kept it with a subtle mystique that lured and then stopped a man in his tracks, before he got too close. By silent command, no one breached her privacy.

Seth had never known her to play games, to lie, or to keep secrets. At least, not until now. But now she thought she was protecting him.

That changed all the rules.

His entire life, he had been the one doing the protecting. He hadn't always succeeded, but he had always been assigned the duty. Yet never, not once in his thirty-seven years, had he been protected. In his Special Forces work, yes. As much as he protected his team, they protected him. But personally? Seth, the man? Never.

Not until Julia.

Something hard went soft in his chest. Hell of it was, he still had no idea why or from what or whom she had been protecting him.

Determined to find out, he walked toward the Lexus. Julia bounced her backside softly against the car door, rubbing at her left arm and staring up into the night sky, as if seeking divine intervention or the devil's reprieve. From the look on her face, she would welcome either, so long as it bailed her out.

Seth's footsteps sounded on the concrete. She swerved a startled gaze at him.

"It's me, Julia." He sounded like a damn fool, but the fear on her face was real.

She relaxed and stepped away from the car. "I thought it would be better if we talked at my place. It's more private. Is that okay?"

Considering he had about given up on their talking at all, anywhere was fine with him. "Sure."

They retrieved her car from the office, then drove south of the base to her apartment. Light from the outside lamps glinted off the two-story white stucco building and spilled onto the patch of grass between the parking slots and her front door. The place looked as inviting by night as it had in full sun. He had driven the realtor crazy, looking at seventeen apartments before finding the right one, but this was for Julia. It had to be special.

And it was. A huge kitchen and living room with a stone

fireplace downstairs and two bedrooms upstairs, all decorated in soft pastels that suited her. Julia loved to cook, and the apartment's gourmet kitchen had settled it. As soon as he'd seen it, he had known that this was the one.

Julia dropped her keys on the kitchen bar and her purse on the bar stool's flowered seat pad. "Can I get you something to drink?"

Solemn. Serious. She dreaded what she was about to tell him. He couldn't imagine why. They had always discussed anything and everything—except her marriage and his childhood. Both were topics she had never brought up, and both were facts Seth would rather forget. "Something cold would be good."

She walked to the fridge. "Beer, cola, or juice?"

He'd had several glasses of wine. Any more alcohol and he would have to restrict himself from driving. Julia bent to retrieve the cola from the fridge. Her skirt hiked and hugged her hips. The idea of being stuck here had merit, but she wouldn't appreciate it. "Cola."

She passed the can and a glass filled with ice, poured herself some water, and then motioned to the living area. "Let's sit down. This is going to . . . take a while."

The tension in her was impossible to miss. He wanted to put her at ease, but if he did, then he'd never learn anything. A comfortable Julia was a reserved Julia.

He sat on the far end of the sofa and stared into the empty fireplace grate. It looked dark and cold, and outside it began to rain. At first, just light drops tapped against the window. But then the rain grew heavy, like feeder bands in hurricane squalls, beating against the glass, and Julia just sat, as silent and wary as a guilty defendant standing in the courtroom, awaiting a judge's verdict.

HE'D hate her. Consider her a fool. A loser. There would be no more camaraderie, no more joint ventures, no more feeling connected. There would be no more respect.

She had to accept it, to expect it—now, before she saw it in Seth's eyes and heard it in his voice. Before he couldn't bear to look at her, or showed only disgust.

Thunder crackled. Julia shot a glance at the window, saw the raindrops splatter against the pane and then run down the glass in snaky rivulets. How in heaven would she ever get through this?

One demon at a time. One challenge at a time.

One breath at a time.

Sitting at the other end of the sofa, she smoothed down her skirt. Whatever happened, she would not cry. Regardless of how bad it got, or how much it hurt, she would *not* cry. "First, I'm sorry I used your name without your permission. At the time, I didn't know what else to do."

She waited, but Seth didn't say anything, so she went on. "Secondly, I want you to swear to me that you'll never repeat to anyone what I'm about to tell you."

He pursed his lips. "Will you believe me?"

The man had no idea what he was asking from her. No idea. "I'll do my best." She swallowed hard. "That's all I can promise."

"All right." Seth set his glass down next to the can on the glass-topped coffee table. "I swear it."

She closed her eyes, prayed for the right words, the right way to tell him this and not destroy herself in his eyes. "I didn't plan to just up and leave my job, Seth. I told you I had no choice about the way I left, and I didn't." She forced herself to look at him. "You asked why I didn't contact you. It wasn't that I didn't want to, it was that I was incapable."

"What do you mean, incapable?"

"The day I left, I went to Destin, Florida. I don't want to discuss why, so please don't ask. I got there, and stopped to pick up a few groceries." *Immediate shopping.* God, how she hated it now. "When I came out of the store, it was twilight. I've always loved twilight. Nothing is as it seems then, and you can imagine that your life is exactly the way you want it." She let her gaze drift back to the rain-splotched window. "It was a perfect twilight. Balmy and warm, and the sea breeze felt so good. I let down the car windows, cranked up the radio, and hummed along with Jewel. And I imagined that my life was perfect."

"Julia."

"Be patient, Seth. This is . . . hard." *Hard?* Hard didn't begin to describe it. Admitting to yourself that your husband had beaten and nearly killed you, had attacked you repeatedly during your marriage, that was hard. Admitting it to someone else, someone special—whether you wanted them to be special or not—that was hell.

So don't tell him it was Karl, Julia. That's what's got you terrified. There's no law that says you have to tell Seth who attacked you.

"I'm sorry," Seth said. "I didn't mean to push."

"It's okay. This just makes me . . . uncomfortable." Another monumental understatement.

"I understand."

He looked as if he really did. "Everything was fine until I stopped at a stop sign." Memories flashed through her mind. Her chest went tight, and sharp pains streaked through her arm. She rubbed at it and shut out the images. *One . . . breath at a time. One breath . . . at a time. One breath at a time.*

"Julia?"

She darted her gaze to Seth. He stared at her arm.

She stopped rubbing it. "A man jerked me through the car window, Seth. He beat my head against the asphalt street. I kicked, begged, and pleaded with him to stop. I fought. God, how I fought. But I couldn't stop him. I—I just couldn't . . . stop him."

She took a drink of water, pausing to collect herself, her hands shaking so hard she could barely hold on to the glass. "I woke up two days later in the hospital in Intensive Care. I'd had several surgeries. My arm, for one. When he pulled me through the window, he tore some tendons, did some muscle damage, and dislocated the joint at my shoulder. I have a pin in it now." Images snapped in her mind. The hospital. Blinding pain so intense that drawing breath took a Herculean effort. And fear. Always fear. "They didn't know at first whether or not I had suffered brain damage."

Seth's voice dropped to a whisper. "Are you saying you had amnesia?"

"No." She looked over at him. "My brain swelled—trauma induced by my head impacting the street. They had to bore a hole in my skull to relieve pressure. When the swelling went down, I regained consciousness and I knew who I was." And she had remembered the attack in full detail. Only, to her, it was not something that had already taken place, it was happening then. "I spent months in the hospital, and several more months in physical therapy with my arm. It was a . . . grueling experience."

"I'm sure it was." His expression remained deliberately passive. "Are you all right now?"

"A few headaches and occasional muscle spasms. Otherwise, I'm fine." An even more monumental understatement. One of gross proportions, but warranted. Seth looked so worried.

He scanned her face closely. "Were you attacked because of your work?"

"No." No pity in his voice, only deep concern. She could live with concern. It felt good. But she couldn't admit any more about the attack itself than she already had. The tension was building. She couldn't survive another all-night vigil so close on the heels of the last one. "Detective LeBrec arrested the attacker. I had to hide until the trial."

"Protective custody?"

"More or less." She swallowed hard and focused on the placket of Seth's white shirt. As much as she wanted to see what was in his eyes now, she couldn't look. Couldn't risk it. "The man was convicted and imprisoned. He got five years."

"You almost died, didn't you, Julia?"

She had nearly died three times. Once at the scene, twice in the hospital. Tears threatened. She sank her teeth into her lower lip to fight against them falling and humiliating her to the core. "I had to testify."

"Did you know the man?"

She pretended not to hear Seth. "After he was convicted, I just wanted a fresh start. A clean slate where I could begin a new life. Someplace serene and quiet."

"Someplace safe."

"Yes." She looked at the iron grate, the empty fireplace that had never felt heat or the weight of logs. It seemed as empty and wasted as she had felt during her recovery. "Detective LeBrec brought me an atlas. I dragged my finger over a map and it landed on Grace." She blinked hard and managed to lift her gaze to Seth's chin. "It sounds ridiculous, but I needed something good to hold on to—"

"What better place to seek grace than Grace?" Seth dipped his chin to his chest. "I understand, Julia."

"Do you?"

"Yes, I do."

He didn't think her a fool. Or foolish. "I didn't just leave your lab, Seth." The tears again threatened, and she swallowed hard. "I left my life."

"You had to start over someplace that wasn't tainted."

He did understand. Relief swam through her stomach, loosened the bands of fear cinching her chest. "Yes." She met his gaze.

A furrow formed between his dark brows. "Where was Karl during all of this? Did you leave him, too?"

Julia looked away. She could lie to Seth about this but, damn it, she couldn't look at him while she did it. "He was there."

"During the beating?"

"Seth, you're shouting."

"I'm . . . sorry." He lowered his voice. "I just find it difficult to believe a man would stand and watch a stranger pound the hell out of his wife without trying to stop him."

"I was alone in the car." Deceptive. Definitely left the wrong impression, but true. "The point is, my attacker developed a penchant for making threatening phone calls."

"But he's in prison."

"That doesn't stop him."

"You mean they're still going on?"

"Yes."

"Have you reported them?"

"Every single call. At least five a week, including last night." She wrung her hands in her lap. "He's found me here."

"Why don't the authorities stop him? Have you gotten an unlisted number?"

"They've tried to stop him, and I've had fourteen unlisted numbers since I moved to Grace. That's why I used your name for the cell phone. So he couldn't find me. Only now he's made that connection, too." A fat tear rolled down her face.

"Oh, God, Julia." Seth curled an arm around her shoulder, pulled her close. "I'm so sorry this happened, honey. I'm so sorry I made you live through it all again."

"No pity. Please." She went stiff as a board. "I can take anything from you but pity."

"No pity," Seth promised, his own eyes burning. A rage so deep he couldn't pinpoint where it began or ended tore loose inside him. He fought it, focused on holding her, on the feel of her clutching his shirt at his chest, on her face buried in the curve of his neck, and her soft sobs. Yet through the haze of his outrage, resentment, and regret— so much regret and bitterness that this had happened to her—questions penetrated and persisted, running through his mind. She was married to a cop. Why the hell hadn't he put an end to this attacker's tormenting her? What kind of man tolerates his wife being stalked—from prison?

No kind. Unless he *can't* object.

Maybe Karl had been working under deep cover in Destin. Maybe that's why Julia hadn't wanted to discuss why she had gone there. But even if that was so, Karl had no right to put her in that kind of jeopardy; he had every obligation to protect her from it.

Provided he could protect her from it. Maybe the attack had taken him by surprise. Conditions in those kinds of situations could sour in the blink of an eye.

Julia mumbled on, about the agony of healing, the painful therapy sessions that sounded a lot like torture sessions at the Special Forces survival training school, the isolation and fear she had felt about leaving the safety of the hospital and facing the muggers of the world alone. It was as if a spigot had opened full throttle inside her, and more and more anguish and fear and agony poured out. But never a word about Karl.

Nothing about Karl.

That wasn't just odd, it was telling. And Seth didn't give a tinker's damn for what he was hearing. Maybe Karl hadn't been under deep cover. Maybe he had hurt her.

Crazy thought, maybe. But maybe not. She wouldn't be eager to admit her husband had attacked her or had caused her to be attacked. No more so than Seth would be eager to admit his father had been abusive. But this wasn't the time to ask her. Later would be soon enough. Now, Julia needed to vent. It was cathartic, and down deep he knew she never before had opened up to anyone about this. Not to Karl, not to anyone. And that too was telling. They were still connected.

Torn between feeling grateful and humble that their connection remained intact, and angry that she had faced this hell without his support, Seth held her close, rubbing little circles over her back, and let her purge uninterrupted.

They sat there; she softly sobbing, mumbling, and he holding her, listening, hurting with her, and trying to slot the puzzling pieces into their rightful places.

An hour passed, and then another. Her sobs softened to sniffles and her mumbles turned to cohesive sentences. A few minutes more, and Seth could ask her . . .

A phone rang.

Seth ignored it, but the damn thing persisted, though it sounded muffled, and Julia stirred. "Let me get it," he said.

"No, I'm fine now." She pulled away, left the sofa sniffling, and retrieved her cell phone from her purse.

The woman was anything but fine. She shook like a limb being pelted in a hailstorm. But he understood the drill. *Act normal, feel normal.*

Maybe she would pull it off. Even with his training, Seth couldn't. He wanted to beat the hell out of something. Her attacker, for starters. And her husband.

Julia spoke into the cell phone. "Hello."

"Dr. Julia?"

"Jeff?" She swiped at her face, buried her upset. "Why are you whispering, honey?" Attentive and controlled, she frowned. "Are you okay?"

"I don't want them to hear me."

He sounded so scared. Julia shot Seth a worried look. "Who, honey?"

"Dad and the man. I don't know his name." Jeff's voice dropped even lower. "He sounds mean."

Panic twisted her stomach into knots. "What's wrong, Jeff?"

"They're talking about you. Saying bad stuff."

A shiver crept up her spine. This had to be about the report she had filed. "What kind of bad stuff?"

"I—I think they're going to hurt you."

Julia swallowed hard. *Karl.*

No. No, Karl's in jail. Behind bars. Locked up.

She was safe. "Did you hear the man's name?"

"No."

"Jeff?"

"Shh!"

She waited. Sweat moistened her temples, the vee in her bra between her breasts. What was going on at Camden's?

A man's voice crackled in the background. "Hey, your kid's on the phone."

"It didn't ring."

"He's on the damn phone, man."

Oh, God. Jeff had been caught.

"Give me that." Scuffling noises, and then Camden yelled into the receiver. "Who is this?"

Julia should answer. But her instincts warned her against it. She hit the hook button, praying Jeff would call back and let her know everything was okay.

"You're as pale as a ghost," Seth said. "What's wrong with Jeff?"

"He says he's okay."

"Then why the call?"

Julia clutched the phone until her knuckles went numb. "He was worried about me. There's a man there with his dad and Jeff thinks they're going to hurt me."

"Over the report?"

"I don't know." Julia fought panic at having yet another man in her life threatening her.

This one, an unknown.

Chapter Eight

~

SETH'S hunch nose-dived into a logical conclusion.

Whether Karl had attacked Julia, or she blamed him for the attack, something was seriously wrong in their marriage. Yet, regardless of what Seth had thought earlier, he couldn't just ask her about it. He loved her. She was vulnerable. If he intruded, particularly on this, she would resent it. Maybe forever. There would come a time when she felt Seth had taken advantage of her.

By unspoken agreement, they always had respected each other's privacy. He would have to wait until she brought it up. She had vented about the attack and, sooner or later, she would vent about this, too. But the woman had been to hell and back; telling him had to be her choice. She needed to do things in her own way, in her own time. She needed to feel in control of herself and her life. Still, he could offer her an opportunity, let her know he was open to listening. That was about as far as he could take it without risking losing her.

He leaned back against the kitchen bar and opened the proverbial door, hoping she would walk through it. "Julia, why don't you have Karl check out Camden?"

"I can't." Pacing the kitchen, Julia stiffened, but she kept her voice steady. "He thinks I'm paranoid."

"You average five threatening calls a week from a bastard who nearly killed you, and he considers you paranoid?"

She shrugged.

A lie. But one she evidently needed. Now wasn't the time. Her response got him to thinking, though. What logical reason could Karl have for considering her paranoid about an attacker's threats? Maybe Karl had been under deep cover on a case and now it was closed, so he considered the threats empty.

Or, unlikely but possible, maybe Karl was the attacker and the idea of talking to him at all made Julia paranoid. Could be either way, or something else entirely.

"Julia?" Seth blocked her path, felt her rapid breaths on his face. "Do you believe Jeff?"

"Yes." She looked up at him. "Yes, I do."

"You don't think this was just Camden talking with a lawyer, or complaining to a friend about the injustice of the system because he's being questioned about Jeff's abuse?"

"No." She held Seth's gaze. "Jeff isn't an alarmist. He's been through too much. He wouldn't have called unless something they said made him think I was in real danger."

Real danger. The words sounded hollow, empty, shallow. After her accounting of her attack and the subsequent three years of torment and threats of torture, how else could they sound? "Then I suggest you give his warning all due respect."

She slumped back against the bar, clasped her hands to her head, and glared up at Seth, her agony in her eyes. "Just what do you suggest I do that I haven't already done?"

Good question. Sound. Logical. Rational. Because he couldn't answer it, it totally pissed him off. "Nothing." Seth grabbed her phone from its mounting on the kitchen wall. "It's my turn."

He punched in a number from memory and then spoke into the phone. "Camden, this is Holt. Put Jeff on the line."

Julia's mouth dropped open. "What are you doing?"

Seth smoothed the back of his fingers over her soft cheek. "It's okay," he told her, forcing the grit out of his tone. "We've got an understanding."

"Dr. Seth?" Jeff's voice sounded tiny. Tiny and scared.

"Hey, buddy. How's it going?"

"Okay."

"Is your dad right there?"

"Uh-huh."

"All right. Just listen then."

"Okay."

"Dr. Julia told me about your dad and the mean man. Have either of them hurt you?"

"No."

Relief poured through Seth. He rubbed at the back of his neck. "Are you scared they might?"

"No."

Okay. Okay, this he could handle. His training couldn't do Jeff a damn bit of good with Seth nearly two hours away from the boy. "But you're scared they'll hurt Dr. Julia, right?"

"Uh-huh."

Julia was where Seth could do her some good. Better and better. "Do you know who the mean man is?"

"Uh-uh."

"Is he still there?"

"Uh-uh."

"Can you tell me what he looked like?" Seth quickly added, "Just say yes or no."

"No."

Seth stared at a little bisque angel on the kitchen window's sill. *A little help here would be appreciated.* "You didn't see him?" he asked Jeff.

"No."

Following his instincts, Seth probed. "You just heard him, right?"

A very enthusiastic "Uh-huh."

Obviously, the man had been shouting. "Did you hear his name?"

"No."

Seth frowned. "Are you all right, buddy?"

"Yeah."

He dropped his voice and turned toward the fridge so its whirring motor would muffle his words and Julia wouldn't hear. She'd go postal. "No bruises?"

"No."

Seth's heart rate slowed down. "Okay, then. I'm going to stay here and take care of Dr. Julia tonight, so you don't need to worry about her. But that means I can't drive over to see you until tomorrow. Is that okay?"

"Yeah." Relief flooded Jeff's voice.

He wanted Seth watching over Julia. "Okay, buddy. Now don't tell your dad I won't be there. That's important."

"Okay."

Seth knew the boy needed something, but he didn't know enough about kids to know what would put him at ease. The little angel caught his gaze, and he remembered how as a kid he had hungered for an adult who seemed calm and in control. Unsure if that would work for Jeff, Seth gave it a shot. "I won't let them hurt her."

"Promise?" Jeff's voice cracked.

"I promise, son."

Jeff hung up the phone.

Thick-throated, so did Seth. He turned, and nearly bumped into Julia.

She stood staring at him. "You drive over every day to check on Jeff?"

Oh, hell. Seth scratched at his nape. "Didn't I mention that?"

"No, you didn't mention that."

"Well, yeah, I drive over or else call." He grabbed a glass out of the cabinet, filled it with water at the sink.

"And Camden lets you see him? Talk to him? You have an understanding?"

"Yes." Snagging a dishcloth, Seth swatted at a water spot on the tile counter.

She crossed her arms over her chest and gave him a suspicious look. "Okay, what did you do to him?"

"Nothing." Seth swore and then shrugged. "I promised Jeff I wouldn't hurt his dad, and I didn't."

"Why was he scared you would?" She gasped and her voice hiked up a notch. "You two didn't get into a shouting match in front of Jeff."

"Would I do that?"

"I don't know." She walked to the living room, grabbed a throw pillow from the sofa, and then squeezed it against her chest. "Would you?"

"No." Seth let his gaze drift, stuffed his hands in his pockets. "I sent him inside to wash his face first."

Julia slapped at her thigh. "And then you threatened Camden."

"I did not." Seth gave her a solid frown. "I merely informed him that I would be checking on Jeff daily."

"Checking on him, come hell or high water?" Julia speculated.

Seth let out a huge sigh. "More or less."

Looking disgusted, she slung the pillow back on the sofa and muttered something under her breath.

He should tell her about Jeff's bruise, but now wasn't the right time. Before Jeff's call, she had been really upset. Then the call had upset her more. Telling her about the bruise now would only push her over the edge. She'd definitely cry. He could take Julia being angry, but seeing her in tears ripped him to shreds.

Logically, he shouldn't feel he had failed her. She was a married woman. But her husband had failed her, and Seth felt the guilt. Nothing about emotions depended on logic. He loved her. She'd been hurt. He'd failed to protect her. It was that simple. That simple, and that complex.

Midway back to the kitchen, she stopped and glared at him. "You're checking on Jeff for me."

Damn if that didn't sound like an accusation. "And for him," Seth admitted, bristling. "We're buddies."

Julia gave him a breathtaking smile and then did the

strangest thing. She slammed against him, hugged him hard . . . and burst into tears.

Tears. The one thing he had wanted to avoid. What the hell had he done wrong? He circled her back with his arms, felt her trembling. Could be anger, or hopelessness, or something else altogether. He didn't have a clue. But he had the good sense to know sooner or later he'd have to apologize to end the war and get back into her good graces. He might as well do it now, and get the peace process started. He would do just about anything to get her to stop crying. Stress *would* get her arm and head riled up. "Julia, I'm sorry, okay?" He stroked her left arm, shoulder to elbow, soothing the muscles. Already they were tense. "I just wanted to look after the boy. I didn't know it would upset you."

"God, Seth." She reared back and looked up at him as if he'd lost his mind. "You've never been dense. Why start now?"

How could a man answer that and win? He couldn't. No way. And he must be damned dense. Had to be, or three years ago, he would have seen that she had been stressed out and fled to Destin under duress. How had he missed that? Seth held his tongue and just looked at her.

"Do I look upset to you?"

Tears streamed down her face. Her eyes were red rimmed, the tip of her nose cherry-red. If he had a brain in his head, he'd lie. But even in the name of peace between them, that he couldn't do. "Yeah. Actually, you do."

"Well, I'm not." She buried her chin at his chest, looped her arms around his ribs, and squeezed. "I'm happy."

Sometimes women didn't make a damn bit of sense, and that was fine by him. What the hell? If she was happy, he was happy. Why push his luck when he finally had her in his arms where he had wanted her for five years?

Even if there's trouble, she's still married.

Yeah, but it's just a friendly hug.

*   *   *

IT wasn't just a friendly hug.

Well, it was, and it wasn't. Things hadn't gone further, but Seth had wanted them to then, and he'd wanted them to ever since. Hell, he was human and he loved the woman. And he couldn't get the smell of her out of his head. Fresh, breezy, elusive—like the wind up at the cabin after a summer rain.

It had been a long two days.

He had watched Julia and had done his damnedest to put the feel of her out of his mind. It wasn't working. Still, he kept trying. Aside from her being married, she had doubted him on the sensor-codes theft. Fair or not, trained her himself to doubt everyone or not, he still resented it. Her skepticism and lack of faith rankled. Deep. The only saving grace was he doubted her, too.

Between the hug and the skepticism, he'd had a rough couple of long days. True, he enjoyed his work more. When Julia had left his New Orleans lab, his enthusiasm for the work had left with her. He had just been going through the motions, which was why he had welcomed the transfer to Grayton; he had hoped to regain the magic. But he hadn't. Then Julia returned to work with him and, boom, the magic was back. Yet now he couldn't seem to get his mind in gear. He was out of sync, a step off.

Conversely, she seemed unaffected. He had to remind himself that the night she'd told him about the attack really had happened, because since then there had been no evidence of the vulnerability he'd seen in her that night.

Julia had worked efficiently and had gotten to know her team. She'd avoided Marcus but, considering his surly attitude ranked about as welcome as ice in a blizzard, Seth understood that. Just as she understood Marcus was worth the aggravation of his attitude because he was, hands down, the best explosives guy in the world. What Seth couldn't understand, personal physical reactions aside, was how a woman standing in quicksand with multiple hammers arced over her head could act so . . . normal.

She was being stalked from prison and, according to

Jeff, by Camden and his mystery "mean" man. Her marriage was in serious trouble. She was still suffering the physical and mental remnants of being brutally assaulted in Destin. She had a serious security breach on a project for which she bore ultimate responsibility. And she had reasonable doubts about her team members—one of them was definitely guilty of treason—and preventing further corruption without first identifying the guilty one was virtually impossible, though Matthew surely had incorporated every precaution. Yet the woman seemed totally at ease. No perceptible preoccupation. No apparent challenges with concentration or focus, and no evidence of feeling intense pressure.

Until Seth personally had witnessed it, he would have considered it impossible. Even witnessing it, he had reservations about believing it. She honestly had fallen apart in his arms. Normality now simply didn't make sense.

Her emotional reactions had to be manifesting somewhere. That they weren't manifesting outwardly worried him. So much so, Seth phoned Agent 12.

When he came on the line, Seth paused doodling on his blotter and stared at an apple on the corner of his desk. "Any progress, Matthew?" Enough time had elapsed for him to review the Security tapes. Maybe they had gotten lucky and had recorded Dempsey Morse or Marcus using Seth's badge to duplicate the sensor codes, or maybe Matthew had unearthed a motive from Colonel Mason's list of names Seth had passed along.

"So far, we're coming up empty."

Seth frowned into the receiver, shoved a stack of files aside on his desk. "Have we checked everything?"

"Yeah, we have." Matthew sounded ticked off at having to admit that. "Nada."

Damn it. Seth grabbed the apple and bit into it. Whoever had done this had to be sharp to circumvent the system. Someone very good with computers. Swallowing the crunchy bite, Seth let his gaze slide through the glass window into the lab and settle on Cracker. Seated at his desk, he was busy at the keyboard. He was a genius, capable of circumventing the system, but he was innocent. No opportunity. Only Morse, Marcus, and Julia had had opportunity.

Julia, who had protected him, cried in his arms, and now seemed oblivious to any pressure or stress.

Seth turned to the real reason for his call. "I have a question for you."

"Shoot."

"If a convicted felon is making phone threats from jail to his victim, what can authorities do to him?"

"Civilian or military?"

"Civilian."

"What state are we talking about?"

"Florida."

"Florida has antistalking laws," Matthew said. "Is this someone we know, or just a hypothetical situation?"

"It's someone we know," Seth said, wondering if he knew Julia as well as he thought he did.

"The truth is, the laws are in place but it's hell to get convictions. Stalkers are clever. They word things so that the victim knows they're being threatened but when anyone else—like a judge or jury—hears his exact words, they don't sound threatening. It's a challenge."

"So if you reported a guy doing this five times a week for a while, odds are you still couldn't convict him."

"Not if he was clever." Matthew's voice reeked of frustration. "Hell, Seth. Most stalkers know the law better than their prosecutors. More often than not, they walk."

"That sucks."

"Yeah, it does."

"So what does the victim do?" Losing his appetite, Seth tossed the apple into the trash.

"On the record. Continue to file the complaints, get an unlisted number—"

"That's been done. Fourteen times in two years."

"This isn't good news. Stalkers are obsessive, but usually if they're ignored, they'll find someone else to stalk."

"That's a hell of a cure."

"Yeah, but it's what they do, and what we've got. We can't pick and choose dysfunctional behavioral patterns."

So this wasn't a typical stalker, behaving in a typical manner. Karl? Someone Karl busted in Destin? "You said on the record. What about off the record?"

Matthew hesitated. "You on a secure line?"

"Yeah."

"Tell her to buy a gun. A .38, not a .22. And teach her to use it. A guy this persistent isn't going to back off."

"The guy's in prison."

"For now."

The feeling drained from Seth's hand, his arm, his head, and his chest went tight. Matthew knew Julia was the victim. And he didn't sound surprised. But then he wouldn't be. He had the former Black World employee status reports from Intel. Reports reclassified Eyes Only, prohibiting him from sharing them with Seth. "Will he be out soon?"

"I have no confirmation on that."

No confirmation, but not no reports or expectations. Subtle, but important, difference. "Does she know?"

"Not at this time. We can't pass along anything unconfirmed."

In that simple remark, Seth detected a strong warning to keep his mouth shut on this. "Keep an eye on her for me, okay?"

"Professional or personal?" Matthew asked.

An honesty test. One of the tricks of being an excellent investigator was not to ask questions you couldn't already answer. Matthew was invoking that philosophy now. Seth grimaced and met the challenge. "Both."

"Does she know it?"

"No. No choice." She was married and in trouble. Vulnerable. "Matthew, did Karl attack her in Destin?"

"I can't answer that. Direct violation of the Privacy Act."

"Can you tell me it wasn't Karl?"

No answer.

It'd been worth a shot. "Thanks."

Matthew cleared his throat. "Seth?"

"Mmm?"

"About her stalker. If the time comes and she shoots the son of a bitch, tell her to shoot to kill. If she just injures him, she'll end up supporting him for the rest of his life, and probably doing time. Lawyers harp on his medical expenses—he looks pathetic and weak now—and his diminished employment potential, if any potential exists, and juries buy into it and hold her responsible. That's the way it often turns out."

Julia? Kill a man? Seth couldn't see it. Not even if the man had been the one who had injured and tormented her. "I'll tell her." Not that it would do any good. "Appreciate the information."

"No problem."

Seth hooked the receiver and worried his inner cheek with his teeth. Exactly how was he supposed to convince a scientist and schoolteacher to arm herself without explaining the danger she could be facing? Worse, to be prepared to commit murder? Because even if she fired in self-defense, Julia *would* see it as murder.

She'd never pull the trigger.

He glanced through the window into the inner lab. Sandlis was out with the flu. Cracker and Julia stood huddled at Cracker's desk, talking animatedly. Marcus watched from his workstation, interested but not participating in the conversation. Seth cursed under his breath. When Marcus paid attention to anything other than his work, something was definitely up.

Dempsey Morse joined the huddle.

The hair on Seth's neck stood on end. Morse had graduated from the old-school style of management: distance from everyone, particularly underlings. Morse got involved only by formal request. Otherwise, he remained a shadow on the project, keeping his thoughts to himself and his person isolated. If he had entered the fold, this had to be serious.

Seth left his office and joined the group. "What's going on?"

Cracker stared at the computer screen. "Someone tried to hack into the vault's computer system."

It was a closed system. Had to be someone in the lab who lacked full access. That ruled out Dempsey Morse. "Were they successful?" Seth darted a warning tug on his ear at Julia.

"Checking." Cracker tapped away at the keys.

Seth's nerves sizzled. "Can you tell what they were after?"

Another screen appeared on Cracker's monitor. He scanned it, and groaned. "Oh, no."

"What?" Julia prompted Cracker to expound.

Morse wedged a shoulder between Julia and Cracker. "Are the key systems safe, or not?"

Cracker didn't answer. Sweat glistened on his forehead, his temples, above his upper lip. "It was a specific sweep."

He entered more data. Waited. Then pulled back his shoulders and went still, locking his gaze with Seth's. "They tried to access all project intel."

All project intelligence? "Everything?" Seth urged, tensing head to heel.

"The good news is, the double firewall I built into the security system held." Cracker eased off his glasses and rubbed at the bridge of his nose. "The bad news is, it wasn't an amateur attempt."

"But they got nothing?" Seth asked for confirmation.

"No." Cracker looked from Seth to Julia. "Nothing."

Morse smiled. "Well, we can relax, then."

"Yeah." Cracker had something else to say, but he didn't want to announce it publicly. "Back to business."

Seth returned to his office. Julia and Dempsey Morse already had full access. They had no need to risk a failed attempt to get it. By the process of elimination, that made Marcus their man.

Any moment now, Cracker would be coming through the office door to brief Seth on what he had discovered and hadn't wanted to reveal publicly.

Ten minutes elapsed. Cracker finally left his terminal,

and Seth steeled himself to hear whatever Cracker had to say.

He walked into Julia's office instead.

And closed the door.

Twenty minutes later, Julia buzzed Seth. "Clear your schedule for an hour or so. Agent 12 wants to chat."

"His office or ours?"

"His."

"Are we traveling together?" If whatever Cracker had told Julia raised concerns with her about Seth, they wouldn't ride over to the OSI offices together.

"Together is fine."

Realizing he had forgotten to breathe, Seth hung up the phone. At least in this, he hadn't been made a suspect.

JULIA sat in the same seat she had occupied the last time she had been in the OSI conference room. Seth sat at her left. Agent 12, across the table from them.

Seth briefed the agent on the hacker's attempt.

Julia interceded, sweeping her hair back behind her ear. "During the search for breaches, Cracker noted that Seth had duplicated the sensor codes. He reported it immediately."

Agent 12 tapped the end of his pen onto a blank yellow legal pad. "If Cracker duplicated the codes, he would report it to focus suspicion away from himself. If he failed to note the duplication, then he would lose his status as resident computer genius." Agent 12 shrugged. "Means nothing."

"Cracker couldn't have copied the codes," Julia said. "I ran a time check. He had no opportunity to get the codes out of the lab and pull the name badge double switch."

Agent 12's eyes widened. "Who did have opportunity?"

"Dempsey Morse and Marcus," Julia said, resisting a sigh. Agent 12 knew all of this already. Seth hadn't told her, but of course he had shared Colonel Mason's list with the OSI. Agent 12 was pulling a credibility check on her.

"Either of them sharp on computers?"

"They both are," Seth put in. "But Morse has full access

already. If guilty, why would he raise a red flag?"

"Same rationale as for Cracker," Agent 12 said. "Maybe Morse wouldn't do it, but maybe he's attempting to divert attention or to elevate himself above suspicion."

Again, either of them. "I don't suppose Morse's reaction proves anything, either," Julia said. "But it still bothers me."

"What did he do?" Seth adjusted his watch.

"Nothing." Irritated with herself for speaking out, Julia frowned. "I just sensed he wasn't surprised by the attempt or relieved it had failed. He said the right words, they just didn't come across as sincere."

"We can't hang a man on that." Agent 12 dropped his pen and rubbed his forehead from temple to temple, leaving white streaks that quickly turned red.

"No, but we can watch him." Seth leaned forward, focusing on Agent 12. "Look, a lot of what we do in the lab comes down to gut instinct and intuition. Because that's the way we work so much of the time, our instincts are honed. We might not consciously recognize significance, but that doesn't mean we should dismiss instinctive urges."

"I haven't suggested we dismiss anything." Agent 12 lifted a hand. "We rely heavily on instinct, too. All I'm saying is, what we've got isn't enough."

Julia hated it, but she had to agree. Cases could be built for time-delay devices being incorporated, for high-tech transmissions that circumvented the security system. Factoring in those things, most of the staff looked guilty. Dempsey Morse's insincere concern. Marcus's loner attitude and frosty disposition fit the profile of one capable of treason. Linda seemed preoccupied with her husband's absence and with trying to keep her kids in line, but that could be a cover, and Greta seemed immersed in her work and lost in another world, which could also be a false façade. Yet whenever something like a hacker attempt occurred, everyone knew it meant tighter security and more intense scrutiny. No one welcomed with open arms living in a 3-D fishbowl.

Agent 12 cleared his throat. "Considering this project has been up and running such a short time and we've already had two attempts to breach—one, we consider successful—I need to brief you two on a delicate complication. It's classified, of course." Matthew straightened in his chair. "For your own protection, we had hoped to keep you out of the need-to-know loop, but I think the gains on that have ceased to outweigh the losses."

"If it pertains to this project, we should know it." Julia spoke softly, but her tone smacked of resolve and reprimand.

"I happen to agree, Dr. Warner. Unfortunately, higher headquarters only just arrived at that same conclusion." He stood up. "Let me grab a file," he said, then left the room.

Julia and Seth waited in silence. Her watch ticked like the timer on a bomb, though that was impossible. It was quartz; noiseless. Yet, she could hear it.

You're weary. Raw-nerved. That's all.

She was. She'd put in grueling days at Grayton and had had nothing but miserable nights. Waiting for Jeff to call back. He never did. Waiting for the new phone number and Karl's threats to stop. The new number was operational, but the threats persisted. Prison guards were just more "brothers in blue," glad to turn a blind eye to Karl's calls. They considered him a cop wrongfully imprisoned by his corrupt wife's slick lawyer. Simply put, he'd conned them. Even the warden. So she was waiting for nightmares of the attack to stop waking her in the middle of the night drenched in a cold sweat. Those hadn't stopped, either. And now Seth was a victim in them, too.

Seth saw Jeff and, of course, assured her he was all right. But she wanted—*needed*—to hear his voice, to know for herself, for sure.

Finally, this morning, she had given in and phoned the substitute, Olivia Hawthorne. A general inquiry had netted a positive but general response. Jeff appeared fine and clearly missed Julia. He mentioned her a dozen times a day. Waffling on sending him a message to call, Julia had decided against it. Ms. Hawthorne would consider that unusual enough to report, and Julia didn't dare to risk doing anything that could result in questions being asked that she couldn't afford to answer. Or in doing anything to arouse the wrath of Camden that would be unleashed on Jeff.

"Julia?" Seth asked from beside her. "Where do you go when you do that?"

"Do what?"

"Blank out."

"I didn't." Uncomfortable because she had done exactly that and he had read her so easily, she squirmed on her seat. "I was thinking about Jeff."

Seth reached over and patted her hand. "He's fine, honey."

Honey. Nice. Really nice. "I know. I'm just concerned." As much as she hated to admit it, Seth's show of support and empathy felt good. It was nice to have someone share your worries. Scary to want someone to share your worries, but . . .

"Got it." Agent 12 came back into the briefing room and shut the door behind him.

As if caught stealing, Seth snatched back his hand. His tanned skin flushed, and heat flooded Julia's face. They both had to look as guilty as sin.

Agent 12 stopped dead in his tracks. "Is something wrong?"

"No."

"No."

"Okay." He let it slide and returned to his seat, dropping the inch-thick file on the table before him. "From all indications, we're going to be in close contact for a while. 'Agent 12' is getting cumbersome, Julia. Privately, just call me 'Matthew.'"

He'd omitted directing Seth, addressed only her.

They already knew each other on a first-name basis. Stood to reason. Otherwise, her vouching for Seth never would have been enough to get Matthew to leave Seth's clearances intact. *Rusty skills.* Otherwise, she would have recalled that by guilty-until-proven-innocent policy, Matthew should have pulled the clearances.

A silver of resentment spiked up her spine. More games. She didn't know which was worse. Men in general, or the military in particular. Both had proven to be ace game players.

But not pulling Seth's clearance proved something else, too. Something important. Julia glanced at Seth and tugged her right earlobe. He tugged back.

The message received had been understood. In Matthew's book, they were both in the clear. Ultimately responsible, yes. But not guilty of crimes.

Matthew opened the file tagged "Benedetto, A. 2 West Freedom Coalition" and passed a photo. "Intel reports have heightened our concerns about this specific-sweep attempt on the vault's computer system."

Julia took the picture. The man in it looked sophisticated. Mid-forties, traditional black suit and red tie, and strong facial features. A thin scar slashed across his right cheekbone. One like a child might get going over the handlebars on his bike, trying to learn to ride "no hands," though her instincts suggested its jagged origin had been a knife slash.

"Who is he?" Seth asked.

"Anthony Benedetto." Matthew's tone turned bitter. "Remember his face. I'm afraid you're going to see a lot of him. Not literally. Just his handiwork."

"Why?" Julia asked, committing the photo to memory.

"He's the head of the suspected terrorist group, Two West Freedom Coalition."

"Suspected?" Seth asked for clarification.

"Only officially," Matthew said. "The group exists, though a lot of people, including me, would sleep better at night if it didn't. Two West is a large organization based on a thousand-acre estate in rural Alabama. Property's been in the Benedetto family for four generations. Locals call the mansion 'the Palace.' We think somewhere around two thousand members are based nearby. Maybe more. Definitely more of them scattered throughout the country, and some outside it. And lots of money."

"Drugs?" Julia speculated.

Matthew gave her a negative nod. "Benedetto made a fortune in technologies and inherited another one from his father, Philip. Philip was a political activist and the alleged previous leader of Two West. He played dirty, but he was as slick as glass. It took a lot of resources to pin anything on him that would stand up in court."

Failing to make the connection between the Benedettos and Project Home Base, Julia asked, "Why is this terrorist group significant to us?"

Matthew's expression turned from solemn to grim. "Because we have reason to suspect Anthony Benedetto has a mole assigned to your project."

Seth spoke first. "Do you know who?"

"Not yet." Matthew took back the photo from Seth. "But project specifics have been referenced inside Benedetto's organization."

Julia grasped her chair arm and squeezed. So someone from Intel, the CIA, or some other intelligence-gathering agency considered the threat against the United States serious enough to risk ordering an operative to infiltrate Benedetto's organization. This was definitely bad news.

"That concerns us," Matthew went on. "But what worries us more is that we suspect Benedetto recently gained access to the Rogue."

"Oh, God." It slipped out before Julia could stop herself.

Seth paled. A white line circled his mouth. "How strong are these suspicions?"

"Damn strong, but not conclusive. We haven't confirmed with a visual, and it hasn't been formally announced to the coalition's council, but Rogue access is common knowledge inside Two West."

"What the hell does he plan to do with a Rogue?"

"That, Dr. Warner," Matthew said, "we don't know. Which is why we're so nervous."

"Nervous?" Seth dragged a hand through his hair. "You should be damn terrified."

Matthew didn't respond, just turned his gaze to Seth and waited for him to expound.

"If Benedetto has the Rogue and Home Base's sensor codes, he has the capability to create more havoc than you can imagine—even in your worst nightmare."

"I can imagine it, Seth." Matthew stared, owl-eyed. "I know the Rogue's capability. What I don't know is the man's."

"Has Intel run a personality profile on him?" Julia asked the question, not at all certain Matthew would answer. He knew the answer, but he might choose not to reveal it, or he might be under orders not to reveal it.

"He's been profiled," Matthew said. "He's stable. Respected both in and outside his organization, and he has powerful friends. Unfriendly-to-the-U.S. powerful friends. Philip was street-smart. Anthony Benedetto is educated, clever, attuned, street-smart, and a little paranoid about security. In his business, I consider that paranoia a healthy asset. He's also judiciously ruthless. So far, we've never known him to act violently out of anger, only out of what he deems 'necessity paramount to the protection of my coalition.' No one crosses his lines and lives, though his personal conduct remains above reproach, which is why we've failed to nail his ass to the wall."

Tapping a finger against the tabletop, Seth grimaced. "Henchmen do his dirty work."

Matthew nodded confirmation. "Loyalists. And he has two thousand of them who are known to us—and only God knows how many who aren't. Every one of them stand ready, willing, and able to execute his orders without question." Matthew hiked his brows. "His people trust him implicitly."

Julia frowned, and spoke from experience. "That kind of trust can get you killed."

"Sometimes it does," Matthew agreed. "But that doesn't slow down the other loyalists. They go to him with everything from domestic disputes to financing college educations and home and business loans. He treats them all equitably."

"Superior leadership skills." Seth grunted. "Sounds like he should run for President."

Matthew raked his forehead with his fingertips. "I wouldn't rule that out."

"You're joking." Julia blurted out.

"Unfortunately, I'm not." Matthew grimaced as if he had bitten into something sour. "He's got major political connections."

That revelation put a bitter taste in Julia's mouth. She swallowed hard. "Anything else?"

"Two things," Matthew said. "First, Benedetto operates under a strict code of ethics. No organizational wars ever affect the loyalists' family members. Wives and children are revered. Untouchable."

"A terrorist with ethics." Julia rolled her gaze.

"Definitely," Matthew agreed, missing her sarcasm, or choosing to ignore it. "Two West loyalists have the strongest code of honor I've ever seen in any group, and that includes our own military forces. They don't fall victim to typical vices—like drugs or alcohol—they're educated and dedicated, protect their families and each other, and they never leave the coalition."

"A financial mafia and members for life." Seth rubbed at his chin, assimilating. "Like a damn cult."

"Similar," Matthew said. "Most are born, live, and die in the coalition. But it's more like a huge family combining assets in multiple, strategic business alliances."

The protective-family aspect of their code, Julia appreciated, though the terrorist activities negated any genuine admiration. Instead, she feared this Anthony Benedetto. Him and his coalition. Its loyalists would fight to preserve their way of life. The protect-the-coalition organizational threads ran deep, and only death severed them. "What happens if someone breaks the honor code?"

"They have a choice," Matthew said. "Death at the hands

of the members, or suicide." Matthew leaned forward, rested his hands atop the closed file. "That's what happened to Philip. We wrapped up a three-year investigation with enough hard evidence to convict him on illegal weapons charges. Within twenty-four hours, he stuck the nose of a .38 in his mouth and pulled the trigger."

"To avoid a weapons charge?" Julia couldn't grasp the logic in that.

"No, not really." Matthew explained the rationale. "Our Special Forces were part of a task force to disarm him. We did. Because his coalition was disarmed, his loyalists lacked protection. In leaving his people vulnerable, he had dishonored them and himself. That's why he committed suicide."

"They would have killed him, anyway," Seth speculated.

"Yes. But because Philip did it himself, Anthony stepped into his shoes as the natural successor. Intel has rumblings from insiders that he assisted in his father's suicide, and he's definitely devoted massive resources to rearming."

Julia didn't like this at all. Anthony Benedetto and his loyalists were formidable opponents. She had sensed it the first time Matthew had mentioned the man's name, and nothing she had heard since changed her mind. With access to a Rogue, Benedetto's resources, and Two West's loyalists' code of ethics, the coalition could execute a multitude of terrorist attacks. Worse, they had the stomach to execute them with judicious ruthlessness.

That judicious ruthlessness scared Julia right out of her skin. But another attribute that ran coalition-wide she feared even more. Their to-the-death dedication.

Comparatively speaking, her side tended to get bogged down in red tape, political manipulations, and private agendas. Would it measure up?

She didn't know for fact, and that uncertainty terrified her. "We're most vulnerable in this."

"Freedom bears costs." Matthew's eyes narrowed. "But we can hold our own against Benedetto."

"Can we?" God, but Julia hoped so. "Look, no one with the DoD can be around long and not know there's an abundance of courage and bravery and honor in our military. But we've also got service members who are eligible for food stamps—"

"There's a new program going into effect on that."

"Yes, there is, Matthew," she agreed. "And after it does—provided Congress funds it, and it does go into effect—we'll still have eight to sixteen thousand service members who are eligible for food stamps." What the hell? She'd gone this far, she might as well spill out all her fears. "My point is, we've got men and women in uniform because wearing that uniform means something to them. They're definitely not in it for the money. They believe in ideals, in a code of ethics that most Americans seem to have forgotten exists."

"I disagree," Matthew said. "They know it exists."

"Check out the headlines." Seth intervened. "If they know it, they're ignoring it."

They were losing her point in a philosophical meltdown. Julia gritted her teeth and brought them back to it. "The thing is, the warrior in them can take the frequent moves and the long separations from their families. They can handle the dangers and risks and asking their families to take up the slack while they're gone, because what they're doing matters. But the human being in them—the husband, wife, father, or mother—cannot take seeing their kids being hungry. They can't listen to their babies' stomachs growl and feed them ideals."

"What are you saying, Julia?" Seth asked. "That Benedetto will win this undeclared war because he feeds his people?"

"I'm saying we're vulnerable because we don't." She leaned forward against the table. "Everyone has an Achilles' heel. Everyone. Benedetto knows ours." She let her gaze slide to Matthew. "But do we know his?"

ANTHONY Benedetto sat at his ornate desk, surrounded by luxury inside the forty-room mansion. His office was a warm room, smelling of rich wood, old leather, and older money, and cluttered with photographs of his parents, his wife, Elise, a stunning and intelligent woman as compassionate as she was beautiful, and their beloved daughter, Daisy, whom they had named in honor of his mother.

Anthony had been born in this house. Raised in the tradition of Two West Freedom Coalition loyalists, as had his father, and his father before him. His grandfather had acquired the position of chairman in a hostile takeover from Bernard T. Franklin, a flat-nosed German who had founded the coalition but lacked the vision to sustain it or make it grow.

Several of the seventeen council members never had forgiven Anthony's grandfather for unseating Franklin as chairman. But Anthony's father, Philip, had won their unequivocal support by assuring members' personal prosperity *and* delivering it. His philosophy followed three core concepts he had taught Anthony from the cradle, preparing him to take the reins, and he implemented them without hesitation, if not without occasional regret:

One. Revere women. They cement families together and follow their hearts. Their loyalty dictates the loyalty of their husbands and their children.

Two. Protect all of your people with equal vigilance, vigor, and justice. No man's value is greater than any other.

Three. Kill your enemies.

Early on, to preserve coalition solidarity, his father had killed quite a lot of enemies. But in later years, becoming his enemy held little appeal. Loyalists had long memories.

Americans did not. Anthony rubbed a fingertip over the ridged scar on his cheek. Though he was one of them, Americans were his enemy and, while retribution for his father's death and the coalition disarmament must be had, it could not come by simple slaughter. That overt act would require huge sacrifices from his people. But a more subtle plan now in motion would achieve the same justice.

Shortly, the summoned council members would arrive, and he would inform them that Two West now stood eighty-five percent rearmed. And then he would formally announce the coup that would solidify his position as chairman and keep his enemy at a distance. He had secured access to the world's most advanced ballistic missile: the Rogue.

Anthony smiled. "Détente."

Rocking back in his chair, he looked at the photo of his father in its place of honor on the corner of his desk. White suit, broad smile. He would save his coup de grâce—Project Home Base—for another time, one when he needed a victory. A wise strategy Anthony would adopt, considering several unavoidable variables in the plan could cause challenges. Besides, delayed gratification was good for the soul. When the time came, he would have not just détente with his enemy, but the thing he desired most: superiority.

Chapter Nine

"LOCK the door, Seth."

Julia dumped her purse on the bar stool, toed off her pumps, and headed for the kitchen. "I'll get the spaghetti sauce going." She bent down to grab a pasta pot from the lower cabinet, filled it with water at the sink, then set it on the stove. "You make the salad."

"I do great salad," Seth said, his gaze nailed to his hand on the doorknob.

The key in the dead bolt mocked him, and a memory of him at six flashed through his mind. His frantic search for the key. Shouted curses. Hopeless screams. A thin sheen of sweat broke out on his skin.

"Hey, I'm up to my elbows in ground meat," Julia yelled out from the kitchen. "Would you come hand me the salt?"

Seth left the dead bolt untouched, and went to the kitchen, loosening his tie. "Which cabinet?"

"Left of the stove. Bottom shelf." She folded the meat onto itself.

Judging by the containers of spices on the counter, she'd already tossed in everything but salt. He shook the shaker over the meat.

"More."

He dumped more salt.

"That'll do it." She shook a lock of hair from her cheek. It fell right back.

Seth tucked the strand behind her ear. Being in the kitchen with Julia was kind of nice. It helped push the bad memories away.

The pepper tickled his nose. He liked being with her, loved touching her, and he shouldn't do either one. Frowning, he put the shaker back in the cabinet and closed the door. "When we get things going here, I need to call Jeff."

"Great." Julia scrubbed her hands with soap then turned to the sauce pot and tossed in some fresh mushrooms and sweet basil. "I really want to talk with him."

"I know." Already the sauce smelled good. "That's why I told him I'd call from here tonight."

"So you haven't seen him today?" Julia stirred the sauce then turned to the counter and began shaping meatballs and placing them on a cookie sheet.

"You're gonna *bake* the meatballs?"

"Gets the grease out," she said. "So you haven't seen Jeff today?"

"I've never seen anyone bake meatballs."

"For pity's sake, Seth. My uncle Lou was a bona fide Italian—though I think spaghetti is Chinese—and he taught me to make sauce."

She'd never before mentioned her family. Interested, Seth smiled. "Tell me about your uncle Lou."

"He was terrific. Loud. Loving. I could do no wrong in his eyes."

"Unconditional acceptance is a pretty awesome thing." And damned rare. At least, in Seth's experience.

"Yes, it is. Especially Uncle Lou's. He had a million traditions." She added a meatball to the sheet, and her expression turned wistful. "Making spaghetti was his specialty. Before I was tall enough to stir from the floor, he'd pull a chair near the stove—so I could reach the pot. Then, off and on all day, he'd yell, 'Stir the sauce, Julia.' "

She sent Seth a this-isn't-negotiable look. "Uncle Lou *always* baked his meatballs before putting them in the sauce. Always."

"Can't mess with tradition." Seth could see her as a kid,

stirring so much her uncle Lou would warn her not to stir the metal off the pot. "Does he live in New Orleans?"

"No, not anymore." Sadness filled her eyes. "He died in a car accident right before I left there. His, um, brakes went out on the bridge."

"I'm sorry." A tremor in her voice and the withdrawn way she moved alerted Seth. "You don't think it was an accident."

"The police say it was."

"What do you say?" Karl had been a cop there. Maybe a disagreement about her uncle's accident had come between them.

"I say I miss my uncle very much."

Unconditional acceptance. Unconditional love. Damn right, she missed it. Anyone with sense would. "I'm sorry, Julia."

"Me, too." Her smile turned bittersweet. "You would have loved Uncle Lou, Seth. You're a lot alike."

"Really?"

She nodded. "Caring. Special. You laugh a lot."

Not during her three-year absence, he hadn't. "You loved him."

"With all my heart, but not a bit more than he loved me."

How did that feel? To know you were loved with someone's whole heart? Seth didn't have a clue, and probably never would. But her making her uncle Lou's spaghetti now was telling. For her, it was a reminder of her uncle's love. Comfort food.

Julia was not calm or unaffected. She needed comforting, and knowing it eased Seth's mind. Being the victim of an attack and losing her uncle made her an unlikely candidate for treason. She understood loss and pain.

"Are you going to make me ask about Jeff a third time?"

"Sorry." Seth shrugged out of his jacket, draped it across the bar stool holding her purse, and then rolled up his shirt-sleeves. "I got sidetracked."

"Yeah, you did."

"Jeff made me promise I wouldn't leave you by yourself tonight." Seth ducked into the fridge and pulled out the makings for salad. "Where's the cutting board?"

"Lower left cabinet, next to the stove. Top shelf." Julia set down another meatball, forming straight rows. "Did Jeff say why?"

"No, he didn't. Camden stuck to him like glue so the boy couldn't say a whole lot of anything." Damn frustrating.

"Did he say if the mean man has been back to his house?"

"Yes, he has. Several times." Seth grabbed the cutting board and began chopping celery and mushrooms. "But Jeff hasn't seen him. He's only heard him downstairs."

Julia set the oven's temperature dial and then popped the cookie sheet inside. The door clicked closed. "Has he, um, heard the man's name?"

"Afraid not." Something in her tone caught his ear. It hadn't been an idle question. "Why?"

She shrugged without looking at him. "If he's going to hurt me, I'd like to know who to curse."

"He's not going to hurt you." Seth finished the salad, tossed and slid it into the fridge, then cleaned up the mess. They worked well together, professionally and domestically. Did she and Karl?

Seth clamped down on that thought. Suspicions aside, her marriage was none of his business. "Want some wine?"

"No, thanks. Alcohol conflicts with my meds. I have to avoid it. But I'll have some juice."

Seth filled her glass, figured what the hell, a glass of grape juice wouldn't rot out his stomach, and filled his own. Then he grabbed the phone and called Jeff.

Camden put him right on the line.

"Hey, buddy." Seth smiled so Jeff could hear it in his voice. He had studied a couple books on dealing with kids and remembered reading in one of them that if you smile when you talk on the phone, the kid senses it. It was worth a shot. Jeff needed all the smiles he could get.

"Dr. Seth."

The smile turned genuine. Jeff always sounded surprised and so damn happy to hear Seth's voice. He could get used to this kid. Seth let out a little grunt. Hell, who was he kidding? He already had. "Did you have a good day?"

"It was okay," Jeff said, then rambled on about playing football with Travis.

Jeff wasn't a rambler. Something was up.

He dropped his voice to a whisper. "I was getting Dad bored so he'd leave. He hates football."

Lulling him into complacency. Smart tactic. "You okay?"

"Uh-huh," he said. "Are you still at Dr. Julia's?"

"Didn't I tell you I would be?"

"Uh-huh."

"Well?"

"Okay. I guess you are, then."

Jeff couldn't trust. Remembering back and understanding completely, Seth softened his voice. "I am, Jeff."

The boy's sigh of relief swarmed Seth with guilt. He'd just wanted Jeff to understand that when he gave his word, Jeff could trust it. "She wants to talk to you."

"Okay, but you gotta promise me you won't leave her. Promise?"

"Why?"

"Travis said it was the best pass I ever throwed."

Seth frowned. "Is your dad back?"

"Uh-huh."

"Are they going to try to hurt Dr. Julia tonight?"

"I think so."

Julia wiped her hands on a dishcloth and motioned for the phone. Seth held up a finger, telling her to wait a second. "Don't worry, buddy. I'll be here."

"Okay."

"Dr. Julia's trying to grab the phone. Geez, I think she misses you or something." He smiled at her frown. "I'm going to give it to her before she takes it, okay?"

"Okay." Jeff giggled, then turned serious. "I love you."

Seth's heartstrings tugged. "Me, too, buddy." He passed Julia the receiver.

They talked about school, Travis, football, and Julia asked the boy a half-dozen times if he was really all right. In his mind, Seth could hear Jeff mumbling, "Worrywart."

When Julia hung up the phone, her eyes were glossy and overly bright. "I miss him."

"I know you do." Seth looped an arm around her shoulder and gave her a reassuring squeeze. He hoped she didn't start crying. It killed him a little every time she cried, especially since hearing about her attack. "Can I ask you something?"

"Certainly." The stove's timer buzzed. She moved away, pulled on an oven mitt, grabbed tongs from the drawer, and then got busy flipping the meatballs.

The smell of them had his stomach growling. "You've had me scratching my head a little lately."

She closed the oven door and then pulled off the mitt. It had green ivy leaves printed on it. "How's that?"

"You seem calm and normal, but I know you can't be."

Julia looked away, rubbed at her left arm, shoulder to elbow. "I learned from the incident that you can do whatever you have to do, Seth." She set the tongs down on the spoon rest. It too had been imprinted with green ivy. "I told you about the headaches and muscle spasms. If I get upset, then they get raunchy. They last for hours, sometimes days. The more upset I am, the worse they are."

"So you've learned to bury your emotions." That he could understand. Hell, he'd become a master at burying his before leaving grade school. He leaned against the counter. His abuse and her attack. Different catalysts, different circumstances, same reactions. "Can I ask one more question?"

Tension tugged at her expression, and her mouth flattened to a slash. "I suppose."

He wanted to know how Karl fit into all this. Why he not only tolerated the threats but considered Julia paranoid when she recorded up to five calls a week from the jerk who had attacked her. Karl did fit; Seth sensed it. But her armor looked ready to crack, and she was already rubbing her arm. "Never mind," Seth said. "It can wait."

Clearly relieved, she melted butter, minced garlic, and prepared thick slices of French bread, then sprinkled them with parsley. "Why don't you put the meatballs in the sauce?"

Half an hour later, they sat down to eat and talk turned to Benedetto and the Rogue, and then to Marcus and Dempsey Morse. If Benedetto had a mole, then odds ranked high he was one of the two of them. But which one?

Julia twirled spaghetti on her fork. "I know Marcus seems obvious because of his temperament, but you can't accuse a man of treason for having a bad attitude."

"Last I checked, that wasn't a crime."

"And I know Dempsey Morse seems like a good man and he's very bright, but something about him just doesn't sit right with me."

Seth took a bite, chewed and savored, and then swallowed. "Uncle Lou gets an A for the sauce. Damn good."

Julia laughed. "He'd throw it in the trash."

"Why?"

"Because good sauce must cook all day, Seth." She affected a lousy rendition of an Italian accent. "The blending of the flavors cannot be rushed."

"Tastes great to me."

She wrinkled her nose. "It'll be better tomorrow."

"But eating it today makes you feel better."

Surprise flickered in her eyes. "Yes."

Her admission pleased him. So much that he suffered an overwhelming urge to kiss her. Instead, he cleared his throat, dabbed at his chin with his napkin, and turned the topic. "If you've got a gut feeling about Dempsey Morse, then let's take a look at him as a suspect."

Julia tipped her fork tines in Seth's direction. "Four marriages and four divorces. He seems unable to sustain relationships."

"Hard to do when you're always at work. And he is,"

Seth countered. "He's a major stockholder in Slicer Industries. They've invested a bundle in Home Base. If it fails, Morse loses his financial ass and his job."

"Morse isn't a foolish man, Seth." Julia took a sip of juice. "If he were, he would never have gotten this far."

"So we agree. He isn't going to jeopardize his money or his backside."

"Maybe he has an alternate plan."

"Like what?"

"I'm not sure yet." Julia thumbed the rim of her glass. "Is Morse patriotic?"

"I don't know." Seth shrugged. "He's dedicated to his job, and considering his job is defending the U.S., I'd say he probably is."

"But you don't know."

"I'm not sure what you mean."

"I'm trying to see if he's self-sustained or if he depends on others. He doesn't personally. His failed marriages prove that. But sometimes people depend on multitudes rather than just one person. Does he love only his job and his money, or does he love others, too? Does he do this job because he loves his country and wants to protect the people in it, or just because building missiles under government contracts pays well and the sense of power pops his personal bubble?"

In Seth's mind, a lightbulb clicked on. Benedetto's loyalists' to-the-death dedication. "I don't think Morse is patriotic enough to die for his ideals, but I could be wrong."

"I don't think you are. It's his eyes."

"What's wrong with them?"

Julia set down her glass. "They're empty."

"Huh?"

"You sound like Jeff." She smiled. "I like that about you."

Now Seth was really lost and sucking dust. "What?"

Their gazes locked across the tabletop. She started to cup her hand over his, pulled back, and then clearly forced herself to do it. Her warm fingers shook. "I like your honesty. I like it that you're not stuffy, and you don't always have to be right, or to have all the answers. I like how much you care about Jeff, and the way you reach out to others, like Linda and me. I like . . . you."

His heart pounded against his chest wall. "Thank you."

Too serious suddenly, she broke the tension with a barb. "And I especially like the way you wear your sauce." Her lips twisting into a smirk, she got up to refill her glass at the fridge. "It looks good on you."

He glanced down at his white shirtfront, saw the sauce splatters, and groaned. "Terrific." It would stain. Big-time. He shoved back his chair, and went to the kitchen.

Julia was reaching into the fridge. He stretched over her to grab a paper towel. As he stretched, she straightened, and his arm collided with the back of her neck.

She screamed, "Don't hurt me!"

Seth jerked back, saw her drop to a crouch between the fridge and its open door and bury her head to her chest, protecting it with her uplifted arms.

"Julia?" He spoke softly.

She looked up at him, wild-eyed, her breathing heavy and labored. Only once before had Seth seen that much fear in a woman's eyes. Once before, one woman, the night she had died. His throat went thick. "Julia?"

She didn't look away, didn't move, just stared through him. The attack. Memories of the attack had latched on to her.

Seth slid down to the floor, lifted his arms slowly toward her. "Julia, it's okay. Come here," he said. "Come here, honey. I'd never hurt you. Never. You're safe."

She blinked hard, then blinked again.

"You're safe, Julia." He reached a little closer. "Come here."

"Seth." She scrambled into his arms, clutched at his shirt, doing her damnedest to crawl inside him. "Seth."

"It's okay." He curled his arms around her, smoothed her blouse over her back, and whispered soft, soothing words against her hair. "It's okay. Shh, I've got you now."

She let out a little whimper, and then sat quietly for long minutes, just holding on.

When her heart stopped pounding so hard he could feel it against his chest and her breathing quieted, he asked, "Are you okay?"

"No." She sighed. "When does it end, Seth? Does it ever end?"

He wasn't sure exactly what had triggered her memory of the attack. Could have been a similar sound, a similar scent, or the bump of his arm against her neck. Almost anything could be a trigger. He had come at her from behind, but her attacker hadn't. If the man had pulled her through the car window, then he'd come at her from the side. Still, she could have reacted to just the surprise of not knowing someone was that close and getting bumped. Regardless, in his gut, Seth knew the right response to her questions. He lived with triggers, too. "It ends, honey." He brushed at her damp cheeks with his thumbs. "When you choose to make it end, and not a minute before. You have to decide how much power you give the fear. That's the only way."

She leaned her head against his chest. "It's hard."

"Yes, it is." *Hard* couldn't begin to describe it. "But you've got what you need to get through it."

"What?"

He lifted her chin with a fingertip, looked deeply into her eyes. "Courage."

She blinked, then rubbed her nose against his chin. "I trust you, Seth."

He well knew that trust was the hardest thing in the world for a victim to give. Ten times harder than love. "I trust you, too."

For long minutes, he just held her. Then, she sucked in a sharp breath that had her breasts flattening against his chest. "I'm okay now." She touched her forehead to Seth's lips. "Actually, I'm embarrassed."

"No." He pressed a chaste kiss to her forehead. "Not with me, Julia," he whispered. "Never with me."

Tears filled her eyes. She leaned toward him, and Seth met her halfway, placed a gentle kiss to her lips.

She's married. Hurting. Vulnerable. One day, she'll hate you for this.

Wrong. Worse. She'd hate herself. He pulled back. "Honey, I don't think you really want to do this."

Julia stared at him, at his eyes, his nose, his mouth. "I can't believe it, either, but I do. I really, really do." Slowly, deliberately, she circled his neck with a hand to his nape, and kissed him again. Longer. Deeper.

And, God forgive him, he kissed her back.

When she pulled away, she looked as surprised as he felt. "I won't apologize for that," she said. "I probably should, but I won't."

Neither would he. It was everything Seth had always imagined kissing her would be, and more. "I liked it, Julia." Inside he groaned, wishing someone would shoot him. He sounded like a kid just hitting puberty. Worse, he felt like one.

"Oh, God." Her chin quivered. "Me, too."

Did she think that was good or bad? He couldn't tell.

A metallic clang sounded in the backyard.

Julia scrambled to her feet, jerked open a drawer near the sink, and pulled out a hammer.

"Calm down." Seth took the tool and set it on the tile countertop. "It's probably just a dog, or maybe a raccoon after the trash. I have to strap down the lid to keep them out of it." He said it, and hoped he was right. But Jeff's warning echoed through Seth's mind.

Julia edged toward the hammer, but didn't lift it. She stared at the glass door leading to the patio. "Don't go out there, Seth. I know what Jeff said." Her voice was pitched high and tinny. "I know about tonight."

"He didn't say anything definitive, and I'm not going to let you stand there scared stiff," Seth insisted. "I'll check it out and then you can relax." He reached for the slider's handle.

"Seth, don't open that damn door!" she shouted, then groaned and grasped her left arm.

The spasms had started. "Honey, don't do this. You'll get sick."

"Sick?" Her gaze remained locked on the door. "No, I can't get sick. I can't . . ."

"No, you can't," he said. "I'll be right back. You're okay. Just stay here."

She nodded, clutching at her arm, her teeth gritted against the painful spasms. Still, she inched her fingers across the counter to the hammer, then clasped it in a death grip.

If holding it made her feel safer, then fine. Seth opened the door and looked outside. Light from the kitchen window spilled out in a strip over the patio and then narrowed into a swatch over the lawn. He saw no one. Heard nothing.

He stepped outside. Checked to the left, to the corner of the building. Nothing. Then he turned right, crossed the yard of the apartment next door. All silent. All still. At the far corner, he paused to check the strip of lawn between Julia's building and the one next door. Nothing except a row of five-foot-high azaleas. He walked around. No one hiding behind them, or—he gave them a shake—between their leafy branches. He frowned. No dogs, raccoons, or cats, either. Nothing.

Something had made the noise.

He headed back, turned the corner to the backyard. The light flooding the grass from the kitchen window and the slider door snuffed out. Julia's scream shattered the pitch-black silence.

His heart pumping hard, Seth ran. Something cracked against his skull. His knees gave out, and he collapsed on the dew-damp grass.

The lights came back on, and in the stream, he saw a crack from Julia's open door. "Are you all right, Seth?"

"Yeah. You?"

"No. No, I'm not all right."

Squinting, rubbing at his head, he saw her, standing just

outside the slider door on the patio. Her chest was heaving. But it wasn't pain or fear burning in her eyes.

It was anger.

"You didn't lock the front door." Rigid, she held her hands fisted at her sides. "Why didn't you lock the damn door, Seth? I specifically asked you to lock the damn door."

He rubbed his head. Already a goose egg had lifted and his pulse still throbbed at his temples. "What happened with the lights?"

"I don't know. I heard someone on the stairs, so I went to see who it was. He must have come in the front door—you didn't lock it. The next thing I knew, a man was running toward me and out the back door. I thought—"

Seth rolled to a sitting position, and under his knee saw the damning evidence. Her hammer. "You threw this at me?"

"I don't think so." She came toward him. "I don't know. One minute I was holding it and the next minute it was gone."

And she had screamed to warn him. Okay. Okay. Seth hauled himself to his feet. She'd also come outside. That didn't fit. Unless her intent had been to protect him. Whoever had been in the apartment had already come outside. No one had entered since they had arrived. He would stake his Special Forces training on that. The intruder had to have already been inside, hiding upstairs. "Are you sure the apartment is empty now?"

"Yes. He ran out the back door. He knocked me off balance, so I know the angle. Definitely out the back door."

"He?" She'd said *he* repeatedly. Seth stood up, dusted the grass and grit from his palms.

"Whoever." She looked at Seth's head, examined the goose egg. "It was dark. I didn't see. And to tell you the truth, I'm really fuzzy on everything that happened after you went out the patio door."

He believed her. She had been pretty panicky. "Let's go call the police." He guided her back inside.

"I don't think we should do that." She sounded calmer, but she still held her left arm.

"Why not?"

"Because we don't know who it was, Seth." In control now, she began clearing the table. "It could have been Camden, or it could have been Benedetto-related. If we call the police and it's Camden, then fine. But if not . . .". She let her voice trail off, and set their plates in the sink.

"We'd be putting the project at risk." He didn't like it, but she was right. "Matthew needs to know."

"I agree." She poured the spaghetti sauce into a clear container, snapped on the lid, and then set it in the fridge. "Tomorrow."

Tomorrow? Here she goes again with the waiting thing.

Doubt about her reared its ugly head. Having committed to trusting her, Seth did his damnedest to squelch it. He checked the front door. No damage. No windows unlocked, no signs of forced entry anywhere. It didn't make sense. Even if the dead bolt had been undone—and it had—the knob still had been locked.

There were only two explanations in Seth's opinion. The already upset Julia had creamed him with the hammer, or— "Anyone else have a key?"

"No."

The fridge door slammed shut. "Not even Karl?" Seth asked.

"No one." She didn't look Seth in the eye, and guilt oozed from her.

No forced entry and no one else with a key equated to no one else in the house. Julia had freaked out, hit him with the hammer, and had lied about it. That raised a line of thought he had no choice but to consider. She had full access to the sensor codes, had computer savvy and access to the vault's secure system, and she had reacted strangely to the sensor-codes theft. Maybe the reason hadn't been to keep herself on an even keel emotionally to avoid muscle spasms and migraines. Maybe it had been because she knew exactly what had happened because she had made it happen. Maybe she was Benedetto's mole.

So much for trust.

Her being the mole was a leap, one he hated, but a feasible one he would be foolish to ignore without proving or disproving. The key lay in her hammer toss. Had it been accidental, or intentional?

ANTHONY rested his head against the back of his desk chair. Jet lag had him weary. He wiped the grit from his eyes, longing for a hot bath and his bed. As soon as the council meeting was over, he would indulge himself with both.

"Mr. Benedetto?"

Anthony's second in command, Roger Anton, stood at the office door. Sixty-two, spare with words and in form, but hard as nails inside and out. "Your tie is crooked, Roger." How many times had Anthony heard his father say that very thing? Hundreds if not thousands.

"I'm sorry, sir." Roger straightened it. "The council members are waiting in the Green Room, sir."

"Fine."

"Anthony." Daisy Benedetto, pert and tiny and dressed in a sunny yellow dress, skirted past Roger. "I need to speak with you, darling."

"Mama." Anthony smiled and stood up out of respect. "Can it wait? The council members—"

"Let *them* wait. *This* is important." She twisted the single strand of pearls at her neck. "Actually, it's disgraceful."

Anthony frowned. She only twisted her pearls when deeply worried. "What is it?"

"Melissa Branden is here. Her husband works for Nicholas at the glass factory."

Nicholas Franklin. Bernard T. Franklin's grandson. A thorn in Philip's side, and now in Anthony's.

"Do you know her husband has asked for welfare, Anthony?"

"Welfare?" She had to be mistaken. No loyalist ever had to ask any outsider for financial assistance.

"It's true." His mother's worry changed to anger, and then to outrage. "Mrs. Branden says she's asked to see you twice, but someone"—she gave Roger an accusatory glance—"has refused to let her. Both times."

"I do not refuse to see my people, Mama." Anthony looked at Roger, asking for an explanation. "Are you aware of this situation?"

"You were in Europe, sir," Roger said. "I asked Mrs. Branden the nature of her problem, but she insisted she would rather discuss it privately with you."

Europe. The working vacation with his wife and daughter, where he had successfully negotiated for delivery of the Rogue.

"I knew there had to be a reasonable explanation," his mother said. "But the fact remains that Mr. and Mrs. Branden and their two children are in need. Since when do we allow loyalists to live in need?"

"We don't allow it." Hating to see his mother distressed, Anthony gave her hand a gentle squeeze. "Tell Mrs. Branden the matter will be resolved by tomorrow."

"She needs a thousand dollars today."

Anthony nodded to Roger, who left the room to get the money. When he returned, he gave the money to Anthony. "There," Anthony said, passing it to his mother. "Problem solved."

She gazed up at him, the look in her eyes softening. "Thank you, darling."

"For you, anything." He meant it.

She patted his arm and then stepped away. At his office door, she did a double take beside Roger. "Your tie is crooked."

"I'm sorry, Mrs. Benedetto." He straightened it again.

She looked back at Anthony, pensive. "You won't mention Mrs. Branden's visit to her husband. A man needs his pride."

"Not a word, Mama."

She smiled, blew him a kiss, and then breezed out of the room.

Anthony's smile faded. He looked at Roger. "Nicholas has been called down on this before."

"Yes, sir," Roger said. "Twice under your father."

"Good God, Roger. Welfare?" Anthony expelled his disgust in a string of curses. "I will not tolerate this kind of treatment from any loyalist in authority."

"No, sir."

"What were his penalties?"

"Your father fined him."

"And the second time?"

"A heavier fine and tight supervision for six months."

"Lenient," Anthony said. And now, with the change of command the bastard Nicholas thought he could revert to his old ways and get away with it. Anthony needed to set an example. To establish his rules with authority and conviction.

He walked across the office. As he passed Roger, he issued the order. "Kill him."

"Yes, sir." Roger fell into step behind him.

Anthony turned left, crossed the stone-floored solarium, and then turned right, moving toward the Green Room where the council members waited. "Nicholas is married, I presume."

"Yes, sir. Three children."

"Provide well for them," Anthony said. "And make it an accident away from the factory. I won't have my mother or Mrs. Branden upset by this."

"Yes, sir. Of course not, sir," Roger said. "Who should replace him at the factory?"

"Mr. Branden, of course." Anthony paused outside the Green Room's door. "Who better to eliminate oppression than a man who has suffered it?"

Chapter Ten

SETH met with Matthew at ten and explained the events that had occurred at Julia's the previous night, which also necessitated his explaining Jeff's situation and about Camden and the "mean" man.

Matthew leaned back in his creaky office chair and rubbed at his neck. "You didn't see anyone else?"

"No." Seth hated admitting that, felt like a traitor to Julia for admitting it. But what else could he do? This could be related to Home Base and not to Jeff.

"In cases such as hers, it isn't unheard of for the victim to have blackouts, Seth." Matthew leaned forward over his desk, braced the flat of his arms on his desk blotter. "She might not know she attacked you."

She knew. Seth had seen guilt in her eyes, had sensed it in the way she'd refused to look at him afterward. But maybe that guilt stemmed from her kissing him and not from the hammer. "I guess it's possible."

"The only problem with pinning the attack on her is, in your words, she was terrified." Matthew refilled his coffee cup from the silver carafe on the edge of his desk.

"She was," Seth reasserted with conviction. No one could fake that kind of fear.

Matthew lifted his hand. "Then who turned off the lights?"

*　　*　　*

SETH hadn't been able to answer Matthew's question then, and he couldn't answer it later that night, when he returned to the vault to put in some time on his personal sensor project. A terrified woman *wouldn't* douse the lights.

That left Camden or Benedetto's loyalists. But which one?

The lab seemed empty. Only three cars had been in the staff parking lot, one of which belonged to Julia. The other, a blue truck half-hidden under evergreen limbs in Security's section, Seth assumed belonged to one of the guards on duty, though the night shift typically parked in the north lot.

He walked down the maze of corridors to the transporter, inserted his badge into the slot, and then stepped into the cylinder. The clear door slid closed. The airflow stopped.

Damn, but he hated having doubts about Julia as much as he hated her having doubts about him—as much as he hated the transporter. The doubts felt alien and wrong, but only a fool would dismiss them without proof that they should be dismissed. He wouldn't suffer the consequences of being wrong alone.

The door didn't open.

Fighting a stab of panic, Seth waited.

Still, the door didn't open.

Memories flashed through his mind. Memories of him at six, being locked in, unable to find that damn dead-bolt key. The curses, the screams, his slamming a cast-iron skillet against the window above the sink. The glass shattering, peppering his face, chest, and arms and his crawling through the hole, being scraped and stabbed by jagged shards.

In a cold sweat, he turned his mind away from that time; actively worked at shutting out the old sounds, the old smells of fear and blood, the old taste of tears, but the memories refused to be buried. Clammy, tense, fighting them, Seth stiffened and fisted his hands at his sides. Yelling for someone to open the damn door would be futile. The cylinder was bullet- and soundproof.

Where the hell was the guard?

He looked back at the guard's station. Empty. What was going on here? That station was never empty.

Seth turned in a circle. No one in sight. Anywhere.

The air grew dank, stagnant. Logically, he knew that, for the moment, he had enough air to breathe and yet his chest heaved. He sucked in useless air. Sweating more profusely, hot and clammy, he tore his tie loose, unbuttoned his shirt at the neck, and stripped off his jacket. Futile. No fresh air was being filtered into the system: a necessary protective measure against the introduction of biological or chemical properties.

His eyes blurred, his lungs burned, sweat poured down in rivulets all over his body. *Why wouldn't the damn door open?*

He glanced down, and saw why.

On the cylinder's floor lay a small black flashlight.

A flashlight . . . just like Julia's.

JULIA'S arches screamed.

Accustomed to teaching in flats and sneakers, she had gotten out of practice at wearing pumps, and her feet were letting her know they had noticed the difference and objected to it. Coming out of the inner lab, she paused, leaned against the corridor wall and removed her pumps, then walked on in stocking feet.

It had been a day full of frustrations. Professionally, she hadn't gained any new information on Benedetto's mole. Neither Intel, the OSI, nor Julia and Seth, were a bit closer to finding out who was responsible for the sensor-codes theft than they had been when it had occurred. And no one had yet identified possible motives for either Marcus or Dempsey Morse. A concerted effort was being made, but sifting through infinite possibilities took a huge amount of time and manpower resources.

Personally, her frustration level ranked even worse. Had she thrown the hammer at Seth? She didn't think so. Just the thought of committing physical violence against someone else made her sick. How could it not make her sick? She knew the hell of being attacked, the agony of being a victim. But, God help her, she might have thrown the hammer. She didn't know for a fact. She had nearly worked herself into a migraine trying to remember, but once Seth had stepped out that slider door and onto the patio, she got fuzzy. She recalled clutching the hammer. Someone large had whizzed by and knocked her off balance. From that point on, she was blank. Her next memory was of her standing on the patio, raising hell like an idiot at Seth for not locking the door. Had whoever knocked her off balance taken the hammer? Or had she thrown it at him? Only *him* turned out to be Seth?

She had no idea. And having no idea frightened her in ways she'd never before been frightened. Even during the worst of the challenges after the attack, she hadn't suffered lapses in memory. Why now?

She turned down the corridor to the transporter—and saw someone slumped on the floor inside it. What in heaven was happening?

No alert. No security alarms. No lockdown. Her heart thumping, she ran toward the cylinder.

"Seth?" She stopped in front of it. "What are you do ing?"

He looked up at her, pulled himself to his feet. Sweat poured down his face, soaked his hair, his shirt. "Locked in. Get . . . bomb squad."

Julia heard no sounds but, thanks to a teacher's conference course she had taken last year, she read his lips with no problem. Looking to where he pointed, she saw the flashlight. *The terrorists' new weapon of choice.* Her heart slammed into her throat. "I've got to get you out of there."

He stiffened. "Can't expose . . . vault. Security. Hurry." He tapped his chest. "Can't breathe."

Rattled, she only caught some of his words, but she understood enough. He was sheet-white, sweating profusely, and she recalled that not only did the cylinder block airflow, Seth also had an aversion to being in it. Why, she didn't know, but right now it didn't matter. She ran through the other cylinder, grateful it only carded people on entering.

The security station stood empty. Spotting a red alarm button on the desktop's console panel, she pushed it. The open cylinder slid closed. She'd locked down the building.

Guards came running from all directions, armed with M-16s. One of them was Sergeant Grimm. "Seth's stuck in the cylinder with a flashlight," she said. "He has no air. Call the bomb squad—quick." Julia tried to go back to Seth, but a guard snagged her left arm and pulled her back.

Pain shot through her elbow, her shoulder, and she grasped her forearm. "Damn it!" The spasm raised a knot the size of a lemon in her upper arm. She gritted her teeth against the pain.

"Sorry, Dr. Warner," the guard said. "You've got to stay behind the station. For your own safety."

"Then get the damn bomb squad here. He's suffocating, for God's sake."

"We can get him air."

"No we can't," Grimm countered. "If there's a bomb, we have to keep it contained."

In case it was biological or chemical. "Well, damn it, do something," Julia shouted. "I will not stand here and watch the man die of oxygen deprivation."

"Squad's on its way, Dr. Warner."

Two minutes later, a response team appeared in full protective gear and ordered the building evacuated: an order both Julia and Security refused to follow. Wearing black helmets with face masks and body shields—full bomb-retrieval gear—they took control, followed protocol, working efficiently, methodically.

Julia darted her gaze between two guards' shoulders, watching the squad specialists and Seth. Finally, the cylinder door opened enough for a specialist to step inside. Then, it seamed shut. He examined, tested, and then captured the flashlight in a black case. When he nodded, Grimm opened the cylinder door. Two other members met the specialist and they carried the case out of the cylinder and then out of the building. Only then was Julia allowed to go to Seth.

She met him before he cleared the cylinder door. Hugging him to her strong side, she led him away from the transporter. He was soaked through to the skin with sweat, pasty white, and still gasping for air. "Are you all right?"

"Yeah." He nodded. "Yeah." He stumbled.

"Somebody get some damn oxygen."

"No." Seth shook his head. "Just give me a second."

Julia tightened her hold. "Sit right here, against the wall." She guided him to it.

Back to the wall, Seth slid to the floor, gasping. His insides felt like jelly and his mouth, desert-dry.

"Don't breathe so fast," Julia warned. "You'll hyperventilate."

Dehydrated. Hot. "Thirsty."

Julia shouted to Grimm. "Would you get him some water?"

Another guard appeared with a paper cup fill. "We need to ask some questions."

"Give us a few minutes, okay?" She glared over at the guard. "The man's got to breathe before he can talk."

"Colonel Mason's on his way in, ma'am. He'll expect the preliminary questioning to be done."

"And it will be." Her left arm useless, Julia snatched the cup with her right, spilling a third of the water down her jacketfront. "In a few minutes."

The guard nodded and stepped away.

"Here, Seth." Shaking like a leaf caught in the wind, she lifted the glass to his mouth.

He reached for it, his fingers closing over hers, and drank greedily. The cold sliding down his throat felt good.

When the adrenaline rush subsided, he let out a sharp grunt. "I hate that damn thing." He glared at the transporter. "I've always hated that damn thing."

Julia pulled a tissue from her purse and patted at the sweat streaking down his face and neck. "Why?"

Debating whether or not to answer, he looked over at

her and decided he would. She had secrets, and he had condemned her for it. Not outwardly, but she'd sensed his condemnation, just the same. Yet he was guilty of the same thing. He had secrets, too. "I don't like being locked in." He leaned his head back against the wall. "Working in the lab is hard for me, but I do it because I have no choice."

She brushed a lock of his hair back from his ear. It too was soaked. "Why does being locked in bother you?"

Liking the feel of her touch more than he should, he resolved to tell her. But he damn well couldn't look at her while he did it. "My dad used to beat my mother. From the time I was four, my job was to run to a neighbor's and call the police. When I was six, I couldn't do it because I was locked in the house." His voice shook. "Our front door had a keyed dead bolt. The key was always in the lock. Always."

"But that time, it wasn't," Julia speculated.

"No, it wasn't." He stared at the transporter, bitter and angry and riddled with regret. "My mother screamed for me to go, but I couldn't find the damn key. She screamed and screamed." In his mind, he heard the chilling sounds again, relived the fear and agony of being damned to watch and helpless to act. "I finally broke the kitchen window— they'd all been nailed shut. But by the time the police got there, my mother was dead." Seth forced himself to look at Julia then. "She was dead, Julia. I—I didn't save her."

Her whole chest heaved and a tear rolled down Julia's cheek. "It wasn't your fault. You were just a child."

"It was my job."

"Your father inflicted the wounds, not you. The responsibility belongs to him."

Seth swallowed hard, forced his voice to lower an octave. "It was my job."

Sergeant Grimm walked over. "Dr. Holt, Colonel Mason's arrived. Can we ask you a couple of questions before he enters the building?"

"Yeah." Seth hauled himself to his feet. "But I don't know what I can tell you, Sergeant. I didn't see anyone. I put the card in the slot and got in the cylinder. It closed, and never opened. That's about it."

"Except for the flashlight. Any idea who owns it?"

Seth hesitated.

Julia didn't. "It looks like mine," she said. "I carried it on my key ring, but when Dr. Holt told me about terrorists using them, I took it off and put it in my desk."

Seth grimaced. "I told you to get rid of it before coming to the lab."

"Yes, you did," she said. "But I've had a few things on my mind and I forgot."

Doubt flashed through his eyes. Julia hated it. She understood it, didn't blame him for it, but she hated it.

Grimm cast her a suspicious look. "With restricted access, it would be damned difficult for anyone else to get into the building. Other than Security staff and Dr. Holt, you're the only other person here, Dr. Warner."

"It might be difficult, Sergeant, but obviously it's not impossible. It happened."

He gave her a skeptical look.

"I'm not stupid, for God's sake." Julia frowned. "If I were doing something I shouldn't be, would I be so obvious?"

Grimm hiked his chin. "You might."

"I wouldn't and I didn't," she insisted. "Look, I'm guilty of forgetting and bringing the flashlight into the vault, but when I remembered it, I stashed the damn thing in my desk drawer."

"Do you keep your desk locked at all times?"

"When I'm away from it, yes."

"Who has master keys?"

Julia had no idea.

Seth answered. "Dr. Warner, me, Dempsey Morse, and Colonel Pullman."

"Isn't the colonel still TDY?" Grimm shifted his weight from foot to foot and his studious expression pinched into a frown.

"Yes," Seth said. "Switzerland summit."

"Where's his key?"

"Procedure is to turn it in to Security," Seth said, wondering if Pullman had breached protocol. "Anyone on your staff drive a blue truck?"

"No."

"When I came in, there was one in the lot," Seth said. "You might want to run a check on it."

A guard called Grimm aside, whispered something, and then Grimm returned to them and addressed Julia. "According to the access system, you left the building and then returned right before Dr. Holt."

"I didn't." Julia frowned at him. "I've been in my office since lunch."

"Did you maybe run to your car for something?"

"No." Instinctively, she stepped closer to Seth. "Nothing."

Grimm nodded. "I need to see your security badge."

Julia reached into her jacket pocket to retrieve it.

The badge was gone.

"I think you'd better come with me," Colonel Mason said to Julia, and then turned his gaze to Grimm. "Get Agent 12 over here, STAT."

Seth was glad to hear that order issued. Matthew would sort this out.

"Yes, sir." Grimm headed for the nearest phone.

Julia darted a frantic gaze to Seth.

He stepped to her side. "I'm coming, too."

"Yes, you are, Dr. Holt."

None of Mason's affable manner was evident now. He was down to bare bones, serious business, which was a good thing. Ultimately, the security of the lab was his responsibility. He had some explaining to do to the victims and the honchos. The victims, Seth thought, would be far more understanding and compassionate.

In Mason's office, Seth sat down beside Julia. "Colonel, I know it looks damning, but Julia didn't lock me in the transporter."

"I'm glad to hear that, Dr. Holt." Matthew came into the office, then skirted the chairs. "Both of you had better have damn good explanations, or you can kiss your clearances good-bye."

Julia looked up at him. "I don't know what happened. I've been in the lab. I came out and saw Seth stuck in the transporter. I didn't see anyone, so I hit the alarm button on the console at the Security station. That's all I can tell you because that's all I know."

Seth sent Matthew a telling look. "The guard station was empty from the get-go."

"Outside the transporter?" Mason's brows shot up on his forehead.

"Outside the transporter," Seth confirmed.

Mason reached for the phone, punched down the intercom button. "Who the hell's assigned to the transporter station tonight?" He paused, then added, "Tell him to get his ass to my office now." Mason slammed down the phone. "Grimm."

Feeling Julia's gaze, Seth looked over, and saw her tug her ear. How could she be signaling him everything was all right now?

A light tap sounded at the door. Colonel Mason stood up. "Care to join me in the hall, Agent 12?"

The men left the room. Seth looked at Julia and brushed a fingertip over his lip, silently warning her that the room was monitored.

Five minutes passed. Ten more. Finally, twenty-four minutes after they had departed, Colonel Mason and Matthew returned, and the questioning began.

Mason took their statements, followed up with more detailed questions, and then passed them over to Matthew. Nearly two hours had passed.

Matthew's questions took another hour, with first Julia and then Seth reiterating everything they already had told Colonel Mason. It was a pain in the ass, going through it twice, but so long as no one was talking arrests and pulling clearances—which, so far, they weren't—Seth could tolerate it. He was a little concerned about Julia, but she seemed to be holding her own; she had stopped rubbing at her arm a good half hour ago.

When Matthew finished up, he summoned Colonel Mason.

Mason stared at Seth, and then at Julia. "We're getting you a new badge, Dr. Warner. I suggest you hold on to this one."

"Yes, sir."

"I want to tell you both something. I don't like the rumors I've been hearing about strange crap going on in my vault. Grimm says an alarm went off in the inner lab. He went to check on it. You didn't pass him in the corridor, Dr. Warner, so he's convinced you couldn't have locked Dr. Holt in the transporter." Mason sighed and dropped onto his chair. "Agent 12 tells me we've got some . . . challenges . . . going on you two are working to resolve. I don't know the nature of these challenges, and that's fine. But I'm warning the two of you, right now. If anything goes on here Security should be made aware of and it isn't, there'll be hell to pay, and you two will lose a lot more than your clearances."

"Colonel," Julia said. "I gave you my word, didn't I?"

"Yeah, you did." He twisted his lips, gazed at Matthew, Seth, and then back to her. "Now, tell me you're keeping it."

She raised her right hand. "Promise."

The bluster went out of his expression. "All right, Doc." He turned to look at Matthew. "We're running the tapes. I find anything that counters what we've discussed, and you can consider the reports filed with the JCS."

Straight to the Joint Chiefs of Staff? Damn, Mason was skipping a few pit stops in the chain of command. Seth withheld a protest.

Matthew slid Seth an it-better-not-be-necessary look, then turned his gaze to Colonel Mason. "No choice, no problem. I'll pay for the fax."

Seth took that in. The crunch-time code. Matthew was

up against the wall on this, and he'd backed them. He had taken responsibility for both Seth and Julia, and he was putting Seth on notice that doing so had better not become a mistake Matthew would regret.

"Any variance," Seth said, "and I'll fax the JCS myself."

JULIA went home a nervous wreck. She locked the door-knob, but when she went to remove the key from the dead bolt, she hesitated. Seth's story about his mother ran through her mind, and she couldn't make herself pull the key. She left it in the lock. For him, and for herself.

At the kitchen bar, she dumped her purse and shoes, and then went up to her bedroom where she stripped off her clothes, got into a steaming shower, and telling herself she was ditching stress, she slumped against the shower wall and cried until she couldn't cry anymore.

Her arm throbbed, her head ached, but nothing hurt her as much as the doubt in Seth's eyes. Damn it, why did he have to matter so much? *Why?*

Caring was foolish, stupid, dangerous. Definitely not safe. She just wouldn't do it. She wouldn't let herself care.

Turning away from emotions other people considered normal and good and right didn't do a thing to stop the humiliating act of crying. So she cried on. Weeping for caring when she shouldn't, for Seth about his mother, for herself and all she had lost.

When she ran out of tears and hot water, she toweled off and put on a thick terry-cloth robe, and then went down to the kitchen and poured herself a glass of juice.

Needing serious fortification, she rummaged through her purse for her wallet, and pulled out a photo of her and Jeff in the classroom, standing in front of the chalkboard. She'd been illustrating a football play and the school photographer had snapped the picture. He had given her a copy, and even though its edges were curled and frayed from being tucked in her wallet and from being handled so much, she ran her fingertips over Jeff's little face. Whenever things got really bad, Julia pulled out the photo. Just looking at it grounded her and calmed her down. From the first day of school, Jeff'd had that effect on her. He mattered. He made everything else matter. He . . . and Seth.

Seth and his laughter.

Seemed she cared anyway, despite her resolve not to do it. She snatched a tissue from the box on the counter, swallowed an Imitrex pill to thwart a migraine-in-the-making, and then trudged her way to bed and crawled in under the covers.

Her mind raced. Things looked bad for her; she'd have to be a fool not to know it. Even Matthew had looked at her with skepticism. That worried her. Matthew was adept at concealing his feelings. When she and Seth had met with Matthew the first time, he had looked at her without a trace of recognition. Julia *knew* they had met and still had doubted that he wasn't looking at her and seeing a stranger. Matthew was adept, but Seth . . . He was a master. He'd shown her nothing. Not in his expression, in his body language, or in his eyes. Oh, he had stood up for her to Colonel Mason and Matthew but, even now, she sensed Seth's doubt. And she hated it. With passion and conviction, she hated it.

She looked at Jeff's photo again, felt him clutch at her heart, and wished she could talk to him—just for a minute. God, but she hoped Camden was behaving himself.

Scrunching her pillow, she conjured images of him playing football with Travis, fingering his BAMA key chain, smiling up at her. The medicine kicked in and the throbbing in her head eased. She started to relax and, finally, she fell asleep.

Sometime during the night, she dreamed of a phone ringing and thought she had answered it. But the ring persisted, and she came awake.

Sleep-muddled, she stretched over the spare pillow to the nightstand, glancing at the red digits on the alarm clock—two A.M.—and groaned. It had to be bad news. Preparing herself, she clicked on the lamp, and then reached for the receiver. "Hello."

"What took you so long, sugar?"

The hair on her neck stood on end. "What do you want, Karl?"

"Hey, I'm your husband, remember? Try to sound a little more friendly." He paused, then added, "I've got good news for you."

The only good news would be that she would never hear from him again.

"I'm coming home."

Julia sat straight up. He couldn't be out of jail. He'd gotten five years. It had been only three. *How could he be out of jail?* "Did you escape?"

"Now, would I do that?"

He'd do anything. Anything at all.

"I'll be there in a couple of hours. Fix me something to eat, okay? The food in here sucks. Mmm, maybe some of Uncle Lou's spaghetti."

Her blood turned to ice in her veins. Whether or not he had faked the car accident and had killed Uncle Lou, she didn't know. But Karl's taunts certainly made her think he had. That, and knowing her uncle had noticed bruises on her neck only two days before he had died and he had called Karl down on them.

"You know, sugar, prison is hard on cops." Karl sighed, sending static crackling through the phone. "You're going to have to work real hard to make it up to me."

Her throat went dust-dry. "You're not coming here."

He laughed. "See you in a couple of hours."

"We're divorced, Karl." She clamped down on the receiver until her fingers went numb. "You can't come here."

"Marriage is for life." He dropped his voice, gritty and menacing. "You made vows, and you're going to keep them. Accept it."

Terrified, shaking all over, Julia slammed down the phone. He couldn't be out. He had to be tormenting her. This was just like all the other calls. It was. Except . . . Her skin crawled. Something in his voice had sounded different.

It took her a moment to peg it, and another to stop shunning and accept it. That self-righteous, superior sneer he had lorded over her their entire marriage was back in his voice. Good God. He *could* be out!

She tossed back the covers, ran downstairs and grabbed her purse from the kitchen bar, then ran back upstairs and dumped it on her bed. Fumbling through her wallet, scattering credit cards, her driver's license, her calling card, she finally found Detective LeBrec's business card. He would know the truth.

Shaking head to toe, she punched in the number, fumbled and misdialed, and had to do it again. Detective LeBrec worked the night shift. He would be there. *He had to be there.*

A woman answering the phone put Julia right through and, finally, he came on the line. "Julia?"

Relieved to hear his voice, she swiped her hair back from her face. "Is Karl out of prison?"

"Didn't you get my message?"

"Is he out?"

"Yes. I left a message on your voice mail."

Oh, God. Oh, no. Karl was out. He was really out. "I didn't get any message," she mumbled, pushing a hand against her cramping stomach. *Dear God, Karl was free!*

"I called three days ago." LeBrec's sigh crackled in her ear. "I did my best, Julia, but they let him out due to over-crowding."

Three days? Her throat muscles clenched. Spasms started in her arm, and her head throbbed. She paced between the bed and the wall. "When?" Her voice faltered and she tried again. "Exactly when did he get out?"

"Day before yesterday."

"Oh, God." She slid against the rough wall, down to the floor, and crouched in the corner. "He's coming after me. He called and said he was coming here."

"Leave, Julia." Urgency flooded LeBrec's voice. "He conned the parole board, convinced them he's not a threat to you, but we know better. Get the hell out of there and get a restraining order against him."

"He—he could already be here." She scrambled over to the window, squinted out through the slats in the mini-blinds, checking up and then down the street. Nothing moving, thank God.

A stray thought had her chest going tight. Had *Karl* taken the hammer from her, flung it at Seth? Had *he* turned the lights out and knocked her off balance? God knows, if she had sensed he was that man, she would have blocked out the memory.

"We can get local cops to you."

"No. No, he's got something planned. Otherwise, he would've already shown up. He wouldn't have warned me."

"Julia, don't take any chances, okay? We both know what that bastard is capable of doing."

"Yes, we do." Julia stared sightlessly at a weeping iris on her bedroom curtains. "And we both know that no piece of paper is going to stop him."

HIS body clock still attuned to Europe, Anthony Benedetto sat on one of three verandas, eating a predawn breakfast of strawberries, blueberry muffins, and a Mexican omelet, reading the headlines in *The Observer Gazette,* a newspaper far too liberal for his tastes.

Roger joined him. His navy suit crisp and his tie straight. "Good morning, sir."

"Morning." Anthony folded the paper and set it aside, then motioned for Roger to sit down. "Have some breakfast."

"Just some juice, thank you." He poured a glass of orange juice, and began the morning briefing ritual.

On completing the portion of the briefing dealing with loyalists' trials, tribulations, and triumphs, Anthony asked, "Have you spoken to our friend at Grayton?"

"Yes, sir. He has the sensor codes and nearly everything else we need to get up and running."

Anthony poured himself a cup of coffee from the silver pot. "And you've completed the hiring of our lab staff?"

"Yes, sir. All loyalists. The lab is functional."

"Excellent." Anthony sipped from his steaming cup. "Transport the Rogue to the lab tonight."

Roger nodded. "You asked about that woman scientist, Dr. Warner-Hyde."

"Yes?" Talk of the woman made Anthony uneasy. He had taken risks on her he would have preferred not to take. But for the good of his people . . .

"Our friend at Grayton says she's under control," Roger said. "She doesn't have any children of her own, but she's developed a special attachment to one of her students, Jeffrey Camden. His mother died a few months ago—heart attack—and his father is being investigated for abuse."

Abuse. Anthony lost his appetite and dropped his napkin onto his plate, then shoved it away. "If the father disappears, what happens to the boy?"

"I don't know, sir. He has no other living relatives."

Anthony thought on that a moment. Could be important. "What about the scientist? Would she want him?"

"Definitely."

"Thank you, Roger." This new development gave Anthony much to consider. Much to consider.

Chapter Eleven

JULIA jerked on a white blouse and navy suit, stuffed her things back into her purse, then slung its strap over her shoulder on her way down the stairs.

She made it to the car. Halfway down Fairway Lane, she realized she had no idea where to go.

For the fifteenth time, she checked to make sure her car doors were locked, checked her rearview mirror. No lights behind her. None in front of her, or at the crossroads. Fury seethed inside her. A marriage from hell, a divorce from hell, a recovery from injuries inflicted in an attack from hell, and she'd survived. Yet, three years later—*three damn years later*—and just the sound of his voice sent her tumbling back into all the old fears. A stupid phone call, and once again she was a terrified victim.

She stopped at the crossroads. It was decision time. Left to Seth's, or right to the lab?

Her stomach curled, yearning to go to Seth. He would understand. Having lived through what he had with his mother, he really would.

Are you crazy, Julia? He doubts you already.

She gripped the steering wheel hard. Her sweaty palms made it slick, hard to hold on. She snatched a tissue from the box on the console, swiped her hands dry, then tossed the tissue to the floorboard.

Okay, so Seth had just cause to believe she had cracked

him in the head with the hammer—and she had locked him in the transporter, thanks to her forgetting about the damn flashlight. But she hadn't done either one. She had no idea who had taken the flashlight, though her money was on Dempsey Morse—he did have a master key—but Karl could have taken the hammer. He could have thrown it at Seth. Either way, she felt certain of her innocence. And because she did, Seth's doubt ticked her off.

Liar. It hurts you. What he thinks matters. You care about him, Julia. Enough to think he's special, to kiss him, and to want to make love with him—after Karl, and after swearing off men. You care, and that's that.

"Shut up," she told herself, not wanting to care. Angry with herself because she did care. Men could hurt you, deceive you, destroy you to the point where anything is better than being with them. Even death.

You care, Julia.

"Damn it, just—just shut up, and think."

The vault. She hooked a right. She'd be safe in the vault.

Safe from Karl, and Seth. Coward.

Survival.

Cowardice.

Whatever! She had survived once . . . so far. If it took cowardice to survive again, then so be it. Dead women don't get to breathe. Cowards do.

At the entrance gate to the base, Julia flashed her ID and nodded at the guard. He waved her through and she drove on to the lab's staff parking lot. Hopefully, whoever had used her old badge would try to use it again, and then Sergeant Grimm, Colonel Mason, and Matthew could nail him.

Or her.

Linda's anger and frustrations at being a frequent Saudi widow, left behind to deal with the kids and the family crises, wouldn't get out of Julia's mind. She couldn't shake the thoughts, but she resented them. Linda honestly seemed like a good woman.

Even good women can be pushed too hard and too far.

True. The blue truck Seth had mentioned being parked in the north lot earlier was now gone. Two unfamiliar cars were in the staff lot. She parked close to the lab entrance and then went inside, unable to stop herself from checking back over her shoulder. Access to the base was restricted, but Karl had gotten into restricted areas before, and she'd be crazy to think he couldn't do it again.

A lieutenant sat at the first checkpoint station, reading one of Grisham's paperback novels. She didn't recognize the guard, but dredged up a smile, hoping her head didn't explode. The throbbing at her temples had expanded to her nape, and now a solid band of pain circled her forehead. "Morning."

"Starting early today, Dr. Warner?"

She might not know him, but he'd already been briefed on her. "Just getting a jump on things." She looked back at the door. Karl couldn't get into the vault, but he could get into its outer rim, up to this checkpoint.

"Ma'am?"

She glanced back at the guard. From the look in his eyes, he knew her backside was in a sling around here. If not for Colonel Mason and Matthew taking a leap of faith on her, she would be without a security clearance and, without a clearance, she couldn't do anything, including enter the lab. "Yes, Lieutenant?"

"Go on through, ma'am."

Julia nodded and walked on, then made her way through the maze to the cylinder. It mocked her like a tall glass tomb. When she went to put her card in the slot, her stomach filled with butterflies. But not with fear. That cylinder was the one place on earth Karl Hyde, and his cop friends he'd duped into covering up his crimes, couldn't get to her. Karl might get on base, but he could *not* get into the vault.

God, but she was grateful for that.

The door opened, and she stepped out, then grabbed her card and walked on to the lab.

It was blessedly empty, and she felt grateful for that, too. More than anything, she needed to just sit down for a while and let her head calm down. Then she could think. Karl was out. And, unless she found a way to stop him, she would be as much his prisoner now as she had been during their marriage.

Her stomach heaved, her arm ached. She swallowed hard, knowing she couldn't live through his torture again and survive. Surviving it once had been a miracle.

In her office, she dropped into her chair and stared through the glass into the darkened lab. Why in the name of all that's good hadn't she learned to defend herself?

You thought you had more time.

She should have had more time. Two more years. But, no. They let the bastard out on good behavior due to over-crowding.

And in the same fell swoop, they condemned you to hell.

"MORNING, Dr. Holt." The guard nodded.

"Morning, Lieutenant." Seth stopped at the lab's first checkpoint.

"I guess everyone in the zone's getting an early start this morning."

"Excuse me?"

"Dr. Warner came in about three."

Strange. She'd been worn out last night. If anything, Seth would have thought she might arrive late today. "Did she say why?"

He picked up a paperback novel he had been reading. "Getting a jump on things."

What things? Seth wondered. The lieutenant talked on, and Seth diverted his attention back to the man.

"Left about twenty minutes ago. She said to tell you she would be late getting back."

Julia had come and gone? "Did she say where she was going, or why she would be late?"

"No, sir." The guard looked torn, as if he could add something but doubted the wisdom of doing it.

Seth glanced at his name tag. "What is it, Lieutenant Janus?"

"Nothing, sir. I'm probably just tired and seeing things that aren't there."

"What things?" Seth pushed.

"Well, Dr. Warner, sir." Janus thumbed the pages of his novel. "She looked like she'd had a rough night."

"We all did," Seth said. "Didn't they brief you on the lockdown?"

"Yes, sir." Janus stood up a little straighter. "But this was different. She kept checking behind her, like somebody was following her, and she looked . . . I don't know."

The guy's in prison.

For now.

Recalling that snatch of conversation between him and Matthew had the hair on Seth's neck standing on end. "How did she look?"

The lieutenant looked away, lowered his gaze. "Haunted, sir," he said, then returned his gaze to Seth's. "Sounds crazy, but that's the only way to describe it. She looked haunted."

"Thanks for letting me know." Thoughtful, Seth headed toward the lab and checked his watch. It would be a couple hours before he could check with Matthew to see if her attacker was on the loose, and he had no idea where to look for Julia. He'd try her at home and on the cell phone. If she was being followed, she would have stayed put in the vault.

In his office, he made the calls. No answer at either of Julia's numbers. Then, he left a message for Matthew.

Nothing else he could do but stick out the wait. Seth put in a couple hours on his sensor design. One day, maybe Congress would cut loose with the money to fund it. With all the budget cuts, odds looked slim at best. The U.S. needed the capability. Sadly, the honchos who controlled the pursestrings didn't yet realize it. But Seth did. And making sure it was ready when the need arose kept him working at it, despite the odds.

Would that make him patriotic in Julia's book?

*   *   *

JUST after ten, Julia came into the lab. Seth took one look at her and recalled Lieutenant Janus's warning. She did look haunted. Haunted, pale, and raw-nerved.

When she came close enough, Seth whispered, "Are you okay?"

"I'm fine, Seth." She kept walking.

Having learned long ago that any time a woman says she's fine, hell's coming to call, Seth leaned against the lab table and watched her walk into her office, close the door, and plop down in her chair. The glass wall between them couldn't hide the fact that she was haunted and dead tired any more than it could hide the fact that her left arm hung limp across the armrest of her chair. Something had gotten to her in a big way. Was it the lockdown? The sensor-codes theft? The incident at her apartment?

No. She had buried her emotional reactions to those things. He had witnessed that himself. Something else had to have happened. Something that hit her so hard she couldn't bury her feelings about it. But what?

Matthew still hadn't returned Seth's call, but he could just ask her, straight-out. And he would, except Matthew had made it clear that Seth should keep his mouth shut on this, and through the years, Seth also had learned that when a woman says she's fine, a smart man doesn't pry or push until she signals she's ready to talk. He pries or pushes, and she gets her nose out of joint. And a woman's nose out of joint translates to a man living in misery, getting his ears blistered and his ass chewed, until she gets over it.

Life would be easier if trust could be forced. But it couldn't, so he'd just have to wait, and hope it came in under its own steam. And he'd have to hope that whatever had happened to her didn't cause either of them more trouble. Matthew's willingness to go to the wall for them was about at an end. Seth still had no idea why Colonel Mason had gone out on a limb for them. Had to be because of Julia. She clearly had met with the man and had given him her word on bringing him into the loop if the occasion arose. Why hadn't she mentioned that to Seth?

Wait. Wait. She had told him. She had gotten the suspects' time-line list from Mason on the sensor-codes theft.

Seth glanced over at her. Tense, wary, pale, clearly scared stiff—and doing her damnedest to hide it. It was more trouble. Seth would bet his sensor on it. But it wasn't about Jeff.

No, for Jeff, Julia would go to anyone for help, including the devil himself. Could be the attacker, Karl, something related to Benedetto. Hell, there were a dozen possibilities. So which one, or what, had caused this?

JULIA couldn't stay in the vault forever.

She had gotten the restraining order against Karl that morning. Matthew had helped shove through the paperwork. Fortunately, he had connections with the staff judge advocate's office on base and they had connections off base with the civilian authorities who handled legal matters. A judge had signed the order and Julia's had a copy of it in her hand by nine-fifteen.

For what it was worth.

Which was nothing.

During the day, Seth had dropped by the office several times, including to invite her to ride along with him to see Jeff. But as much as she wanted to see him, she had refused. Karl could be watching. The last thing she wanted to risk was leading him to Jeff. There was no doubt in her mind Karl Hyde would do anything, use anyone—even a helpless child—to hurt and "punish" her.

Even Dempsey Morse had ventured out of his hermit hole after lunch and stopped by her office for a short chat, something he had done only once since she had taken over the project. He seemed like a nice man—said all the right things—but something about him set Julia's teeth on edge. That she couldn't peg exactly what had her grinding them.

Mr. Sandlis and Marcus had called in sick with the flu. And about five, Greta and Linda had left to take their kids out for pizza. It was after eight now. The lab had been quiet for hours, and Julia had lingered as long as she dared. She couldn't do anything to arouse more professional suspicion.

Unlocking her desk, she removed her purse from the drawer. There was no place to go but to the apartment. She needed clothes. Maybe she'd just grab some things at the mall and find an obscure motel.

Obscure motel? In Grayton? With Karl's connections? Highly unlikely.

Resentment burned in her stomach. Why couldn't he just leave her alone? Why couldn't he accept the divorce and just leave her alone?

He didn't love her. He had deceived her into believing he did. Maybe even deceived himself into believing it. But he never really had loved her. For him, this was about control. He had married her, therefore he controlled her. Until death they do part.

For Karl Hyde, their relationship was that simple.

Feeling the weight of the world on her shoulders, Julia left the lab, then the vault, and then drove to the apartment.

The lamp she had left burning in the living room glowed, warm and welcoming, but, inside, dread dragged at her.

Just to be safe, she made the block, and then circled two blocks, checking for odd cars or anything unusual. Detective LeBrec had taught her the protective technique, trying to ease her fears during the time between Karl's arrest and his trial. His buddies in blue had bailed him out. To their credit, they had done so before Detective LeBrec had filled them in on the entire story. Still, after they had learned Karl had duped them, they hadn't had his bail revoked. LeBrec claimed it was a protect-your-own kind of thing. Regardless of why, Karl had remained free and she had been the prisoner. LeBrec had stashed her in a women's shelter for safe-keeping.

Less than an hour after Karl had posted bail, Agent 12 had shown up at the shelter and had given her several safety tips. One of which was to get the hell out of the shelter because every cop in the county knew where it was, and within minutes of her arriving there, Karl knew it, too. Matthew had reiterated the "secure the perimeter" technique LeBrec had taught her, and he had rented her a car and helped arrange her escape.

Walking into his office with Seth and pretending she had never before seen Matthew had been difficult. Not impossible, but difficult. She'd only had to block any memories of him from her mind and to keep them blocked. Fortunately, in the past three years, she had become adept at blocking memories. Except when she got the phone calls.

And since hearing Karl was out.

Everything seemed fine, so she garaged the car, walked up to the front door, and then checked the locks. Secure. She keyed the knob, the dead bolt, and then stepped inside, her heart knocking against her ribs. When she closed the door behind her, a little sigh of relief escaped her throat. *Safe.*

Moving to turn the key in the dead bolt, she remembered Seth and his mother, imagined the horror he must have felt at hearing his mother's screams and not being able to find that key. Julia's heart wrenched for the pain of the child, and for the guilt that remained with the man.

Nothing could chew a person up and spit them out like guilt. What she felt about Uncle Lou proved that.

"Hello, sugar."

Julia jerked around. "Karl." *Oh, God! He was in her house? How had he gotten into her house?*

He smiled, but there was no warmth in it. At the foot of the stairs, he leaned, elbow against the banister. "Clever. Running off to the vault—and renting this place in Seth Holt's name. I should've known you'd still be screwing that bastard."

Julia finally slugged through her fear and found her voice. "Get out." She fished in her purse. "I have a restraining order. Get out of my house now, or I'll call the police and they'll put you back in jail."

"Don't threaten me, sugar. It pisses me off." He locked the dead bolt, snatched the key out of the lock, and then stuffed it into his pocket. "You know what happens when I get pissed off."

How in God's name could she forget? He hadn't raised his voice, but she felt as threatened as if he had screamed at her.

He sat down on the steps. His slacks bunched at his thighs and his brown leather jacket was unzipped, split open and hanging loose at his sides.

Oh, yes, she knew what happened when he got pissed. No more than that little reminder, and every nerve in her body stretched piano-wire tight. Fear cramped her stomach, tasted bitter on her tongue, raged through her as strong as it had before she had left him, leaving her feeling helpless. Hopeless.

Three years had passed. *Three years.* Hadn't she made *any* progress? *Any* recovery? How could the fear feel the same? *How?*

Karl draped his arms over his knees. "I've done some checking, and it's a good thing I've come home. You're in a lot of trouble, sugar." He smiled up at her, enjoying this, and then the smile faded. "So how do you like it?"

He'd lost her. Locking her knees to stay upright, trying desperately to think of a way out, she tried to clamp down on her fear that he had killed her uncle Lou, nearly had killed her, and now he had returned to finish the job. "Like what?"

"Being screwed *and* screwed over by your man, Seth Holt?"

Having no idea what he meant, she kept quiet.

"No matter. Those days are over, too." Karl sprawled back on the steps, propping his upper body with his elbows on the steps. "He's using you, Julia. And, being a genius and all, you're still falling for it."

"For what?" God, but her knees wouldn't stop shaking. Any second she'd heave. Her stomach churned and rolled.

"He set you up to take the fall for the security breaches. He's Benedetto's mole."

Shock streaked up her spine. How did Karl know about

this? He *couldn't* know about this. No one could.

He knows, Julia. Accept it.

"You've always been Seth Holt's sucker. He led you around by the nose, and you followed like a stupid bitch in heat." Karl stood up, hitched his pants on his hips. A bar of lamplight slanted across his chin. "But those days are over, too. I'm home now, and you're going to do exactly what I tell you when I tell you. Just like you always did."

Julia swallowed hard. His tone and verbiage resonated of all the intimidation tactics he had used on her. He deliberately preyed on her fears. Damn it, she knew what he was doing. Exactly. So why was he getting to her emotionally? Why couldn't she stand up to him? Why, after going through all she had to get away from him, was she still letting him scare her to death?

Because you know what he's capable of doing to you. What he has done to you. You'd damn well better fear him, Julia.

"Marriage is forever," he said. "Forgetting that could be unhealthy. For you . . . and for Jeff."

Her stomach lurched. Dear God, he knew about Jeff, too? How on earth could he know about Jeff, too? He had to have had some of his cop friends watching her.

What difference does it make how he knows? He knows. He always knows about everything. You know that, Julia.

Impossible.

Oh, really? Well, just when did you tell him you worked in the Black World?

The security breaches and Benedetto. He did know about the breaches and Benedetto.

Uh-huh. So when did you tell him?

She never had. He'd known that she worked for the DoD—but no one outside of high-level Department of Defense personnel and the President of the United States knew she was involved in the Black World. No one else, except the others in it, working alongside her.

So how did Karl know?

She had no idea.

"Jeff's a cute kid," Karl said. "Damn shame I'm going to have to use him to keep you in line. Getting a willful woman to toe the line's a real pain in the ass."

Use Jeff? Over her dead body. "You leave Jeff alone, Karl. I mean it."

"Or what?" He rounded on her. "What are you gonna do, little girl?"

"I am *not* a little girl." She jerked the restraining order, waving it at him. "I'm a grown woman, and I'm not the same woman you used to terrify."

He gave her a wicked smile. "You're standing there shaking in your shoes, and you're gonna tell me you're not scared?" He stepped toward her. "Sugar, let me tell you something. If you've got any smarts at all left in your scrambled head, you goddamn well better be scared of me." He leaned closer, nose to nose, and whispered. "I'm your worst nightmare, and I'm back in your life for good."

Every instinct in her body warned Julia to run. But she couldn't run; the world wasn't big enough to hide her. Not with Karl and his connections. She tried that once and had nearly died three times. Only a fool would try it again.

Dragging up every ounce of courage she possessed, she glared into his eyes. "Leave Jeff alone. His father already makes his life a living hell, and I'll do whatever it takes to keep you from making it any worse."

Surprise flickered through Karl's eyes. "Well, I'll be damned. You love the brat. You, Holt, and the brat. Now, isn't that something? Got you a real little family going here, huh, Julia?"

She held her glare, and said nothing.

"Good. Protect him. Hell, protect them both." Karl rubbed at his jaw. " 'Course, you protected Holt once and that didn't work out too well for you. But, hey, maybe you learned some tips and this time you'll do better."

He stood so close she could smell him; a smell that triggered a memory. The hammer attack. The man who had knocked her off balance, tossed the hammer at Seth. It really had been Karl. His smell. That's why she had blocked the memory.

The stubble on his unshaven face rustled under his hand, and she sensed the wheels turning inside his mind. He would force her into doing what he wanted, using Jeff and Seth as weapons.

When does it end, Seth? Does it ever end?

It ends, honey. When you choose to make it end, and not a minute before. You have to decide how much power you give the fear . . .

She couldn't choose to allow Karl to use force against her, or allow him to use Seth or Jeff as weapons to control her. She had to choose to refuse.

Anticipating Karl's reaction, she braced. "You have no place in my life anymore. I want you out of my house. Now."

He punched her.

Reeling from the blow, she lost her footing, stumbled against the back of the sofa and grabbed hold to steady herself. Her jaw throbbed, her teeth ached, her eyes teared, and she couldn't quite focus.

God, how she regretted not learning to defend herself.

"Don't give me orders, Julia Hyde." Cold fury narrowed Karl's eyes. "Don't you ever give me orders. You tossed my ass in jail and put me through hell. Well, your hell starts now."

He shoved her toward the kitchen. "Get me some food."

She banged a hip and elbow against the cabinet. Pain streaked through her whole left side, hip to shoulder, stole her breath. Tears filmed her eyes and she blinked hard: she was damned if he would get that satisfaction from her, too.

How had this happened? What could she have done differently to have prevented it?

More importantly, what did she do now to get out of it?

Needing comfort so she could think, she grabbed the pasta pot from the cabinet, filled it with water, and then set it on the stove, looking longingly at the phone. If she called the police, she would be dead before they could get here.

She was no match for Karl physically. She had to get out of the house—before he got any more wound up. Already he was pacing. That was his pattern. Get in those verbal digs, slap or punch her, and then pace. After pacing came sitting and brooding, and then the serious cursing. After the serious cursing . . .

No, she had to get out of here before he got to serious cursing. At the stove, she watched Karl from the corner of her eye. He turned the television on ESPN, cranked back in a recliner and put his feet up, the remote in his hand. Some hockey game blared, and Karl brooded, muttering curses on her head.

She watched. Waited. Worried. And watched some more. When he seemed mesmerized by what was happening on the screen, she made it to the sliding door. Her heart pounded hard, threatening to thud right out of her chest. If he caught her, he'd beat her senseless. Maybe, to death.

Stay or go. Either way, you're going to get beaten.

No. She stared into the pot of heating water. No, not again. She turned the burner knob. It clicked off.

Then go, Julia. If you go, at least you've got a chance. Go, Julia. Run!

She inched the door open, slid through, then softly closed it behind her. As soon as the lock caught, she turned and ran blindly into the night.

Stay away from the street. Watch out for the lights. He'll see you!

She hugged the houses, hoping to hell someone didn't mistake her for a prowler and shoot her. Checking behind her, she didn't see him following her. She didn't see anyone. Still, she ran. And ran, wishing she knew where to go, what to do.

Seth.

She had no choice. She had to warn him. Get his help. Karl *would* go after Jeff. Maybe after Seth, too. Karl clearly still believed that they had, and were still having, an affair.

Disappointment warred with a stitch in her side, battling for her attention. She pressed a hand against the ache and ran on. Not contacting Seth during the past three years had done no good whatsoever. The scary part was that if Karl hadn't disabused himself of the idea of an affair by now, a TNT blast wouldn't rid him of the notion. She couldn't let him blindside Seth, and they had to protect Jeff.

Headlights shone behind her. Julia ducked behind a hedge and dropped flat on her stomach on the muddy ground, breathing hard against a sprinkler head, digging into her ribs and still bubbling water, soaking the hedge. Hearing an engine running, she peeked through the thick, wet leaves. A car crept down the street.

Her car.

Chapter Twelve

JULIA stumbled into a service station.

The young man behind the counter, wearing a baseball cap, gave her a wary look. Winded and muddy from running, sprawling on the ground, and sliding under bushes to avoid Karl, she smiled to assure the clerk she posed no threat. "Where's the phone?"

"Outside, around the corner." He motioned left.

"Thanks." She nodded, then went back outside. The lights were bright, making her an easy target.

What was she going to do about Jeff?

She could go to Matthew, but that still left Seth vulnerable. He deserved to know the truth. He needed to know the truth, and he could call and speak directly to Jeff.

God help her, she had to tell him every dirty detail.

First, you have to get to him.

She dialed the operator.

"May I help you."

"I need to place a call and charge it to my home phone."

"Is someone there to accept the charges?"

"No, I'm single." She stretched to peek around the corner. *All clear.*

"I'm sorry, ma'am. Unless someone at your home number authorizes the call, I can't connect you."

Julia stared heavenward. "Obviously, I'm not there or I wouldn't need to forward charges."

"Do you have a calling card?"

"Not with me." She couldn't say it was an emergency. Karl could have a scanner and intercept the call. He had to be Jeff's "mean" man. But why involve Jeff? Julia stared out at the street, at the cars passing by. *So far, so good.* "I can give you whatever information you need, just let me place this call. Please." Julia reeled off her number.

"I'm sorry, ma'am." The operator paused a moment. "Could you verify your home number, please?"

Julia repeated the number. Checked the street. A gangly kid was walking his dog; a woman was pumping gas into her station wagon.

"This number belongs to a man."

Seth had put the phone in his name. "Seth Holt. Dr. Seth Holt."

"Do you have Dr. Holt's permission to make the call?"

"No, I don't, but—"

"Sorry, ma'am." The operator hung up.

Fuming, Julia let her head loll back. *You can't afford more tension.*

Okay. Okay. She'd just call Seth collect, then.

She dialed the number. When the operator came on the line, she said, "Collect, please. From Dr. Julia Warner."

He answered on the second ring. "Holt."

The operator got authorization for the charge, then hung up, and suddenly it all became too much. Julia slumped against the cinder-block wall. "Seth, I need help."

"Where are you?" Worry and fear filled his voice.

She sniffled. "At a gas station on the corner of Sandy Hill and Old Murphy Road. Can you come get me?"

"Where's your car?"

Decision time. Did she tell him the truth, or lie? "Please, just come get me." She swallowed hard. "Hurry, Seth. I—I'm in trouble."

"Five minutes." He hung up the phone.

She set the receiver back on the hook, then stepped back, deeper into the shadows, and watched the cars come and go from the store, praying not to see her own. "Hurry,

Seth," she whispered, folding her good arm over her chest against the damp night air and the fear. "Please, hurry."

Hoping Karl was searching in the opposite direction, toward the vault, she again lifted the receiver. She had to try to warn Camden. Dialing the operator, she placed the call.

Camden answered. "Yeah, hello."

"Will you accept a collect call from Dr. Julia Warner?" Surprise tinged his voice. "Yeah."

"Thank you, sir. Go ahead, ma'am."

Julia swallowed hard. "Mr. Camden, I'm sorry to have to phone collect, but I had to warn you that Jeff may be in danger."

"What kind of danger?"

God, but this was hard for Julia to say aloud. Until now, she never had. Not once. "My ex-husband is trying to force me back into the marriage. If I don't agree, he's threatened to hurt Jeff."

"A crazy married to a crazy." Camden guffawed. "I'm sure he's bluffing, Dr. Hyde."

Julia gritted her teeth, bore the barb. Where was Camden's concern? His fear for his son's safety? "This man doesn't bluff." For Jeff's sake, she had to convince him. "He's already violated a restraining order."

"I see."

Hardly. He sounded haughty, and not at all convinced. What more could she do? "Please take this seriously and keep a close watch on Jeff. You have no idea what this man is capable of doing." Her voice went thick. "I'm afraid for Jeff, Mr. Camden." She was terrified for all of them— Jeff, Seth, and herself.

"Okay, Dr. Hyde. Thanks for calling."

Dr. Hyde. He hadn't heard a word she'd said. "Mr. Camden, don't blow this off. I'm telling you, the man is dangerous."

"I heard you."

"Please tell Jeff . . . to be careful."

"Sure thing." He muttered something she didn't catch, then hung up the phone.

The dial tone droned in her ear. Julia slammed the receiver onto its hook. *Stupid bastard. Stupid, stupid, stupid.*

He wouldn't tell Jeff. Wouldn't do anything except gloat because she was having domestic difficulties. He was accustomed to domestic difficulties. Hell, he'd perpetrated them in his own family.

The wind whipped her hair into her eyes. Smoothing it back, she brushed against her jaw, and winced. It was already sore. Angry, resentful, scared stiff, she looked around the corner of the building to the street. Still no sign. By now, Karl had to realize she had avoided going to the lab or to Seth's house. "Damn it, Seth. Hurry!"

SETH swerved into the gas station and slammed on the brakes. A truck and two cars outside—neither was Julia's. He shoved the gearshift into park and got out of the Lexus.

Julia ran toward him from around the corner. Mud and bits of grass clung to her blue skirt and white blouse—the clothes she had worn to work that day. She stepped into the light. Wet and barefoot? No, she had on stockings. They looked like shredded wheat. "What happened to you?"

She ran around to the passenger's side of the car. "Were you followed?"

"No." He stood beside the car.

"Get in, Seth. Please."

She slammed her door shut, reached for her safety belt.

Seth got back in the car, noticed her left arm lay crooked and limp, braced against her side. "Julia, I'm not moving this car until you tell me what's going—" He stopped suddenly, his eyes narrowed, and his voice elevated. "Where did you get that bruise?"

"Don't yell at me." She buried her face in her right hand. "Just go. *Please.* I'll explain in a minute, just get me away from here."

Seth popped the gearshift into drive and took off, automatically checking his rearview mirror to make sure he wasn't being followed. "I want to know what happened to your face, Julia."

"I got mugged." She wrenched around to look behind them. "He took my car."

"Did you call the police?" Seth braked for a stop sign.

Julia darted her gaze side to side, front to back. "I couldn't."

"Why the hell not?"

Tell him, Julia.

Put him in more danger? Explain once loving and marrying a man capable of Karl Hyde's atrocities? She had believed him, for God's sake. What kind of woman did that make her? Seth had placed his future in her hands. His faith, his financial security, and his credibility. She couldn't tell him this. Not until she proved herself to him.

"What if it was one of Benedetto's loyalists?" She held the door's armrest in a death grip. "I can't explain that to civilians."

Seth frowned at the dashlights. A lie. Reasonable, rational, but from her body language and shaky voice, a lie. Why lie about this? And why worry that a mugger would follow her?

"I'll report it to Matthew." She sucked in a sharp breath. "You're turning left. Why are you turning left?"

"My house is left. I'm taking you home. You're going to take a shower and get warm and dry. I'm going to make you a cup of hot tea. And then we're going to have a long talk, Julia, and you're going to tell me what the hell is going on."

"We can't go to your house."

"Why not?"

"Because we need someplace safe to talk. It's likely I'm not the only target. It's . . . highly probable he's also coming after you."

Seth pulled into a driveway, made a U-turn, and headed away from town. She knew who was after her.

"Where are we going?"

"I have a cabin on a lake not far from here. We can talk there."

"Does anyone in the lab know you own it?"

"Linda." So this was work-related, not personal. Confused as hell, he punched down on the gas pedal. "I haven't mentioned it to anyone else."

Julia fell silent.

Weed-infested ditches hugged the sides of the two-lane road. Its shoulders were soft, and loose grains of sand spun up and hit the car's undercarriage.

Soon, the lights from town shone behind them, and Julia looked over at him. "Seth?"

"Mmm?"

"I didn't hit you with the hammer. And I didn't lock you in the transporter. I swear it."

How did he answer that? "Okay."

"No, it's not just okay." She reached over with her right hand and clasped his arm. "I need for you to believe me. At first, I wasn't sure about throwing the hammer. I was fuzzy and I thought maybe I had panicked, but now I know I didn't do it."

Strangely enough, Seth believed her, despite Security's certainty that she was the only person not on the Security staff in the building at the time he had been locked in the transporter. Without evidence, and with her badge missing, Matthew had agreed it improbable. He and Colonel Mason had backed Seth, which was the only reason either of them still had a security clearance. "I believe you, Julia."

She let out a little moan. "Thank you."

They rode on through the night in silence. Seth glanced over to see if she had dozed off, but she hadn't. She stared straight ahead, blanking out. This time, he didn't disturb her. She had been mugged again, and she hadn't dissolved into tears. He would just as soon she stayed collected.

"Seth?"

"Yes?" He checked his speed and then his mirrors.

"I know it's an imposition, but I need another favor. A big one."

Her voice sounded strange. Gravelly and strained, as if the words themselves choked her. "What do you want, Julia?"

"I—I need for you to teach me how to defend myself."
She stiffened, but she didn't look his way. "I need to learn
how to kill a man."

Stunned, Seth looked over. Her jaw was set, no rapid
blinking. She was dead serious. "Matthew suggested you
learn to shoot a .38." He opened the door for her to tell
him if her attacker was free. "I can teach you."

"I would appreciate it very much," she said, leaving the
door shut. She swallowed hard and then cleared her throat.
"But I also need to be able to . . . do it . . . without a gun."

Do it? She nearly strangled on saying it. How could she
do it? "Okay. I can teach you some hand-to-hand combat
techniques."

"Thank you."

"We'll call Matthew from the cabin and work on it this
weekend." It was Friday. "We can cover a lot of ground
by Sunday night, provided you work at it."

"I will." She nodded, lending weight to her claim, and
sent him a shattered look. "I'm tired of being a victim."

Because there were no words he could give her to take
the anguish out of that remark, Seth clasped her hand, gave
it a gentle squeeze, and then held on, resting their linked
hands on his thigh.

THERE were no locks on the doors.

Julia stared at the knob, panic seizing her stomach. How
could a man own a cabin on a lake that he only visited
occasionally and not have locks on the damn doors? Karl
was free, after her—and probably after Seth and Jeff—*and
there were no locks on the damn doors*?

"Take a look around and get familiar." Seth closed the
door behind him.

Rather than argue, she did it. The cabin was rustic. Two
bedrooms, living room paneled in rough-hewn wood, one
bath, and a decent kitchen with a back door. There was no
lock on it, either.

God help her, they were sitting ducks.

Seth shrugged out of his jacket and hung it on a wall

rack next to several baseball caps. One was red with the BAMA insignia, reminding her of Jeff. She hadn't known Seth was a fan, too.

"Why don't you take a shower and warm up? I'll scrounge up some clothes for you."

Not even a twist-turn lock on the knob, for God's sake. Or one of those sliding bolts with a chain. Nothing.

"Julia?" Seth stared at her.

"Shower. Yes, I'm going." She walked to the bath. It was small. One window. No lock on its door, either. Good grief, Seth was a trusting soul. He shouldn't be. He really shouldn't be, and she was going to have to tell him why.

God, but she hated it. With every atom in her body, she hated it. She stripped out of her clothes, dumped what was left of her hose in the trash, and got into the shower. The hot water sluicing over her shoulder took some of the cramping out of her arm. She was thankful for that, particularly since she didn't have her medication with her. But unless God was napping, she shouldn't need it. She had made it this far without it. No small miracle, that.

She snatched up the soap and rubbed down her chest, her shoulders and thighs, working up a fresh-smelling lather. During the ride, she had forced herself to calm down and think. Karl would never leave her alone. She had no choice but to accept it. The therapist had said abusers often back off when faced down. Julia had serious doubts about Karl Hyde fitting that profile, but if she could face him down without all of her old fears chewing her up, if she could—just once, damn it—get mad instead of scared, then maybe, just maybe, she would not be paralyzed by fear. Maybe she could force him out out of her life.

She had to try. For herself, for Seth, and for Jeff.

Karl couldn't hurt Jeff. He couldn't hurt either of them. She would never forgive herself, and she would never be able to live with the guilt. Guilt about Uncle Lou already filled her every crevice. She couldn't hold any more.

Karl Hyde will never back down and leave you alone, Julia. So what are you going to do? Murder the man?

Her stomach flipped over. She lifted her face to the shower nozzle, let the water beat against her cheeks, protecting her bruised jaw from a direct hit with her cupped hand. Could she murder Karl?

After all he had done to her, the answer to that should be simple. And yet the idea of taking a human life—any human life, even his—repulsed her. It violated everything she believed.

So you'll let him hurt Jeff and Seth, just like he hurt Uncle Lou.

Her chest went tight. She suspected, she didn't know for certain, that Karl had killed her uncle by rigging the brakes on his car. But Uncle Lou had been a fanatic about keeping his car in top condition. He would have noticed any signs of the brakes wearing or becoming sluggish. Karl had to have cut the lines. The police said no, but she had proof that they took care of their own. True, not typically in something as serious as murder. But all it would have taken was one cop who owed Karl a debt. Either way, Karl was capable of killing. She knew he was capable of killing.

The question is, are you capable of killing him?

A rap sounded on the bathroom door. "Julia, are you okay?"

She shook, slinging water off her face. "I'm fine, Seth. Be out in a minute."

"I'm putting some clothes right outside the door."

"Thanks." God, how could she be weighing the merits of murdering a man and still sound so normal?

Twisted. Because of what Karl had done to her, she'd become twisted.

Resenting that, she rinsed away the soap, toweled off, and then dressed in a pair of jeans three sizes too big and a worn-out black Saints football team T-shirt. At the mirror above the sink, she finger-combed her hair. Seeing the bruise on her jaw infuriated her, and she met her own eyes in the mirror. Sometimes a woman could be pushed too hard and too far.

"If I have to, yes," she told her reflection. "To stop him, I'll kill him."

"Julia?" Seth tapped at the door again. "Tea's ready."

"Be right there." She held her stare into her own eyes in the mirror. She had to tell Seth about Karl, but she didn't have to tell him now. She couldn't tell him now. She was already too stressed. She'd trigger a migraine and muscle spasms, and she didn't have her medication.

Coward.

Damn right. Damn right. It takes a sick woman to marry a bastard like Karl Hyde. Sick or pitiful.

Or protected and innocent of knowing people like Karl exist. Be fair, Julia. You were not sick or pitiful. Just innocent.

Even if that were true, what woman could pull such filthy skeletons out of her closet and parade them before a man who mattered—whether or not he should. Seth already doubted her. She cared for him and he didn't yet know she was divorced.

You don't trust him to understand? Knowing what he went through with his mother? Ridiculous.

It wasn't ridiculous. That was different. He had been a helpless child. She had been a grown woman, supposedly one with a good mind and common sense. Children can't choose their parents, but she *had* chosen her husband.

Julia, he deceived you. Seth will understand deceit.

What if he didn't understand? No, she couldn't tell him now. After she calmed down. Then she'd tell him. When she felt strong enough to handle his reaction, either way.

SETH put the gun in the middle of the scarred-oak kitchen table, between Julia's teacup and his coffee mug.

She saw it, flinched, stiffened, and then sat down, staring at it.

Seth let her drink half her tea before saying a word. When she had, he spoke softly, knowing the risks he was running in prying, yet determined to take them. "What happened to your face?"

She lifted her hand and covered the bruise with her fingertips. "He hit me."

Seth clenched his fists under the table. "Who?"

"The guy who took my car."

Not *the mugger*, or *the carjacker*, but *the guy*. She knew him, all right. "While you were in the shower, I phoned Matthew. He's calling back to talk with you in a few minutes."

She shifted on her seat, but Seth couldn't tell if she was relieved or worried. "He's also contacting the Grace Police Department. I asked why, but he refused to explain. My guess is he's going to request that they keep an eye on Jeff. Does that conclusion sound reasonable to you?"

"Yes, it does." Her cup wobbled. She grasped it with both hands to steady it.

Definitely all connected. Seth tested the water. "Matthew's calling back for a physical description of your mugger. Any details you can give him might tie the guy to Benedetto. Maybe he's a loyalist."

She stared down at the table. Her face had been pink from the hot shower, but now it deepened to red. She definitely knew him. Could be professional or personal but, either way, Julia was hiding the truth. And she was intentionally hiding it from him. Why?

Matthew had been out of town, but so far as he knew, her attacker was still locked up in jail. If it had been Camden, she would have said so. That left Benedetto. If she had hooked up with him—which Seth's gut said was impossible—then Benedetto was not happy with her performance. Actually, to have her mugged, he would have to be unhappy enough to violate his own code of ethics. Two West revered women. Benedetto revered women. Slugging a woman hard enough to immediately bruise her jaw didn't exhibit much reverence in Seth's opinion. So it seemed unlikely Benedetto or his loyalists were behind this, either. That left Karl.

"You already have a gun." Julia looked up at him from across the table.

Seth wanted to pursue the truth, but breaking through Julia's defenses required patience, particularly if Karl had attacked her. "I want you to handle it." Seth nodded toward the gun. "Get used to the feel before you start learning to shoot."

She picked up the gun. It too wobbled. "What kind is it?"

Silver. Pearl grips. "A Smith and Wesson .38 detective special."

She stared at it. Turned the gun over in her right hand. Held it up and aimed at the handle on the refrigerator. More wobbling. "It's heavy."

Seth walked around the table, leaned over from behind her, and then showed her how to grip the gun with two hands. His fingers curled around hers. They were ice-cold. "Hold it like this."

She swallowed hard.

Her hair tickled his cheek. She smelled fresh and clean, soapy and scared. Nothing covered the smell of fear. Not in the jungle, in the desert, or in the cabin's kitchen. Fear smelled distinct, potent, and her feeling it offended him. "You're safe here, Julia."

"There aren't any locks on the doors."

That response, he hadn't expected. The gun in her hands shook as much as if she had actually fired it. She'd be lucky to hit a barn, much less its door. "No, but you're safe here." He wanted to hold her to reassure her, but she was married and vulnerable, and he had to remember that.

He returned to his chair, his throat thick and the smell of her lingering in his mind. "We'll get started on your defense training first thing in the morning." He had questions. A lot of them. But she looked exhausted and brittle enough to snap. Now was a lousy time to push for answers. "Tonight, let's cover some safety tips."

Clearly relieved, she slumped in her chair, propped her feet on the rung of the chair to her left, and she seemed more at ease than he had seen her look all day.

His patience would pay off. Soon she would answer all

his questions and—unless his gut instincts were way off, which they rarely were—she would tell him a lot more than he expected.

She walked to the stove and refilled her teacup. "More coffee?"

His pulse rate quickened. How could a woman look so sexy wearing baggy jeans and an oversized T-shirt? He liked her being here. Liked her in his kitchen, in his clothes. In his life. "No, thanks."

She smiled and returned to the table. "Okay, I'm ready."

Seth couldn't think. Damn it, no woman had ever taken his thoughts right out of his head. He mentally shook himself, ordering his libido into a deep freeze and his logic front and center. Guns. Safe handling of guns. That's right.

He began briefing her on handling and maintaining firearms, and then specifically on the .38's capability. When she had a firm grasp, he moved on to the things a holder should never do. "And lastly," he said. "Never pull a gun on anyone you don't intend to kill."

Julia nodded, attentive and alert, but from the frown creasing the skin between her brows, a question lingered in her mind.

"What?" Seth asked.

She looked up from the gun on the table to Seth. "I was just thinking that I need to buy a bigger purse. If I try to pull it out of the one I use now, it could get stuck."

If she had been carjacked, hadn't she had her purse with her? She hadn't had her purse when he had picked her up from the service station, and it seemed unlikely she would drive without at least her wallet. But she hadn't had that, either. So why was she worrying about a gun getting stuck in a purse that had been stolen?

More and more it appeared she hadn't been carjacked. She hadn't gotten muddy and wet and covered with grass taking a single punch, and she didn't move as if she were sore from tangling with the man.

Seth shoved his questions aside and considered giving her a lecture on carrying a concealed weapon—including informing her that she would need a permit to carry—but then decided against it. She had been mugged and injured twice. More seriously the first time, but still, twice. He could stomach paying a fine for her carrying without a permit a lot easier than he could stomach the possibility of a third mugging. "Shoot through it."

Her eyes widened. "Through my handbag?"

Seth nodded. "Stick your hand down inside, aim, and fire. No lost time, and the bullet will penetrate the leather."

"It'll also blow a hole in my purse."

"Julia, if you're firing the gun, you're firing it to blow a hole through a human being. Comparatively speaking, ruining a purse doesn't matter much."

She lowered her gaze to the table. "No, I suppose not."

"Don't you want to call Karl?" Seth asked, opening the proverbial door one more time. "Tell him where you are so he doesn't worry?"

"No."

Seth waited, but she didn't elaborate. Telling, that. Only one reason she wouldn't want to call Karl. He already knew. He knew because he was the sorry son of a bitch who had done this to her.

It was time for the truth. "Julia, don't you think it's time—"

The phone rang.

Frustrated, Seth slid back his chair. Its legs scraped against the wooden floor. At the wall, he lifted the receiver. "Holt."

Grateful he hadn't gotten to finish his question, Julia stared at the gun and took in three deep breaths. Just the sight of it made her queasy. She didn't have to like it, but she did have to learn to use the gun. And she'd better learn to use it well. Karl was a trained professional, and he would definitely use one on her. Or on Jeff. Or on Seth.

"Yeah, she's okay," Seth said into the phone. "A bruised jaw, but—" He paused, listened, and his expression turned grim. "I understand. I'll get her." He turned to Julia and held out the receiver. "Matthew."

Julia walked over and took the phone. "Hello."

"You doing all right?"

"I look like a squirrel with nuts stuffed in my cheek and I'm mad as hell but, yeah, I'm all right."

"Karl?"

"Yes." She stared at Seth.

"He found the apartment?"

"Sure did." She forced herself to smile to hide some of the anger she felt about that. The system sure had failed her. Justice was indeed an illusion. She was the victim, and yet she was the one in prison. It didn't have walls, but that only made it the worst kind of prison. She lived with the illusion of freedom, and nowhere felt safe.

"Julia," Matthew said. "You're going to have to tell Seth. He needs to know. Karl *will* confront him. You have to know that. Seth should be prepared."

"I know." She turned her back to Seth, squeezed her eyes shut.

"He'll understand."

"Really?" She stared at a knothole on the paneled wall, wishing she could shrink down and crawl inside it.

"Give the man some credit. You know what he's like."

She did. The problem was, he didn't have a clue what she was like, or who she really was.

Hearing only line static, Matthew sighed. "He matters to you."

Did he really expect her to answer that? She didn't want to acknowledge it to herself, much less to anyone else.

"Would it help to know you matter to him, too?"

Don't believe it. Don't.

She managed a whisper. "It's different."

"I don't think it is."

Hope flickered inside her. She tried to snuff it out. Hope leads to disappointment, to rude awakenings, to pain. *Do you want to feel more pain?* "It's different," she insisted, grating out the words.

"It's not," Matthew insisted. "Seth hounded me for three years, trying to find out where you were."

"That's not an asset." She nudged the angle where the wall and floor met the tips of her bare toes.

"It should be."

"I don't see how." *Hounded* sounded a lot like *stalked*. She'd had a gutful of that, thank you very much.

"Maybe I can help explain. I've known Seth a long time. We worked Special Forces together on more rough-ass missions than I care to recall. He's a good man, Julia. You can trust him."

Seth had been Special Forces before going civilian? She should be surprised, she supposed, but she wasn't. He was highly skilled, capable on so many fronts. Still, he doubted her and she had doubted him. Before she had left his New Orleans lab, she felt she could trust him. She hadn't taken anyone into her confidence but, back then, her trusting someone else had been an option. Now, she wondered if she would ever again be able to trust anyone—including herself. She *had* blanked out after the hammer incident and hadn't been certain whether or not she had hit him.

"Look, Julia." Matthew softened his voice. "After what happened, I know trusting anyone has to be hard for you. But—"

"I understand." She did. It was Matthew who didn't have a clue. She glanced back at Seth, who was sitting at the table, listening avidly and pretending to be stone-deaf.

"Learn what he teaches you," Matthew said. "Work at it, Julia."

He was telling her something important. Silently cursing because the cabin didn't have a secure-line phone, she improvised. "I know he'll be back."

"Yeah, he will." Matthew's disgust carried through the phone line. "You'd better give me a current description."

Was he helping her cover from Seth? Or did Matthew really need one? She reeled off a quick physical description of Karl, knowing Matthew had more he could tell her but couldn't speak freely. "Is Jeff okay?"

"Fine. Grace PD is keeping an eye on him."

"With his father's consent?"

"Unfortunately, no. Camden doesn't want his privacy invaded, so the cops are forced to hang back. But they're as close as they can legally get, Julia."

"Thank you." The tightness in her chest eased. "Can someone talk directly to Jeff? I don't want him frightened, but he needs to be on his guard."

"I've taken care of that."

Not at all surprising. "I wish we could get Jeff out of there and take him somewhere safe."

"Without Camden's permission or a court order, we can't, and we don't have sufficient grounds for a court order. I just got off the phone with his case worker not ten minutes ago."

"So Grace's police observation is an informal thing, then?" Oh, she didn't like this. Not at all.

"Yes, but don't worry. They take cases of kids being threatened as personally as we do. I logged Jeff in as a Bravo-One."

"What is that?"

"One of our own kids under threat," Matthew explained. "Same priority as any other kid, but our agents pull duty and as many extra volunteer hours as they can and still stay upright." Matthew paused. "Funny. They do that on non-Bravo-One designations, too. I guess we just do it to signal each other that it's family under attack."

"I appreciate it."

"We can't do anything personally until Grace calls us in, but we're on alert and ready to move."

"You explained everything to his case worker? I mean, they know this is child endangerment, right?"

"They know," Matthew confirmed. "Talk to Seth, Julia. Tell him the truth. All of it."

Her fingers tightened on the receiver. "I'm not sure I can do that."

"You'd better try," Matthew said. "Otherwise, you're leaving him wide open to a surprise attack. My guess is he's up to the challenge but, if it isn't necessary, letting him get blindsided so you can keep your secrets isn't right."

Seth stared at her from the table. She couldn't say what she wanted to say, so she said nothing.

"Julia, not knowing could get him killed."

And she'd have to live with his blood on her hands. She clamped her jaw shut. "Don't you think I know that?"

"You'd better know *and* believe it because it's fact."

She clutched at her chest with her free arm. It felt as tight as if someone had clamped metal bands around it. "Trust me, Matthew. I have no illusions. Not anymore."

"He's armed."

Karl. Armed. Her mouth turned dust-dry. An armed man who had nothing left to lose. "How do you know that?"

"Grace spotted him leaving Camden's earlier today."

"Jeff!"

"He was at school. He never saw Karl."

But he would be back. That's what Matthew had been trying to tell her. Karl would be back—for Jeff.

"Don't worry. Grace's got him covered," Matthew said. "Worry about Seth. Right now, you're hanging him out to dry—blindfolded."

The image sickened her. She had been left vulnerable to attack. How could she do it to anyone else, much less to Seth?

Just how much is your pride worth, Julia? Is it worth Seth's life?

It wasn't. Her heart felt squeezed. Nothing was worth that. Not her pride. Not her own life.

ANTHONY Benedetto stood on the green on the thirteenth hole at Fair Oaks Country Club, eyeing a shot that was going to be a bitch to make. Hearing a golf cart heading his way, he turned and saw Roger approaching. What was wrong now?

Roger pulled to a stop. "Sorry to interrupt, sir."

"No problem." He was having a lousy game, anyway.

"There's a complication." Roger crawled out of the cart. "The new loyalist from Starke is causing some unhealthy challenges for the woman scientist."

Starke. The home of Florida State Prison, and the former residence of his newest recruit in this venture. Damn it. Complications were exactly what Anthony had hoped to avoid. "What kind of complications?"

"Ones preventing her from focusing on her work and sidetracking Dr. Holt from finalizing the launching sequence."

"I'll handle it." Anthony put his club back into the bag on his cart. "And run a complete profile on her. I'm especially interested in anything that could convince her to commit treason."

"Yes, sir." Roger rubbed his brow, clearly worried. "Mr. Benedetto, are you planning to launch the Rogue?"

He laughed. "No, Roger. Having it gives us détente. Using it would force retaliation. That would not be in our best interests."

"No, sir."

Anthony eyed the golf ball, the hole, and debated between putters. Choosing his favorite, he got into position. He should be offended by Roger's question, but Anthony wasn't. The man wasn't questioning his authority, only wanting a fix on the coalition's official position. And he would know soon, when the transaction had been completed on the sale of the Home Base technology to Two West's Eastern associate.

The United States would be helpless.

Smiling, Anthony swung the putter.

Chapter Thirteen

~

JULIA hated the gun.

She hated the feel of it in her hand. Squeezing its trigger, and its recoil jarring her to the bone. She hated the smell of it when it fired, the sound of its bullet exploding. She hated everything about it. Every single thing. But most of all, she hated *not hating* the images in her mind of the bullets whizzing past the cans Seth had set up on the fenceposts and exploding in Karl Hyde's chest.

In a clearing between the cabin and the lake, she and Seth had been practicing shooting for hours. The best she could say was that she no longer feared the gun. Now, she respected it.

Tipping her head against the chill wind, she reloaded the .38, pulling bullets from the third box. Two empty boxes lay in the dirt near her feet. When she had stopped missing the cans and had started hitting them, she had felt a shameful sense of elation. And with each target she hit, she whispered a victory chant inside her mind. *Victim no more.*

She fired the gun rapidly six times. Knocked four cans off the fence, and winged two.

Seth stepped to her side. "Much better."

"You were right." She lowered the barrel of the gun, aiming toward the ground, then turned toward him. "Not jerking the trigger is the key."

He finger-combed his hair back from his face. The damp

wind reddened his cheeks. "You're a quick study."

"Not really." She looked back at the cans and imagined Karl facing her down, his gun aimed at her forehead, hammer cocked and ready to fire. "I'm motivated."

Seth took the gun, showed her how to clean it, and then passed it back to her.

She slid it inside a brown pouch. "What next?"

"A few evasive skills." Seth reached down and grabbed a sports bottle filled with water. "Sometimes it's smarter to run than to fight." He sprinkled water into the dusty dirt, grabbed a broken piece of branch, and stirred. "Sometimes it's not so easy to run. You can find yourself outnumbered, or civilians stand in your way."

"Civilians?" Odd term for him to use. No. He'd been in Special Forces with Matthew. It wasn't odd at all.

"Innocent bystanders," he amended. "Anyway, at those times, shooting a firearm carries risks you don't want to take. So you have to learn evasive tactics, ways to extricate yourself from the situation."

She stared down at the ground. "And you do this by making mud pies?"

"No." He dipped his hands into the mud, then stood, pecked a kiss to her startled lips, and smeared her face. "You do it by becoming invisible."

"Seth!" Julia groused, but stayed still. Had his eyes always been that deep a gray? Held that amused twinkle? She really liked that twinkle. Attempting to diffuse a sudden sensual awareness, she backed away. "Geez, all this training and a facial, too."

Seth grinned. "No extra charge."

THE evasive tactics came much easier to Julia than the offensive ones. She had escaped and evaded a million times in her mind, replayed each and every attack—especially the one that had hospitalized her—over and again until she had found a way for it to end with her safe and unharmed. But when Seth began teaching her hand-to-hand combat skills, she ran into trouble quickly.

Squared off and facing her, his feet spread, his jeans pulling tight across his thighs, his face as mud-smeared as his shirt, he went still. "What's wrong?"

The dried mud caked on her skin, made her face feel tight. "My arm's too weak." Pain rippled through her left arm, across her shoulder, down her spine. "I exercise it nearly every day, but it's just not strong enough for this."

"Julia, we all have challenges and limitations. The key to survival is to make them work for us instead of against us."

"How, Seth? Either I can use my arm, or I can't. And I can't." It wasn't a matter of will, damn it. Her will had saved her life many times. She had inner strength—except when it came to risking losing Seth again. It was physical strength she lacked.

"Block with it, like this." He demonstrated, hiking his arm, crooking his elbow. "Then use your leg and foot to compensate." He kicked out, pulling back to keep from knocking her flat. "Will that work for you?"

She tried it and, not expecting her to carry through, Seth took the full brunt of her thrust to his stomach. The air in his lungs gushed out, and he fell to the ground.

Stunned, Julia stared at him.

He stared back, equally as surprised.

She stepped closer, smiled down at him. "Yeah, I think that'll work fine."

"Smart-ass." He stood up and swiped at his muddy seat with his hand. He didn't smile, but his eyes had a pleased twinkle in them.

She definitely liked the warmth in that twinkle. It had been a long time since a man had looked at her with warmth and appreciation. At least, that she'd noticed. Actually, she liked it a lot. She liked Seth a lot.

You love him.

Queasy, she lowered her gaze. It couldn't be love. Love would *not* be a smart move for a woman in her position. In fact, it would be damn stupid. Julia refused to be stupid. Again.

Do you honestly think you have a choice? You feel what you feel, Julia.

No, she could refuse. She chose to refuse to survive.

"Okay, foot queen," Seth said. "Let's go at it again. Only this time, you won't catch me off guard. I'm bigger and stronger than you, so you're going to have to outthink me."

"Yeah, right." She raised her arms and lifted onto the balls of her feet, posturing. "You're forgetting you're a genius. How am I supposed to outthink a genius?"

"Shouldn't be a problem." He shrugged. "You're a genius, too."

She blinked hard, as if stunned by the reminder. "True." She feigned a left jab, crossed with her right, and connected with his forearm. "I forgot."

Seth went statue still. His voice deepened, husky and low and serious. "Maybe it's time you remembered exactly who you are, Julia."

His meaning wasn't lost on her. It stopped her dead in her tracks. The next thing she knew she was flat on her back, looking up at the sky.

Seth reached out a hand to help her up. "I thought maybe that would reinforce my reminder."

She flipped him.

He smiled. "You're learning."

"Like I said, I'm motivated." She extended a hand.

Seth clasped it, and pulled her down to the grass. Half covering his body, Julia sucked in a sharp breath. His expression turned serious. "Maybe it's time you learn who I am, too."

"Who are you, Seth Holt?"

"A man who trusts you. A man you can trust with anything. A man willing to go to the wall for you, Julia. Any wall, anywhere, anytime."

Her heart melted and, knowing she shouldn't, knowing she first owed him the truth, knowing once he knew that truth he wasn't likely to want anything to do with her, she accepted that the gulf between emotions and logic was broad and deep.

One breath at a time.

Chest to chest, thigh to thigh, she stared down into his face, and emotion won. Wise or not, whether she wanted to or not, safe or not, she loved him. "Maybe it is time." Slowly, she lowered her head and pressed her lips against his.

Seth closed his arms around her and kissed her deeply. Her response seemed different; more open, less tentative. She cared about him, too. He felt it in the touch of her hands on his shoulders, his neck, his chest; sensed it in his soul.

The time for truth had come.

Turning, he hovered above her, tense and serious. "I'm not opposed to kissing you, Julia. I think about it a lot. I love doing it even more." Again, he opened the proverbial door. "But one of us needs to remember something significant."

She lifted a finger to his shirt. Ran it along the placket between his second and third buttons. "What's that?"

"You're married," he said. "I know you, and I know you're not the type of woman to engage in affairs. So what's happening here, Julia? What is this between us?"

It was the perfect opening, and she started to take it; started to, and stopped. Why had she stopped?

"I know I need to explain some things, and I will, Seth. I promise. But can we not talk about them right now? Right now, I need to focus on survival skills."

Disappointment rammed through him. Trust couldn't be demanded, but he felt he had earned it. Yet she had a point about slivered focus and survival. "All right, we'll wait." Clasping her hand, he helped her to her feet. "Time is short, and we've got a lot of ground to cover."

Seth worked her hard, then harder, until they both had worked up a respectable sweat. He was angry. With her for not being honest and open with him, and with himself because, dishonest and closed, and married and vulnerable or not, he wanted her anyway.

She paused for a drink of water and squirted her face to

cool down. The mud streaked her skin, reminding him of Jeff's face-washing. Julia had put effort into learning. Seth knew why. At least two dozen times during combat training he'd heard her mumble, "Victim no more."

She *was* motivated. But was she motivated to defend, or to attack?

JULIA crawled into bed groaning.

If a square inch anywhere on her body wasn't sore, she had yet to find it. But it was a good kind of sore. With each tactic Seth had taught her, she had felt stronger, more confident of her ability to defend herself. And more competent to help defend him and Jeff.

She lay in the dark, pulled the comforter up around her shoulders. It was quiet here. If there were locks on the doors, she might actually be able to sleep. But, as much as she needed locks to feel secure, she understood Seth's aversion to them. After what had happened with his mother, how could he not hate locks? Still, her understanding wasn't going to do a thing to help her sleep. Not with a guilty conscience gnawing at her. In the morning, first thing, she had to damn the consequences and tell Seth the truth. She had this inkling he had already figured it out. If he had, it said a lot for him that he wasn't pushing her for an admission. For tonight, she'd lie here aching and sleepless. She'd watch the sun rise, just as she had this morning, and not sleep a wink. Not . . . a . . . wink.

THE woman slept like the dead.

Seth eased her bedroom door nearly closed and then sat down on the floor just outside it. Stretching his legs across the hallway floor, he lifted his mug. The hot coffee burned going down his throat.

She needed a good night's sleep and, after today's workout, she should get one. If she caught him guarding her door, she would think he had lost his mind. But after Matthew's two-word warning during their last phone call, Seth didn't much care if she thought he was nuts so long as he kept her safe.

Stand guard.

Matthew hadn't expounded, but cryptic was enough. Earlier, Seth had asked Matthew to keep an eye on Julia. The warning proved he was doing it, and that she wasn't just under threat. She was under siege.

Direction or nature didn't matter. Forewarned was forearmed, and Seth stood armed to the teeth. To get to Julia, any attacker had to go through him.

He only wished she would come to him. Several times that day she had started to tell him the truth; he'd sensed it. But suddenly she had stopped. He hadn't pushed her, though he wondered now if not pushing her had been a mistake. Julia wasn't like most women. Maybe she was different about pushing and prying, and getting her nose out of joint, too.

A comfortable Julia is a reserved Julia.

He sipped from his steaming mug and stared at the ray of light streaking from the den across the hallway's wooden planks. But an uncomfortable Julia wasn't acceptable to Seth. Not after her attacks and injuries. When he thought of her being in the hospital and then in rehab for months, it ripped him up inside. And it hadn't escaped his notice that she still hadn't said a damn thing about Karl.

She had to know Seth would realize something was wrong there and he'd be reasoning through it. Scientists operated that way, including Julia. She would know Seth was thinking that if she were his wife, she wouldn't have to ask another man for help learning to defend herself—especially since Karl was a cop, trained in defensive and offensive tactics and techniques. And that Seth would be shaking his head at Karl's not teaching her to defend herself after the first attack. And certainly she would know Seth was wondering why Karl hadn't objected to her spending the weekend alone with another man, learning what he had chosen not to teach her. She had to know all those things. And because she hadn't addressed them, and because she had kissed him several times, Seth felt certain Karl had been her attacker. If they were at odds over her uncle Lou's accident or she felt Karl was responsible for her attack by putting her in a vulnerable position, she would be more at ease revealing the truth to Seth. Karl's being her attacker, however, was different. An abuse thing. One that would take an act of Congress to admit because the wounds cut so damn deep and a lot of them were self-inflicted: an unfortunate but natural result of constant attacks on victims' self-esteem.

Seth bent a knee and braced his arm atop it, watched the steam lift from his mug and curl up into the shadows. Then again, she'd had a lot on her mind, personally and professionally. Maybe Seth's observations and deductions, or even his curiosity, hadn't occurred to her.

Seth mulled on that. Impossible. She was too sharp. She'd learned to bury strong emotions and function normally. No, it had occurred to her. All of it. And she had chosen to deceive him. What he didn't know was why.

"NO. Don't. Stop it. Oh, God, please. Stop it!"

Seth barged into Julia's bedroom, tripped over her shoes and banged a shin against the bed frame. "Julia?"

Light spilled in from the hallway, formed a bright bar across her bed. She lay curled on her side, gasping in deep, labored breaths as if trying to feed starving lungs.

"Julia, what's the matter?" Seth stepped closer. "Are you okay?"

"Nightmares." She shoved at her hair. Sleep-tossed and tangled, it fell right back over her cheek. Seth's white T-shirt hiked high on her thigh and clung to her breasts with the rise and fall of her rapid breaths.

Never before had he considered a T-shirt on a woman sexy. But on Julia . . . "Nightmares about the incident?" That's how she had referred to the first attack.

"More or less."

How did he respond to that?

Her breathing steadied and she stared up at him, the light

slanting across her chin. "I think, more than anything, I'm suffering from a guilty conscience."

"Why?" Seth asked, but now he wasn't at all sure he really wanted to know the answer. Her confession had to be professional. Why would she have a guilty conscience for anything personal?

The sensor-codes theft ran through his mind. It couldn't be that. He couldn't live with knowing Julia was a traitor. She couldn't be a traitor.

"Sit down, Seth." She patted the bed next to her hip. "We need to talk."

If she wasn't being honest about Karl, what else was she lying about? "Do you want to talk in the living room?" He was human, damn it. Just a man. He needed distance. "Or I could fix you something to drink in the kitchen."

"No." She flatly refused. "This is going to be hard. I need . . . darkness."

Seth's stomach soured. Julia wasn't a coward. She'd gone nose to nose with honchos dozens of times. This wasn't about guilt. It had to be about shame. It was about the sensor-codes theft.

He sat down. The mattress sank under his weight, and her hip shifted, coming to rest against his side. Knowing instinctively his illusions about her were about to be shattered, he steeled himself to hear what she had to say.

"I'm not married to Karl anymore, Seth."

Shock pumped through him. "What?"

"We're not going to get very far if you shout at me."

"I'm not shouting."

"You are."

Okay, maybe he was, but she'd stunned him, damn it. Here he'd been terrified that he had brought a traitor into an extremely sensitive program and, worse, he'd been feeling guilty for loving her, knowing she was another man's wife, and she was *not* another man's wife, and—

"I divorced him right after he went to prison."

"Prison?" Christ Almighty. He had attacked her. He really had.

Or he was under deep cover.

"You're shouting again." She stared up at the ceiling. "Maybe this isn't a good time to tell you this, after all. Maybe we'd better wait—"

"Oh, no." Seth grimaced, grappling to get a grip on how these developments fit into the big picture of things. She wasn't married anymore. Karl was in prison. Was he under deep cover or an abuser in prison for attacking Julia? And was she innocent, or a traitor? "I want to hear it all now. Right now."

Julia sank her teeth into her lower lip. That was the trouble with opening a Pandora's box. Once you lifted the lid, you were committed to exposing everything inside. "The thing you most need to know is Karl is out of prison now, and he's trying to force his way back into my life. He's using Jeff to do it."

"How?"

"I don't know." God, but she hated telling him this as much as she hated handling that gun. "He threatened to hurt Jeff unless I do exactly what he says."

"Matthew knows this," Seth speculated. "That's why he's got Grace PD watching Jeff."

"Yes. They have jurisdiction. But Camden isn't cooperating. He doesn't want his privacy invaded."

"His son is threatened and he's worried about privacy?"

Tears burning her eyes, she didn't trust her voice, and so she nodded.

"Something's wrong there."

Agreeing, Julia tugged at the comforter, tucked and pinned it under her arm. "I have a restraining order against Karl, but it won't stop him. Nothing will stop him, Seth."

Restraining order? No deep cover. The bastard was guilty of the crime. "Julia. Honey." Seth clasped her hand and gentled his voice. "I know Karl pulled you through the car window. I know he attacked you."

Her heart thudded hard. God, how she wished she could deny it. A man doing that to his own wife. A woman so blind she had married that kind of man not knowing his true character. Humiliation washed through her, shrouded her, smothered her. But she couldn't deny the truth. Not anymore. Not to herself, nor to Seth.

Reaching deep, determined to face this head-on, she answered. "Yes, he did." She paused, dragged in a reinforcing breath, praying more courage would come with it. "I'd left him. He reported my car stolen and used his cop connections to track me down. It didn't take long. The same day I left, he found me in Destin and . . . and nearly beat me to death." Remembering this was hard, and talking about it hurt like hell. Hurt, humiliated, and embarrassed.

You've got to do this, Julia. For his protection and for your own peace of mind, too. It wasn't your fault. You didn't deserve this. You're not dirty because of it. Let the truth out. Once it's out, it can't hurt you anymore.

But letting it out wouldn't hurt her any less. "When I came to in the hospital, Karl was there." Her hands shook. She clutched at the edge of the comforter. "He warned me that I could never leave him. That he'd always find me. And if I tried to leave him again, he would kill me."

"So you pressed charges against him."

"Actually, I didn't." She clutched at a bigger bunch of the covers, rubbed the fabric folds between her forefinger and thumb. The nubby fabric grated, felt good. Comforting. "I was too afraid of him. I knew what he could do."

"So how did he end up in prison?"

"Detective LeBrec figured out what had happened and turned the case over to the DA. They pressed charges."

"And Karl was convicted."

She nodded. "They sentenced him to five years. But he got out a few days ago, because of overcrowding. LeBrec said Karl conned the parole board into believing he was no longer a threat to me."

Seth frowned. "Even with all the phone threats?"

"Yes."

"And the parole board knew about them?"

"They didn't consider what he said threatening."

Still frowning, Seth sighed. "You said you left to protect me and you. How did I figure into this?"

She squeezed the quilt hard. "That's not important, Seth."

He clasped her hand, rubbed her fingers with his thumb. "It's important to me."

She swallowed hard, dug deeper still for the courage to answer honestly. This, she had never wanted anyone to know. Ever. Especially Seth. "Karl thought we were having an affair. I tried to tell him we weren't, but he never believed me." Insane jealousy. Insane man.

"He beat you for it."

Because that was too difficult to answer, she turned the subject. "I really do think he killed Uncle Lou." Her voice cracked. "I can't prove it, but he taunts me with it. I—I think he did something to the brakes that made him crash through the bridge's guardrail."

"I know." Seth scanned the room. The dresser, the bedside lamp, the gingham curtains at the window. "And you left me to get away from him. Because he abused you."

Her eyes burned, her throat went thick, and something hard and heavy weighed down on her chest. "Yes."

"And you agreed to come back to help me, thinking you would be returning to New Orleans?" Seth wished to hell he could see her eyes. She had agreed to face all those old ghosts, all those bad memories, to help him. She had agreed to trudge through hell for him. *For him.*

She turned away, toward the window.

Seth paused, thought back to the day they had met at the beach, recalled her relief on learning she would be going to Grayton and not New Orleans. Now, he understood the enormity of that relief in ways he couldn't understand it then. Now he knew how much she had been willing to sacrifice for his sake, how many more burdens she had put on herself to ease his load. And he loved her for it. It, and much more.

"Seth, it wasn't my fault." Her voice sounded thin,

thready. "I'm not a bad person. I really tried to be a good wife to him."

"Julia, don't."

"No, please. It's important to me that you understand." She let out a little humorless laugh. "I married him but, back then, I didn't know what he was really like. He fooled me. He fooled everyone. I didn't even know that men hit women, then. That sounds crazy and naïve now, but then I didn't know it, Seth." Blinking hard, she stared out the window into the night sky. "My parents were clones of June and Ward Cleaver. They were rational, logical, work-everything-out-peaceably kind of people. I never, not once, heard my father raise his voice to my mother. They sheltered me from the ugliness of abuse. I didn't know it existed until I married Karl and became a victim of it."

"When did it start?"

The beatings. He meant the beatings. Julia clutched at the covers, wadded them in her fist. "Less than a month after the wedding."

"A month?"

"Twenty-four days," she said. Specifically, twenty-four days, six hours, and fifteen minutes. "We went to the policeman's ball, and I smiled at his captain. When we got home, Karl accused me of coming on to the man. I'd done nothing wrong, but in his eyes I had committed adultery. He . . . went a little crazy."

She skipped over the actual conflict, unwilling to relive it again in her mind. "Afterward, he was sorry. Genuinely sorry. And I felt so guilty. I thought maybe I *had* looked at the man wrong, or I'd done something to give the wrong impression. I *must* have done something wrong because men just didn't hit women. They just didn't."

Seth looked at her as if she'd lost her mind. "You blamed yourself?"

How could he be so shocked? "In my case, wouldn't you?"

Seth paused to mull it over, and then sighed. "Without

a frame of reference, I guess I would." He dragged a hand over his neck. "So you forgave him."

"Yes, I did. And things went along okay until the next time, and then the next, and then the next. He worked at breaking me down, Seth. Little by little. And he did it."

She searched the sky through the window for a star to focus on, but there were too many clouds. "No one sets out to let something like this happen to them. Abusers are just damn smart at going about their business. They work on you in little ways until you start believing them, and by the time you realize they're wrong, they're not wrong anymore. You've become exactly what they accused you of being. And you don't know how it happened, or even when it happened, only that, now, that's the way it is."

"I've suspected Karl attacked you for a long time. I knew he was involved, but I thought maybe he had been responsible and hadn't done it himself." What she had told Seth about her uncle Lou substantiated that. Seth reached out and gave her shoulder a reassuring squeeze. "I understand how abuse works, Julia."

"I wish you didn't." His touching her with gentleness was her undoing. A tear rolled down her cheek. "I wish I didn't, too."

So did Seth. He let the silence rest between them, giving them time for the reality of their broken dreams and shattered lives to settle and become easier to bear. Then he asked, "When did you realize the abuse wasn't your fault?"

"I realized it early on, but we'd been married six years before I dared to believe it and began planning my escape. Right before I left for Destin, we were at his station's Christmas party." Julia sniffled, feeling stronger, less afraid of the truth's ability to destroy her relationship with Seth. Less afraid that exposure could destroy her. "One of the wives came into the rest room and saw the bruises on my neck. She put together what was happening."

"What brought on that attack?"

"I'd made the mistake of mentioning you the night before. Karl . . . took exception."

He had beaten her because of him. More than once. Guilt Seth hadn't earned lay heavy on his shoulders, soured his stomach. He clasped Julia's hand in silent apology.

She held on hard. "The woman told her husband, who talked to Karl's captain. He and a couple other officers took Karl into the locker room and showered him down. Actually, I think they worked him over. The captain wanted Karl to know how it felt to be trashed by his own."

"Did Karl tell you that?"

"No." Julia pulled a pillow from behind her head and clutched it to her chest. "The captain's wife warned me. I knew I had to leave fast. Karl would be humiliated by what they had done, and he'd take it out on me. I threw some things in the car, and left for Destin."

"Why Destin?"

"I chose it like I chose Grace. With a fingertip on an atlas. What better place to seek your new destiny than a town named Destin? I'd been planning to escape for a long time." She plucked at the pillowslip with her finger and thumb. "I just needed more money first. Karl kept a tight leash on our funds. But when I got my last raise, I had Personnel divert a part of the increase to a secret savings account, so the amount didn't change much. He never knew I was skimming."

She had to skim her own money? Seth wanted to vomit. Karl physically and emotionally dominated her, controlled her money, her actions, and her life—and made her think he had to do it, that she was incompetent to handle things for herself, and that his abuse was her fault. What a sorry son of a bitch. What a typical, sorry son of a bitch. "And then he found you in Destin."

"Yes." She swallowed hard. "And now he's found me in Grayton. He was in my apartment when I came home from work Friday night. I escaped and called you to come get me."

"Karl punched you?" Seth asked, but only for verification. During this conversation, he had come to see Matthew's warning to stand guard in a whole new light.

"Yes."

"I wish you had come to me right away, Julia. Back when all this started." He felt like a damn fool for not realizing what was going on with her then. "We could have spared you a lot of hell."

"Don't you see?" She turned over to face him. "I couldn't. He was angry with you already. Only God knows what he would have done."

The last of the puzzle pieces clicked into place. Protecting him. "You're afraid he'll come after me now. That's why you're telling me this."

"I *know* he'll come after you, Seth." Julia prayed for more courage, knowing her low-level light had begun flashing hard the moment she had opened this Pandora's box. "I have to divert him. Leave here and never come back." The thought of never seeing Seth again shattered her, and tears rolled down her face.

Seth pretended not to see them. "You can't leave."

"It's the only way," she said. "He won't stop. Nothing will make him stop. If I'm ever going to have peace in my life, I've got to disappear."

"What about me?" His voice dropped low, gritty.

"Once I'm gone, he'll leave you alone. You'll be safe."

"Julia, I'm not worried about my safety, I'm worried about your being out of my life again."

"Don't." She wanted to weep her heart out, felt so close to weeping her heart out. But if she started, she was afraid she would never stop.

You let down your defenses and you're weak. You can't just put them up again.

"He won't go away, Seth. Ever. I can't do that to either of us."

"What about Jeff?"

"Maybe I should take him with me."

"That, you can't do."

"Why not?" She sat straight up. "He has no one else, and Camden doesn't want him. He's being abused. I called to warn Camden about Karl, and he was so cool, and not at all worried about Jeff. It gave me chills, Seth. Absolute chills. If I don't take Jeff away, Karl will hurt him. He'll do anything to anyone to get to me. You can protect yourself, but Jeff's just a little boy. He can't fight Karl."

Seth clasped both of her hands in his and held them tightly. "Julia, listen to yourself. Just listen to yourself." He paused, to give her a moment to think beyond her fear. "Honey, the truth is, you're no kidnapper and you'd be lousy at living on the run."

"I've got to try."

"No," Seth contradicted her. "That's no kind of life for you, or for Jeff."

"What else can I do?" She looked at him through blurry eyes.

"There's only one thing you can do," he said. "You're going to have to back him down."

"Karl doesn't back down. Haven't you realized that yet? If he did, when he got out of prison, he would have stayed away from me. He hasn't done that." She pulled her hand from Seth's, sat up, and rubbed at her left arm. The tight muscles threatened to spasm. "I can't live every moment of my life waiting for his next attack. I can't do it, Seth. I have to run."

Seth caressed her face, cupped her chin in his palm, and softened his voice. "Honey, you can't run. There's nowhere to hide." He circled her back with his arms, pulled her close to absorb some of the sting of his words. "But it's going to be okay. You won't have to hide. You're not facing him alone anymore."

She pulled back, her eyes glossy with tears. "I can't involve you more than you already are. I can't—"

"Julia." Seth stroked her cheek, lightly touched her bruise. "Haven't *you* realized yet that wherever you are, I am?" Seth smiled into her solemn brown eyes. It was all so clear now. She wasn't a traitor. She'd just been afraid of telling him the truth. Afraid he would blame her for what Karl had done to her. Understandable, but she should have known better. And soon she would know better. He pulled her back into his arms, felt her trembling, and slid on the bed until she lay beside him, cradled in his arms.

They didn't talk. Didn't move. Just lay there, drawing strength and comfort from each other, until finally, Julia's trembling eased and she slept.

Seth rubbed little circles on her back, swearing she would have her peace. Her serenity. And she would feel safe.

With what Karl had done to her and what he had threatened to do to Jeff—the only two people in the world that the adult Seth had dared to love—Karl Hyde had sealed his fate.

Once, Seth had failed to protect a woman he loved. He wouldn't fail again.

IN his estate office, Benedetto read the profile on Dr. Julia Warner-Hyde and wanted to weep. How could a man do to a woman what her husband had done to her?

Roger shifted on his seat. "The council will never accept this man being an employee of Two West, much less a loyalist."

"Would I employ a man who does not revere women?"

"Not normally, sir, but to solidify your position with the council, and with this woman scientist playing such a key role, I thought—"

"Wrong. Never. He doesn't work for Two West." The pages shook, revealing Anthony's inner turmoil. He set the report down on his desk. "He works for our friend at Grayton."

"But he's still been given loyalist status. That will be a problem with the council."

"No it won't." Anthony glanced over at his father's photograph, remembered the three concepts for ruling. "Mr. Hyde is unfit for coalition association." His wife had nearly died three times. Three times. At his hands. "He's unfit to breathe."

"I wholeheartedly agree, sir." Roger straightened his tie.

"I assume you want to wait until we get all we need on the project."

Torn, Anthony debated and then nodded. "Unfortunately, yes." If the scientist resisted, they had to have leverage. Karl Hyde could provide it; she feared him. "We do what we must to preserve the coalition, Roger. Without hesitation, if not occasionally without regret."

"Of course, sir." Roger stood up. "Will you be advising the council on this matter?"

"No." Anthony's father had died for less than Hyde had already done. "We can't risk any association whatsoever."

Nodding, Roger left the office.

Watching him go, an uneasy feeling came over Anthony. He lifted his father's photo and stared at it, long and hard. *You did not die in vain. You did not.*

Chapter Fourteen

AT the house in town, Seth pulled the Lexus into his garage. "I just want to check to see if Matthew's left any messages. Then I'll take you over to the apartment to get some things."

"Get some things?" Julia pushed at the sleeve of the flannel shirt she was wearing. The cuffs hung over the tips of her fingers.

Seth cut the engine. "You need to stay with me until Karl is contained."

She put a hand on his thigh. "Seth, I really appreciate everything, but Karl will never be contained. Not as long as there's a breath in his body."

Seth stared through the windshield at the door to the house and debated responding. He agreed with her, yet telling her he intended to kill the man would only upset her. To Seth's way of thinking, she had spent more than enough time being upset already, so he settled for an alternate truth. "Matthew's concerned."

She groaned and swiped her hair back behind her ear. "He isn't alone."

Seth swerved his gaze to her. "I'm concerned, too."

"I know you are." Her voice went soft. "But you've done so much to help me already. I can't ask you to take on even more risks for me."

"You can ask me for anything, Julia. Anything, anytime." He cupped her hand on his thigh. "If I can give it to you, I will."

Her gaze went molten, then speculative. "Why haven't you ever married?"

Karl had found her first. But this wasn't the time, and sitting in the car in his garage certainly wasn't the place, for a declaration. "Bad timing." Seth reached for the handle and cranked opened the door.

Julia got out and walked toward the door leading into the house. "What do you mean, 'bad timing'?"

At the front of the Lexus, Seth again debated. Heat radiated off the car's hood. "The woman I wanted was already married."

Julia stepped up behind him, her expression guarded. "That must have been rough."

"At times." She had no idea she was that woman; the disappointment flickering through her eyes proved it. How could a woman so smart miss a truth so simple and obvious? He opened the door, and stepped into the house.

"Oh, dear, God." Julia gasped.

Seth came to a dead halt. His home had been ransacked, ceiling to floor. The light fixture in the den dangled. Sofa cushions lay tossed, bookshelves dumped, paintings that had been hanging on the wall had been slashed and now lay ruined on the floor. "Stay here," he told Julia, then walked through the house.

The kitchen was a disaster area: Pots and pans strewn on the floor, boxes of cereal sliced open and dumped, macaroni crunching under his shoes. Even the refrigerator had been emptied. Cracked jars of mayonnaise, mustard, and sweet pickles littered the floor.

The bedrooms and baths were no better. Every single thing in his home had been methodically damaged or destroyed.

Outrage at the invasion, the violation, pumped through his veins. *Bury it, Holt. Emotions get you killed.*

Detaching, he looked at the damage through the eyes of a Special Forces soldier. Systematic. Methodical. Definitely done by a pro, but too thorough for Karl to have pulled off alone, unless he felt certain he had plenty of time. "Looks like Benedetto's loyalists paid me a call."

"It's all ruined." Julia's voice trembled, thready and weak. "Everything's ruined."

"It's all right, Julia," he said. "It's insured, and it's just stuff."

"Yes, but it's *your* stuff."

Her indignance charmed him as much as everything else about her. He smiled. "It's okay." He rubbed at his neck. "Actually, it's not. It's damned confusing. Anyone involved in Project Home Base knows everything on it stays in the vault."

"Maybe Benedetto's loyalists didn't do this."

Seth turned to look at her. "What other professional would go to this much trouble? It had to be Benedetto's men," he said, certain odds were fifty-fifty it had been Karl, but not wanting to worry Julia even more, or for her to feel more guilt. And she would. Unjust, but she would. If there was one thing Seth Holt understood, it was guilt.

Julia wanted to look away. Resentment and guilt and regret seethed inside her and she didn't want to battle them. Convincing Seth would take all she could manage. Maybe more than she could manage. How could she trust him with more? She'd given him the truth, if only the bare bones of it. But to take this leap of faith, to trust that he could know everything, understand, and still care for her . . .

He did care for her. She felt it in the warm way he looked at her, heard it in his voice, felt it in his touch. Damn it, she didn't want to lose him, too.

You can't lose what you never had, Julia. Truth omitted is a lie. How can the seeds of anything good grow in a bed of lies? Seth is Seth. Seth is not Karl.

Faith. One more time, this was all about faith. She'd had faith and told him about Karl. Seth hadn't run. He hadn't turned morose, or looked at her with pity. She couldn't blame him for Karl's sins, and she couldn't compare them as if they were the same. They weren't. Quickly, before she could turn coward, she blurted out, "I think Karl did this."

Seth frowned, rubbed at his neck. "Honey, I know the man has earned his black marks, but what would he gain by doing this?"

Julia's mouth went dry. What if she was wrong? What if Karl hadn't done this? Oh, but it felt as if he had. She could almost smell him, among the cinnamon and pickle brine dumped in the kitchen floor. "He still has connections. He used them when he was still in jail to get my new phone numbers. He traced my car through three registrations in three different states and got my address. He found the apartment here and the phone number and the cell phone number, though all of those things were in your name."

"And he thinks we're having an affair," Seth added. "So you're telling me that he went into some insane jealous rage and did this?"

"Seth, don't make light of this. He's a skilled professional. You don't really know what he's like. Not really. He's capable of anything." She willed Seth to believe her, to realize she wasn't just a terrified woman demonizing a man who had terrorized her. "When Karl broke into my apartment, he knew I'd gone back to work in the Black World." She held up a hand. "Don't glare at me, Seth. I never, not once *ever*, told him I worked there."

"Then how did he know it?"

"I told you, he has connections." She leaned back against the hallway wall. "All kinds of connections. A cop working the street doesn't exactly deal with the cream of society, you know?"

Understanding lit Seth's eyes. "You think Karl is somehow connected to Benedetto, or to his project mole."

"I don't know what to think, Seth," she answered honestly. "Karl claimed you were setting me up to take the fall for the security breach. That you're the project mole working for Benedetto. He knew Benedetto's name."

Seth didn't say a word, but he'd definitely picked up on her doubt. His mouth flattened to a thin line.

She stepped closer, hating to hurt him this way, but unable not to do it. She had to know the truth and to put this matter to bed. She had to ask him, straight-out.

Touching a hand to his chest, she looked up into his eyes. "Acting on faith alone is really hard for me. You know why. But I'm asking you for the truth, Seth."

Go on, Julia. Take that leap of faith. He's a good man. You know he is. You love him. Do it!

Julia leapt. "Whatever you tell me, I will believe you. But I need to hear you say it. I need for you to tell me Karl lied and that you have nothing to do with any of this."

"I didn't steal the sensor codes." Seth loosely gripped her arms. "I didn't attempt the specific sweep on the vault's computer system. And I'm not Benedetto's mole."

That cost him a lot of pride. His honor being questioned hurt him; she could see that it did, and she hated it. But she had to hear it from him, firsthand. "Neither am I, Seth. I swear it."

He looked down at her. His eyes flashed fury and then regret. "I know."

"You didn't know."

"I had doubts. You were acting strangely. No one under ten tons of pressure acts calm, Julia. But now that I know about Karl and what stress does to you, I know why you acted strangely." Seth hugged her. "I won't doubt you again."

"Me, either." She hugged him back, relieved and so damn grateful she had taken the risk and leapt. "Who do you think is Benedetto's mole?"

"Dempsey Morse."

She looked up, confused. "But you said he wasn't a logical candidate. He does have millions invested in Home Base, Seth."

In the living room, he closely surveyed the damage. He had been collecting oil paintings all of his adult life. The bastard had slashed through every single one of them. "True, but Dempsey Morse is the only candidate who makes sense."

"Sense?" Julia started to pull the trash bin out from under the sink.

Seth stopped her. "Don't touch anything, honey. You could destroy evidence."

Honey. Soft and endearing. Her heart skipped a little beat every time she heard it. She liked the feeling. Maybe even she *could* heal. Seth made trying worth it. "Sorry." She let go of the bin, scanned the living room. "I don't see Morse doing this damage. We failed to find a motive. So did Matthew."

"We weren't looking in the right direction."

"Oh?"

"Grimm ran a check. The blue truck in the lab's parking lot the night I got stuck in the transporter is registered to Morse."

"He could have lifted my badge," Julia said. "He came out of his hermit hole for a chat earlier that day."

"In your office?"

She nodded.

"Bingo. Access to the badge and to the flashlight."

Probable, with him having that master key. "But why would he risk a lifetime in Leavenworth for treason and losing the millions he's got invested in Slicer Industries? And isn't it a little obvious for him to use his own truck?"

A broken bottle of ketchup had splattered on the pickled cabinets, the once-white wall. "Sometimes the best place to hide is in plain sight. It has to be Morse. Aside from you and me, he's the only other person in the inner lab with full-project access. Someone without full access would have considered that and not raised a red flag. Morse had to have copied the sensor codes, which means he has nearly everything."

"He couldn't download anything to a declassified area." The lab's computers were on a closed system.

"Right. But he could copy almost everything if the system was diverted, performing a specific sweep. That's how Cracker broke the CIA's system."

"Did Morse know that?"

Seth nodded and stuffed his hands into his jeans pockets. "So Morse has most of Home Base, and Benedetto has the Rogue."

Julia aligned things. "All they need is the tracking sequence and they'll have everything necessary to develop Home Base. Morse has access to everything else. Designs. Specs. Schematics. Intel." The only reason Morse didn't have the tracking sequence was because Seth was still refining it and hadn't yet approved it being included in the project.

"Exactly," Seth agreed. "Marcus doesn't have full access, which is why Benedetto would recruit Dempsey Morse."

Julia slumped against the counter. "Home Base could be obsolete before it's even developed." She swerved to look at Seth. "You'll be ruined."

"It's worst than that, Julia." Seth let his gaze drift from the mountain of books dumped on the floor to her. "The technology will be worth millions to all hostiles. If Morse and Benedetto black-market it, they'll make ten times more money on it than Slicer Industries will make on Home Base."

"Morse profits from both."

"Provided he shields himself from guilt behind someone else."

"Like Karl?"

"Maybe." Seth grabbed a paper towel and used it to snatch up the phone. "We need to get Matthew in on this. If we're right, then we're facing huge challenges."

She clasped her hands, resisting an urge to wring them. "Seth, are you thinking Morse or Benedetto recruited Karl, too?"

"I don't know, honey. Someone got him out of jail. Morse doesn't have that kind of political pull, but Benedetto does. And someone told Karl about your working in the Black World. If you didn't—"

"I didn't."

"Then maybe he has connected with one of them. Or

maybe Karl just found out about your working in the Black World through his own connections and he went a little crazy about our affair."

"Possible."

Seth dialed Matthew's number and then listened to the phone ring. "Julia?"

She turned toward him. "Mmm?"

"About that affair."

Her pulse pounded in her ears. "Yes?"

The look in his eyes warmed. "I think we should start it now."

Julia's heart shot up to her throat. Before she could respond, Seth held up a shushing finger. "Matthew, it's Seth. You need to get over to my house right away—and bring a forensics team."

"Bodies?"

"No. Someone just trashed the place. But we've got a few theories to explore."

"Ten minutes."

The line went dead and Seth hung up the phone. Julia still stood, just staring at him. He'd shocked her, he supposed. He kind of liked that dazed look in her eyes.

They stood staring at each other for a solid five minutes. Seth had given her absorption time, but clearly if he didn't make the first move, they'd still be standing there on the Fourth of July. "Well, do you agree or disagree?"

Wary, skittish, she frowned at him. "With what?"

"Our affair." He stepped closer, let his hands slide over her hips, around to her back. "I think it's a good idea, Julia."

"I . . . don't."

"Why not?" He leaned toward her, pressed kisses to her neck, whispered at her ear. "You know I'm crazy about you."

"I know you're crazy if you think that's a good reason to have an affair."

"It's not." He could say aloud now what he hadn't been able to say out loud for five long years. "But wanting you is. And I've wanted you for a long, long time."

"Seth."

Hearing a protest coming, he nixed it. "Honey, don't."
He rubbed their noses. "Sometimes you think too much
when you should just feel." He covered her mouth with his
and kissed her long and deep, tasting her surprise, her hes-
itancy, and, finally, her hunger.

When she let out a little moan and slumped against him,
he knew they had won the battle over fears from their pasts.
There would be wrinkles from time to time, but they had
gotten on the right path.

"Ahem." Matthew cleared his throat. "Well, I see I'm
interrupting."

Julia gasped and tried to pull away. Seth refused to let
her go. Circling an arm around her, he kept her anchored
her to his side. "Great timing, Matthew."

"Yeah." Grinning, he looked at the kitchen. "You two
making up from a little lovers' quarrel?"

"Not quite." Seth managed a smile. Julia, conversely,
looked mortified. Her getting comfortable with caring about
him was going to take some time. Some time, and a lot of
nurturing, and even more trust. "We evidently had a visitor
while we were up at the cabin."

"Mmm." Matthew pursed his lips, looked around. "Your
visitor's a little on the sloppy side."

He seemed distracted, but he wasn't; Seth knew the drill.
He was systematically scrutinizing, just as Seth had done.

A sergeant dressed in camouflage gear appeared at the
kitchen door. Matthew opened it. "Bring in the team, Sawyer. Check everything."

"Yes, sir." The man turned and waved, and four others
dressed as he was, carrying cases of gear, entered the house
and then disbursed to different rooms.

Julia found her voice and began filling Matthew in on
their suspicions.

He listened attentively, and then voted with Seth. "Benedetto and most likely Morse. He has the most to gain,
though we haven't yet found a substantial link."

"You will," Seth predicted.

"Maybe." Matthew walked through the den. "One thing I'm certain of is, if those two have joined forces, Benedetto will use this technology against the U.S."

"If he builds Home Base, we're dead in the water," Seth said. "Whatever we throw at him, he'll deflect, evade, and use against us."

"I understand." Matthew put a cushion back on the sofa. Tossed a pillow atop it. "But hating any- and everything American, anything he can use against us, he will."

"All because his father committed suicide." Julia resisted a sigh. It was difficult to imagine hatred running that deep. Not impossible but difficult, even for her.

"All because we disarmed his father and he felt forced to commit suicide," Matthew corrected her. "And because he's backing himself into a similar corner."

Blaming America seemed twisted yet, in a way, natural. And with their code on family—Julia shuddered. "There's nothing he won't do."

"Nothing." Matthew's expression turned from grim to bitter. "A couple of hours ago, I received an Intel update on Two West. We have confirmation. Their arsenal has been rebuilt."

"Satellite, or visual?" Seth asked.

"Both."

"Including access to the Rogue?"

"Everything but a visual confirmation on the Rogue and one hell of a lab. Makes ours look like a training ground for amateurs."

Julia took it all in, spun scenarios, and found one that fit. "Benedetto knows you're coming after him. He doesn't want to be forced to commit suicide, like his father."

"He's too ambitious to let that happen," Matthew said. "And too clever. We'll never pin anything directly on Benedetto."

Julia tried but couldn't follow Matthew's logic. "I understand all this, but none of it gives us indisputable proof that Dempsey Morse is working with Benedetto."

"That's true," Matthew said. "But the Morse alliance is a logical deduction."

Julia crossed her arms over her chest. "How did you eliminate Marcus, Seth?"

He stepped around the end of the bar, into the dining room. His mother's crystal was destroyed. Every fragile glass had been broken. "Marcus lacks a comprehensive understanding of the project. He knows only his specific assignment—explosives. Sensors don't explode, they gather info. Marcus would have needed verification of the sensor-codes theft, yet not once has he attempted to get it. Morse doesn't need confirmation. He knows the codes are accurate, so Morse has to work for Benedetto."

Julia weighed it out and came to the same conclusion. "But how do we prove it?"

"Let's think on that, get some people geared in that direction, and meet at noon tomorrow to discuss it," Matthew suggested. "Right now, we need to explore the Karl connection. To tell you the truth, I'm not convinced there is a Karl connection."

"Maybe he isn't connected." Julia shrugged, obviously disagreeing. "But he's threatened me, Jeff, and Seth, and he knew about my work in the Black World and he called Benedetto by name. *Someone* got him out of prison two years early. Knowing Karl's appetite for my blood, I don't doubt he got himself involved, Matthew. I'm not sure how he got involved, or through whom, but I know Karl *is* connected."

"I don't doubt your sincerity, but his connection just doesn't fit the profile." Matthew leaned back against the stove. "It violates Benedetto's code. They never involve families."

"Karl and I are divorced."

"Two West doesn't acknowledge divorce. To them, you're still his wife. And they never touch kids. If Benedetto did bring in Karl and he used you or Jeff, then Karl and Benedetto would lose honor with the loyalists. Benedetto might sacrifice Karl but he would never risk himself."

"Maybe not," she said. "But maybe Dempsey Morse would. He could have recruited Karl."

"Or," Seth interjected, "maybe Benedetto's loyalists don't know Karl is working for Two West and involving Julia and Jeff." Seth tugged at his right ear.

Julia saw it, and stopped cold. *Desperate men commit desperate acts.* Benedetto could feel forced onto a ledge. "Could be."

"We can't discount the possibility." Matthew glanced down at the floor and his expression turned curious. "Seth, when did you become a lunch-toting BAMA fan?"

"What?" Seth turned his gaze and saw a lunch box—one he had seen before. The bottom dropped out of his stomach. "It's not mine."

"Sawyer! Get a bomb squad in here," Matthew shouted. "Now!"

"No." Julia pressed her hands over her chest, let out a little whimper. "It's not a bomb."

"How can you know that?" Matthew glared at her. "You can't know that."

"Yes she can." Seth stared at Matthew. "It's Jeff's."

BENEDETTO took the nickel tour of the factory. The people looked content, the work was going well, and production was up. Mr. Branden appeared to be doing a good job, and Anthony told him so.

"Thank you, sir."

"Any problems?" Anthony stepped outside, preparing to depart, and paused by a trash receptacle. On it, was written: "It's your factory. Keep it clean."

"No, sir." Branden, a lean man with a broad forehead and intelligent eyes, smiled. "Not a one."

"If you need anything, don't hesitate to call." Anthony returned to his limo, where Roger stood waiting.

Roger shut the door, then walked around and got in, worry in his eyes. "Hyde has kidnapped the boy."

"What boy?"

"The scientist's student, Jeffrey Camden."

Son of a bitch. First the lunatic attacks a woman and now he kidnaps a child?

"I recommend you notify the council immediately, sir. This will be public. There's no way to keep it from them."

Anthony stared through the tinted window, feeling his world start to crumble. Hyde, the idiot, had created a catch-22 situation for himself and for Anthony. He needed time to think of a way out. Surely there had to be a way out.

"Sir," Roger said. "Should I call a meeting?"

"No."

"No?"

Anthony buried his temper. "We can't. Not yet. We don't have everything we need."

Thoughtful, Roger stared at Mr. Benedetto. The man rarely became rattled, but he was rattled now. In twenty-two years, Roger had never seen Anthony's father rattled. But then that chairman had never been foolish enough to violate the coalition's sacred code. He had never, not once, compromised his honor.

This chairman had said Hyde worked for the coalition's friend in Grayton. But did he? Roger wondered. The news of this kidnapping hadn't exactly taken Mr. Benedetto by surprise. He seemed to have anticipated it as a possibility. Perhaps not, but perhaps he had expected the scientist to resist, and he had surmised Hyde would use the boy to encourage her to cooperate. Hadn't Mr. Benedetto asked for a detailed investigative report on her that included information on what it would take to get her to commit treason?

Definitely an ethics violation. The council would never believe Anthony Benedetto hadn't authorized the kidnapping, or that any loyalist, even a green recruit, would commit one without his authorization. He was finished, even if he didn't yet realize it.

The council would remove him from power. He would lose everything in disgrace, without honor. There would be no détente. No superiority over the United States. No retribution for disarming the coalition and Mr. Philip's death.

Anthony too would die.

And his mother, Daisy, would again mourn.

That, Roger couldn't allow; he'd given Mr. Philip his word.

Miss Daisy. Everyone loved her, sought her advice. She was a wise woman and had often counseled Philip.

Roger would seek her advice on this matter. If a way to protect her son and the coalition could be found, Miss Daisy would find it. Hadn't she protected Mr. Philip, assisted him in his suicide?

Chapter Fifteen

M ATTHEW declared Seth's house off-limits and sent Julia and Seth to Julia's apartment to await word on Jeff.

When two hours had passed and they had heard nothing, Julia's panic nearly overwhelmed her. Pacing alongside the bar stools, she stopped and looked at Seth, sitting there drinking a glass of juice. "We've got to call Camden. We can't just keep on sitting here and doing nothing. The not knowing is driving me crazy."

"Honey, we can't fly by the seat of our pants on this. We could get Jeff hurt." Seth set down his glass and reached out.

Julia slid into his arms, curled her fingers deeply into his sides. "He's just a baby."

"I know." Seth tucked her head against his shoulder. "I'm worried, too, and I don't like it, either. But Matthew's intervened. We've got to trust him."

"Grace's PD is probably throwing a fit."

"Probably not. Matthew's a pro at these things. He knows what he's doing."

"He'd better not screw up." She muttered against Seth's neck. This was Jeff. Her tiny Jeff with the big heart and sad eyes who desperately needed peace, who envisioned his mother burning in hell every time he closed his eyes and still had the courage to love her and Seth.

"Matthew will do his best," Seth said, clearly believing it.

Would his best be good enough?

Worried sick for Jeff's safety, they alternated between pacing the floor and reaching out to each other for comfort and reassurance. Hours passed. And long after dark, the phone finally rang.

Julia scrambled and answered it. "Hello."

"Finally home, eh, sugar?"

Her stomach muscles clenched. She pressed a hand against them, mouthed to Seth. "Karl."

"You shouldn't have run away from me. Especially not to Seth Holt."

She cocked the receiver so both she and Seth could hear. "What do you want?" she asked Karl.

"I want you. You're my wife, Julia." He paused, and when she didn't say anything, he added, "Evidently, you've forgotten that, but I've found a reminder for you so you won't forget again."

"I'm not your wife." She leaned against Seth, grateful for the feel of his arm around her. "Not anymore."

"You'll come running to me, sugar. That's a promise."

"I can't imagine how." He had to be suffering delusions—or planning a new version of hell he felt confident of dragging her through.

"Didn't you find the present I left for you?" Karl let out a humorless laugh. "Ah, never mind. Hold on a second."

The line went silent. Julia cast a fearful look at Seth. Then she heard a weak little voice.

"Dr. Julia?"

Jeff! God, how she prayed Camden had listened. But he hadn't. And now Karl had Jeff. Her knees went weak. Frantic, she squeezed Seth's side.

"Stay calm," Seth mouthed, holding her tighter. "Be strong for him."

Her pulse pounded in her ears so hard she had to struggle to hear. "It's me, honey. Are you all right?"

He sniffled, then began crying. "I'm . . . scared."

Julia's heart slammed into her throat. "Is he the mean man?"

"Uh-huh."

Seth talked into the phone. "It's okay, buddy. We're going to help you."

Karl came back on the line. In the background, she heard Jeff crying. "Shut up, kid," Karl said. "You still there, Julia?"

"I'm here." Her arm muscles went into riot. Clenching her teeth, she leaned heavily against Seth. "Karl, do not hurt that child. I mean it."

"Well, I'd say his safety is up to you, sugar."

Cocky bastard. The spasms intensified. "What do you want?" She hissed in air, fighting against the pain, and Seth began massaging her arm.

"Meet me in two hours at Holt's cabin." Karl paused to yell at Jeff. "Come alone, Julia, or I'll kill this squalling kid—and bring me everything on Home Base."

Julia stared into Seth's eyes. She'd been right; Karl *was* connected. Seth nodded for her to agree. She blinked hard. "Will Jeff be there?"

"Yeah, he'll be there." Karl dropped his voice, deep and menacing. "Don't hold out on me, Julia. I want it all. Everything you've got on it."

"Why involve Jeff in this?" she asked. "He's just one of my students."

"Don't try to con a con, sugar." Karl guffawed. "You love the brat. Your mistake," he said. "You promised to love me, but you lied. Now, you're gonna make it right with this Home Base stuff, or everyone you love is gonna die."

Julia clutched at Seth's side, knowing Karl meant it. He would kill everyone who mattered to her.

Everyone.

Jeff and Seth.

Chapter Sixteen

A pin dropping in Julia's apartment would have sounded like a brick of C-4 exploding.

She stood in the kitchen with the phone in her hand, glaring at Matthew and Seth, certain both men had been invaded by idiot aliens. "Look, I don't give a damn what either of you say, I'm calling Camden. Jeff is his son. He has a right to know the child has been kidnapped."

"This is my fault." Seth leaned a shoulder against the door frame and crossed his chest with his arms. "I knew he was a latchkey kid. I knew it. But I thought in his neighborhood, he'd be okay. I thought with Grace PD watching him, he'd be safe."

"No one Karl Hyde targets is safe, Seth." Julia let some of the steam seep from her voice. "But you couldn't know that. It's not your fault he got Jeff. I warned Camden that Jeff had been threatened. If anyone's to blame, it's me. I knew Karl was going after Jeff and I didn't get him out of there myself."

Seth gave her a negative nod. "No, I knew Camden was abusing him. I saw the bruise. I should have gotten him out of there."

"Bruise?" Julia clamped the phone in a death grip. "What bruise?"

"The one Camden gave Jeff."

"Oh, God." Julia turned her back to Seth and Matthew

and began dialing. "How dare that bastard hit Jeff? How dare he?"

"Hold it a second." Matthew hit the hook button. "You calm down before you call anyone."

"Calm down?" Julia guffawed, feeling as if the top of her head were going to explode. "He bruised Jeff and you want me to calm down?"

"Yeah, I do." Matthew paused and the look in his eyes showed both his own anger and his understanding. "You call Camden, making accusations, and you're liable to make things worse."

Julia tried to be rational, to hear Matthew with her head, but her heart wouldn't let her. "Jeff is *not* going back to that man. Ever."

"We'll deal with that," Matthew said. "But first—"

Julia glared at Seth. "You should have told me."

He lifted his hands in supplication. "You would have cried."

That had to be the most ridiculous remark ever to come out of Seth Holt's mouth. "I'd cry, so you leave Jeff there to get beaten?"

"I wouldn't do that. I had no choice but to do what I did, Julia." Seth walked toward her, where she stood at the wall phone. "I called his social worker. She's involved, okay?"

The truth hit Julia like a sledge. "You saw the bruise. That's when you sent Jeff to wash his face and you threatened Camden."

"For Christ's sake, Seth," Matthew interrupted, his voice elevating. "Have you forgotten your hands and feet are lethal weapons?"

"I didn't put a hand on him." Seth reeled his gaze to his ex-Special Forces team member. "We came to a verbal understanding."

"Yeah." Julia grunted, "Camden didn't hit Jeff again or you'd hit Camden."

Seth shrugged. "Actually, I said I'd kick his ass, but that's close enough."

Matthew's relief was obvious. "Look, at the moment all of this is academic. Before we can adjust Camden's attitude toward kids, we've got to get Jeff back alive."

Julia stiffened against the wall. "Karl won't kill him."

"How can you be sure?" Seth raked a hand through his hair, more worried than Julia had ever before seen him.

"Because if Jeff is dead, Karl can't use him to torture me."

"He could torture Jeff." Seth looked up from the floor. "Would he torture Jeff?"

"To get to me"—she blinked hard—"he'd do anything." God, but it hurt to admit it. It hurt even more to know it was true. "Matthew, get your plan together. We've got less than an hour."

She picked up the phone.

"Don't blow this, Julia." Matthew's warning came out low and controlled, but it carried a huge punch. "Jeff will pay the price."

She swallowed hard, harnessed her rioting emotions and sending them to that place strong emotions belonged, and then dialed the phone.

Camden answered on the second ring, and Julia licked at her lips, her mouth stone-dry. "Mr. Camden, this is Dr. Warner."

"What is it now, Dr. Hyde?" He sounded exasperated.

"Jeff's been kidnapped."

"Don't you ever give up?" He grunted. "Jeff is playing football at Travis's house."

"He's not." She stared at the wall above the phone. "My ex-husband just called. He has Jeff."

Camden grunted. "You're one crazy lady. Karl hasn't put a finger on Jeff."

Even now he didn't believe her. Silently screaming, she remembered Matthew's warning, stared into Seth's worried eyes, and forced herself to calm down. "I talked to him. He—"

Wait. Wait. Karl?

The truth body-slammed her, and her world spun out of

control. "I've—I've warned you. That's all I can do."

"Whatever." Camden dropped the receiver.

The dial tone droned in Julia's ear. She couldn't make herself move, yet she needed to sit down before she fell. She dropped the phone, lunged at a bar stool and held on.

"Julia, what's the matter with you?" Seth helped her get on the seat.

She leaned forward, ducked her head between her knees, and forced herself to breathe slow, even breaths. "Dear God."

"Julia?" Seth stood at her side, placed a hand at her shoulder. "What the hell is it?"

"Camden let Karl kidnap Jeff," she gasped out. "He *let* him do it."

Matthew frowned at Seth. "Did Camden admit that?"

The dizziness subsided. Julia straightened, then slumped over the bar, smoothing her face with a shaky hand. Her left arm was so full of spasms she couldn't tell when one stopped and the next one started. Grimacing against the intense pain, she told them. "He used Karl's first name and he denied the kidnapping. They're working together on this."

Seth understood and explained to Matthew. "Camden never wanted Jeff. The boy told me only his mother wanted him. Camden never loved him."

"So Camden gives Karl permission to kidnap his son?" Matthew shook his head, unable to imagine it.

"No." Seth disagreed. "He gave Karl permission to kill Jeff."

"Good God." Matthew frowned. "Wait, I can see it. Karl uses Jeff to manipulate Julia on Home Base and Camden gets rid of his unloved burden and never dirties his hands."

Julia went for her purse, pulled out the .38.

Seth grabbed her arm. "What are you doing?"

Tears rolling down her cheeks, she jerked out of his grasp. "I'm going to kill that son of a bitch."

Seth took the gun, passed it to Matthew, and pulled Julia into his arms.

She slumped against him. "How could he do this? How could anyone? The man has no soul, Seth."

"Honey, we'll deal with Camden. I promise you that. But first we've got to help Jeff."

She pulled back, looked up into Seth's face. "No, not *we*. *I* have to help Jeff. Karl said to come alone or he'd kill him. If I go alone, Jeff's got a chance."

"Julia, you can't do that."

"I have to, Seth. If I don't, Karl *will* kill Jeff. I didn't think so, but he has Camden's blessing, and I'd have the guilt—forever. Karl knows it. He will kill him. How am I supposed to live with that? I can't live with that."

"Honey." Seth softened his voice, hoping to soften the blow, and stroked her hair back from her red-rimmed eyes. "Karl plans to kill Jeff, anyway."

"I know that, damn it. Don't you think I know that? I have to stop him. I have to try, Seth."

Matthew cleared his throat, interceded. "I agree with Julia, Seth. She's got to go in alone."

"What?"

"She's Jeff's best shot." Matthew reached for the phone.

Seth disagreed, but he recognized the signs. Things were not as they seemed. Matthew was trying to save Jeff and Julia's life, and he'd have to do it in spite of her. "Who are you calling?"

"Colonel Kane. He's working the AID angle of this operation. For what I've got in mind, we're going to need a little assist."

No one brought in the Air Intelligence Defense for a "little assist." Julia pulled away from Seth. "What exactly do you have in mind?"

Matthew's eyes gleamed. "A covert operation to extricate Jeff and take Karl down."

"No." Julia put her foot down. "I'm the reason Jeff is in this situation and Karl will know I'm not alone. I won't risk it. You listen to me, Matthew, because I swear I'll shoot anyone who gets between me and that baby."

"Would you stop threatening to shoot people?" Seth

frowned at her. "Look, let's talk turkey. You go in alone, your odds of getting Jeff and yourself killed are about ninety-nine percent. With Kane's Special Forces assisting, we stand a chance of getting him and you out."

Unconvinced, Julia persisted. "What are the odds on that?"

Matthew answered. "A hell of a lot better."

Ignoring Matthew's cryptic answer, she turned to Seth and lifted a questioning brow.

"I don't know. But they're trained specialists, Julia. They're better equipped and they're not emotionally involved. You go into situations like this with your emotions engaged, you get killed. You get other people killed—usually, the ones you're trying to save. You've got to shut down. That's a fact."

She folded her arms over her chest. "Speaking from experience?"

"Yeah, I am."

Surprised he'd admitted it, she sighed. "Are you going to be on that team?"

He nodded.

"Well, we're screwed then." She frowned at Seth. "When it comes to Jeff, you're as emotionally involved as I am. So where does that leave us—and our baby?"

"I'll shut down, Julia. I've had plenty of experience."

He was talking about his family. "Haven't we all?"

Matthew hung up the phone. "Let's go. Colonel Kane's meeting us at the OSI office in ten minutes. He's scrambling a team."

ANTHONY sat on the veranda, staring out over the gardens. Not much was blooming, but the evergreens gave him a sense of peace and solitude absent in his life lately. This whole matter was about to blow up in his face. He knew it as well as he knew his name. As well as he knew Hyde was out of control.

Killing Hyde wouldn't stop it. Not now. Not with the boy involved, and not with Anthony missing the deadline to transfer the technology to his Eastern associate, as promised.

Nothing would stop it now.

"Anthony." His mother touched his shoulder, then walked around to his side. "We need to talk, darling."

Roger had gone to her. She was twisting her pearls. "About what, Mama?" Anthony saw the worry in her eyes and the resolve. Inescapable. It was the beginning of the end.

"Elise tells me you aren't sleeping. And your daughter looks at you and cries."

"Why?"

"Have you checked a mirror lately, son? They're terrified. You look like death." Daisy sat down beside him and her pink skirt flared around her calves. She clasped his hand. "I don't know what your challenges are, but I do know that you must pull yourself together. If you learned nothing else from your father, you should have learned that a leader doesn't have the luxury of falling apart during crises. Too many others depend on you."

"I am not falling apart, Mother," he said stiffly.

"I'm glad to hear it." She paused, then went on, her resolve even stronger. "I've buried a lot of people I've loved, Anthony. I refuse to bury you, too." She reached into her skirt pocket and pulled out a prescription bottle. "Dr. Stanley recommends these for you."

"Drugs and alcohol are not permitted. Not to the chairman. You know that, Mother."

"The chairman is not denied prescription medication. I know that, Anthony." She pressed the brown bottle into his hand, curled his fingers around it. "Take them. Promise me you'll take them."

Anthony looked at the bottle. Xanax. For anxiety. Three per day. A weak dosage. It seemed important to her, and he had experienced trouble sleeping and eating lately. And he supposed he had frightened Daisy, being short-tempered. "I'll take them."

"Thank you, darling." She stood up, kissed his forehead, then went back inside.

Anthony walked to his office, asked Roger for a glass of water, and sat down at his desk.

When he passed the glass, Anthony said, "Get me our friend at Grayton on the phone."

"Yes, sir." Roger stepped into the outer office.

The intercom buzzed. Anthony punched down the lit line and lifted the receiver.

"Yes. Mr. Benedetto?"

"What are you doing down there?" Anthony demanded to know. "I need that system operational."

"I'm doing my best."

"Your best is lacking. You have the finest lab and staff money can buy, so what—"

"Things just aren't working as they should."

Not working as they should? The idiot had been fed false information. Had to be. The bastards were on to them. "Do what you have to do, but get that system operational now."

He slammed down the phone and, feeling his blood beat at his temples, he unscrewed the cap on the bottle and took a pill. That inept idiot was going to screw around and cost Anthony everything. Why couldn't a loyalist have been assigned to the project at Grayton and spared him from dealing with a damn inept idiot?

Frustrated, Anthony looked at the prescription bottle and tried to remember whether or not he had taken a pill. Unsure, he swallowed one, and then looked at his father's photograph. "I'm doing this for you, but if I go down, I am not going alone." Unlike his father, he had no son. No successor. Damn Elise for her inability to have more children. Damn America. Damn them all.

"Mr. Benedetto." Roger walked in, his face pale and waxy. "The council has called an emergency meeting in one hour."

"For what?"

"To talk to you about the kidnapped boy, Jeffrey Camden."

Someone had made the connection, damn it. Anthony would have to forfeit their friend at Grayton. But first he needed the rest of the project intel. "Fine."

"There's more, sir."

"More?"

Roger nodded. "While you were on the line, your Eastern associate called. He said something . . . puzzling."

"What?" Anthony asked, knowing the news could only mean more trouble.

"He said you missed your delivery date on the exchange. He gave you the Rogue and you promised to deliver Home Base and didn't." Disdain edged into Roger's voice. "He's disappointed that you broke your word."

Roger's distaste for the lapse was clear. Anthony attempted to reassure him. If any one person in the coalition could hang him, aside from his mother, it was Roger. "Odd. I thought I had notified them. There's been an unavoidable project delay. The scientists are working on it. Call and explain, Roger."

"Yes, sir. But they've given you a second deadline. Forty-eight hours. Either you produce then, or they seize assets."

Roger was puzzled by the seizure threat.

Anthony was not. The Eastern associate would seize Two West's arms. And Anthony would die, just like his father.

He wouldn't do it. He wouldn't!

"Forty-eight hours should be fine, Roger. But tell them it really depends on the scientists. I can't deliver what they haven't yet developed. If they want what we already have, I'll be happy to pass that along now."

"Yes, sir." Roger turned and went back to his office.

Having no intention of turning anything over before the package was complete, Anthony debated strategies.

And dry-swallowed two pills.

Chapter Seventeen

JULIA sat down at the OSI conference table.

Her stomach in knots, she looked over at Seth, and then at Matthew. They both appeared calm. How could they be calm? Karl, the bastard, had Jeff.

Matthew dropped the point of his pencil to the yellow legal pad. Along with the scribbles only he and God could decipher were peppered dots where he had dropped the pencil point over and again, as if venting a nervous tic. "We've got the project intel ready to go."

"You can't be serious." Julia's skin crawled. Had they lost their minds? She stared at Seth. "With the Home Base intel—"

"Benedetto can launch the Rogue and he can return any U.S. missile to its launch site," Seth interceded, leaning forward and lacing his hands atop the table. "We know, Julia."

"And," a man said from the doorway, "we have no idea where he'll target."

Julia looked over at the man. Blond, early forties, weary eyed and dressed in Class-A blues. He stood very erect, even more so than the habitual military posture, and she figured he had to, to keep from tipping over due to the weight of the medals on his chest. From the eagles on his shoulders, she knew he was a very young full-bird colonel, but she'd rarely seen that many medals on anyone's uniform, including most generals.

"Colonel Kane." Matthew stood up and offered his hand. "Come in, sir."

The AID officer handling the intel aspects of the Benedetto operation. Definitely Special Forces. She sensed it in him, and in the way Seth looked at the man while not looking at him.

Colonel Kane walked over and took a seat. "Dr. Warner." He nodded. "Seth. Wish we could have had this little reunion under different circumstances." Something akin to pain flashed in Kane's eyes. "I understand the boy is Bravo-One."

"Yeah." Seth's misery and worry over Jeff surfaced. "He's mine—and Julia's."

That remark surprised her, but once it sank in, it felt good. Actually, it felt right. Jeff should be theirs. They loved him . . . and each other.

"Whatever it takes." Kane nodded his understanding. "Benedetto's up against the wall. We figure he's going to launch. What's your best guess on his target?"

"D. C." Seth hiked a shoulder. "He can take out the Pentagon, Congress, and the White House."

Julia's skin crawled. Targeting the seat of America's federal government would severely damage the nation's operations and, in Benedetto's eyes, would vindicate his father's death. But even with a gutful of hate, how could he justify the utter chaos and extensive destruction he would create?

"D. C. would cover most of his objectives," Kane said.

"Unfortunately," Matthew added, "I agree."

"Intel is reporting disturbing news." Colonel Kane straightened in his seat, next to Matthew.

"About the Rogue?" Seth asked.

Julia glanced from Seth to Kane and waited for his response.

"About Benedetto." Kane gave Seth a concerned look laced with deep worry. "He's getting frustrated."

"Why?" Julia didn't get it. "If he's got Morse, he's got everything, so what does he have to get frustrated about? And why does he need Karl?"

Matthew answered first. "He doesn't. Morse needs Karl to protect his façade of innocence. Karl goes down—I think the original plan called for him to go down with you—and Morse sells Home Base to hostiles. Probably to the same hostiles who sold Benedetto the Rogue. He makes millions, Morse makes millions and he holds on to Slicer Industries, staying lily-white."

But Morse didn't have the launching sequence, which is why Karl had demanded everything on Home Base. "That explains Karl," she said. "But not Benedetto's frustration."

Colonel Kane answered. "Having the project info and intel is one thing, Dr. Warner. Putting it into operation is another. Aside from the tracking sequence, Morse has all technology and technical info, but he lacks your skills. Yours and Seth's.

Seth rapped the table. "Benedetto being frustrated raises some hairy possibilities."

Julia looked at Kane. "Can't you just arrest him?"

"We could, but we don't know the location of the Rogue or the project intel. And we don't have enough evidence on Morse to assure a conviction." Kane shifted on his seat. "Initially, Benedetto didn't intend to launch the Rogue."

"He only wanted the ability to launch it," Seth speculated. "To prove to his people that he could protect them."

"Right." Kane shifted his gaze to Seth. "Benedetto had two objectives. To rebuild his arsenal, and to get the Home Base technology. But he did intend to sell the technology to hostiles without developing it. Money for him, headaches for us."

"Then Morse came along," Seth said.

"And Karl Hyde," Kane added.

Matthew had been silent. Now, his worry shone clearly in his eyes. "If Benedetto feels frustrated by failed attempts to get Home Base operational, he could get violent."

"He could get desperate." Seth pursed his lips. "Each failure puts his honor at risk."

"We're certain of one thing." Kane let out a sigh, rubbed at his neck. "He's breaking down. We picked up a prescription issued for him. Xanax. It's an antianxiety drug."

Julia's stomach lurched. "There's another thing you can be sure of, Colonel. Anthony Benedetto is not going to follow in his father's footsteps and commit suicide without exploiting every possible alternative. He wouldn't recruit Karl, or allow Morse to, if he considered it a risk to his honor."

"The profilers agree," Matthew said.

"So does Intel." Kane grimaced. "Hyde covers for Morse, and Morse for Benedetto. Benedetto is protected. That was the plan. But things haven't gone off as planned."

Finally, Julia thought. Common sense. "Which makes it totally asinine to even consider giving Karl project intel to get Jeff back." The words hurt her throat. "We have to get him back somehow, but we can't jeopardize the country to do it."

Seth turned on his seat to face her. "We'll give Karl project intel, Julia, just not Home Base's intel."

Julia processed that, saw the wisdom and the risks in it. She rubbed at her temple. "What I don't understand is why they want everything rather than just the launching sequence. Morse has access."

"But he's only had access to bogus reports," Kane said.

Surprise rippled up Julia's backbone. "Since when?"

Matthew responded. "Since the sensor-codes theft."

Her blood chilled. "Benedetto knows it."

She darted a fearful look at Seth. He didn't tug at his earlobe. "I know you want to do some covert operation on this, but I won't allow it, Seth. Benedetto, Morse, and Karl know Matthew's involved; they'll expect one. Jeff would be in even more danger." She looked at each man at the table. "I'm meeting Karl alone."

Colonel Kane shot her a level look. "Can you kill him?"

Julia hesitated, then answered honestly. "I don't know.

But I do know he'll expect a covert-op trap. I'll do my best for Jeff. That's all I can promise." And she'd pray her best was good enough.

"That's an acceptable response, Dr. Warner." Kane nodded. "We'll be in the distant vicinity with a team. With the lack of mental stability going on in the Two West camp, I think that's best. The risks of us moving in are unacceptable. After you secure Jeff's release, then we'll pick up Karl and advance on other fronts."

Other fronts. Morse and maybe Benedetto himself. "Fine."

Seth watched Kane, doing his damnedest to remain passive and not feel disloyal to Julia. It was difficult because Colonel Kane was lying through his teeth. But his rationale was honorable—he was trying to save her life, and Jeff's—which was the only reason Seth *could* keep silent. If brought into the covert-op loop, Julia would give away the fact that the team was near. Her actions would reflect their presence and, trained, Karl would pick up on it. Julia wouldn't intend for that to happen, but it *would* happen. And Jeff would lose his life. Julia might, too.

She wouldn't see the situation that way, of course. But that's the way it was and, after this was over, Seth would explain his rationale for maintaining secrecy over and again until she forgave him for not telling her the truth.

Odds of her forgiveness were iffy at best. Particularly if anything happened to Jeff. But in that case, the point would be moot. Regardless of what she did, Seth would never forgive himself.

THEY'D lied to her.

Julia knew it. Sensed it as surely as she sensed Benedetto was about to lose it and go on a killing spree. She felt it as strongly as she felt the Camry's steering wheel under her clenched hands. Colonel Kane, Matthew, and Seth had all lied.

She could forgive Kane and Matthew; with them, lying wasn't personal. But Seth? She loved him in a way she thought she would never again love any man. Not after Karl. And that made Seth's deception not only personal. It hurt. Deep.

Okay, be fair. He doesn't know you love him.

She wasn't crazy enough to tell him. Hell, she'd just accepted it herself. Loving again, after Karl, was scary. Hard. But Seth's knowing or not knowing didn't change anything. He had lied to her.

Checking the rearview mirror, she pressed a hand to the project disks in her bra and frowned, grasping for the first time exactly how Seth must have felt when she had left New Orleans without saying a word. She had regretted leaving him, resented having to leave him, missed him, but only now did she feel the sense of betrayal he must have felt then. She hated it.

The weed-infested ditches gave way to the turnoff to the cabin. Julia hooked a right, her heart rate hiking a healthy notch, and checked for signs of anyone following. The dirt road kicked up a mountain of dust behind her. A herd of elephants could be tailing her and she wouldn't know it.

But Karl would know. He would have night vision gear. From the cabin, he would be able to separate dust clouds.

She began to sweat. Fear and doubt that she was up to this challenge swarmed through her, shrouding her.

You can't fail, Julia. You have to stand up to him. You can't let the old fears intrude. Not this time. Not with Jeff's life in your hands.

She inched into her purse, felt the gun, and prayed Seth was right, that the bullet would penetrate the leather, because she had finally accepted the inevitable. Hate was a burden too heavy to carry. It was dark and ugly and it consumed everything good until only hate was left. She had to let go of the hate—and she could. She could forgive Karl for what he had done to her. If he would just leave her alone, she could accept what had happened and put it to bed in her past. Chalk it up to lessons learned. But she could not and would not forgive him for what he'd done to Jeff, or for what he intended to do to him.

Not now. She positioned the barrel away from a seam in her purse, toward smooth, less dense leather. Not ever.

He'd pushed her hard and far for a long time. No more denying the truth. In kidnapping Jeff, Karl had pushed her too hard, and too far. He had left her no choice.

FIVE years had passed, but the camouflage gear still felt as natural to Seth as his skin. He looked over at Matthew's greasepaint-smeared face. Colonel Kane sat at Seth's right.

They made a circle and came at the cabin from across the lake by boat. From the shore, they moved in on foot, snaking their way through the darkness, listening for abnormal sounds. Colonel Kane signaled and a Special Ops team fanned out into the woods and took cover at their designated positions in the dense underbrush.

About seventy-five yards out, Seth saw a marking on a tree and stopped cold. "Son of a bitch."

"What?" Matthew whispered from Seth's side.

"C-4." Seth examined the plastic explosives attached to the tree. "Trip wires at ground level, two, four, and"—he swayed, hoping the moonlight would glint on any overhead wires—"and six feet. Maybe more."

Kane joined them, swearing softly, then spoke into a lip mike attached to a lightweight headset fitted in his ear. "Alpha, back down. We've got C-4 all the hell over the place. Trip wires level, upper—and probably below. Status report," Kane said, tight-jawed. "Chandler?"

"North's wired, sir."

"Madison?"

"Yes, sir. All the hell over the west side, sir."

"Paddy?"

"Bastard got the south, too, sir."

And they were coming in from the east. Seth's stomach furled. It would take hours to undo this handiwork. They could detonate it, but a brick would take out a house. They had seen enough to know that if it were detonated, they would take out the cabin and blast in a new lake. Karl would be gone, but so would Jeff and Julia.

"Seth?" Colonel Kane looked him straight in the eye. "We can call in air support, fly over the damn stuff. Your call."

Sweat trickled down Seth's face, from fear and from the humid heat. "You do that, and Julia and Jeff are dead."

"That's my take on it, but I wanted to consider all options."

Matthew's eyes brimmed with concern . . . and understanding. "She's on her own."

"Yeah." Seth's throat muscles clamped down. She, who'd had one weekend of training in self-defense. Had sustained near-fatal injuries from the bastard she now had to confront, a bastard who had hospitalized her for months and still caused her challenges. She—who, for the life of him, Seth couldn't see ever inflicting injury on another human being, much less killing a man—was on her own.

The only hope he could latch onto was something she had said at this very cabin. "Victim no more."

Determination and conviction could carry a person a long way in accomplishing missions deemed impossible. But those facing those impossible missions usually had undergone extensive training that honed their instinctive reactions. With only a weekend of training under her belt, Julia simply didn't possess those skills. And she had sustained injuries that imposed physical limitations on her others confronting these challenges just didn't possess.

Would her resolve, determination, and persistence be enough to save her life and Jeff's?

THE pills made the world a less scary, shitty place; gave him more control and focus. Anthony stretched out on the sofa in his office, soothed by the smell of the leather and its soft, buttery feel.

"Mr. Benedetto?" Roger stepped near. "Are you awake?"

Why couldn't Roger just leave him alone and let him

enjoy a few more moments' respite before the pills weren't numbing him anymore? "Yes."

"Your friend from Grayton just phoned. He's still waiting for the launching sequence."

"Why doesn't he have it?"

"Dr. Holt hasn't yet approved it."

Anthony lowered his arm from over his eyes. "Tell that bastard to get us operational or I'll pluck his heart out."

"Yes, sir."

"Tell him we're out of time." Sitting up, he shouted. "Do you hear me, Roger? We're out of time."

Knowing that better than Mr. Benedetto, Roger walked to the desk, opened the top drawer, pulled out the prescription bottle, and then returned to the sofa. "I heard you fine, sir." He shook three pills into his hand. "Your mother asked me to remind you not to forget to take these."

Anthony downed the pills without water.

Uncivilized. Uncouth. Roger put the bottle back in the desk, turned out the light, and closed the office door. Anthony Benedetto's days were numbered.

And Daisy Benedetto didn't seem so wise, not anymore.

Chapter Eighteen

LIGHTS glowed amber inside the cabin.

Julia cut the engine and stared through the windshield, searching the windows, hoping for a glimpse of Jeff.

Nothing.

Something moved in the darkness. Squinting, she saw Karl, dressed all in black and standing alone in the grass, just in front of the cabin's front porch. The light at his back silhouetted him; he looked huge. And she felt small. Small and helpless.

Memories of Destin and the attack, the pain, every threat he had made rushed in on her, carrying all her old fears. She wanted to ease her hand inside her purse, grip the gun, but she couldn't do it. He would notice her hand being stuffed inside her purse, and only God knew what that could mean to Jeff.

You have to face him, Julia. You have to back him down.

She left the car, slid her purse strap over her shoulder, and stopped about twenty feet in front of Karl. The fear was strong. Bitter, and as strong as her resolve.

Dear God, she didn't want to kill anyone. She knew how to kill. But to actually do it? To actually, in cold blood, commit murder? No, she didn't want to commit cold-blooded murder. Not even against Karl.

When does it end, Seth? Does it ever end?

When you choose to make it end. You have to decide how much power you give the fear . . .

"Where's Jeff?" Her insides shook. She lifted to the balls of her feet, attempting to prepare for anything. Karl always had attacked her from behind, but if pushed and in a pinch . . .

"He's in a safe place." Moonlight caught the metal on Karl's gun and glinted.

With him, how could anything or anyone, anywhere, be safe? No way. But obviously he believed what he was saying. She had to reason with him.

Reason? With Karl Hyde? Don't be ridiculous, Julia.

She had to try. For her own peace of mind. If she ended up having to kill him, then she was going to have to live with it. She wanted—no, *needed*—to know she had explored every possible alternative.

Fear lumped in her stomach. She pressed the flat of her left arm against it. "Karl, how can you justify kidnapping a child?"

"Camden suggested it."

Once, Julia had believed that. So had Seth, Matthew, and Colonel Kane. Hell, the entire Intel community had believed it. But they had all been victims of Karl's propaganda, his psychological warfare. And they had all been wrong.

Camden and Karl were abusers. Their strength came from terrorizing those weaker. Just as Karl didn't want her dead, Camden didn't want Jeff dead. He'd have no one left to torment. "You're lying."

"Watch it, sugar." Karl stepped closer. "I'm about out of patience with you."

"Benedetto told you to get Jeff—to get to me."

He guffawed, but there was an uneasy flicker in his voice. "Benedetto doesn't mess with families. You ought to know that. What? Your Intel assholes can get you out of a women's shelter but now they're slipping on you?"

She was on the right track. She felt it down to the marrow of her bones. "Benedetto got you out of jail. He bought you out. That's messing with families."

"That's reuniting a family. It's different."

So it had been Benedetto himself and not Morse who had brought Karl into this. "No, it's not different. It's Benedetto getting desperate." Seth's words ran through her mind. *Desperate men commit desperate acts.* "He's a terrorist on a power trip, hell-bent on proving he can protect his people. But why are you letting him use you? Don't you understand that millions of people—including you—could die?" Seth and Jeff and she could also die. Seth, without knowing she loved him. Regret twisted in her stomach, churned, and, not for the first time, she wished she had told him. "Millions *will* die, Karl. It'll be your fault."

"My fault?" Anger flattened his mouth to a grim slash. He rushed her, grabbed her left arm, got into her face. "Whatever happens is your fault, you ungrateful bitch." He expelled a sharp breath. "You made the bomb, and you made me what I am."

"Oh, no." She jerked away. "I haven't done anything to you. You've beaten, attacked, stalked, and tormented me. Once, I bought into your lies. I didn't know any better then, but I do now. No more, Karl. You're responsible for what you do."

He turned toward the light. His eyes brimmed with hatred. "You're pissing me off, sugar. Maybe you'd just better give me what I came for before I have to remind you why pissing me off's a bad thing for you to do."

Julia stepped back. "You're getting nothing from me until I get Jeff."

He lunged at her, swung at her purse. It thudded to the ground, out of reach. She maneuvered, resisting his weight, blocked with her arm and kicked, connecting with his lower abdomen. Expelling air, Karl flew backward and landed on the ground with a dull "Umph."

Julia scrambled to her feet. She had caught him off guard once, but that wouldn't happen again. Where was her damn purse? She needed her gun.

You won't shoot him.
I will if I have to.
You won't.
Shut the hell up!

Karl clipped her left shoulder, sent her sprawling. She tried every move—every single move Seth had taught her about attacking a man's most vulnerable points, and a few of her own. But nothing worked. Karl was too strong. And her purse was too far away.

He grabbed her by the neck in a chokehold and jerked her to her feet. Her stomach hurt from his punch, her shoulder felt as if someone were driving nails through it. And the top of her head threatened to blow off. *Where the hell was Seth?*

Karl dragged her toward the porch. "I want the disks, Julia."

"Not until I get Jeff."

He flung her to the ground. Grabbed her purse from a weedy clump of dirt and dumped its contents on the ground. "Where are they?"

"Where's Jeff?" *Come on, Seth. I know you're out there. Intercede, for God's sake—before the bastard kills me.*

But Seth didn't come. No one came. She prayed hard, and still no one came—except for the ghosts of her old fears. They arrived in force, bombarding her. Terrifying her.

Dear God, help me. I can't fight them and him, too. I . . . can't.

Run, Julia. Run.

I can't leave Jeff!

He can't hurt either of you without the disks.

He couldn't. Something had gone wrong for Seth. But any delay she could wrangle would give him and the team more time to move in.

Karl dug through the purse. "A gun, Julia?" He laughed. "This has to be a joke."

At the moment, it seemed to be a bad one.

On his knees in the dirt, rifling through her things, he

examined the gun and tucked it into the waistband of his black slacks. "I'm going to ask you one more time, sugar. Then I'm going to beat the hell out of you. Where are the goddamn disks?"

Julia ran. She ran blindly, skirting the edge of the cabin, heading toward its back.

A man stepped out, tripped her. She fell spinning, rolled in the sandy dirt, and crashed a hip against the metal trash can.

A gun fired and a bullet whizzed past her head.

"Hey!" a man called out. "What the hell are you doing, Karl?" As he came closer, dry leaves crunched under his shoes. "It's me."

Camden. Dear God, Camden had tripped her. He too wore all black and, buried in shadows, she'd had no idea he was there until she had heard his voice.

Karl rounded the corner, his own gun drawn and aimed at her.

"Hey, this wasn't in the plan." Camden's voice rattled. "You said no one got hurt."

"And you believed him?" Good grief. Even Camden couldn't be that dense.

"No one got hurt. That is what you said, Karl," Camden insisted.

Karl cursed. "Cowards with no guts really piss me off. Especially stupid ones." He lifted the gun, aimed at Camden, and fired.

The impact of the bullet drove the man back, against the outer cabin wall. He crumpled to the ground. Dead.

Dead.

Julia couldn't move. Fear paralyzed her. She needed to run, to get away. Good God, Karl had just killed Camden! But she hadn't seen Jeff—she had to find Jeff—and her damn arms and legs wouldn't work. Nothing would move. *Why wouldn't anything move?*

Karl sighed. "Benedetto isn't gonna like this."

He wouldn't. In fact, it could toss him over the proverbial edge and, over the edge, his desperation would manifest in concrete action. Hostile, criminal, deadly, concrete action.

Something flashed in an arc over her head. It cracked against her skull and pain exploded from her temple to her nape. Before she could life a hand, she was out.

SCRAPE. Swish. Thump.

Hearing the sounds, Julia came to and opened her eyes. She was in a metal coffin, about four feet below ground. Karl stood outside the hole, a shovel in his hand. It scraped the sandy dirt, swished as he dropped it over her, and thumped when it hit bottom.

"You're burying me alive?" Her heart thudding hard against her chest wall, she shook dirt from her face and felt something strange at her nose.

"I wouldn't mess around with that," Karl said. "It's oxygen. You've got twelve hours' worth, sugar."

He couldn't do this. She needed Jeff. He needed the disks. She felt for them, but the disks were gone.

Don't panic, Julia. You can't panic. You need to stay calm. To find Jeff and get him out of here.

"If the info is good, I'll be back for you. If not, then you'll die of oxygen deprivation—just like your favorite little student."

Every muscle in her body clenched at once. Ice-cold fear crippled her, freezing her where she lay. *He'd buried Jeff? The son of a bitch had buried that baby?* "Karl, no! Tell me you didn't. Tell me you haven't hurt that child."

"Buried. Not yet dead, but buried."

"You can't do this!"

But even as the protest left her mouth, another shovelfull of dirt fell over her body, and another. She clutched at the edge of the coffin, tried to pull herself out. She had to find Jeff. God, he had to be terrified. What if he panicked and pulled out the nosepiece to his oxygen? What if he bumped the oxygen bottle and shut it down? What if . . . ?

Oh, God, she had to get out of here. She struggled to

grasp the ledge, but it was slick with sand and moist earth. Her fingers gripped and slid.

"Stop it!" Karl hit her hand with the back of the shovel.

Her knuckles stung. She cried out in pain. "Karl, do this to me, but not to Jeff. He's—he's just a little boy."

"You love him."

The implication that she loved Jeff and didn't love Karl wasn't lost on her. "Please, Karl. I've asked you for few things. Now I'm begging you. Don't hurt Jeff. Please don't hurt Jeff. *Please!*"

"Too late." He dropped another shovelfull of dirt. This one on her head.

Shaking off the dirt, her hand still stinging, she dared to again reach for the edge. She had to get to Jeff. Had to save herself so she could save him.

I'm scared of the dark, Dr. Julia.

She heard Jeff's voice inside her head; a conversation they'd had just after his mother had died.

Bad stuff happens in the dark. People hurt you then. I don't like the dark. I don't like hurting.

Nightmares. She and Jeff both suffered nightmares. Only this nightmare wasn't a dream. They were both awake. And yet her instincts warned it would be the worst nightmare of all.

Her fingers still throbbing, she again stretched, struggled to grab hold, and locked onto the edge of the metal coffin. Pulling hard, she sprang to a squat.

Karl dropped the shovel. "Damn it, Julia." He clutched at her shoulders, shook her, and then shoved.

She fell. Cracked her head against the edge of the coffin. Pain shot through her skull. She ignored it and tried harder, fighting him, determined to survive, to get out of here, to get to Jeff.

One more time, she got her feet under her and scrambled toward the far side of the hole, away from Karl.

He grabbed her hair, jerked, and she lost her footing. His fist collided with her jaw, and she crumpled, falling back into the coffin, seeing stars. Her head fogged. She

shook it, trying to clear it, trying to get rid of the spots
dancing before her eyes. They got thicker . . . and thicker.
Blind rage infused her. She couldn't give in, couldn't give
up. Her left arm useless, she curled on her side and shoved
herself up.

Karl kicked the lid.

She saw it falling, tried to block it with her left arm, but
it crashed down over her.

The lid slammed shut.

Pitch-black darkness surrounded her.

He had won. Once again, she was helpless. And hopeless. Once again, she had failed to protect herself from him.

Resignation, resentment, regret, and self-ridicule spread
and seeped through her every cell.

The dirt spattered atop the coffin, and each pinging
sound brought her a step closer to death.

She'd failed. Again. This time, herself and, God help
her, Jeff.

"I'm so sorry, honey." Tears filmed her eyes. "I'm so
sorry."

*You have to decide how much power you give the
fear . . .*

Seth was right. She had to choose.

And she chose to fight.

She hit the top of the coffin, pummeling it with her fists,
crunched and shoved at the lid with her feet. The weight
of the dirt was too heavy. She scooted, shifted, and finally
turned on her stomach and then tried shoving against the
lid with her back.

It cracked open.

Dirt poured in. She kept going, hoping it didn't bury
her.

You might die, Julia.

She might. But, by God, this time she would die fighting.

Victim no more.

Chapter Nineteen

‎

"WE'VE got an in."

Seth turned from dismantling a timing device's detonator to Colonel Kane. "Where?"

"West." Kane held up a finger, then spoke into his lip mike. "No. Do *not* approach. Repeat, do *not* approach. Follow him." He shoved the mike away from his lips. "Hyde's leaving the cabin."

Seth swiped at the sweat rolling down the side of his face. "What about Julia and Jeff?"

"They're not with him. We're picking up one heat source in the car—Karl."

Matthew walked over. Brittle leaves and twigs crunched under his boots. "Seth, prepare yourself. Paddy's reported hearing gunfire. Two shots."

Julia and Jeff? Seth's heart slammed into his throat. "Let's move in."

THEY couldn't be dead.

They couldn't be. Seth's nerves stretched tight, threatening to snap. Never before on a mission had he hung on to control by such a thin sliver. But never before had Julia and Jeff been involved.

Julia. The woman he had silently loved for five years. The woman he had only kissed and never had made love with, or slept next to, or had Christmas dinner with. He'd never even brought her flowers or told her he loved her. No. No, she couldn't be dead. She couldn't.

And Jeff. He had promised to help Jeff, the kid mentally tortured, emotionally and physically abused, who dared to love, knowing the costs. Who loved through the fear. He loved Seth, damn it. No, Jeff couldn't be dead.

They couldn't be dead. He'd lost his mother, paid for it all his life. He couldn't lose Julia and Jeff, too. Not them, too.

"Colonel Kane," one of the team shouted out. "Over here, sir."

Seth sprinted across the front of the cabin toward the voice. He had heard that specific pitch before, recognized it, but never before had he hated it as much as now. It signaled his worst fear being realized. A body had been found.

Kane squatted low to the ground. Above his head, Seth saw blood splatters on the side of the cabin and stopped cold. Seeing the blood had seemingly rooted his feet to the ground.

Matthew walked over, stood directly in front of Seth, blocking his view and forcing him to look into Matthew's eyes. "Seth, it's not Julia or Jeff," Matthew said firmly. "It's not Julia or Jeff."

Seth heard him, but he was afraid to believe him. Wanting something—*needing anything*—so badly terrified him.

"Seth." Matthew clasped his shoulder, forced him to focus his eyes. "It's Camden. Hyde must have killed him. No .38 does that kind of damage."

Camden? It was Camden. "Where's—" His throat thick, he cleared it, and then tried again. "Where's Julia and Jeff?"

"We haven't found them yet," Matthew said softly. "Julia is here, somewhere. She has to be. She didn't leave with Hyde."

"Maybe she did. Maybe they both did." Just speaking the thought had Seth feeling as if an elephant had stepped on his chest. "Maybe the reason the heat sensor didn't register them was because—"

"No," Matthew insisted. "Their bodies would still be warm. They weren't in the car. Julia's here . . . somewhere."

Barely able to breathe, he did his damnedest to bury his emotions. "What about Jeff?"

"No idea." Regret flooded Matthew's eyes. "We're on Grace PD, but it appears the last sighting was Camden leaving home with Jeff. The bastard pulled some smooth moves and Grace PD lost him. They're deducing Camden brought Jeff to Hyde."

Seth walked up to the body. Camden lay back against the cabin wall, looking as if he had stopped to rest and maybe to do a little stargazing, except for the red staining his shirt and the gaping wound in the center of his chest.

Camden. It really was him. It wasn't Julia or Jeff. And if the bastard wasn't already dead, Seth would've had to kill him. He *brought* Jeff to Hyde?

Breathing easier, now that he had seen for himself, Seth began searching, plowing through the cabin, then through the surrounding grounds, circling out from the cabin, that reported second shot haunting him. On the trail to the lake, loose dirt clung to his shoes. It felt softer, and he slowed down and hit the ground with his flashlight to see why. Tracks. Distinct shoe prints. One person. Dense, heavy. Karl carrying Julia?

Seth followed the path doggedly, skirted a skinned palmetto. Some small animal ran in the undergrowth, scurrying through the darkness and staying out of sight. Seth moved on, following the tracks by the light of the moon and the flashlight.

He saw the shovel first. Its bowl was clumped with dirt. Rushing over, he looked at the ground around it. No leaves. Freshly turned earth. *Jesus, God, the maniac had buried her!*

Lifting his Glock, Seth fired twice into the night sky and then began digging. Frantically, he shoveled at the dirt, and soon others joined him.

Finally, they unearthed the box. Staring at its lid, Seth felt his heart thunder a deafening tattoo.

"Open it up."

He heard Colonel Kane, saw Paddy bend forward.

"No." Seth stepped forward. "I'll do it."

God, but he was terrified at what he would see. She had been buried at least two hours. They'd been searching for what seemed ten times that long. There was no way she could have survived.

Julia, dead? *Dead?* The weight of losing her, of living in a world she was no longer in, crushed down on him. Seth blinked hard. Then blinked again, gripped, and lifted the lid.

Julia sprang out of the box, gasping, clutching at Seth, ripping at the oxygen mask. The canister attached to it dangled and then fell back into the box with a clank.

"Seth!" She clutched at him, wadding huge fistfuls of his camo gear in her hands. "Seth!"

"It's okay, honey." Seth wrapped his arms around her, pulled her to him. His eyes burned, his nose and throat tingled. Julia was alive. *Thank you, God. Thank you.* "It's okay now. Shh, you're okay now."

"No. No!" She backed away, tears washing down her face. Her left arm lay limp, hitched at her side. "He's buried Jeff!"

Every nerve ending in Seth's body sizzled an alert simultaneously. "Where?"

"I don't know." Her knees gave out. "Oh, God, I don't know."

Holding Julia upright, Seth looked at Kane. "You'd better get some more men up here."

Kane nodded. "Already on it."

JULIA tromped around an oak, shoved at a small branch in her path. "Seth, it's been six hours." The branch popped back into place behind her. "He's not here."

"We don't know that, honey." They didn't. Not yet. Not until every inch of ground had been examined.

"I do." She stopped in front of him, watched him swipe at the sweat rolling down his greasepainted face. "I know it, Seth." Hysteria elevated her voice. "Kane and Matthew have half the people assigned to Grayton crawling all over this ground. Jeff is *not* here. I . . . feel it."

Seth couldn't make himself openly agree with her. That would be admitting defeat. Admitting he had again failed to protect someone he loved, someone who loved him. And, if not here, then where was Jeff buried? Where?

Julia reached up to Seth's face, her hand trembling, her eyes red from crying and cold. "We've got to get Kane and Matthew to pick up Karl and force him to tell us where he buried Jeff. If we don't, Jeff is going to die." A sob crawled from her throat. "We can't let him die, Seth."

The pleading in her voice tore at him. "Julia, I'd do anything for you, honey. Anything. But—"

"I know you love Jeff, too. Don't you dare tell me you don't."

"Hell, yes, I love him. I don't deny it." God, but Seth hated to hurt her. It wasn't right. She had been hurt so many times, more times than any one person should have to endure, but he had no choice. Damn it, he had no choice.

"Seth, please."

He cupped her dirt-streaked face in his hands. His throat went thick and every atom in his body rebelled against refusing her. "I can't do it, Julia."

"He's going to die." A huge tear rolled down her cheek.

"God, I hope not. We'll do everything we can, you know that. But we can't pick up Karl. If we do, Benedetto and Morse are going to walk away with the Home Base technology and the Rogue, scot-free. Millions will die, Julia. Millions."

Matthew stepped out of the shadows beside a bush. Its limbs and leaves swished against his thigh. "Seth's right, Julia."

If Matthew had come to find Seth to deliver good news, he would already be relating it. So his news had to be bad. "What's going on?"

"Colonel Kane just got an Intel update. The news isn't good, Seth."

"Jeff?" Julia asked, fear twisting her face.

Seth glided a protective arm around her.

"Sorry. No word on him yet." Matthew shifted his gaze from Julia to Seth. "It's Benedetto. His people have found out about Karl."

Which meant all hell was about to break loose on the Rogue. "Do they know about Jeff?"

"Yes. Benedetto's convinced his council Karl is a new loyalist recruit and he was attempting to reunite him with his wife. That, the loyalists swallowed, since they don't recognize divorce. But they didn't swallow Jeff's kidnapping. Now they're questioning Benedetto's ethics and doubting his ability to protect them."

"Because Morse has failed to get Home Base operational?" Seth asked.

"And because of poor judgment on Jeff, and the drugs."

Julia leaned heavily against Seth for support. "It's only a matter of time."

"Until what, honey?"

She looked up at him. "Until the loyalists find out Benedetto deliberately broke the honor code not for any family but for the technology. He's damned to an emotional downward spiral, Seth. It's inevitable, especially with the drugs altering his perceptions."

Seth followed her line of thought. Benedetto was a trapped rat with no exit strategy that left him upright. He was out of options. "Desperate men commit desperate acts."

She nodded. "Capable of anything." *One breath at a time.*

"There's more," Matthew said. "The last transmission Intel received from the operatives inside Two West projects that Home Base will be operational within forty-eight hours. They're that close."

"But they don't have the launching sequence."

"Evidently, they've come up with one on their own."

Julia braced her forehead against Seth's chest, inhaled

sharply. He tightened his hold on her, knowing exactly what she was thinking because he and Matthew were thinking it, too.

Cornered rats attack.

Julia stared up at him. "Seth, we've got to do something."

"I know." He did know. But the U.S. had no operational missile-defense system and Congress wouldn't fund his damn sensor system. So what exactly could they do? "Let's talk to Colonel Kane."

"NO." Colonel Kane flatly refused, then sent Julia a sympathetic look. "I understand, okay? You love Jeff as if he were your own. I have kids, too, so I really *do* understand. But I can't save one child and jeopardize a nation, and that's what you're asking me to do."

Julia glanced down her mud-streaked arm to her wrist at her watch. Nine hours—that was how long they knew for certain Jeff had been buried. It could be longer. Karl had to have buried Jeff before coming to the cabin. It had to have taken him a couple of hours to wire the area with bricks of C 4, but he could have done that before burying Jeff. When, *exactly,* he had buried Jeff now became critical. Jeff could already be out of oxygen.

Think, Julia. Think!

She licked at her lips. "Colonel Kane, I suggested this before, and I understand why you didn't do it then, but we're out of time. Jeff could be out of time. You've got to check the grounds around my apartment and Seth's house in town."

"Why would Hyde risk that?" Colonel Kane asked. "He'd be exposed in neighborhoods, Julia. Being seen burying a kid in your front yard just doesn't fit his professional profile."

"Oh, but it fits his personal one," she countered. "Karl has always flaunted his superiority over others by dominating them. He builds his power by draining it from others.

He would risk it. He'd get a royal high out of burying Jeff alive right under everyone's noses."

Because that was true, and she once had married him, once even had loved him, venom filled her voice. "He'd see a poetic justice in it. Either place—my apartment, or Seth's house. If Jeff's near my apartment, then Karl's rubbing my face in it. I love Jeff, and his death is my fault. If he's near Seth's, well, Karl always has believed Seth and I were lovers—which we're not, although he still believed it. So it would be Karl's way of punishing me for being unfaithful. He doesn't recognize divorce, either."

"I agree with her, Colonel." Seth stepped to her side, put his arm around her waist. "Either place does fit Karl's personal profile."

Colonel Kane blew out a breath, looked off into the distance, and weighed the matter. "Okay. We'll try it."

Hope lifted in Julia and she gave Seth's hand a squeeze. "Thank you."

Kane nodded and adjusted his lip mike. "Paddy, scramble two teams. Send one to Dr. Warner's apartment to nose around, and the other to Dr. Holt's home in town."

"Let's go, Julia." Seth guided her toward the Camry.

She followed but cast him a frown. "Where are we going?"

"To your apartment." The car door opened with a squeak. "We learn what we can from our abuse and shut out the rest. It's how we survive, right?" When she nodded, he went on. "Something you said about Karl struck one of my shut-outs. My father used to be just like Karl. He never eased up on my mother. Constantly, he proved to her that she deserved being 'punished.' He'd leave her little reminders that she'd forced him to do what he'd done to her. Karl would do that, too. And if he runs as true to form as my father did, he'll do it at your place, not mine. Maximum guilt."

WHEN Julia and Seth arrived at her apartment, the team was already on-site, scouring the grounds with electronic equipment. Heat-seeking sensors, Julia supposed, and only God knew what else.

A dog handler arrived. He had the dog smell Jeff's lunch box, and then turned him loose. Julia grimaced. So many people had handled the box. It would take a miracle for the dog to actually track Jeff from it.

"Dr. Holt?" A sergeant dressed in fatigues came up to Seth. "We've been over every inch of the yard." His forehead filled with creases. "Nothing."

Julia clasped Seth's forearm, urging him to look at her. "He's here, Seth. I feel it."

Seth knew exactly what she meant. His own instincts were screaming it as loudly as if Jeff himself were shouting. "I know."

"Check again," Seth told the sergeant. "The guy who buried him is a trained professional with nothing left to lose. He might not have broken the sod or left the typical evidence. Look for the unusual."

"Yes, sir." The sergeant turned and issued orders to the rest of the team.

Seth looked over at Julia. "You start on the left. I'll take the right. Look for anything, Julia. Anything at all."

Already walking away, she nodded, and Seth watched her go. His heart felt heavy and full at the same time; a damn strange feeling. He had loved three people in his life. One was his mother, and she was dead. Julia was the second, and he had nearly lost her. The third was Jeff.

Jeff, who had chosen to trust Seth above everyone else. Who had hugged Seth, and had sounded so awed and surprised and so damn happy to see him. Jeff, who after being betrayed by his father had shown more courage than most adults, telling Seth the truth about the bruise, and then had shown still more courage by opening his heart and looking into Seth's eyes, and saying, "I love you."

He couldn't lose the boy. He couldn't . . . lose the boy.

Seth turned right, strode past the patio and down the lawn from the lot line to the row of azaleas. He backed into them, stepping between two bushes.

His feet sank down a good six inches.

Seth riveted his flashlight. Broken branches between the two bushes. He swept down to the ground. Wet soil, but freshly turned. Something red. His skin prickled, the little hairs on his neck lifted. Jeff's BAMA key ring. "Jeff? Can you hear me, son?"

No answer.

"Jeff, hold on, buddy. Just hold on." Seth dropped to his knees, began digging with his hands. "Julia!" he shouted. "Over here."

Julia ran the width of the yard, clipped the corner of the house with her right shoulder. Pain streaked down her arm, across her back, but she kept running. "Where are you?"

"Under here." Seth didn't pause digging. Dirt flew out from his cupped hands. "Get help. Get a shovel. I think he's down here."

"You *think*?"

"Damn it, I know, okay?" Seth threw her an ornery look. "I know the same way I know I love you and you love me. Now would you get me a damn shovel?"

"Yeah." A little stunned by his declaration, Julia turned, spotted the sergeant, and yelled her request.

Within half a minute, the dark side of the apartment between buildings was flooded with men and spotlights and the sounds of shovels scraping dirt.

One hit something metallic. "It's here, Dr. Holt."

On his knees, Seth shifted toward the spot. So did Julia. Standing behind Seth, she looked over his shoulder, elated and full of fear. What if it had been too long? What if Karl hadn't left Jeff oxygen? What if . . . ?

"Open the damn thing." Seth's elevated voice proved his fears matched her own.

The lid opened.

And Jeff lay inside, tucked into a tight little ball.

Seth reached in, felt for a pulse. For a second, nothing registered. He swiped the mud caked to his fingertips away, then tried again, pressing his fingertips lightly against Jeff's carotid.

"Seth?" Julia couldn't stand it. Jeff lay so still. So utterly, lifelessly still.

The beat felt more like a flutter. But it was the most beautiful feeling Seth had ever felt. "He's alive, honey." Tears filmed Seth's eyes, choked his voice.

The oxygen mask put out no air. It was only blocking Jeff's breathing. Seth removed it, tossed it on the grass. "Get the medics in here—STAT."

Seth lifted Jeff's little body out of the box, laid him flat on the grass. Julia dropped to her knees at Jeff's head, smoothed his hair back, her smile devastating and devastated.

Seth swiped a finger through the boy's mouth, making sure nothing blocked his airway, gave him a few breaths to jump-start him, and then checked his pupils and his pulse.

It took only moments to see that Jeff was in trouble. Julia sniffed back tears. "Is he breathing okay?"

"A little shallow. Pulse's weak and thready," Seth whispered so only she could hear, then leaned forward, close to Jeff's ear. "Come on, buddy. Come back to us. Dr. Julia's going to have to fit if you go to heaven and leave us here."

A little groan escaped Jeff's mouth.

"That's it, honey," Julia said. "Come on, Jeff. You've got to fight to come back to us." She looked over at Seth. "CPR?"

"No, just a little time." The oxygen canister was nearly empty. Jeff likely had been functioning on diminished oxygen for a short time. Unfortunately, it didn't take long for symptoms to appear. He was slow to come around. But inside, Seth knew the reason wasn't physical. "He needs to know—"

"He's safe," Julia finished, understanding perfectly. She bent low, pressed butterfly kisses to Jeff's muddy forehead. "It's okay, honey. Dr. Seth and I are here. We're always going to be here for you."

Jeff grunted and whispered something she couldn't make out. "What did he say?"

Seth smiled at her, tears shining in his eyes. " 'Promise?' "

She laughed. "I promise, honey." She nuzzled him and reached for Seth's hand. "We both do."

Jeff wiggled his fingertips. They clasped his hands and held tight.

WHILE the paramedics were looking Jeff over, Colonel Kane arrived. "Is he okay?"

"Yeah," Seth said. "They're going to transport him to the hospital for observation, but everything looks fine."

Julia glared at Kane. "When Seth found Jeff, he barely had a pulse."

Though it wasn't her intention, Colonel Kane's tense expression proved he had taken her remark as a backhanded way of saying he should have listened to her earlier. And just scared enough by her own burial and by Jeff's close call, Julia didn't correct him. Maybe next time he would be more open to suggestions.

The medics put Jeff on the stretcher. He looked so tiny. She left Kane and Seth and went to Jeff, clasped his fingertips. "Hey, caught your breath yet?"

"Uh-huh." He looked worried. "Dr. Julia, where's Dr. Seth?"

"He's talking to Colonel Kane, honey. He hasn't left."

"We're ready to transport," one of the medics told her.

Julia nodded.

"No, wait." Jeff's face was pinched with worry. "I need to talk to Dr. Seth first."

"Just tell me, honey."

"Uh-uh. I want Dr. Seth."

Julia felt a twinge of jealousy, and chided herself for it. She hadn't been replaced in his affections, merely dislocated by the man who had protected him from his father and had pulled him out of his intended grave. It was natural. "Seth!" she called out to him. "Come here. Jeff needs you."

Seth ran over and smiled down at Jeff. "What is it, son?"

He crooked a finger, motioning Seth closer, then whispered. "I need to tell you something, but you gotta make Dr. Julia leave. She'll worry."

Seth nodded. "Tell me you're thirsty."

"Huh?"

"Trust me, Jeff."

"I'm thirsty."

Seth turned to Julia. "Honey, could you get Jeff a glass of water? He's thirsty."

One of the medics started to object. Seth silenced him with a glare he couldn't misunderstand.

When Julia moved out of hearing range, he looked back to Jeff. "Okay, spill it, buddy."

"My dad brought me to the mean man. He told me he was sending me to my mom."

Seth felt the familiar rage stir and threaten to erupt. He swallowed it back down. "I'm sorry. But it wasn't your fault, okay?"

"Okay."

"Really, Jeff. It wasn't your fault." Seth clasped his hands. "I have something bad to tell you. I was going to wait, but I think it might be better that you know it now, so you can stop worrying."

"The mean man killed my dad, didn't he?"

Startled, Seth met Jeff's gaze. "How did you know?"

"I just did. In here." He thumped his chest. "Like I knew you'd find me."

"I'm glad I did. Dr. Julia would have been really, really upset."

"She loves me." Jeff looked away, then back at Seth. "You do, too."

"Yes, we do, Jeff."

"Dr. Seth?"

"Mmm?"

Worry flooded Jeff's eyes. "What's gonna happen to me?"

"You're going to go to the hospital, and they're going to watch you for a while and make sure you're okay."

"No, after then?" Jeff blinked hard, wide-eyed and worried.

When it was time to come home. He had no other family. At least, not legally. "I'm not sure how it'll all work out yet."

"I got nobody."

"Wrong." Seth disputed him in no uncertain terms. "You'll always have Dr. Julia and me."

Julia passed the water glass to Jeff. "I'm going to adopt you. Actually, Dr. Seth and I are going to adopt you. You'll live with us."

How could she tell Jeff that? "Julia—"

Her chin set, she glared at Seth. "We'll get a judge to let us adopt you, Jeff."

"What if he won't let you?"

"Now that would be ridiculous, wouldn't it?" Julia grunted. "No one in the world could love you more than we do."

And her tone made it pretty clear a judge would agree or wish to hell he had.

"Promise?"

"Yes, we do," Julia said.

When Seth nodded his promise, too, the worry melted from Jeff's face.

"We need to get him to the hospital." The medic at the head of the stretcher began to move.

Seth backed away.

Julia stepped forward. "I'm coming with you."

Colonel Kane intervened. "No you're not, Julia." He motioned for the medics to go on.

Julia stood, torn.

"Don't even think about going anyway," Colonel Kane warned her. "You could get Jeff killed."

She turned to stare at him.

"Right now, you're both listed MIA."

Missing in action? "Why?"

"The plan calls for you both to stay missing in action," Colonel Kane continued, ignoring her question. "Hyde won't want witnesses, Julia. He'll eliminate them."

The colonel made sense. She didn't like it, but she had to agree with him. Still, she felt torn between being with Jeff and seeing him go to the hospital alone. He had just been buried alive and nearly murdered. And even though Camden had been a bastard, he had also been Jeff's father. Jeff would mourn. Someone needed to be there to comfort him.

"I'll take care of Jeff," Colonel Kane promised. "You have my word on it."

"Okay." Julia glared at him. "But do *not* disappoint me on this. *Please.*"

"I won't."

"So what now?" Seth asked.

"Take Julia to your house. Keeping her under wraps is your domain. Just sit tight and wait."

"For what?" Julia asked, perplexed.

"For Hyde to contact Seth." Colonel Kane frowned. "He'll want to either gloat about your death or to negotiate a deal—the real Home Base data in exchange for your life. Either way, Hyde will call." Colonel Kane's eyes flinted like steel. "When he does, we'll get him."

They would. Provided Seth didn't get to Karl Hyde first.

ANTHONY Benedetto drifted in the warm haze induced by the Xanax. Resting on the sofa in his office, he let his mind wander back to when he was a child and he would rush to his father and share something that would have been insignificant to a grown man but was of consequence to a boy. His father had stopped what he was doing—*always* had stopped what he was doing—to listen to Anthony. And Anthony wanted to talk to his father now. To go fishing with him again. He had been the best speckled-trout fisherman in the world.

Voices. His father?

Anthony twisted his head, cocked an ear. No. Roger. Roger and . . . *Mother?*

"The council knows about the drugs," Roger said.

"They're a legal perscription."

"Yes, but he's not taking them as prescribed, Mrs. Benedetto."

"He's going through a difficult—"

"Yes, ma'am, I know that," Roger said. "Unfortunately, Jason Franklin does, too."

Franklin. Anthony tried to focus. Bernard T. Hostile takeover. Nicholas, his grandson. Abusing the loyalists. Murdered on Anthony's orders. Jason. Jason? Anthony couldn't recall a Jason Franklin, but it didn't matter. Nothing mattered. Not really.

"Who is Jason Franklin?" Anthony's mother asked.

Anthony smiled. Wonderful woman. Always anticipating his needs.

"Nicholas's younger brother," Roger said.

"The same Nicholas who used to take advantage of the factory workers?"

"Yes, Mrs. Benedetto."

The one I had killed, Mother. Anthony shivered. It was a little cool in his office. A blanket would be nice. And a real pillow. He opened his mouth to ask Roger to get them, but his mother's voice stopped Anthony cold.

"Why is the council calling for a special meeting?"

"Drug abuse is expressly forbidden," Roger said. "Franklin is insisting the council call for a vote."

"On what?"

"Electing a new chairman."

"Over my dead body," she said.

Thank you, Mama. Anthony closed his eyes, let his mind drift. All was well. His mother would see to it.

She always saw to everything.

Chapter Twenty

THE bathroom door opened with a distinct creak.

Standing naked under the shower spray, Julia went rigid. "Who's there?"

"Me. Can I come in?"

Seth. *Seth?* Her heart slammed into her throat. She shoved her dripping hair back from her face. *About that affair. I think we should start now.*

Did she want to do this?

It's crazy. You'll be vulnerable again. Didn't you learn anything from Karl?

He's not Karl.

Is any man really that different?

"Julia?" Seth asked from the other side of the shower curtain. "Just say the word and I'm out of here. I thought—" he stammered. "That is—" He faltered again. "When you told Jeff we'd be adopting him, I thought—Well, never mind what I thought. Your silence speaks volumes."

She pulled the shower curtain open. Seth stood naked on the white half-moon rug. The sight of him captured her breath. "You, um, thought what?"

"I thought we'd be . . . together." He looked at her, so solemn and serious. "You know. A . . . family."

She couldn't read him. Why, of all times, did he have to go into statue-face mode *now*? "Is that what you want? To be a family with me?"

The look in his eyes warmed. "Yeah."

Yeah? That's it? That's all he had to say?

It wasn't enough. Not for her, not now. Not after Karl. "Why?"

Seth stared at her a long moment, then, as if he had gotten a fix on her, he stepped into the shower and wrapped her in his arms. "Because I love you, Julia. I've always loved you."

"You have?" *Always?* How could she believe a blanket declaration like that? How could any woman? When they had worked together, he'd never made the slightest over-ture.

You were married. Seemingly happily married. Would you really want a man who came on to you believing you were happily married?

She wouldn't. She lifted her hands, the spray of water hitting her firmly on the back. "Are you sure it's not just for Jeff?" It could be, and she'd understand that totally. Hadn't she asked herself that same thing? Told herself that no judge in his right mind would refuse the two of them adopting Jeff, provided they were married?

Seth pulled her closer, let her feel how much he wanted her. "I'm sure." He rubbed their noses. "I love Jeff, Julia. But I've loved you longer."

His body pressed against hers. She looked up at him and smiled. He was the most amazing man. Gorgeous, head to heel, inside and out, and he loved her. Her, Julia Warner, scarred inside and out. *Scarred.*

She dropped her left arm, held it close to her body to hide the scars on her arm and the ones on her side that ran from her armpit nearly down to her waist.

Seth stared into her eyes, lifted her arm, and looked at her scars. Her face went hot. The ones on her arm were godawful. Just one was seven inches long. Jagged. Ugly.

He kissed it.

Then he kissed the scar on her ribs. And then he kissed her, sweeping her mouth with his tongue, washing her fears right out of her heart. Breathless, she held on, suddenly not feeling scarred and ugly. Suddenly feeling beautiful . . . and desired. Suddenly, desiring.

She wrapped her arms around his neck, pressed her body to his, and kissed him deeply. "I want you, Seth. I never thought I would want to be intimate again. But I do. I want you."

He lifted her to him, kissed her long and deep. "I know this has to be hard."

"Seth, I—"

"Shh, let me finish." He pecked a kiss to the tip of her nose. "For people like us, trust is harder than love. Making love is physical, but it can come from the heart. Then, it's pure and nothing else intrudes. No one else intrudes." He stared deeply into her eyes. "Love me from your heart, Julia. That's how I'm going to love you."

Understanding passed between them, and Julia opened her heart to him, and then her body, and they made love.

When satisfied and still warm in the afterglow, she nuzzled Seth, accepting what he had told her as truth. When you loved from the heart, lovemaking was pure and nonintrusive. And noninvasive. It was a scared time of communion between bodies, minds, and hearts. It was magical, mystical, and marvelous.

She curled her arms around his neck and whispered, "Seth, love me again."

GOOD things come in threes.

Julia had heard that saying all of her life. Today, she had learned the truth in it for fact, firsthand. Loving the feel of Seth with her in bed, she curled closer to his side and rested her head on his shoulder. She had survived. Jeff had survived. And Seth loved her and Jeff.

It was almost too good to believe.

Don't wimp out now, Julia. Not now, when you can finally realize your lifelong family dreams.

God, but she wanted them. Desperately. So scary, that. Needing some serious comfort food, she scooted toward the edge of the bed.

"Where are you going?"

"To the disaster area once tagged your kitchen." Where were her slippers? She touched her toes to the floor along the side of the bed. Matthew'd had someone drop off a suitcase of her "essentials" from the apartment.

"What for?"

"I'm hungry." She checked under the edge, but the slippers weren't there. Maybe she had left them by the sofa.

Seth rubbed at his neck, the sheet scraping against his skin. "Uncle Lou's spaghetti?"

Not surprised by his insight, she admitted the truth. "Yeah."

He braced an elbow and lifted himself. "Tell me you're not sorry about us, Julia."

"No, I'm not." She crawled back in bed and curled up next to him, closing her arm around his side, then stroked him rib to hip. "I'm just scared."

"Me, too." He wrapped his arms around her, took in a sharp breath against her shoulder. "I've never loved anyone else. Not since my mother."

"Think we'll get used to it?"

"It'll take a while, but, yeah. I think so." He stroked her back. "Thought you were hungry."

"I'm too comfortable now to get up."

Hands down, one of the nicest compliments he had ever received. Seth smiled against her hair and, in each other's arms, they drifted back to sleep.

Sometime later, the phone rang.

Without jarring her, Seth reached to the bedside phone and answered it, sounding fully awake. "Holt."

He paused, then said, "No, not a word."

A smile entered his voice. "Tell him we're holding him to it." Another pause, then, "She's fine. Sleeping right now." He sounded relieved by that.

Insecurities crept in. Did he regret them making love? This shift in their relationship? Or was he just glad to see her getting some rest?

Damn it, woman, the man loves you. Don't go destroy-

*ing it by doubting his every move and word. What you're
really doubting is yourself. Your fear is the fear of loving
again. Of being vulnerable and hurt again. It takes courage
to love, Julia.*

It did. God, but it did. She could be crushed.

For God's sake, Seth doesn't crush. He isn't Karl.

She knew it. And she knew it wasn't fair to compare
them. On anything. Ever. Yet it was nearly impossible not
to do it. Viewing everything through your own frame of
reference, your own perspective, was normal. How could
she *not* rely on her own past experience?

*So rely, already. But rely on your experience with Seth.
Only with Seth.*

Seth. He was kind and funny. Caring, honest, and brave.
Courageous, fair, and strong enough to be gentle and to
admit fear. That was Seth. Wounded and struggling to come
to terms with his past as much as she was, and with guilt
he hadn't earned but still carried.

Poor Seth needed Uncle Lou's spaghetti, too.

She rested her fingers on Seth's chest. Stroked him. She
needed a little time to adjust, that was all. Time for her
head to accept all her heart already seemed to understand.
Just a little time.

"Yeah, I'll be in the vault shortly," he said into the
phone. "I've got some work I need to do. Keep me posted."

He hung up, then nibbled at her neck. "I have a message
for you from Jeff."

She opened her eyes and looked at Seth. Light from the
bathroom sliced across his chin and left eye. "What?"

"He says—and I quote—'Tell Dr. Seth and Dr. Julia
they gotta get married and then adopt me cuz the nurse said
that's the only way it's legal and nobody can change it.' "

Julia's heart drummed. "How do you feel about that?"

He drew in a slow, deep breath, and caressed her arm.
"I love you, Julia."

His eyes said more. Far more. And she loved what she
was hearing and seeing. "I want a house on a few acres. I
don't like crowds anymore," she warned him. "I'm bitchy

as hell early in the morning, and sometimes I like to just sit and be still. Not do anything, not say anything. Just . . . be."

He bit back a smile. "I don't snore, cheat, lie, and I swear to God, I'll never raise a hand to you."

"I'm going to hold you to that." Her voice sounded steady, but inside she trembled. "And if you ever do—"

"I'll shoot myself to spare you the trouble." He lifted a hand. "I promise."

He would. She knew it wasn't idle talk but a sacred vow. "Seth, I know when your dad went to prison and you went through all those foster homes, you learned to be self-sufficient."

"More like self-contained."

She had become that way with Karl. "I learned not to need anyone or anything from anyone, too. And it worked fine, until you and Jeff came along. It's scary, Seth. I need to know it's not all one-sided. I know Jeff needs me, but do you?"

"Oh, yes. Definitely. Always." He sat down beside her on the bed. "I still have trouble showing it, but I'm working on it. You'll have to help me, Julia."

"I will, if you'll help me, too."

"Deal."

"Deal." She pecked a kiss to his lips and stroked his face. "I still have a hard time visualizing you in Special Forces. It didn't surprise me; I'm just used to seeing you in a lab coat."

"I saw myself in the lab coat, too, which is why I made the shift. Research and development has always been my professional first love. I still have this vision of creating something that will finally assure peace. It's an idealistic pipe dream, but—"

"So was electricity, the telephone, and personal computers until someone did them, Seth." She hugged him and planted a kiss to the salty skin on his neck. "I like your dream, and I hope you never give it up."

"I can't give it up." he said, satisfaction in his tone. "I'm a family man now. Everything is . . . different."

More at stake, more at risk, more to lose—personally. "Yeah." She pecked a kiss to his neck. "I want to tell you some things, so you understand me better."

"Okay."

"In the kitchen that night, when I got so upset—"

He'd reached over her to get the paper towel. "I remember."

"Karl always attacked me from behind. I get a little freaky when someone sneaks up on me, so let me know you're coming, okay?"

"I will." Seth laced their fingers.

"For a long time, I was kind of like a prisoner. Breakfast had to be ready at precisely seven A.M. If it was late, Karl would take my plate and put it in the sink, and run water over it to ruin the food. When he went to work, he would take the phone with him, so I couldn't call anyone, and when I got home from work, he'd check the mileage on my car. If I was a tenth of a mile over, I had to have a receipt or some documentation to explain the difference and where I had been."

"Damn, Julia."

"I know. It was crazy. But it happened gradually, and I thought it must be my fault because normal husbands didn't act that way. Finally, I saw the light, and I found a way out. It was a rough exit, but I survived it. It's not easy to remember these things, much less to talk about them, but it's important. You need to know I'm never going to be anyone's prisoner again."

"Damn right you're not."

"I know you're not him, okay?" She gave Seth a bittersweet smile. "But sometimes—if just for a second—at least for a while, I'm probably going to forget. When I do—"

"I'll understand." Seth hugged her hard. "Julia, I *will* love you enough to make you forget the bad times."

"No, I can't forget them and neither can you. We can't outrun our pasts, and we shouldn't try. If we forget, we open ourselves up to letting it happen again. As hard as those experiences were to get through, we learned valuable lessons from them. We learned what not to do and how to be strong enough to build good lives in spite of them. I want Jeff to know that, too. That he can thrive in a loving home. I want us all to have that."

"We will," Seth promised.

They talked for over an hour, and Julia saw a side of him she felt sure no woman before her had ever seen: Seth's soul. He opened up his most secret self and laid it before her, trusting her completely. Her heart filled and, and, feeling tender and poignant, she reached for him. They made slow, sweet love, and then Julia slipped into a restful sleep.

Sometime before dawn, Julia missed his warmth, and awakened. "Seth?"

"Right here, honey." Dressing in the shadows, he stepped into a pair of Dockers. Tugged on a shirt.

"Where are you going?" She glanced at the clock. "It's not even daylight."

"Karl hasn't called."

"He's not going to call." She wadded up the covers. "I tried telling you and Matthew and that hardheaded Colonel Kane that, but none of you would listen."

Seth sat down on the bed, stroked her hair. "I'm listening now." Loving the smell of her hair, he bent low, pressed a kiss to her neck. "Why won't he call?"

"He decided to kill me after all, Seth. We both know it now." She turned over, sat up, dragging the cover with her, and then tucked the sheet under her armpits, over her breasts. "He has no reason to call."

"He thinks you're dead."

"Yes. And that means you know it. He knows you know. That's enough."

"What about the right Intel on Home Base?"

"Jeff and I are both dead. Karl has no leverage to use against you to get it. Morse sure isn't going to go toe to toe with him and expose his involvement."

"You could be right." Seth brushed her sleep-tossed hair

back from her eyes. "I'm going out to the base."

"Why?"

"To work on my sensor."

"Now?" She sounded shocked, but damn it, she was shocked.

"You're safe here. Matthew has men watching the house."

It wasn't that. "Why now, Seth?"

He stared at the curtained window a long second. "Gut instinct," he said, turning his gaze to her. "I need to run simulator studies on my sensor. We're going to need it, Julia."

"We don't have it available."

"Yes, honey, we do. I've done a prototype. But I don't know—"

"You haven't even done simulator studies. Seth, honey, how can you even consider implementing this without so much as the simulator studies?"

"I'm going to do the studies now," he said. "Look, if Intel is accurate on this—and Matthew swears by all that's holy, it is—then Benedetto's beyond desperate. The loyalists found out about Karl burying you and Jeff and they're holding Benedetto personally responsible."

Julia's heart ricocheted off her ribs. "He'll attack soon."

"Yeah, he will." Seth pressed a kiss to her forehead. "Which is why I have to move fast and pray hard my technology is solid. If he launches the Rouge, it's our only defense."

"What will it do?"

"What Home Base can't—I hope."

Julia kicked off the covers and slid out of bed.

Seth stared at her. "What are you doing?"

"I'm going to help you."

Seth stood up, gripped her firmly by the shoulders. "You can't."

"I have to. The two of us can accomplish far more—"

"Julia, you're missing. Just like Jeff. I'm not exposing you to more danger."

"Instead you'll let half the country get torn up?"

"No. I'll handle it. Just cooperate, okay?"

"Can you handle it?"

"Yes. The studies, I can do alone."

"Okay. For now, you go alone." She dropped back onto the bed. "But if you see that it's close and you need help, you'd better bring me in, Seth."

"I will." He kissed her hard and quick, then headed for the door.

"Seth?"

He stopped and looked back at her.

"I mean it. If you let me sit here and die without you, I'll be mad at you forever."

She didn't want to die without him. She loved him. She hadn't gotten involved with him just for Jeff. She hadn't yet given him the words, but Seth knew how hard that could be. When she felt she could, then she would say them. And God, but he hoped that would be soon. He'd waited a lot of years to hear them. "I refuse to die without you."

"Promise?"

"You sound like Jeff."

"Where do you think he got it? Now, promise me. Yes, or no?"

"I promise." Unable not to, Seth smiled. "You know, I think it's going to be easy loving you."

"Hold that thought."

"For how long?"

"Oh, I don't know. A couple of lifetimes should do it." Her expression turned saucy. "And don't think you'll always get your way by giving me that sexy look."

"How long will I get away with it?"

"Truthfully?"

He nodded.

"Maybe a lifetime." She wagged a warning finger at him. "But just one."

Yeah, she loved him. She really did. "I think I'd better watch myself or I'll be the one in trouble here."

* * *

RUNNING the simulator studies had been low priority. Now, every instinct in Seth's body shouted they were a crisis priority.

He worked through the rest of the morning, through lunch, and on into the afternoon, pausing to attend a progress-report briefing with the team, less Mr. Sandlis and Marcus, and to listen to Linda lecture him on the benefits of having a well-rested mind when dealing with five thousand pounds of explosives on bombs-in-the-making. What didn't surprise him was Dempsey Morse cornering Seth at the water fountain. God, how Seth wished they had enough hard evidence to nail his ass to the wall now.

"Julia hasn't shown up again today," Morse said, sounding tense and wary.

Seth took a long, cool drink. "Has she called in?"

"No. No one's heard from her." Morse darted his gaze. "Can we talk a second, in the conference room?"

The most secure place in the inner lab. "Sure." Seth walked over, entered the conference room, and then took a seat. "What's up?"

"It's Julia." Morse sat down across from Seth. His forehead wrinkled in a frown and he folded his hands over his round belly. "I know you've worked with her before and you have a lot of respect for the woman, but, well, frankly, I'm concerned."

The son of a bitch was going to tag Julia with the blame for the breaches. "About what?"

"We've had more than a few . . . oddities . . . around here, and all of them have happened since Julia took over the project." He couldn't hold Seth's gaze. "I have to be careful here. You know Slicer has millions invested in Home Base. Protecting its interests is my number one priority."

"A successful project is your number one priority, Dempsey," Seth countered. "Without that, you've flushed your millions."

"True." He nodded his agreement. "But I'm worried

about her sudden absence. Something could be wrong."

"What do you recommend we do?"

"I think we should contact the OSI."

The guy was a real piece of work. Seth leaned back in his chair. "If we call the OSI on an absent employee, we could look like total fools."

"Why?" Dempsey shrugged. "She's not a regular absent Dod employee. She's Black World."

"She also has a history of leaving without notice or warning." Seth gauged Morse's reaction. The damn fool didn't bother to hide his relief that Seth had rejected the wisdom of contacting the OSI. Serious, serious tactical error. "If she's just taken a couple of days off and we report it, then she gets fired and we look like idiots. We can't afford that. Who's going to continue to fund a project run by idiots?"

"Good point." Morse stood up, began pacing alongside the conference table, end to end. "She's put us in a compromising position. We report it, and we look like idiots. We don't report it, and her absence turns out to be involuntary, then the OSI is going to cut us up into little pieces and feed our livers to Colonel Pullman and the brass at the Ballistic Missile Defense Organization."

Seth fed Morse's fears. "Higher headquarters would take us not filing the report personally. They've become real sticklers on security since the Los Alamos incident. We're still dealing with the fallout. And you should know that Colonel Mason's already threatened to take any discrepancy directly to the JCS."

At the mention of the Joint Chiefs of Staff Morse paled.

Relieved to see it, Seth went on. "Bottom line is, if some hostile is responsible for her absence and we haven't reported it, then we're guilty by association. We'll do time in Leavenworth, no doubt about it. So, do we risk it?" Seth shrugged. "It's your call, Dempsey."

"I don't know." Morse paced faster and faster. "I'm just not sure."

"Make the call, Dempsey."

He stopped, stared at Seth. "I say we wait a while. See if she shows up."

Delay was one tactic, Seth supposed. Morse was looking for a way to pin Julia's absence on Karl. But he wasn't supposed to know Karl existed, so that threw a wrench in the works. One Morse should have already worked out and hadn't. Evidently, he had planned on Karl being caught red-handed, which kept Morse uninvolved. Now, Morse expected Seth to investigate Julia's absence, which would again keep Morse totally on the outside. A piss-poor plan, but since the matter was academic anyway, why not let him delay? "Waiting a while works for me."

"I'm heading out," Morse said, rubbing his stomach. "Think I'm getting Marcus's flu."

"Keep in touch."

Morse left the conference room moving double time. He was definitely the project mole working for Benedetto, but he was also either a lousy strategist, or he was in the dark on the Hyde facet of Benedetto's strategy. Seth's instincts shouted it was the latter. Morse recruited Karl. Benedetto arranged for Karl's release from prison and struck a side deal with him. Morse didn't know about Jeff's kidnapping and the burials. If obtaining information from Julia by force failed, then Karl would take the fall for the ethics breach, insulating Benedetto and Morse. At least until Benedetto was through with Morse. Then he'd have to die. Benedetto couldn't risk letting Morse live.

Thoughtful, Seth went back to his office and dialed the phone. "Agent 12, please."

"One moment, Dr. Holt."

Mrs. Anderson. Seth recognized her crisp voice.

"Don't you ever sleep?" Matthew grumbled. "I close my eyes for the first time in thirty-four hours and you call. This had better be good, Seth."

"Morse just paid me an exploratory visit about Julia's absence. He's definitely our man."

"We've already determined that."

"Yeah, we have. Now, we've confirmed it."

"So what's your point?"

"I don't think he knows about Karl burying Julia and Jeff." Seth had second thoughts. "Actually, I don't think he knows about Karl at all."

"You sure?"

"It makes sense. Benedetto needs data from Julia. Julia fears Karl. Benedetto gets Karl out of jail to get the data." Seth twiddled a pencil on his blotter.

"Logical, so far," Matthew said.

"It stays logical." Seth stared at the dimpled ceiling. "If the loyalists find out about Karl burying Julia and Jeff—which we now know they have—then Karl takes the fall. A new loyalist who doesn't make the grade. Honor code breach insists on Karl's death. Benedetto has Karl killed, keeping with the code, and he stays protected. He can't blame Morse for bringing Karl into Two West; he needs him to get Home Base up and running. This way, if Karl fails, Morse is protected—until his services are no longer required."

"There's value in telling Morse. Hyde switched cars at a Winn-Dixie grocery store about half an hour ago. We lost him."

He was a pro. A capable, skilled one, to have outmaneuvered Matthew's men. "Does Julia know?"

"No. Colonel Kane's orders. She's stressed to the max."

"He's been reading the Intel reports on her."

"Yeah," Matthew said. "But the two operatives watching her know Karl's on the loose. They're prepared."

Seth had mixed feelings about that, but Julia *was* already stressed to the max. Should Seth give her a heads up, anyway? "We could let Benedetto lead Morse to Hyde."

"The risks are too high."

The news kept getting worse and worse. "Benedetto's a loose cannon already, eh?"

"Worse than you can imagine. He's losing it, Seth. The profilers are going crazy, trying to figure out what he's going to do next. The drug abuse only makes their job harder."

Seth grimaced. Stared through the glass wall at Cracker working the computer. Benedetto's next move was decidedly easy to figure, regardless of the drugs. "He's going to launch the Rogue."

"We'd better hope not."

"It's coming. Bank on it."

"Why are you so sure?"

"He's an addict on the edge with firepower and a lot to prove—to us, and his loyalists—and even more to hide. His best bet is to bury his skeletons in rubble, Matthew."

"Crunch time."

"Yeah, crunch time." Karl hadn't died as a result of the operation, as planned. The truth that Benedetto had recruited him would come out. Benedetto knew he was damned to die—by the loyalists' hands or his own—and he wasn't going to die alone. He was going to take as many people with him as he possibly could. "Is Jeff okay?"

"He's fine. Beating the socks off Colonel Kane at poker."

Seth blinked hard. "Kane's pulling duty watching Jeff?"

"Yeah, his wife, too. He promised Julia."

Seth understood. The man felt honor bound to personally keep Jeff safe. And he felt a little guilty for not listening to Julia sooner and checking out the apartment earlier. When he couldn't be there, his wife would. They relied on each other, like Seth and Julia.

"Keep me posted, Matthew. I've got some more work to do before I check out of here." Seth hung up the phone and went back to his simulator studies, hoping to hell he had gotten the technology right because, from all indications, he wasn't going to have much time to make any adjustments before he needed the system to be operational.

With Benedetto crumbling, Seth might have no time at all.

ANTHONY had a hangover. He'd never had a hangover before, and he wasn't finding the experience pleasant. His head hurt, his eyes ached, and his stomach felt queasy. It was the drugs.

After hearing his mother and Roger discussing the council electing a new chairman, he had quit the pills. Cold turkey. God, but he'd been sick. Now, he was just hung over. Maybe if he took just one, he would feel well enough to do what he had to do.

He couldn't wait much longer.

Opening his desk drawer, he pulled out the bottle and took out one oblong pill. Kind of pink. He popped it into the back of his throat and dry-swallowed.

Within a few minutes, he began to feel better. Not good, but better. It was time to deal with their friend from Grayton. Except for an obligatory progress-report briefing at the base, he had been in the Two West lab nearly around the clock. That the United States DoD was paying him sick leave while the man was here, working in his lab, amused Anthony in ways little else these days could.

Elise had threatened to leave him and file for divorce.

His daughter hid from his sight.

His mother called him a disgrace to his father's memory.

Anthony looked at his father's photo. They were all wrong, of course, and he was about to show them just how wrong. Them and that mouthy bastard, Jason Franklin. Anthony dialed their lab.

Finally, their friend from Grayton answered. He sounded harassed and irritable. "Yes, what is it?"

Anthony was irritable himself. "I need to see you in my office immediately."

"That's not possible. Not now. I'm at a crucial point—"

"Make it possible," Anthony insisted. "We need a Plan B. Plan A's been blown to hell and back."

"I'm sorry to hear that."

"You'll be even sorrier if your ass is parked in Leavenworth for forty years."

"I'm on my way."

Anthony hung up the phone. Plan B was drastic. But he was desperate. Everything was fading away. He didn't know how to be anything other than the chairman of Two West Freedom Coalition. He had prepared for this role his entire life, and he was losing it.

Plan B would bring it all back. Stronger and better.

He gave his father's photo a wink. "Stronger and better."

Chapter Twenty-one

~~

"POKER?" Julia pulled the phone away from her ear and stared at the receiver.

"Yeah, but it's okay," Jeff quickly assured her. "We're playing for throat sticks, so Colonel Kane says it ain't illegal."

"Isn't illegal."

"That's what I just said."

Julia grabbed a dishtowel and swiped at water droplets puddling on the rim of Seth's kitchen sink. She had been cleaning for hours and the place still looked as if a tornado had hit it. "What do you mean, throat sticks?"

"The things the doctor shoves down your throat before you get the sucker."

"Ah." Tongue depressors. Julia smiled. "So are you okay there?"

"Yeah. But I'm ready to go outside."

Julia stopped wiping and leaned against the cabinets, stared sightlessly out the window at the sunshine. "I know." Being buried in darkness with nothing but fear for company created a powerful yearning for open spaces, light, and fresh air. "It won't be long."

"Dr. Seth told me." Jeff asked uneasily, "Dr. Julia?"

The worry in his voice pulled hard at her heartstrings. He needed now what he had needed since his mother's death. He needed peace. And come hell or high water, when this Benedetto/Karl Hyde matter was resolved, Jeff was going to get it. She and Seth would see to it. "What, honey?"

"Do you think my dad's burning in hell?"

That question she hadn't expected. But Jeff's distress came through loud and clear. He was mourning, and worried. "What do you think?"

"I dunno."

"Remember your talk with Dr. Seth about your mom, honey, and then tell me what you think."

Jeff paused a long moment, working through his thoughts and feelings. "I think, even if you do something very bad, God still loves you," Jeff said. "So I don't think Dad's burning. I think he's maybe in detention."

Detention. Julia smiled. "You could be right."

"Yeah." Jeff's tone lightened. "He's just getting yelled at for what he did. God'll let Dad go to heaven after he gets it."

"After he gets what, Jeff?"

"That he did bad things."

Camden had to know what he did was wrong and yet she had heard him herself. "He didn't know anyone would be hurt, Jeff. I heard him tell the mean man so."

"Is that when Dad got shotted?"

"Shot," she automatically corrected him. "Yes, it is. He didn't want anyone hurt." Camden had to realize there was a chance of it, though. But Jeff didn't need to hear that, or to be forced to deal with it, too. Not now. Maybe never.

"What if he did want someone hurt?"

Camden had said something to Jeff. She propped her hand on her hip, the dishtowel dangling against her side. "Do you think he did?"

"Yeah, but he probably didn't really mean it."

"You mean, he only thought he meant it when he said it, right?"

"Right."

"Well, I think God would take that into consideration. We all say things we don't mean at times."

"Yeah, and He loves us no matter what." Jeff sounded relieved. "I'm sure he's just in detention."

"Yeah," she agreed. "Me, too."

"I gotta go. Colonel Kane says it's time for me to deal. I don't much like it. The cards are slick and they fall all over the place, but we can't go outside to play football."

Smiling into the receiver, Julia ripped a paper towel from the holder, mounted under the cabinet, then swiped at the stovetop, marveling at Jeff. Here she was still a bundle of nerves, skittish about every creak and bump, and he was together enough to play cards and wanting to play football. "When everything's okay, Travis can come over and play ball with you. You be good, okay?"

"I will." He paused, then whispered, "I love you, Dr. Julia."

He didn't want the guys to hear. "I love you, too."

She cradled the receiver on the wall, then tossed the paper towel into the trash. The bag was nearly overflowing. And it smelled.

Wrinkling her nose, she pulled the bag from the bin, tied its top, and then headed to the back door. Moving the chair blocking it, she clasped the knob and hesitated. Seth didn't have locks on the doors here, either. Apprehensive, her stomach knotted. Karl was still on the loose. Being watched and tracked, but loose. Still out there, and still coming after her.

Matthew's profilers insisted Karl had buried her and that signaled he was through with her. But Julia knew better, and she knew Karl Hyde far too well to be duped into believing that he had buried and then forgotten her. Not him. He didn't want a pound of flesh. He wanted *every* pound of her flesh *and* her blood and bones. And he wouldn't stop until he got all he wanted any more than he would have buried her and not gone back. He had gone back—if only to gloat over her body. And from all the activity, he had to know she was no longer in her intended grave.

He could be outside Seth's house right now.

She looked through the window, but saw only the unmarked car parked two doors down. Matthew's men. She spotted them, and Karl would, too. And with his training, he would know how to get around them.

Obviously, Matthew still felt she was at risk. Otherwise, why would he waste the manpower of having her guarded? Morse was hardly capable of coming after her himself. Oh, he had motive. Definitely, he had motive. But if he got caught, he would lose Slicer Industries and be arrested. Foolish move, and he was not a foolish man.

Karl and Morse are being watched, their every move monitored. So why are you terrified to go outside to put a bag of trash in the can? Damn it, Julia, you can't live your life fearing everything. You can't give anyone that kind of power over you.

Julia grimaced at the door, glanced back over her shoulder to the bar. Her purse lay atop it. A new .38 was in it, loaded, and ready for use. Matthew's OSI agents were watching the house. Others were watching Morse and Karl. There were no signs or sounds of trouble outside. She was safe.

She cranked the knob, walked across the patio to the concrete pad upon which the trash can sat, and then lifted the lid and dropped in the bag.

Something scraped the concrete behind her. Before she could react, Karl jumped her from behind, grabbed her left arm, jerked, and twisted it behind her back, shoving it up toward her shoulder blade.

Blinding pain seared her. Julia saw stars. Her stomach heaved, and she broke into a cold sweat. In her mind she screamed, but the sound leaving her throat barely registered as a whimper.

"You blew it, sugar." Karl pulled her arm up higher.

Wrenching spasms racked through her shoulder, bolted down to her fingertips. Her left arm was useless.

Compensate. Use your feet and legs, Julia. Use your feet and legs!

Seth's voice. Yes. Yes. *Victim no more.*

She twisted into Karl, shoved, and kicked, aiming for his groin. Her foot connected with his body. He stumbled backward, bent double, clutching himself, groaning, and cursing her.

Julia ran for the door. Grabbed a chair and tried to wedge it under the knob.

Karl's reddened face appeared in the door's glass panel. He twisted the knob and shoved with his shoulder.

Julia slid backward. Her spine collided with the corner of the bar. Pain streaked through her back, down her arms and legs. She saw her purse. The gun.

She didn't want to kill anybody.

It's kill or be killed, Julia. Choose.

Snatching at her purse, she fumbled for the gun. If she could fire it, then Matthew's men would hear the shot. She didn't have to kill Karl, only to fire the gun. *If she could get the damn thing out of her purse!*

The wooden door slammed back against the wall and cracked, hanging loose on its lower hinge. Karl bulldozed through, coming at her.

Terrified, she fumbled, dropped the bag onto the floor, and she dove for it. Karl got there first. The pain in her arm and shoulder doubled, blinding her. Knowing she couldn't use her feet—he'd be expecting that now—she rammed into him. He barely moved, but he dropped her purse.

In a tangle of arms and legs, they thrashed on the floor. His cursing roared in her ears. The spasms in her arm and shoulder tightened, remaining constant, compounding and inching up her neck. She had to do something. *Now.* Or he'd kill her. She scrambled, screamed, and this time, there was sound. Shrill and earsplitting, it pierced her pain, and startled Karl.

She got the bag, the gun, and it slid easily from her purse. She dropped the handbag. Its contents spilled, and a tube of lipstick rolled across the floor. Change spilled from her wallet and clanged dully against the tile.

Julia whipped around, aimed for Karl's chest, and watched the fight drain out of his face.

"What? The little girl's gonna shoot me?" He grunted.

"Don't come any closer." Shaking, running on sheer adrenaline, she gained her feet, took her two-handed aim.

Surprise flickered through Karl's eyes.

Victim no more.

"So he's taught you how to shoot, eh?" Karl taunted her, but he didn't move.

He was afraid of her. Karl Hyde was actually afraid of her. The truth hit her suddenly, settled over her slowly. "I'm good at it, too."

"Knowing how to pull a trigger doesn't mean you've got the guts to kill a man."

"It doesn't take guts to kill you, Karl. You'd better pray to God that I have the courage to let you live." She met his gaze, swearing she would rather die than to be his victim one more time. She'd rather face anything than that. Anything. "I wouldn't bet a nickel on it myself. I look at you, and I see a bastard who tried to feel like a strong man by beating up on me. I see a bully with no discipline or self-control. A weak shell of a human being with no honor and no respect. I see you for what you really are, and every time I see you, I remember what you did to me. I relive every single slap, punch, and kick, Karl. You have no idea what that's like, do you? No idea how much it hurts or how angry it makes you." She swallowed the thickness from her throat. "Trust me"—she cocked back the hammer—"I can kill you. My fear is in letting you live."

Sweat beaded on Karl's forehead, above his upper lip, and fear seeped into his eyes.

"That's right." She didn't dare relax. Didn't dare to show him that her knees felt like water and her arm cramped so badly she swore it was about to fall off. "I'm not afraid of you anymore. I'll never be afraid of you again."

She inched back, against the counter. "It's a big decision—whether or not to shoot you. I should. My hell would end instantly. If I don't shoot you, then you could nag me the rest of my life. God knows, you've tried often enough to kill me."

He lifted a hand. "It wasn't personal, Julia."

"The hell it wasn't. Who do you think you buried in that grave?" She guffawed, glared at him. "You kidnapped and nearly killed a precious little boy you didn't even know just to get back at me, and you dare to tell me it's not personal?" Seeing red, she raised the gun, clamped her jaw. "I *should* kill you for that. For what you did to Jeff."

You're losing it, honey. Seth's voice. *Calm down. He's looking for an opening to attack you. If you shoot him, shoot to kill.*

What would Jeff think of that?

"Okay, okay. I lied." Karl huffed. "Don't blow a gasket."

Death or jail. Do what you have to do to stay safe and let go of what he did to you, Julia. He's taken everything from you once. Don't give him any more. It's our turn. Yours, mine, and Jeff's.

She tipped the barrel ceilingward and pulled the trigger three times in quick succession. Karl instinctively hit the ground, clutching at his chest.

Julia watched him wallow on the floor, feeling a giggle threaten her throat. A totally inappropriate response—to giggle. Ridiculous. Nerves, she figured. Had to be nerves.

Karl tested his chest with his fingertips, seemingly amazed to find them bloodless. "You didn't shoot me."

Where the hell were Matthew's guards? "Given a choice, I've decided you're not worth the bullet. But push me, and you'll be a corpse." She motioned with the gun. "Get up."

Julia led him to the bathroom and locked him inside. Bracing a chair under the doorknob, she silently swore that when she married Seth Holt, he was damn well going to have to get used to having locks.

She grabbed her cell phone and called the lab.

Seth answered. "Dr. Holt."

"It's me," she said. "You'd better get home."

"I'm right in the middle of the simulator study—"

Julia snapped. "Karl Hyde is camping out in the bathroom as we speak, Seth. I debated killing him, but I didn't want to have to mop the damn floor again. Now, are you coming home, or do I need to call Matthew to get rid of this guy?"

"He got into the house?"

"He sure did." She kept an eye on the hallway leading to the bath. Karl had a penchant for attacking from behind, but he wasn't going to get the chance. Not this time.

"Where are Matthew's men?"

"Good question. Why don't you call and shout at Matthew and stop shouting at me, because I don't have a clue, and I don't like the yelling."

"I—I'm sorry."

"To hell with sorry, just get home." The adrenaline rush was subsiding fast and it was all that was keeping her frayed nerves together. "He moves and I'm shooting him, Seth. We'll have to find another way to get Benedetto. I mean it. I swear, I do."

"Three minutes. That's all I need."

Matthew arrived in two. He hit the pavement running, and nearly paused at the car where his two men had been stationed. *Empty.* Where the hell were they? He started shouting. "Julia!"

She opened the front door. "Karl's locked in the bathroom. I don't know what happened to your men."

"Are you okay?"

"I hurt like hell, Matthew," she said honestly, watching more and more of Grayton's Security Police cars arrive.

"Is Karl armed?"

"I don't know. I don't think so, or he would have challenged me when I aimed the gun at him."

Matthew walked down the hall, drew his own gun. "Hyde, I want you to come out of there, nice and slow. Arms behind your head. Hell, you're a cop. You know the drill."

Silence.

"Do it now, Hyde."

Julia's nerves sizzled. "Careful, Matthew. He's up to something."

"Hyde, I'm counting to three."

Seth came up behind Julia. "He's not there."

"Yes he is." Julia frowned. "I locked him in, Seth."

He didn't quite meet her eyes. He didn't have to; the sinking feeling in her stomach said it all. Julia slumped back against the wall. There were no locks. On the doors, or on the windows.

A man dressed in camouflage gear cleared his throat to let them know he was there. Matthew looked back at him. "What is it, Paddy?"

"Cramer and Thurston, sir." His grim expression mirrored his tone. "We found them."

"The guards watching the house?" Seth speculated.

Matthew nodded and cursed softly.

"What?" Julia looked from Seth to Matthew and then back to Seth.

He let his head loll back, paused and swallowed hard, then met her gaze. "They're dead, Julia."

"I'm moving you both to a safe house."

Matthew said it before she could openly react, but not before guilt that these men had died while guarding her assaulted Julia. She slumped against Seth.

"Not necessary, Matthew. Karl won't be back," Seth said. "Not here."

"You're being stupid."

"Look, Hyde's a coward. A sorry-assed, woman-beating, kid-burying coward. He won't be back. Not while I'm here. He takes out Julia and me, and he's got no one left around to grieve."

Matthew slid Seth a what-the-hell-are-you-talking-about look. But Julia understood perfectly. "I want to see the men."

"That's impossible. They're off-limits until after forensics completes its investigation, Julia."

"Don't protect me." Julia looked Matthew right in the

eye. "I know I'm responsible. I have to see them."

"You're not responsible," he insisted.

"They died guarding me."

"Yes, they did. Because they relaxed and got sloppy," Matthew said. "They were professionals. They knew their jobs and the risks and considered them worth taking."

"They died for me," she stubbornly insisted.

Seth turned to her, gripped her by the shoulders. "Yes, they died guarding you. But the reason they were here had nothing to do with you personally. It had to do with the job. The ideals."

Like Benedetto's loyalists. Tears brimmed in her eyes. "To-the-death dedication?"

Seth nodded.

"It's a hell of a way to find out that, eligible for food stamps or not, your side measures up."

"Yeah." He rubbed her arms, shoulders to elbows. "Yeah, it is."

THE council was there.

In his house. In his own house, talking about him.

They knew that hellhound Hyde had buried Julia and Jeff. And they were holding Anthony responsible. *You have no honor, Anthony . . .*

He looked around the Green Room, made eye contact with each of the seventeen, and let his gaze stop on Jason Franklin, who was addressing the council. He looked disciplined, sounded authoritarian. Dangerous combination— for Anthony.

"Considering the flagrant violations," Franklin said, turning his gaze to Anthony, "I don't see how the council can request any remedy short of your resignation."

Anthony's blood ran cold. From the corner of his eye, he checked Roger's reaction. It had always been an excellent gauge of the council climate.

Stone-cold remote. Roger agreed with them.

"Shortly, you'll understand that things are rarely what they seem," Anthony said. "And that asking me to step down is not in the coalition's best interests."

"I beg to disagree," Franklin said.

"You would." Anthony put an empathetic edge on his tone. "Understandable, considering the circumstances. But within twenty-four hours, even you, Mr. Franklin, will grasp the truth." Anthony looked away, to the other members. "Is twenty-four hours an unreasonable request from a man who has devoted his life to serving you?"

The council members mumbled among themselves and finally agreed to the wait. Then they departed.

Roger followed Anthony to his office. "Mr. Benedetto, what happens within twenty-four hours?"

"Armageddon." Anthony dismissed Roger, then lifted the phone and dialed the lab. When their friend from Grayton got on the line, he issued the order. "Activate Plan B."

"Seriously?"

"It's that or Leavenworth."

"Yes, sir."

Anthony hung up the phone, opened his desk drawer, and pulled out the prescription bottle of pills. He started at the bottle and then gave it a little shake. About sixty or so tablets, he estimated.

He poured himself a glass of water, put his father's photo directly in front of him on the desk, and then swallowed down the pills, one by one, reliving all the high points of his life. His happiest moments, greatest triumphs, and most sterling successes. Elise giving him her vows at their wedding, her eyes shining love and admiration. Daisy's birth, her first step, the first time she called him Daddy. His mother's gratitude the night his father had died. God, but she'd had courage. His father's had faltered, but his mother had been right there to help him. She'd curled her fingers over his, kissed him good-bye, and then pulled the trigger, keeping his honor intact. Anthony had taken the gun and had held her while they wept and mourned.

Without hesitation, if not without occasional regret.

The bottle of pills stood empty. Anthony went up to bed. Elise was already asleep. He snuggled to her warmth between the silk sheets, under the comfortable weight of the satin comforter, buried his face in her sweet-smelling hair, and then closed his eyes.

The battle would not be won in his manner of choice, but it would be won. The United States had cost him his father. Cost him the respect of his people and the love of his family. It had isolated him. Made him a widower in his heart.

Now many Americans would be widowers. And widows. And orphans. And many, many more would simply be dead.

On that final thought, Anthony Benedetto went to sleep.

Chapter Twenty-two

∼

AT three A.M., the phone rang.

Seth shook loose from the scented, tangled sheets, reached over Julia to the nightstand, and answered. "Holt."

She scooted toward him, nuzzling and complaining at the interruption with a little groan. He couldn't blame her; they hadn't slept much.

"Dr. Holt, this is Lieutenant Swede at the Battle Management Command Center. You and Dr. Warner need to report STAT, sir. THREATCON Delta."

Threat Condition Delta was reserved for the most severe threats. "We'll be there in ten." Cradling the phone, he shook Julia awake. "Julia, get dressed. All hell's broken loose."

She tossed back the covers, slid to the edge of the bed. "What's happened?"

"I don't know." There wasn't a secure-phone line to the house. "THREATCON Delta."

"Delta?" She snagged some clothes on her way to the bath. "It's got to be Benedetto."

Jerking on his slacks, Seth agreed with her.

THE command center was hopping.

Three rows of continuous desks stretched across the dimly lit sixty-foot room. Men and women, wearing a mix of traditional blue uniforms, Class-As, and fatigues, filled every seat, staring at computer monitors. Seth automatically looked to two large illuminated screens on the front wall. Pinpoints flashed red on the world map, depicting current hot spots and active operations. The second screen displayed a map of the northeastern United States and Seth focused on it. That was the location of their immediate challenge.

Colonel Kane shouted at some major, picked up the receiver to the red phone—a hot line to the honchos—and began giving a concise briefing. Could be the general, the commander of the Ballistic Missile Defense Organization, the Joint Chiefs, who were no doubt in the Pentagon's Tank, or the President.

Matthew stood beside Colonel Kane, and his expression said more than Seth wanted to hear. Bluntly put, he was scared shitless and, knowing Matthew's penchant for being cool under fire, that made Seth worry more.

Seth and Julia caught Matthew's eye. He rushed over and launched into briefing them. "Benedetto's gone off the deep end."

Seth braced, knowing what was coming. So, he noticed, did Julia; she was already clutching at her left arm.

"The loyalists demanded Benedetto resign."

"Resign?" That didn't fit.

"Do the honorable thing." Matthew cast a worried look back at Colonel Kane, who was still on the red phone. "Suicide."

Seth grimaced. Events were unfolding as expected, and as feared.

"Benedetto refused. He got them to give him twenty-four hours to turn things around," Matthew went on. "They pushed him, and the crazy bastard pushed back."

Julia sucked in a sharp breath. "He launched the Rogue."

Matthew nodded and, though Seth expected it, hearing it acknowledged had his heart slamming against his ribs. "From where?"

"The Chesapeake Bay." Matthew's expression soured from grim to morbid. "They launched from a commercial tug. Morse assisted, Seth. That's verified. One of our operatives was on the boat and reported in before it went down."

"Benedetto's loyalists blew up the tug?" Julia asked.

Matthew nodded.

Seth scanned the map. Little change. "With our people on it?"

"No, they evacuated before the hit."

"What's the distance between D.C. and the launch site?"

"It's within a hundred kilometers, Seth."

Could the news get any worse? "Has the Puzzle Palace been notified?" Seth automatically reverted to the slang name for the Pentagon.

"Kane's on the phone with the Joint Chiefs now. The President will be on line with them momentarily."

He should be on Air Force One, out of the line of fire. Why the hell hadn't he evacuated?

Kane hung up the phone. "GPS," he shouted to the global positioning system satellite monitor. "Status report."

The third man in the first row of desks answered. "Nothing's showing up, sir. I've got a clear screen."

The GPS system was supposed to offer an early warning that a hostile missile had been launched and alert the ground-based radar systems.

"Ground-based radar?" Kane shouted out.

"Nothing, sir."

Seth's stomach curled. Nothing on the GPS or the ground-based radar systems?

Kane stared at the GPS monitor. "Do we have a satellite in the appropriate sector, Sergeant?"

"Yes, sir."

"We got visual confirmation of the launch from the tug. So why the hell can't we track the damn thing?"

"I—I don't know, sir." He gave Kane a perplexed look. "There's nothing there."

Julia answered, shouting over to Colonel Kane. "I can fix that."

Seth looked at her and Julia met his gaze. "They've enabled the stealth feature."

"Can you do that, Dr. Warner?" Colonel Kane yelled back.

"Yes, I can." She turned to look at him. "I designed it."

Kane nodded. "Then please remedy this situation now. I'd like to know where the son of a bitch is going and how it's armed."

Chemical, biological, or nuclear. That she couldn't fix or tell him. Where, she could manage. Tense, she looked at Matthew. "I need a computer with full access."

"Pick one," Matthew said. "They're all wide open in here."

Julia went to the first desk. The lieutenant scrambled out of his seat and she sat down and went to work. She wound through the firewalls, the safeguards and encryptions, and finally got to the Rogue, then disabled its stealth.

"We got it, sir!" the GPS monitor bellowed.

Julia looked to the large screen, saw the red blip.

"We've got to intercept that missile, Seth." Matthew stared at him.

"If we do, it'll detonate." Seth glanced over at Julia. "If the warhead is WMD, millions are going to die."

"We can't just sit here and let the bastards take out D.C."

They couldn't. They would lose the White House, Congress, and the Pentagon.

"What about Home Base?" Matthew darted his gaze between Seth and the screen. "We've got the prototype."

"We can't use it on this. If we return the Rogue to its launch site, we'll still lose D.C. and most of the federal government." Seth tracked the trajectory on the screen, a thin red line. The Rogue had turned west, toward Los Angeles.

"What the hell is that thing doing?" Colonel Kane demanded to know.

The radar specialist responded. "It's erratic as hell, sir. Something's destabilized it."

"Dr. Warner, could disabling the stealth do that?"

"No, Colonel. It couldn't."

Kane held up his hands. "Then what the hell is happening?"

"The Rogue is performing as advertised, Colonel," Seth said. "You aren't supposed to be able to project its trajectory with standard countermeasures. That's why it's called a Rogue."

"But the damn thing's zigzagging."

Seth got to a computer, began seeking a pattern. Tense minutes passed, with Kane answering the red-line phone again and again.

"Give me something to tell them, Holt." Kane slammed down the phone, frustrated. "Anything to tell them."

"Working on it." Seth didn't spare the colonel a glance.

Tension pulsed through the command center. Everyone felt it, and everyone suffered its pressure.

Finally, the information processed and the computer had enough data to draw a hypothetical conclusion. A new screen popped up on Seth's monitor. "It's not going to L.A. If it maintains its current pattern, it'll hit in three hours."

"Three hours?" Colonel Kane frowned at the screen, and then at Seth.

He nodded.

"Where, for God's sake?"

"New York City." Seth grimaced. The most densely populated area in the country. And at eight A.M. Eastern time, it would be damn densely populated.

Seth looked over at Julia. Their gazes met, and the regret he felt he saw mirrored in her eyes. This morning, normal everyday-average people were feeding their kids breakfast, dropping them off at school, and going into work, thinking this was just another typical day. Except today millions of them would die. Men, women, children. Parents, grandparents, and cousins. Lovers. Friends. And Uncle Lous.

And a nation would mourn the worst tragedy ever suffered on its soil.

But which millions of blissfully unaware people would die?

"What are our options, Seth?"

He looked at Colonel Kane. "New York City, or D.C.—and everything within a hundred kilometers of either one. If the warhead falls into the WMD classification, then, of course, the anticipated damage assessments escalate proportionately."

"Can't we tell if it's carrying a WMD warhead?"

"No." Seth's bitterness tinged his tone. "The Rogue's constructed from a new metal alloy that requires a specific sensor to determine warhead type."

"Then why the hell don't we have it?"

"The budget didn't allow for it."

Julia came over to Seth. "We can't disarm the Rogue, but we can create interference and scramble its trajectory. We won't know where it'll detonate, but odds are in our favor it will be in an area less populated."

"We can't do it." Seth gave her a level look. "Are you willing to dump bio or, God forbid, chemicals? Because you damn well could be doing just that."

"It's going to hit somewhere, Seth. If it's biological, we can't inoculate the entire country before symptoms occur."

If it turned out to be chemical or nuclear, there would be no one left to inoculate. "We can't just intercept it. Not without knowing it it's live ordnance or a decoy, or its type of warhead."

"Home Base can tell us if it's a decoy."

"Yes, but if we disrupt it, it'll detonate."

Matthew lifted his hands. "We built the damn thing. Can't we disarm it?"

Seth nodded. "We always build in safety features, factoring in that only we'll have the technology but preparing just in case someone else gets their hands on it. Yet—"

"Morse has that technology, too," Colonel Kane interjected.

Seth again nodded.

Julia crossed her arms over her chest. "So what *can* we do?"

He looked her straight in the eye. "We've got to reprogram the Rogue and change its target."

"Can we do that?" Matthew asked.

"Seth. That's impossible." Julia guffawed. "Conventional seekers won't work. The Rogue's alloy prevents it. Even with Home Base, we can only reverse its existing trajectory. Any attempt to alter it and we alter the magnetic energy field. The Rogue will detonate."

Seth disputed her. "We have the technology."

"Then why the hell aren't we using it?" Colonel Kane stepped into the fray.

Seth's chest went tight. If he was right, great. If not, well, he'd be glad to be dead with everyone else. "We've got the technology, I said." He looked at Kane. "But it won't be operational or incorporated into our defense capabilities for at least five years."

"Why the hell not?"

"Budget." Seth let his bitterness show. "Talk to Congress and our Commander in Chief. They get righteous about our lack of preparedness, but they hold the damn purse strings. Without the funding, we're stymied."

"Stymied, hell. We're screwed," Matthew said.

Seth stared at the screen, at the blip. "We've got a shot."

"What shot?" Julia stared at him, perplexed, then caught the twinkle in his eye. "Your sensor?"

He nodded. "It's ready—and it should override the metal alloy in the Rogue."

"What are you talking about, Holt?" Colonel Kane folded his arms across his chest.

"A technology project I've been working on for years—on the side. Congress refused to fund it, so I've been limping along on my own. I altered the design so it can piggyback on the Home Base system."

"And your sensor is operational?"

Seth hedged on that. "Theoretically, with it, we can determine the type of warhead the Rogue's carrying. We can also reprogram its trajectory without detonating it—at least, we can in theory and in very limited simulated studies.

But—and it's a big one, Colonel Kane—the studies haven't been extensive and the sensor hasn't been field-tested. At best, deploying it will be a close call timewise, and it might not work."

"Trial by fire," Matthew said.

"It has to work." Julia looked from him to Seth. "We don't have anything else."

"Well, Colonel?" Seth said. "Your call."

Kane stared at the screen, the red-lined path, then turned a steely gaze back to Seth. "Do it."

"Don't you want to check with the honchos?"

"What are they gonna do?" Matthew growled. "Say no when there's no other option."

Ignoring Matthew, Colonel Kane addressed Seth. "I'll tell them. They'll just have to sweat it out with the rest of us."

"Yeah, well, notify Congress, too, sir," Matthew said. "They're the ones who wouldn't give us the money."

Seth turned to Julia. "Get the team in here. We're definitely going to need Cracker. And make sure Lieutenant Swede"—Seth motioned to the GPS monitor—"keeps a satellite glued to the Rogue. I need as close to zero time delay on transmissions and receptions as he can squeak out—and tell him to find me a ship-free sector in the Atlantic where we can detonate the Rogue, if it's not WMD *and* we can reprogram its trajectory." Seth headed toward the door.

"Where are you going?" Julia called out to him.

"To install the sensor on the Home Base prototype." He glanced at Matthew. "The sensor only activates on an air-to-air launch. We need a F-16. Voluntary mission. High risk."

Julia's heart shot up to her throat. A pilot to volunteer for what could well be a suicide mission.

"I'm on it." Matthew stepped to the nearest phone.

Her emotions threatened to riot. She ordered them back to that secret place, and then headed for Lieutenant Swede. This couldn't be happening. It just couldn't.

Dear God, it couldn't, but it was. And for a moment, she resented knowing and understanding the potential impact when others remained blissfully ignorant. She imagined Jeff and Seth and the life they could have, all of the people who could be hurt by this. And in her mind, she saw them, face by face, each of the victims who one minute would be here and the next minute would be gone. Standing, hands linked, in a line that stretched back and forth across the country, they reached from coast to coast. And then she saw the people whose lives had been touched by those victims. Those who loved them, and those who had been loved by them. And then she saw those who would never be because the victims were no longer here to parent them.

The mass of people linking hands grew larger and larger and, inside, she wept.

SETH returned to the command center, winded and worn.

Julia met him at the door. "We've got forty minutes— and a projected flight time of thirty-four minutes."

"Where's Cracker?" Seth headed into the pulse of the center.

"He's here. They're all here." Julia grasped his arm. "Seth, Linda's husband is piloting the F-16."

"Mac?" Seth felt his energy deflate. "I thought he was in the desert."

"He was. It wasn't a regular remote tour. He was filling in for a critical staff member. He got back two days ago."

"He volunteered for this mission?" Seth wanted to spit nails. Guilt swarmed his stomach. "If this fails, Linda will never forgive me."

"Seth." Julia cupped his face. "Honey, they're all *somebody*'s husband or wife."

"I know." Seth walked on. "I just—"

"I understand." Julia and Seth stopped beside Matthew and Colonel Kane, who held their gazes fixed on the screen, on that damn red line that had come to represent hell.

Sparing Seth a glance, Colonel Kane asked, "What do we do now?"

"We wait."

And we worry. Julia looked up at Seth. "I want to call Jeff."

He nodded.

"Dr. Warner." Colonel Kane lifted a staying finger and dropped his voice to a whisper. "You do that, and everyone in this room is going to shut down. They're looking to you two to see how much to worry about this. Make that call, and they're going to interpret it to mean we're already mourning our dead."

Julia stared at him, torn between doing the right thing and what her heart wanted her to do. The battle ran its course, and finally, she nodded. "Of course."

"Agent 12," Lieutenant Swede called out. "Line two, sir."

Matthew grabbed a phone, talked quickly and intensely, then cradled the receiver and returned to the group. "Karl Hyde is in custody. He's looking at life in prison for this."

Julia corrected Matthew. "He's looking at the death penalty. I witnessed him shoot and kill Camden."

"You actually saw him do it?" Seth asked, stunned that she hadn't told him.

She nodded. "But even if he gets life, I think his days of threatening me are over."

"You can bet on that," Seth said.

Matthew agreed. "Even if he skips the chair or the needle, any contact with you will be prohibited, Julia."

Finally Karl was the prisoner and she was free. "What about Dempsey Morse?" Her anger at him ran as deeply as her anger at Benedetto. No, deeper. With Benedetto, you got what you saw. He didn't hide his treasonous, murderous acts beneath the respectable façade of a civil servant.

"Our operatives plucked him out of the Chesapeake before the tug went down. He's not talking yet, but he will." Matthew glanced back at the screen. "Last report, they were closing in on Benedetto. The loyalists are in an uproar.

Things at Two West are pretty chaotic right now."

Seth stepped away, went over to Linda. "I understand Mac volunteered for the mission."

"He did." Worry etched her face, and she was breathing hard.

"I'm sorry he's at risk, Linda."

"I am, too. But it goes with the turf." She mustered a hint of a smile. "I married Mac because I admired his courage." Her gaze turned wistful. "Sometimes it gets in the way of our lives, and sometimes it makes my damn hair gray, but this is who Mac is, and I love him for it."

Seth clasped her shoulder, gave it a gentle squeeze. "He's lucky to have you." The woman had every bit as much courage as Mac. If this went badly, she was the one who would be left behind to pick up the pieces for the family.

"Damn right, he's lucky," she said. "And, I assure you, I remind him of it—frequently."

"I'm sure you do."

The bluster went out of her voice. "Seth, is this going to work?"

A shiver ran through his body. God, but he wished he could be certain. "I can't say for fact, Linda. Studies have been too limited. But I think it will."

"Then it will," she said emphatically.

Feeling the weight of her faith bear down on him, Seth looked past her shoulder and saw Cracker pounding away at the computer keyboard. "What's he doing?"

"Familiarizing himself with the system."

Seth nodded, then walked over. "Anything strange?"

"No, just getting oriented." Cracker didn't look up and his fingers never slowed down, rapping consistently against the keys.

Seth stared around the command center. Work went on, but every eye with a second to spare watched that red blip on the screen.

He looked at Julia. Like everyone else, she was clearly tense and wary, weary of watching and waiting and silently praying the projected flight time was longer than the actual. Six minutes wasn't much operational time. But it was enough, provided his sensor worked against the metal alloy and adjusted for the magnetic alterations of Mac's physical proximity and it didn't detonate the Rogue.

Kane was on the red-line phone again. He motioned to Seth. "Holt, come here."

Seth went over. Kane held the phone out to him. "The chief."

Not the Chief of Staff, the Commander in Chief. The President. Seth positioned the receiver at his ear. "Mr. President."

"Dr. Holt. I just wanted to thank you for your efforts. Regardless of how this turns out, you went to a lot of trouble on your own, developing that system."

"Yes, sir, I did." Seth frowned, and his irritation with the President got the better of him. "Sir, with all due respect, why aren't you on *Air Force One*?"

"I sent the veep." His voice dropped a notch. "If this fails, I'm taking personal responsibility. I'll be with my people."

"But sir, the Vice President—"

"The truth is, Dr. Holt, I couldn't live with this." He paused, then added, "Is your sensor going to work?"

"I wish I could say for certain, but the truth is I don't know. I never had the funds to field-test the system."

"I understand. At the moment, I can't tell you how much I regret slicing the DoD budget to the bone."

Didn't they all regret it? "Yes, sir."

"How is it supposed to work?"

"It's supposed to determine what type of warhead we're dealing with and let us alter the in-flight trajectory."

"I must be confused."

"Sir?"

"It was my understanding that even with Home Base, any trajectory alteration would detonate the Rogue."

"The sensor tricks the Rogue into thinking its magnetic energy field hasn't been altered. It's the alteration that detonates the Rogue. As long as the Rogue thinks its field is stable, we can change the trajectory."

"And you can do this without a major power source?"

"I had to, sir. The power source exists, but current arms treaties prohibit us from using it."

"I see." The President cleared his throat. "Either way, Dr. Holt, thank you for your personal efforts."

"You're welcome, sir."

The dial tone buzzed in Seth's ear. He passed the phone back to Colonel Kane.

Cracker yelled out. "We've got the sensor tap!"

Seth scrambled to a computer, went through the paces, trying to determine the type of warhead. "Julia," he shouted.

"Right here." She appeared at his side.

"Run down the target codes."

She sat down at the nearest computer, and got busy.

Lieutenant Swede began the countdown. "Five minutes until impact."

Seth needed more time. Not much, just a little more time.

"Four minutes until impact."

Damn it, where was the data? Where—the firewall. "Cracker, give me the double-firewall-bypass code!"

"You'll leave the system wide open to hackers."

"If I don't get around the son of a bitch, we won't have any living hackers."

"2143839 Bravo Zulu 273."

Seth keyed in the code.

"Two minutes until impact."

Seth scanned the screen, then double-checked. "No evidence that it's biological, chemical, or nuclear."

A collective sigh filled the room.

Julia worked frantically, reprogramming the Rogue's trajectory, sending it into the cleared shipping lane in the Atlantic. "I got it!"

"The Rogue is eastbound," Lieutenant Swede announced. "It's made the turn and is now over the Atlantic."

War whoops echoed through the command center.

"Mac? Is he all right?" Linda asked Lieutenant Swede.

Swede held up a finger, paused a long second, and then grinned ear to ear. "He's returning to base, ma'am."

Linda let out a shuddery sigh and swiped at a tear no one was meant to see.

Everyone looked relieved. Everyone except Julia and Seth. Their gazes met and held.

"Swede?" Seth didn't look away. "Give me a distance."

"Sir, eighty-seven kilometers offshore—and less than two minutes until impact."

Colonel Kane picked up on the tension, stared at Seth. "Is that enough time?"

"It's going to be close. The Rogue travels at roughly 8.33 kilometers a minute. The coast could take a direct hit within the damage zone."

The command center went silent. Intensity returned. Tension thickened the air and settled wall to wall like heavy fog.

Lieutenant Swede spoke up. "Thirty seconds until impact."

Seth swallowed hard, clasped Julia's hand.

"Twenty seconds."

His breath catching in his throat, he stared at the screen.

"I love you, Seth," Julia whispered.

She didn't look at him, and he didn't look at her. "I love you, too." Five years, he'd waited to hear those words from her. Wasn't Fate wicked to withhold them until now?

"Four seconds." Swede's voice wavered. "Three. Two. One. Impact."

The blip on the screen flashed.

In silence, everyone watched, knowing they were witnessing massive destruction.

Seth cleared his throat. "Swede, distance?"

He looked at Seth, his eyes shiny, and smiled. "One hundred seven kilometers, sir."

Julia tugged at her right earlobe. Seth tugged back, and

she let out a little squeal, then swept him into a hug. "You're brilliant."

"I'm relieved." Seth smiled. "And brilliant."

"Damn modest, too." Julia laughed hard and deep. "But I'll forgive you, this once."

Seth looped his arms around her waist, smiled down at her. "In that case, I have some news for you."

"What?"

"We've got temporary custody of Jeff."

Her heart leapt. "We do? How—"

"Matthew arranged it through the staff judge advocate's office and the same civilian attorneys who worked your restraining order."

"That's wonderful news." She smiled from the heart out, knowing he hadn't told her earlier in case things didn't go well.

"We'll file the petition for adoption as soon as things settle down."

"After you marry me, right?"

"Right."

Kane held the red-line phone to his chest and answered a second one. "Benedetto's out of the picture."

More giddy laughter and victory shouts flooded the center. But something spiked a warning in Julia. It was their code of honor and ethics, nagging at her again. She softened her voice, so it didn't carry. "Colonel Kane?" When he looked at her, she went on. "Benedetto's dead, isn't he?"

Kane nodded. "Drug overdose."

"But loyalists don't do those kinds of drugs."

"His prescription," the colonel clarified. "He wiped out a bottleful."

"The guy's got everything in the world, and he opts to O. D." Matthew shook his head. "Well, Julia, I'd say that proves my point. Are you ready to admit it?"

"Admit what?"

His eyes twinkled. "That our side's got the right stuff."

Julia looked at Linda, talking via headset to Mac, who

was about to land the F-16. "Two West loyalists don't have a thing on us."

"Damn right." Matthew smiled.

"Damn right." Seth looped an arm around her shoulder. "Come on. Let's go see our boy."

Julia fell into step beside him. "About this marriage thing."

He stopped in the center of the hall and stared at her. "What about it?"

"There's a condition."

Seth frowned. "I'll never hurt you, Julia."

"That's a given." She squeezed his side. "But it's not my condition."

"What?"

"I want locks on the windows and doors." Before he could protest, she added, "It's not safe, Seth. Anyone could just walk in off the street."

"Okay. For you and Jeff, I'll do it. But no locks that require keys from inside the house. I just can't do that."

The scars of abuse ran deep for both of them. They would for Jeff, too. But as hard as those challenges had been, Julia conceded, they deserved respect. They had given her, Seth, and Jeff insights into each other that those who had never experienced abuse could never understand. Together, they could heal.

She slid into the Lexus beside Seth. Together, they *had* healed, enough to take the ultimate risk. To love again. Without healing, there could be no self-love much less love for another, and there was a lot of love between them. Which proved that living without love had been an insult to life.

She sat back on the seat, watched Seth get in behind the wheel and crank the engine. In searching for Jeff, in watching that screen and envisioning Benedetto and Morse's penchants for death and destruction—and in daring to risk loving again after the abuse—they had both come to fully appreciate the value of life.

And they chose to live, giving life and love all due respect.

Epilogue

J EFF'S still having trouble sleeping inside." Seth cast a worried look across the kitchen table at Julia.

"It's the combination of darkness and being buried." She understood completely. "But it's getting a little chilly to be sleeping outside."

"We've been tiptoeing around him, Julia." Seth poured himself a cup of coffee and sat down at the kitchen table, across from her.

"He's been in a fragile state."

"And our tiptoeing makes him think he still is."

"Good point." Julia sipped from her cup of tea. "Well, Dr. Seth, what do we do?"

"We need to make Uncle Lou's spaghetti," Seth said. "I think it'd do us all good."

Lips pursed, Julia stared at Seth, reasoned through his suggestion. While she would never know for sure whether or not Karl had caused her uncle's accident, she knew well the legacy Uncle Lou had left her. Normalcy. The peace, security, and serenity that comes with the common, every-day, average; the comfort, calm, and acceptance of unconditional love. She wanted that for Jeff, and for Seth. Until now, neither of them had known it. She had lived it, and then had lost it for a while. But, together, they could all live it from here on out. "Yeah." She smiled at Seth. "We need to make Uncle Lou's spaghetti."

Ten minutes later, Jeff stood on a chair pulled near the stove, a dishtowel tucked into the neck opening of his shirt to protect it from sauce splatters. Seth stood behind him, guiding his hand, stirring with the big metal spoon. "Would I lie to my best buddy?"

"She *bakes* the meatballs?"

"That's what I said, isn't it?"

"Yeah, but—"

"Her uncle Lou was a real Italian, and that's how he taught her to do it. You gotta respect family and traditions, Jeff. They're nothing to sneeze at."

"I don't think we had any traditions."

"We didn't, either," Seth said, an odd catch in his voice. "But Dr. Julia's a nut about them. We'll both have a million of them now."

"We get her traditions?"

"Sure." Seth licked at a splatter of sauce clinging to his thumb. "She's our family."

Jeff grinned. "They can't change anything, can they? I mean, we're married and I'm adopted forever, right?"

"Forever," Seth promised. "Maybe longer."

Jeff cocked his head.

"Hey, you know how Dr. Julia is. Can you imagine her ever letting you not be adopted?"

"She is a worrywart." Jeff looked relieved about that.

"Yep, she sure is."

Julia debated on who had the biggest smile, Jeff or Seth. Or maybe her. Finally, life felt good and right. As perfect as it should be . . . almost.

She stepped back behind the bar, out of Jeff and Seth's line of sight from the stove, and then called out, "Stir the sauce, Jeff."

"I got it," Jeff yelled, then whispered. "Worrywart."

Seth's laughter filled the kitchen.

God, how she loved Seth's laughter. Filled with hope, Julia smiled, snitched a gumdrop from a candy dish, and popped it into her mouth. She had survived. *One breath at a time*. Now, she would flourish. They would all flourish.

Finally, she had love and laughter in her home, and her son in her kitchen with her husband, carrying on tradition . . . stirring Uncle Lou's sauce.